What Others Are Saying about The Wandering series by L. B. Graham

"The heart of Lewis and the world-building of Tolkien dwell richly in the works of L. B. Graham. Prepare yourself for high fantasy charged with suspense and intrigue. . . ."

—Wayne Thomas Batson, bestselling author of The Door Within trilogy

"There is a completeness to L. B. Graham's literary imagination that I don't see very often. He's a world-maker. Barra-Dohn, with its strange technologies and ruthless tyrants and wandering priests, feels like a whole world, a world you can immerse yourself in and not come out for a long time."

—Jonathan Rogers, author of The Wilderking trilogy and *The Charlatan's Boy*

Regarding *The Darker Road: The Wandering, Book 1*

"Intricate world, intriguing characters, and incredible pacing equal fascinating reading. L. B. Graham has created fantasy in *The Darker Road* that draws the reader in and won't let go. Fun reading, but be ready for those heart-thumping pages. There is danger between these pages and the heroes needed to fight a scourge of corruption."

—Donita K. Paul, author of The Dragon Keeper Chronicles and Chronicles of Chiril

THE LESSER SUN

The WANDERING: BOOK 2

LIVING INK BOOKS
Writing Worth Reading

L. B. GRAHAM

The Lesser Sun
The Wandering: Book 2

Published by Living Ink Books, an imprint of
AMG Publishers, Inc.
6815 Shallowford Rd.
Chattanooga, Tennessee 37421

This is a work of fiction. Names, characters, places, and incidents either are the product of the author's imagination or are used fictitiously. Any resemblance to actual persons, either living or dead, events, or locales, is entirely coincidental.

Print Edition: ISBN 13: 978-0-89957-773-9
EPUB Edition ISBN 13: 978-1-61715-340-2
Mobi Edition ISBN 13: 978-1-61715-341-9
PDF Edition ISBN 13: 978-1-61715-342-6

First Printing—January 2015

THE WANDERING is a trademark of AMG Publishers.

Cover designed by Daryle Beam at Bright Boy Design, Chattanooga, TN.

Interior design and typesetting by PerfecType, Nashville, TN.

Interior illustrations by Abe Goolsby, Nashville, TN.

Edited and proofread by Veronika Walker and Rick Steele.

Printed in the United States of America
20 19 18 17 16 15 –V– 6 5 4 3 2 1

For Ella, my Olli, who's a lovely and talented young woman—
never forget that you are deeply loved.

Contents

Prologue

The Wonder and the Terror

Emin stared at the magnificence of the Temple of Kalos, the sunshine gleaming off its shining white walls. High above the Temple, a single hawk reeled, a small dark shape visible against the bright blue of the cloudless sky that stretched from horizon to horizon.

It occurred to Emin as he watched the hawk that nothing else around him seemed to be moving, an odd thing since he was standing in one of the busiest streets of Zeru-Shalim. He lowered his gaze from the Temple and the sky above it, and only then did he notice that the steps of the Temple, the open courtyard beside it, and the street around him were all littered with the bodies of the dead.

He stepped over to the body closest to him and stooped down. It was the body of a woman, he thought, but it was hard to tell, as the face was so emaciated as to be little more than skeletal. Wisps of dark hair flitted around in the slight afternoon breeze, dancing like loose threads barely anchored to her skull. Emin didn't know much about the rate at which a body decayed, but he thought that probably this woman had been dead for quite some time.

As if to confirm his suspicion, the skeletal face began to flake and blow away in the wind. Living in Zeru-Shalim, a city surrounded by sand, Emin had seen many sandstorms. The sudden disintegration of the woman's body and the small, swirling grey cloud it formed as it blew away on the wind seemed like that, like a storm of flesh and bone turned sand and swept away in a single moment.

Only, the swirling, grey cloud wasn't so small. It was large, and growing. Emin glanced around, beginning to realize that all the bodies were collapsing at the same moment and making their own contribution. He pulled his shirt up over his mouth to avoid breathing any of it in, and for the first time since noticing the myriad of bodies, he started to think that perhaps he should make his way home, get away from the gruesome scene around him.

Emin turned away from the Temple, and much to his surprise, saw that the rest of Zeru-Shalim had disappeared. There were no more buildings, no more streets, no high, strong city walls. There was only desert sand, dotted here and there with the inevitable sage bush, stretching endlessly away in every direction. Panic struck Emin, as the strangeness of the situation finally began to dawn on him. The decaying bodies, the disappearing city—what was going on?

Where was Armond, his father, one of the most important and powerful priests in the Kalonian Priesthood? Where was Calsura, his oldest brother, also a priest of Kalos? They both served in the Temple, and part of Emin wanted to run in, even though to do so was forbidden. At the same time, he was afraid to go in. What if they were dead too? What if their bodies had crumpled into dust on the Temple floor?

Emin was paralyzed with indecision. He looked back up into the open sky, searching for the reeling hawk. He found nothing. He screamed at the empty sky, and as he screamed, the world went dark.

Emin woke, the image of the endless sand surrounding Zeru-Shalim lingering before his eyes. He did not stir from his bed, but rather he lay still, trying to regain and hold onto the memory of the Temple of Kalos. Whenever his dreams took him home, took him into the past, they seemed to turn out badly. Even so, he loved the clarity with which he sometimes recalled the city of his youth, and he sought that clarity in his waking moment, afraid that if he moved, it would slip away like sand through his fingers. At last he sighed, letting the dream go, and rose from his bed.

He pulled back the curtain that hung across the front of his small "house," and he descended the stairs into the afternoon sun that shone brightly on the small but growing settlement of Amh-uru here in Azandalir. The years had slipped away since he and his brothers had picked this small island to be their new home—if indeed a place he had only visited occasionally for the better part of forty years could be called a home.

Yes, the years had slipped away, and the memories from those transient years grew dim with time—one reason he tried to hold onto his dreams of the past, even when they were bad dreams. The memories in his dreams seemed clearer. In fact the older the memory, the clearer the images when he dreamed them. It sounded odd, and backwards, Emin thought, but it was true nonetheless.

Given that odd inversion, where the more distant memories still lived in his mind the most clearly, it didn't surprise him terribly much that the memory of the Temple of Kalos had been so clear in his afternoon dream. He'd only been a young boy when he and his brothers had left Zeru-Shalim. Now he was the only one of them still left, but he could remember the Temple where his father had worked—and died—as clearly as anything else he remembered from those days.

Today was not a day to look to the past, though, but to the future, although Emin thought increasingly that one must always view the future through the lens of the past. Indeed, it seemed inevitable that it should be so. The only real question was whether you would learn anything from your past experience and keep those lessons in perspective so that your vision of the future might be more accurate. If you didn't do both of those things—learn from the past and keep it in perspective—then Emin believed you were doomed either to make the same mistakes as you had made in the past or to replace them with different, perhaps worse ones, because you were overreacting to them.

Emin sighed. He knew his time was short, having already outlived his next oldest brother by more than five years, and he wanted to chart as clear and as wise a course for the Amhuru to follow in the years to come as he could. Hence his constant attempts to learn from the past but not overreact to it. And yet he knew, deep down inside him, that for all his efforts, he could not see the challenges that lay ahead, could not prepare for every eventuality, could neither avoid mistakes himself nor tell his children and his children's children how to avoid them. They would be made, and if they were serious enough, they would spell doom for them all.

Marzin, Emin's son, greeted him as he approached. "Father, did you sleep well?"

"Well enough," Emin said, embracing his son. The great heartache of this calling Kalos had placed upon them was the physical distance it so often put between the Amhuru and those they loved. How much time with Marzin had Emin lost over the years, with all their wanderings? And now, quite possibly, a more permanent division might lie before them, for Emin had not yet decided between the Northlands and the Southlands, though the time for deciding would come soon.

"Are Tajira and Balamiin both here?" Emin asked.

"Tajira has come, but we are still waiting for Balamiin."

Emin nodded, and they turned to walk together among the small buildings of Azandalir. Several new houses were being built nearby, for their numbers were growing. This was true both because their families were expanding and because they had recently decided to accept apprentices from outside the family.

It was long overdue, Emin thought, but at least the Council had finally seen the sense in allowing it. After all, the precedent had really been set years ago when Calsura's daughter married a man from Alaxundra. Since then, many had found their spouses outside the family, as had been inevitable.

Kalos had entrusted the six fragments of the Golden Cord to the sons of Armond, and now that Marzin wore the fragment Emin had borne for so long, those six fragments had each been passed on to the next generation. The Amhuru would never be a large people, but Emin knew they must grow and thrive if they were to survive the challenges ahead. When suitable apprentices were found in their wanderings—men and women who were willing to make the sacrifices it required and who could be trusted with the weight of their responsibilities—they must be embraced and welcomed.

"Is it true what they say about Zeru-Shalim?" Emin asked, not sure why the question had suddenly popped into his mind. "The name has changed?"

"Yes," Marzin said. "The city is now called Barra-Dohn."

"Barra-Dohn," Emin said. The words felt strange in his mouth. He shook his head as he added, "No longer the city of life and peace, then."

"No, it is the city of might and power," Marzin replied. "Mordain's grandson now holds the throne, and I think the change was his idea."

"I think, perhaps," Emin said, "that the change was proposed once before."

"Ah, well," Marzin said, shrugging, "I may be wrong."

"What do you think of him?" Emin asked. "Mordain's grandson, that is."

"Not much," Marzin said simply. "What lessons might have been learned back when the plague struck the city when you were a boy seem to have been forgotten. Now, both Barra-Dohn and its king ride the wave of wealth and influence its recent discovery has provided. How long that wave will last, though, who can say?"

"Is it really true, the rumors of this wonder-metal?"

Marzin stopped, and for a moment he stared straight ahead. Emin could see the look in Marzin's eyes, and he wondered what he was thinking right at that moment.

Marzin turned to face his father. "They call it meridium, and yes, I would say the rumors are true. From what I have seen they are, anyway. I think meridium is going to change the world."

"So," Emin said, nodding, "it's like that, is it?"

"I think so," Marzin said, nodding too, and running his hand through his hair at the same time.

"How does it work? What kinds of things can it do?"

Again, Marzin hesitated. "I only know a little. While the people of Barra-Dohn wish to demonstrate meridium's power, they also guard the secret of its production zealously—for fear, I think, that others will learn to replicate their success and they will lose control of its production. It is a curious balancing act between showing its power and hiding its secret.

"What I do know," Marzin continued, "is that I have seen men walk above the ground wearing meridium soles on their shoes, I have seen lights made from meridium illuminate the night, and I did not see this but have heard that there are ovens that do not need wood, but rather generate heat by use of meridium, too."

Emin blinked, looking at Marzin to see if perhaps his son was teasing him, but there was no hint of humor there. He appeared serious. "How can this be?"

"I do not know," Marzin said. "There was a rumor, among some of the merchants who have begun to trade in meridium, that it has something to do with how the metal is mixed. Apparently, it must be combined with something else. The merchants seemed unsure about just what that something else is, and I heard all kinds of ideas—sand, sage oil, sea water, and even, believe it or not, blood."

"Blood?"

"Yes, some say that the butchers in the city are paid well for preserving the blood from the animals they slaughter and selling it to men who work for the king."

Emin shook his head. "Well, whatever the secret is, it won't be a secret forever. Secrets have a way of finding the light."

"Yes," Marzin said as they resumed walking. "They do indeed."

"So, this meridium reacts in some way to the Arua," Emin said, thinking about the examples Marzin had used. "Perhaps we should acquire some, to investigate and compare its uses and limits with the power of the Cord."

"I think we should," Marzin said. "It is very expensive, though, at least right now. Perhaps the cost will go down as—"

"Elder! Elder!"

Emin and Marzin both turned to look at the child who had interrupted them. It was Raltan, a boy of no more than ten. "Come quickly!" he shouted breathlessly. "Simanto is doing something . . . terrible."

Raltan turned and ran, and Emin and Marzin ran after him.

It didn't take long to size up the situation. Simanto stood with his right arm outstretched, the Zerura he wore wrapped around his right forearm. Not far away, another boy stood, trembling, staring not at Simanto but at the vines that were wrapping their way slowly up his legs, having almost reached his waist. Emin could see the vines growing as he looked at them, spreading up and around the other boy's legs, inch by inch, could see the look of concentration on Simanto's face, and more to the point, could feel the Arua field being manipulated.

There were other children standing nearby, and while they had been calling out to Simanto to stop, they had fallen silent once Emin and Marzin arrived. Emin walked forward.

"Simanto," Emin said, his voice soft and steady as he approached, "I think you have made your point with young Halman. Let go of the Arua, Simanto."

"I'm tired of being teased," Simanto said through clenched teeth. He did not let go of the Arua. "I told Halman to stop."

"I am sorry that Halman has been teasing you," Emin said. "He should not have been. But as I said, I think you have made your point. Let go of the Arua."

"He'll just do it again," Simanto said. "Tomorrow, or the next day."

"What are you saying, Simanto? Will you silence him for good? Would you murder to avoid being teased?"

Simanto's arm wavered, and Emin could feel his grip on the Arua falter. For the first time, the boy took his eyes off Halman and looked at Emin. "No, Elder, I didn't mean that. I wouldn't kill him, or anyone, I just . . ."

"You just what?" Emin asked. He returned Simanto's look calmly, letting the silence between them grow until it was almost audible.

Simanto released the Arua. His arm dropped to his side. His head drooped down. The vines around Halman's legs stopped growing, and Marzin walked over to the other boy and cut the vines off of him. Emin walked over to Simanto, put his arm around the boy's shoulder, and started immediately to lead him away from the others; Marzin could handle them. This would be tricky enough without having an audience. Simanto had done what was forbidden, and he would be embarrassed. For a child that already struggled to fit in, Emin feared the boy had just made his life much more difficult than it had already been.

They walked in silence through the calf-high grass until Emin heard a quiet sob. He looked down. Simanto was wiping tears away from both eyes with the heels of his hands. Emin opened his mouth to say something, but Simanto spoke first.

"I'm sorry, Elder," he said. "I know I shouldn't have done that. Now they'll just hate me even more."

"No one hates you, Simanto," Emin said, squeezing the boy's shoulder. "And you are right, you shouldn't have done that. You are an Amhuru, and we do not use what we bear for revenge, no matter how much we feel it is deserved."

Simanto nodded. "Yes, Elder."

They walked on awhile in silence, and Emin decided it was finally time to ask. "Simanto, I will need to think awhile about how this incident should be handled, but I need to ask you—how did you do it?"

"I don't know, Elder," Simanto said, and Emin thought he heard genuine confusion in the boy's voice. "I just . . . I reached out, calling the grass to grow, to become vines that would wrap around his legs, and it did."

"You turned grass into vines?"

"I . . ." Simanto hesitated. "I think so."

Emin tried to process what he was hearing. More than sixty years of bearing a fragment of the Golden Cord, and yet so much of it and its power was still a mystery. What the boy said sounded impossible, and yet he had seen the vines stretching up Halman's legs with his own eyes. More to the point, those vines only grew in one place on the island that Emin knew of, near the sapling talathorne trees, and there weren't any of those anywhere near this place. Was it possible that Simanto could have altered the very nature of the grass to become a vine and then made it grow?

"Simanto," Emin said, "have you experimented with this before? I mean, have you tried to make grass or flowers or anything else grow faster? Have you tried to alter them?"

Simanto walked beside Emin, but he did not answer.

"You need tell me the truth, Simanto. It is important."

"Yes, Elder."

"Yes, you will tell me the truth? Or yes, you have done this?"

"Yes, I have done this before."

Emin nodded. He would need time to think about how to handle this, but what he needed to do now was clear enough. He reached out his hand. "You know I need to take it, Simanto."

Simanto nodded and removed the Zerura from his arm. He handed it to Emin. "Will I get it back, Elder?"

"I don't know, Simanto," Emin said, and he could see from the look in Simanto's eyes that Emin's answer surprised him. The boy probably thought Emin would assure him that he would, eventually. Emin couldn't do that, though. He hoped he would be able to return the Zerura one day, but experimenting on living things, even grass, and using that power against another—these were serious things. Things that were forbidden. Things that could not be tolerated among the Amhuru, the Keepers of the Cord.

"Are you ashamed of me, Elder?" Simanto asked, looking at him. Emin felt the boy's eyes searching him.

"I am your great-uncle, Simanto," Emin said. "I love you."

"You are everyone's great-uncle here," Simanto said.

"Not quite everyone," Emin said, smiling at that. "But this does not make the fact that I love you any less true."

"I am sorry that I scared Halman, Elder," Simanto said.

"That is good to know," Emin said. "But you will need to tell him that."

"I know."

"Come," Emin said, "let's go back. We will need to face your mother and father eventually. Might as well do it now."

Emin sat crosslegged by the fire. The nights were cool in Azandalir this time of year, and it seemed to Emin like it was much harder to get and stay warm than it had been when he was a younger man. He scooched a little closer.

His son Marzin and two of his nephews, Tajira and Balamiin, joined him at the fire. They each bore original fragments, the three that had been chosen to go north. What they were preparing to do would change not only their community and their task, but it would change the world. It was momentous in ways even Emin couldn't fully understand. He knew that, and yet he found his mind wandering back to the seemingly much smaller matter of an angry boy, misused by his peers and in turn misusing his power to punish one of them. He wondered if it wasn't a portent or harbinger of some kind of dark future, though he knew he might be making something out of nothing.

"Marzin," Tajira said, as he glanced across the fire at his cousin, "your father has that look again. His mind wanders far away from here, I think."

Emin smiled and looked up. "Not too far away. Just far enough to wonder how vines that only grow in the shade beneath a talathorne tree came to be in the middle of a grassy field, miles from any tree at all."

Silence. The other three looked thoughtfully into the fire, too. None of them said a thing. Tajira and Balamiin had not been there, of course, but word of what had happened had spread, as inevitably it would. Emin suspected it would take a long time for Simanto to repair the damage he had done to his reputation, and he wondered, not for the first time, why it was that those who most needed to be loved and accepted were the most prone to doing exactly the thing that made love and acceptance difficult?

"Do you think it possible," Emin said, "that he could change grass into vines? Or do we think he simply found vines among the grass and made them grow?"

There was another moment of silence, and Emin started to think he should simply turn their attention back to the matter at hand, when Balamiin said, "I am not sure if taking grass and altering it, replicating another plant that is perhaps near enough to the grass in its structure to be altered in such a way . . . I'm not sure if that is possible, but the fact that he could make it grow, visibly, is itself alarming, is it not?"

"I don't know," Tajira said. "I haven't paid close attention to the growth patterns of the vines, but they do seem to spring up around the trees pretty quickly. To accelerate that pattern a bit, that doesn't seem too extraordinary. After all, think about what we are planning to do."

"Yes," Emin said, "think about what we are planning to do. Think about that, and consider both the wonder and the terror of the Cord."

"This is why we are here," Marzin said. "It is why we are doing this. It is why we are making the Madri, to keep it safe."

"I know, son," Emin said. "But even though our motives are good, the Madri will do harm to some. We know this. There will be towns, maybe even cities, which will have to be abandoned once the Madri is created. Trade routes, too, since crossing will be so difficult. Those cities and trade routes, they are the homes and livelihoods of real people, and we are going to destroy them."

"Trade routes can be altered and cities can be rebuilt elsewhere," Balamiin countered. "The world will adapt, and even if there is hardship because of the Madri, if it keeps the Cord safe, then it is in the world's best interest."

"Besides," Tajira said, and Emin could hear the impatience in his voice, "this matter has already been decided. The timetable is set. We are here to finalize and confirm, not secondguess."

"Yes, you are right," Emin said. "We should turn to the business at hand. I take it from what Tajira just said that a date has been set?"

"Thirty days," Marzin said. "We want to make sure there is enough time for the others to gather, but not too much."

"All six of of us will need to be close enough that we can seize and control the Arua together," Balamiin added, "but we'll need to be as far from the Madri on our respective sides as possible. We don't know exactly how unpleasant passing through will be for one of us, and we don't want to find out."

"When do you leave?" Emin asked.

"In three days. By law, we cannot be here when the others come, so we will gather our families and go. There won't be enough time to scout much of the Northlands for a new home, but that's all right—we already have a few ideas and can investigate those further after we complete the work."

"Will you join us, Father?" Marzin asked.

The question, at last. Emin had been avoiding it, but now that it was here, he knew the answer.

"No, Marzin, I will stay."

Marzin nodded. Emin knew his son would believe his decision was because of Marzin's sister, Emin's daughter, who was buried here on Azandalir. That was part of it, certainly, but it was only part. Emin could feel that his time was short. Maybe not weeks short, or months short, but certainly only a few years at most. He was too old for the journey that lay ahead for the Keepers of the Northland fragments.

He would stay, and one day, not too long from now, he would be buried beside his little girl.

The night grew late, and when they had discussed those things that Emin would need to pass on to the Southland Keepers when they came, they adjourned. But Emin stayed by the fire long after the others had gone.

Simanto. He just couldn't push the boy and the image of the vines growing around the legs of the other child from his mind.

All the defenses they had built and were building to protect Azandalir, all these things were designed to protect the Amhuru from threats outside the clan. What about the threats inside?

He thought of the Madri, and beyond that, of the series of remarkable discoveries and breakthroughs in their use of the Cord that had convinced them that such a thing was possible. Could they—could anyone—wield that much power indefinitely without being corrupted by it?

He saw the Temple of Kalos again with all the clarity of his earlier dream. The power of the Cord had not just corrupted Kartain, but it had corrupted the Kalonian priesthood itself. His father had resisted, and his brother had supported him, even if less openly, but if Armond and Calsura had been in the majority, then Kartain would never have been selected by the others to be the Amhura. And if the Kalonian priesthood could be corrupted, could not the Amhuru also be?

"Kalos, will we fail as they did?" he murmured, half out loud. "And what will happen if we do?"

Again the images. This time of the plague, but not this time from the dream—from his actual memories. The bodies in the streets of Zeru-Shalim. Rotting. Decaying. Stinking. The bodies waiting to be gathered and either buried or burned. Would that happen again? If the prohibition to gather and unite the fragments of the Golden Cord was broken, would the whole world pay the price this time?

That day must be prevented, of that Emin was sure. Whatever else went wrong, however else they failed, all six fragments of the Golden Cord must never, ever be brought back together.

Whatever misgivings he had about the Madri, Emin had ultimately agreed to the plan, though for a reason that he had never voiced. No, he had kept it to himself, and he would take it with him to his grave.

All the other safeguards that had been put in place over the last fifty years, all the laws and protocols, and even the defenses of this island—all of them depended on the fidelity and cooperation of the Amhuru, and all of them would collapse like a burning house if the Amhuru abandoned the charge they'd been given and succumbed to the lure of the power of the Cord. None of these things could save them—or the world—from themselves.

The Madri, though, was a real thing, a physical thing, a thing that the Amhuru would make and that once made would be impossible for a lone, rogue Amhuru to unmake. It was impartial and impersonal and did not care who your father or your grandfather was, and if it succeeded in keeping any man, Amhuru or otherwise, from bringing the six fragments together, then it was worth whatever disruption it would create in the world.

But could such a day ultimately be prevented? Where the will was strong enough, where the desire of a man was fixed and focused and the goal so immense and alluring, could that day really by stopped? Could the Madri actually do that? Could anything do that?

No, Emin admitted, it could not. He was the last of the six brothers, the last of the sons of Armond, the last who remembered the plague that had struck Zeru-Shalim. He knew that he and his brothers had done the best they could, the best they knew to do. He also knew that the future was unwritten, and that he would have to trust the wonder and the terror of the Cord into the hands of his descendants and hope that when the challenges of tomorrow came, that they would be equal to them.

If not, then Kalos help them all.

Part 1

The Lesser Sun

1

Surprise

Kaden quickened his step as he walked along the dark wharf. He'd been detained at the inn longer than expected and left for the trip back to *The Sorry Rogue* too late. Getting what he'd come ashore for was great, but—

The sound again.

He knew if he glanced over his shoulder he'd see nothing but the faint glow of the too sparse streetlights and deep banks of shadow, but someone was definitely there. He couldn't be sure of how many, but he was being followed.

Brexton was one of the busiest ports in the Maril Islands, but it was notoriously rough. By day the harbor crawled with city guards and port authority agents who ran the surface business of the port with ruthless efficiency. Under the cover of night, however, Brexton became merely ruthless, a home to almost every form of illicit trade known to man.

Captain D'Sarza had warned them of all this before they decided to come here. As an ideal place for getting information, they'd agreed that coming to Brexton was worth the risk. And, until tonight, they'd played it safe. No one had ventured into the city alone, not even Tchinchura.

Perhaps having been here a few weeks had made Kaden complacent, but he'd hoped to come ashore, get what he was after, and head right back. He'd not intended to be quite so long or stay so late into the night. Now he was on his own, not a guard in sight and none likely to appear—at least not in their official capacity. In Brexton, it was well known that most of the guards who secured the port by day roamed it at night with less than lawful intent.

Kaden scanned the wharf ahead. Jetty after jetty extended out into the harbor, where the dark shapes of ships and their masts rose up into the night. The jetty where *The Sorry Rogue* lay tied up at the end was at least a hundred yards ahead, but with any luck Kaden would reach it before the footpads behind him made their play. Once there, he was confident he could make the ship without incident.

Kaden wasn't afraid for himself. He felt the metallic band he wore on his left bicep, cool under his fingertips. He'd fight if he had to fight, and unless they'd brought an extra large gang with them, he'd win. But if he was pressed into a fight, he would have to do whatever was necessary to defend his life, and it might be hard to avoid hurting any of his attackers seriously, or perhaps killing some of them.

He didn't want to do that, but Tchinchura had stressed from the beginning of Kaden's training that, while Amhuru always did whatever they could to avoid the unnecessary taking of life, the fragments of the Golden Cord and their replicas had to be protected at all costs. Now that the Jin Dara had two of the six originals, the need to keep the other four and their replicas safe had only become all the more important.

Thinking about the Jin Dara made Kaden uneasy. He was alone, at night, in a dangerous city, being followed by who knew how many stalkers. Almost certainly, the men following him were some variety of the basic cutpurses who haunted all the big cities of the world at night, but there was always that chance—no matter how remote—that they were something else entirely.

The Jin Dara was surely seeking Tchinchura and what he carried, even as Zangira and his company of Amhuru were seeking the Jin Dara.

Three large men moved out from behind a warehouse on Kaden's left. Kaden, rather than retreating, pulled the axe from his waistband and ran toward them. They seemed taken by surprise. They had undoubtedly expected to drive Kaden back along the wharf toward their companions who were following behind, but now they faced an unexpected charge from a man with an axe. They each had short cudgels, useful in close quarters, and now raised them in their own defense.

At the last moment, Kaden veered to his right, ducked under the swing of the man who was on that side, and struck him on the other elbow with the flat of the double-bladed axehead. He felt the crack of a splintering bone and, standing up to his full height, struck the same man another blow on the head, again with the flat of the axe. The man crumpled to the ground, and Kaden moved quickly to retrieve his cudgel before the other two assailants could regroup.

He backed up a few steps, holding firmly onto both weapons. Beyond the two men who remained on their feet, he could see three more men running along the wharf. His pursuers seemed eager to join the fracas, and Kaden thought it prudent to deal with the two men in front of him before the numbers got even more lopsided.

The two men separated and began to circle, hoping to flank him, all the while watching him warily. He took a breath, moved his hands together in a flash to switch the weapons, then stepped toward the man on his left as he threw the cudgel point blank into his forehead. No sooner had he let it fly than he reversed direction with his left arm held high to block the blow coming from the other man.

He managed to get up under the blow enough that it wasn't a direct hit, but the man was big and the swing strong. Kaden was knocked back a step and couldn't swing his intended counterblow with his axe. The man, sensing his advantage, either overestimated how badly he'd hurt Kaden or underestimated Kaden's ability to recover, or likely both. As he cocked his arm way back, probably hoping to swing with enough force to knock Kaden right off the wharf and into the harbor, Kaden regained his balance and dodged.

The blow missed, and Kaden moved in, striking several sharp blows with the flat of the axe in strategic places, drawing painful grunts from his opponent and leaving him on his knees in pain. Out of the corner of his eye, Kaden saw the man he'd hit with the thrown cudgel moving toward him, and he leapt out of the way, rolling as he hit the ground. When Kaden came up out of the roll, the man changed direction and charged again.

This time Kaden took the direct approach. Again moving forward rather than back or to the side, he cut the distance between them rapidly, while his attacker's big swing was just beginning. Apparently, no one had taught these thugs the folly and predictability of always swinging with all their might. Kaden didn't make that mistake. Instead, he jabbed with the end of the axe, short and quick, right into the big man's chin, splitting it open and breaking his jaw.

Returning his axe to his dominant hand, he spun to face the three additional men who were just then arriving. They seemed to hover a short distance away, as though held back from him by an invisible wall. The two on the ends surveyed the men who lay either groaning or unconscious around Kaden and then glanced at their comrade in the middle, as though looking for direction. For his part, the man in the middle kept his eyes steadily on Kaden.

"I appreciate your rushing to my rescue, friends," Kaden said, fixing a smile on his face and adopting a friendly tone. He tossed his axe almost casually in the air so that it rotated a few times before he caught it again by the handle. "But, as you can see, I'm quite unharmed. These men, however," he added, gesturing to the wounded around him, "might require some assistance."

Again the two men on the ends glanced at the man in the middle, clearly waiting for his signal. The man in the middle remained still, watching Kaden. "Who are you?" he said finally.

"A traveler," Kaden replied.

"Well, traveler, let's not play games, shall we?" He stepped toward Kaden, who held his ground, resisting the urge to step back. "I saw you with Nassar tonight, and his merchandise is never cheap. Hand over whatever you bought from him and any coin you have on you, and I'll let you go unharmed."

"I don't think so," Kaden said as he smiled again. "I'll make you a deal, though. Toss your cudgels into the harbor and help your friends off the wharf, and I'll let you go unharmed."

"Don't be a fool," the man snapped, eyes blazing with fury. "You're still outnumbered and alone. You won't get lucky twice."

Kaden's smile disappeared. He hardened his face and voice, gesturing with his axe toward the three wounded men on the wharf, one of which was struggling to his feet. "These men were lucky. Lucky I disabled them without having to use lethal force. If you press the issue, I can't guarantee I'll be able to do it again. So, if my luck runs out," Kaden said, stretching out his arm and jabbing the axe at them to accentuate the point, "it will be you who suffers for it."

The standoff continued, silently. Then, as though unable to bear the tension anymore, the wounded man who had regained his feet started to limp as quickly as he could down the wharf, away from them. The two men opposite Kaden who had not yet spoken glanced after him, as though very much wishing to follow.

For the first time since his arrival, the man in the middle stole a peek to either side. Kaden knew, and he knew the other man did too, that he had lost control over his followers and the situation.

The man pointed to the two men who were still on the ground as he spoke to his accomplices. "Get them up and move back."

Before they could respond, Kaden stepped forward, gripping his axe and holding it up. "First, your clubs. Into the harbor."

"What for?" their leader sneered. "We'll just get more."

"Even so," Kaden said, "throw them into the water."

The man wavered, as though reconsidering his decision to retreat, but then he nodded and motioned to the others. All three of them tossed their short clubs into the harbor, where they disappeared in the darkness with an unceremonious *plunk*.

Kaden started to move slowly backward, keeping his eyes on them. As he moved away, the two who had said nothing throughout the entire exchange came forward to help the others. The one in the middle did not. He stood, keeping his eyes on Kaden.

"Perhaps we'll meet again, traveler."

Kaden smiled and shook his head. "Careful what you wish for, friend."

And with that, Kaden turned and jogged away along the dark wharf. It was long past time to be back onboard *The Sorry Rogue.*

Even before Captain D'Sarza opened her mouth, Kaden knew she was furious. Her hands were planted firmly on her hips, and though Kaden was taller, she leaned forward, glaring up at him with a fiery intensity in her eyes, strands of her dark dyed red hair hanging down in wisps, having escaped from the rest that was so carefully tied back under the bright green scarf.

"What exactly do you think you're doing?" she said. "We were this close to sending out a search party. Into Brexton. At night!" She glared at him, as though stunned silent by the incomprehensible stupidity that would have required such a thing.

"I'm sorry about the lateness of the hour," Kaden said. "I had business that—"

"Business! I don't care what business you had," D'Sarza interrupted him. "I'm the captain of this vessel, and at the very least, if you're going to be out after dark at a port like Brexton, you need to keep me informed."

"I'm sorry, Captain," Kaden said. "I never intended to—"

"Your father may have been a king," she said, moving right along, "but we're a long way from Barra-Dohn."

"Captain . . ." Kaden said coldly, doing his best to restrain himself. "Which part of 'I'm sorry' didn't you understand? Or do you simply enjoy reminding me how far I've come down in the world?"

"Don't think that being apprenticed to Tchinchura makes you an exception, either," D'Sarza said, not even acknowledging Kaden's words, except perhaps to glare a little more. "Even Amhuru have to follow the rules on *The Sorry Rogue*."

Kaden clenched his mouth shut. He wasn't going to win this fight, and he didn't care. He had no real stake in it. He just wanted it to end, and he knew the fastest way to ensure that happened.

"Captain," he said after gathering himself to make sure there was no trace of anger left in his voice—though he couldn't help the slight patronizing tone that remained—"I'm sorry about any worry or difficulty I've caused. You are the captain, and I will do a better job keeping you apprised of my intentions when I go ashore."

"Yes, well, see that you do," D'Sarza said. She hesitated a moment, as though considering whether to say more, then stalked off, barking commands at the small group of sailors unfortunate enough to be huddled around the mast a short distance away.

Kaden watched her go, then started across the deck toward the cabin he shared with Nara. Before he got there, though, Tchinchura emerged from the shadows enclosing the port side of the ship. He glided quietly out into the moonlit portion of the deck, where Kaden stopped to greet him.

"I suppose you heard that," Kaden said wryly. The elder Amhuru never missed anything, so Kaden had no doubt that he'd heard every word.

Tchinchura smiled at the joke, his white teeth gleaming in the faint light, a stark contrast to his dark skin. "I've spent a lot of time at sea," he said. "I learned a long time ago that captains are much like the sea they love. When a storm blows up, you won't make any headway sailing against it, so you might as well get out of its path until it blows itself out."

"I tried to."

"I know," Tchinchura said. "I was commending you."

Kaden offered a weak half-smile.

He'd been apprenticing under Tchinchura for almost the entire time since their escape from Barra-Dohn some two and a half years ago, but the elder Amhuru's words of praise still made him self-conscious. It wasn't that Tchinchura was too sparing or too effusive—it was simply that his own father, Eirmon Omiir, the last king of Barra-Dohn, had rarely praised him in any genuine, meaningful way. He still wasn't comfortable with the experience.

"You ran into some trouble, I see," Tchinchura said, changing the subject.

Kaden didn't ask how he knew; he'd stopped doing that a long time ago. There'd be some detail the Amhuru had noticed—maybe the sweaty clothes or a mark on his axe or something else Kaden would never have thought of, maybe all of the above.

"Yes, I was set upon by three thugs. I handled them before their three friends could join them, and then I managed to talk myself out of any further mischief."

"Handled them?"

"Yes, but I don't think anyone was seriously hurt. Some broken bones and wounded pride, but they'll live."

"Good," Tchinchura nodded, showing his approval again. "Of course, if you'd been back earlier, you wouldn't have had to fight at all."

For Tchinchura, that simple, soft-spoken comment served as an unusually strong rebuke, and it stung far more than Captain D'Sarza's harangue. "I know," Kaden said. "I put what I wanted ahead of my responsibility."

"I know it was important to you," Tchinchura said, "but as an Amhuru, you have more to consider now."

Kaden nodded, hanging his head. He stole a glance at Deslo's cabin, which was dark.

"He's still awake, I think," Tchinchura said. "He was up with me until just a little while ago. Seemed worried about you."

Kaden looked up. "Thanks. I better let Nara know I'm back first."

"Good idea," Tchinchura said, grinning again. "Though I suspect she already knows."

"She just might," Kaden acknowledged, glancing around at the rest of the dark deck and feeling somewhat relieved that he couldn't see Captain D'Sarza. "Still, I'll just pop in to see her before checking on Deslo."

"Goodnight," Tchinchura said. "Big day tomorrow."

"Yes," Kaden agreed. "He's excited. Nervous but excited."

Tchinchura nodded as he turned and disappeared back into the shadows. Kaden turned and crossed to the small cabin he shared with Nara, slipping quietly inside. There was Nara, at the little desk in the corner. She was reading by lamplight, absorbed.

"Another of Marlo's books, I see?" Kaden said.

Nara rose at his voice, setting the book down and crossing with a warm smile. She embraced him, and he held her close. When he relaxed his hold, though, she still held him tight, lingering.

"I'm all right," he whispered.

She let him go.

He glanced at the book on the desk and its faded pages. "How many of those are you going to read?"

Nara raised an eyebrow. "I wonder if Tchinchura knows his apprentice is a skeptic."

"I'm not a skeptic," Kaden said, a little indignant. "Just not a fanatic."

"Oh, so reading books from the past—books that take Kalos and the Old Stories seriously—that makes me a fanatic, does it?"

Kaden, having already run afoul of one woman tonight, made a decision to avoid doing so with another at all costs. He did have a stake in this discussion. A big one. "Not at all," he said. "I was just teasing."

"I know," Nara said, whispering. She leaned in as she put her arms around his neck and ran her slender fingertips through the hair on the back of his head. "So was I."

"Oh, right," Kaden said, looking at Nara suspiciously. She was in a surprisingly good mood. His late return had earned him two rebukes so far, and he'd expected a third. Instead, she held him tenderly and gazed up at him with something approaching pure happiness in her eyes.

"Nara?" he said finally. "What is it?"

For a long moment, she didn't answer. She just stood, holding him, looking up into his eyes. In that moment, a handful of things flashed through his mind, most of them connected to Deslo's birthday the next day. None of them prepared him for what he was about to hear.

"Kaden . . ." Nara said. "I'm pregnant."

2

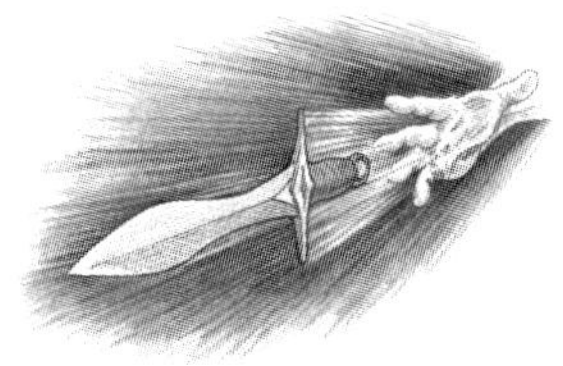

Gifts

Kaden blinked, looking at his wife. "Did you just say that you're . . . ?"

"Pregnant," Nara said, smirking as she looked up at him. "The word you're looking for is 'pregnant.'"

"But . . ." Kaden said, searching for something to hold onto as the world swirled around him. "How . . . I mean, how could that be?"

"Do I really need to answer that?"

Kaden ran his hand through his hair. He felt warm. He swallowed and took a deep breath. "Nara, it's just . . . you know, Deslo's thirteen tomorrow, and we're not exactly young anymore—"

"Speak for yourself," Nara said, with mock indignation. "You may have attained the ripe old age of forty, but I won't be there for almost two more years. And besides, young or old, expected or not, it's true. I'm pregnant, Kaden. We're having a baby."

"We're having a baby," Kaden repeated, the plain fact of it finally dawning on him. "I'm going to be a father again."

"Yes, you are," Nara whispered.

Kaden smiled and looked down in wonder as he placed his hand on Nara's belly. It was smooth and warm, no different than it normally felt, and yet everything was different. "I don't believe it. After all this time, a brother or sister for Deslo. He doesn't know yet, does he?"

"No," Nara said. "I've only just felt sure of it myself. I thought we could tell him together."

"Sure," Kaden said, "but we should probably wait a little while, so he doesn't feel his birthday and the ceremony are being overshadowed."

"Absolutely," Nara said. "I didn't mean we should tell him right now. I don't want to share this with anyone just yet. It's our secret for now."

Kaden nodded, some sober realizations hitting him about the nature of their situation. Nara saw the change come over him and asked, "What is it?"

"It'll be a lot different this time, won't it?"

"I don't know, I think the process is pretty much the same, even at my advanced age." She smiled coyly.

"I mean this," Kaden said, motioning around him to indicate the tiny cabin. "Not exactly a palace, is it?"

"No, but most babies don't get palaces. And no baby needs one."

"True, but we're exiles with no real home and no idea where the road ahead will take us," Kaden said. "Living on a ship and roaming the world are less than ideal circumstances to bring a child into, don't you think?"

"Maybe, but let me ask you something," Nara said, reaching down and taking both of Kaden's hands in her own. "Do you love me?"

"Yes, Nara, of course I—"

"Did you love me when Deslo was born?"

Kaden, who had been looking at Nara as she spoke, lowered his gaze. A hint of sadness had appeared in her eyes. Perhaps he'd imagined it. They'd come a long way since fleeing Barra-Dohn, slowly building the marriage they'd never had while they lived there. Despite how far they'd come, though, it still shamed Kaden to think about how he'd neglected both his wife and son.

"Nara, I—"

Nara reached up and placed her finger gently on his lips. "That's behind us, now. I just need you to understand something. I've been happier these past few years than I ever was in the palace of Barra-Dohn, and it isn't even close by. I don't care that I'm probably going to have this baby on a ship. As long as I'm with you, as long as we're finally a real family, that's all the home this baby needs. It's all the home anyone needs."

Kaden nodded and smiled again, squeezing Nara's hands. "Point taken. We'll take this one step at a time." He let go of Nara's hands and motioned in the direction of Deslo's tiny room. "I want to pop in and see Deslo, if he hasn't fallen asleep yet."

Before Kaden could turn back toward the door, though, Nara had reached out and taken hold of his arm. "You aren't going anywhere yet. Not until you tell me that this makes you as happy as it makes me."

Kaden turned back toward Nara and wrapped his arms around her. Leaning down, he kissed the top of her head and stroked her hair. "It may take some time for me to get used to it, but never doubt that I'm happy about it." He turned her head up so their eyes met. "I'm delighted."

They stood holding each other, and after a moment, Nara eased Kaden away. "Go. I know he was trying to stay awake until you got back."

"Thanks," Kaden said, smiling. "Back soon."

Deslo's "cabin" had been a small storage room before being put to its current use. The back half was just big enough for the hammock that hung across it from wall to wall, and the front half held only a small stool, pushed to the side so no one stumbled over it upon entering. Kaden slipped into the dark room quietly and sat down on the stool. As he lifted his candle, he could see Deslo's eyes flicker open.

"Sorry to wake you," he said.

"I wasn't asleep yet," Deslo said, but Kaden had his doubts.

"Big day tomorrow," Kaden said, setting the candle on the floor.

"I guess," Deslo said, adjusting himself in the hammock and looking up at the ceiling.

Kaden smiled. Deslo might not technically be thirteen yet, but he'd been a teenager at heart for a while now.

"Nervous?"

Deslo shrugged. "Not really."

"Good," Kaden said. "Don't be. It'll be fine. Just do what Tchinchura says, and it'll be fine."

Deslo didn't say anything else, so Kaden reached into his pocket and pulled out the small, wrapped bundle he'd risked his neck and D'Sarza's anger for in Brexton. Deslo noticed the motion and turned to see what Kaden had.

"Turning thirteen is kind of a big deal anyway," Kaden said. "A special birthday deserves a special present."

Kaden stretched out his hand toward the hammock. Deslo sat up, reached out, and took hold of the bundle. He looked puzzled, seeming to weigh the small but heavy object in his hand. "What is it?"

"Open it and find out," Kaden said.

Deslo unwrapped the bundle, dropping the loose packaging on the floor. In his hand was a small, dark red figurine of a man holding some sort of tool in his hand. Deslo turned it over in his hands a few times, then looked up at Kaden again, still puzzled. "Who is it?"

"I'm not really sure," Kaden said. "I think that's a trowel he's holding, so it's probably a mason."

"A mason," Deslo said, frowning. "This is my special present?"

"It's not special because of who it is," Kaden said. He'd anticipated a reaction like this. "It is special because of what it is."

"A statue?"

"What it's made of," Kaden said, reaching out so that Deslo could put the figurine back in his hand. Kaden ran his fingertips along the statue, feeling the cool, smooth marble. "This isn't just any stone, Deslo. This marble was quarried in Aralyn, just north of Barra-Dohn."

That got Deslo's attention, and Kaden handed the figurine back. Deslo gave it closer look.

"Finest red marble in the world," Kaden said quietly, almost reverently. "I really wanted to give you something that would . . . I don't know, connect you somehow with home. But I didn't know what to get. I looked a long time, port after port, but nothing seemed to be just right.

"When I saw this, though, I knew I'd found it," he finished as Deslo clasped the small statue in both hands in his lap. "A piece of home you can hold."

Deslo stared at Kaden, the look in his eyes unreadable. Then he reached down and set the small figure on the floor.

"It isn't home anymore."

Kaden was surprised. "Why do you say that?"

"It's been two and a half years," Deslo said. Kaden couldn't decide if he heard sadness in Deslo's voice or perhaps something else. Maybe anger. "We're never going back."

"We may never go back," Kaden said, and the words almost caught in his throat. He'd thought them before, but it was another thing to say them, to admit this to his son, to Deslo Omiir, who was to have been the heir to that great city and its empire after Kaden was gone. "Nevertheless, Barra-Dohn is home. It's a part of me. It's a part of you, and we carry it with us, always. It lives in here."

Kaden reached up and touched his chest, tapping it lightly several times.

Deslo watched him for a moment, and then looked back at the ceiling. "Am I still not old enough?"

"Old enough for what?"

"To know the things you wouldn't tell me when I was younger," Deslo said. "About what Zangira found."

Kaden clasped his hands and leaned forward on the stool. He looked at Deslo, lying on the bunk, gazing at the dark wooden ceiling. He thought for a moment, to make sure.

"You're old enough."

Deslo looked over, and Kaden thought there might have been a glimmer of surprise. It was late, and he had probably expected Kaden to at least put it off. Kaden didn't want to put it off, though. It seemed somehow oddly appropriate, tonight of all nights, before Deslo turned this page in his life, to look back with him at what had happened.

"You know what Tchinchura wears," Kaden said, "and you know that your grandfather had one too. You know what he did to get it."

Kaden almost never talked about Eirmon, but he knew that Deslo had figured out some of what had transpired around him during the final days of Barra-Dohn. There was no hiding from their family's part in it.

"You also know about the Jin Dara, how he attacked the city. You know that we're pretty sure he took the fragment of the Golden Cord that Eirmon had." Kaden took a deep breath before he continued. "One of the reasons we're so sure is that when Zangira and the Amhuru he took with him returned to Barra-Dohn, it was so completely devastated, they concluded that the power wielded there must mean the Jin Dara had both pieces."

Deslo wasn't staring at the ceiling anymore. He had turned on his side and was watching Kaden intently. "Was nothing left? Were there no people?"

Kaden shook his head. "They found ruin and rubble, lots of sand, and lots of dead bodies."

Kaden had held back until now from telling Deslo the truth about the total annihilation that Barra-Dohn had suffered. He hadn't wanted those images of home in his son's head. But that had been Deslo the boy. Tomorrow, Deslo would leave that childhood behind. More than that, he would give himself to a far greater purpose, one that might cost him his life, and he deserved to know the truth about the city he'd been raised in and the cruelty of the one who had destroyed it.

"Like Garranmere," Deslo said, breaking the silence and interrupting Kaden's musings. Kaden looked at Deslo with surprise, and Deslo added, "We destroyed Garranmere. The Jin Dara destroyed us."

"Yes," Kaden said, nodding almost reluctantly. Garranmere was not a happy memory. "But even the damage we did to Garranmere doesn't really compare to the complete annihilation of Barra-Dohn."

Deslo seemed to ponder that for a moment. Then he asked, "Did they find any trace of the Jin Dara?"

"Yes and no," Kaden said. "He left his mark, beyond the destruction of Barra-Dohn. Almost the entire northern half of Aralyn was abandoned. Amattai, though not physically destroyed, was empty. Zangira suspects that though they had allied themselves with the Jin Dara against Barra-Dohn, the people of Amattai must have realized after what they witnessed that something worse even than Eirmon had come among them, and fled.

"Perhaps they have returned now, or perhaps they one day will, for Zangira thought it clear that the Jin Dara had moved on. Where he went and with what purpose, well, that remains a mystery."

"Zangira is still looking for him, isn't he?"

Kaden nodded. "He searches for the Jin Dara and the missing fragments of the Golden Cord, even as we search with Tchinchura for clues about the Jin Dara's past in hope that they may also shed light on his future."

Deslo reached down and picked the small statue up again. He wrapped his hand around it and held it tight. "Thanks."

"You're welcome," Kaden said. He wasn't completely sure if he was being thanked for the figurine or for finally telling Deslo what Zangira had told them over a year ago when they'd last met with him, but he didn't really care. He'd accept gratitude in any form from Deslo these days.

"Get some sleep," he said, rising from the stool. "Big day tomorrow."

"Dad?"

"Yes?"

"Doesn't it bother you? Not being a king?"

Kaden sat back down. "Honestly, no. It doesn't bother me at all. I'm sad about what happened to Barra-Dohn. It was my home, our home. But really, not being king is almost a relief. I've got you and your mother. That's all I need."

"You didn't want to be king?"

"I didn't want to be like my father," Kaden said quietly, his voice unexpectedly shaky.

"You could have been a different kind of king," Deslo said. "I would have been."

"You would?"

Deslo nodded. "The night after we toured Garranmere, I vowed that when I was king, I'd release the other cities of Aralyn from Barra-Dohn's control. I vowed the empire would end with me."

Kaden stared at his son, trying to really see this boy who seemed so capable of completely surprising him sometimes. He smiled, rose again, and said, "You'll make a fine Amhuru, Deslo."

"Thanks," Deslo said, and Kaden slipped out of the room.

Kaden stood on the deck, his arm around Nara. The sun was out and the day bright, but a sharp breeze was blowing at the moment, and he wanted to keep any chill from the wind away. Strange, he thought, how different the world felt this morning with the knowledge that a tiny life was stirring inside Nara.

Waiting with them for Deslo were Captain D'Sarza and the others who had been with them since the day Barra-Dohn had fallen: Tchinchura, standing quietly with his arms folded across his broad chest; Marlo and Owenn, the two Devoted, in their usual black robes; and Rika, her hair pulled tight and her clothes colorful. Rika noticed Kaden looking and smiled, directing a friendly nod of the head his way.

Much had changed in the time they had been traveling together, but Kaden thought few things had changed as much as Rika. They had all been affected by the stunning and dramatic destruction of Barra-Dohn, but none of them had seemed more overwhelmed by it than her. She'd suggested, at the time, that seeing Deslo's other tutor, Gamalian, killed in front of her eyes had been just too much for her, and even though Kaden hadn't thought the two had been especially close, he could imagine how something like that would make an impact on someone who wasn't well-acquainted with the more violent propensities of mankind.

In the nearly three years since, though, Rika seemed to have shaken off those tragic events and adapted quite well to life onboard *The Sorry Rogue.* In fact, she seemed to relax far more than Kaden could remember her ever relaxing in Barra-Dohn, even opting over time for more festive attire than she'd ever worn before, similar to D'Sarza's look. Nara, though, saw the changes in Rika's clothing choices less in terms of her becoming more festive and more in terms of her becoming less reserved.

Kaden glanced from Rika to Nara now and saw that not only was Nara watching Rika too, but she was frowning as she did so. There'd been a definite coolness between both women since leaving Barra-Dohn, which Kaden assumed had been rooted in the "open secret" that Rika had been Eirmon's mistress—the most recent of many. Whatever it was between them had taken a turn for the colder in recent months, but Nara wouldn't tell him what it was about. He took for granted, then, that he didn't want to know, and happily left the matter alone.

The sound of Deslo's door opening diverted Kaden's attention, and he turned to see his son emerging into the morning sunshine. Knowing that the ceremony would not include them, Captain D'Sarza and the others greeted him warmly, wishing him a happy birthday. After their greetings and well-wishings had been given, Rika, the Devoted, and Captain D'Sarza went on about their business, and Deslo stood now with just his parents and Tchinchura.

Nara embraced Deslo, hugging him tight and kissing him gently on the head. "Thirteen and embarking on the journey of a lifetime," she said. "I'm very proud of you, Deslo."

Deslo nodded and mumbled, "Thanks," shifting his stance awkwardly as though suddenly forgetting how to stand or what to do with his hands. He looked from his mother to his father and the Amhuru and back.

Nara took the cue and hugged him once more before stepping away. "I'll let you get on with things. We'll talk later. If you want to," she hastened to add, almost as an afterthought, and Kaden reached out to take her hand as she started away. He smiled and squeezed it, trying to reassure her that he'd talk to her at least, even if Deslo didn't have much to say.

Kaden hadn't had a close relationship with Deslo until after fleeing the destruction of Barra-Dohn, so the boy's growing recalcitrance this past year hadn't affected him nearly as much as it had Nara—she felt it more keenly. He'd tried to reassure her that it was fairly natural, even if undesirable, but Nara had found that comfort threadbare.

"Let's go up," Tchinchura said, speaking at last, and he turned to climb up onto the upper deck where they'd have a bit more privacy. Tchinchura walked to the stern rail and stopped, as did Kaden and Deslo.

Though both were broad, neither Kaden nor Deslo were very tall. The Amhuru was both tall and broad, and Kaden felt as he often did in Tchinchura's presence—a little bit in awe. The Amhuru's golden eyes were fixed on Deslo, though, and as Kaden looked at his son, he could see that if he himself was a little nervous, Deslo was more so.

Tchinchura held out his hand, and Kaden looked at the replica of the Amhuru's fragment of the Golden Cord wriggling in it. As Tchinchura kept his hand still, the replica rose slowly into the air above it and began to move and dance in a slow, graceful, rhythmic pattern.

"For a thousand years, the Amhuru have kept and cared for the fragments of the Golden Cord, to the best of our ability," Tchinchura said. "It is a sacred trust we hold from Kalos himself. It is a responsibility that comes with great power, for bearing even a replica of a fragment will give you that power. This responsibility should never be entered into lightly. Are you resolved, Deslo, that you want to become an apprentice? You must be ready to die to protect the fragments and their replicas, and with the Jin Dara out there, with two pieces already in his possession, this is perhaps a very real eventuality, a decision that may confront us all."

Tchinura paused, keeping his penetrating gaze on Deslo, but Kaden was pleased and proud to see that Deslo did not falter under the look, and Tchinchura continued.

"Your father chose this freely, and you must as well. It must be your choice."

"It is," Deslo said at last. "I know what the Jin Dara did to my home. I know what is at stake. I want this."

Tchinchura examined Deslo closely, then nodded. "Very well, then we'll proceed."

He placed his right hand on Deslo's head and nodded to Kaden, who placed his right hand on Deslo's shoulder. Deslo bowed his head a little bit, not because of the weight of Tchinchura's hand, but because of the weight of the moment. Kaden understood that weight, having felt it himself when he went through this ceremony.

While listening to Tchinchura lead Deslo through the same vows, his mind drifted back to the moment when he stood before Tchinchura and Zangira. He hadn't known that someone who wasn't born an Amhuru could become one, but once he had discovered it was so, it had been a relatively easy decision for him to ask Tchinchura if he could. The end of Barra-Dohn had meant the end of all he'd trained and prepared for, and while committing himself to establishing that relationship he'd never had before with

Nara and Deslo was important, he had needed a larger purpose in life. Becoming an Amhuru had filled that void.

Now Deslo was joining him as an apprentice, and he couldn't be happier. Deslo's future had collapsed along with his own, so there was no reason Kaden's new, larger purpose shouldn't become Deslo's too. Besides, though Deslo had been delighted at his father's new interest during their first year or so at sea, things had been harder of late. Kaden told himself the strain between them was due to the same growing pains that plagued Nara's relationship with Deslo, but deep down he wasn't sure. He wondered if he was reaping some of the bitter harvest he'd sown by his early neglect of his son, now that Deslo was older and might be feeling less charitable about his father's past mistakes. Perhaps both of them being apprenticed to Tchinchura would help bridge this new divide.

Tchinchura directed Deslo to remove his shirt, and Deslo did, tossing it down onto the deck a few feet away. Their years at sea had left Deslo nearly as dark-skinned as Tchinchura. Kaden looked at his son standing firm, and he thought how much he had changed in the last year. His muscles were hard and his baby face gone—Kaden found it easy to see the man replacing the boy he had barely known. He intended to know the man, no matter what.

"Lie down," Tchinchura said, and Deslo did. The sun was bright and the decking hot, but Deslo did not complain. He lay still, and Tchinchura stooped down, setting the replica of his fragment of the Golden Cord on Deslo's chest. The replica squirmed and moved and wriggled, and Kaden recalled as he watched it what he had felt at that moment—the wonder and amazement as the Zerura felt for and found his heartbeat and then synced its own rhythmic pulsing to that beat. He continued to watch as the replica moved up Deslo's chest and over his shoulder, then down his left arm until it wrapped itself around his left bicep.

Deslo, who had been lying very still and alternating between closing his eyes and peeking to watch the replica move across his body, now looked up at Kaden and Tchinchura as though to inquire about what to do now.

Tchinchura smiled and clapped Kaden on the back. “It is done, my friend. Let us help my new apprentice to his feet.”

They bent down, took a hand, and pulled Deslo up. He sprang to his feet, and Kaden thought perhaps he could sense in his son a hint of that new energy and life he had felt when this had been him. He glanced down at the replica he also wore on his left bicep, trying to remember what it had felt like before it had come to rest there.

He didn’t get far with that thought, for at just that moment, a piercing shriek ripped through the morning calm and shouts of confusion and dismay erupted behind them on the main deck. Soon, all three of them were racing from the stern to see what was going on.

3

Setting Sail

Kaden paused at the rail looking down over the main deck. The center of the disturbance was easy to spot, as a sailor was down on his hands and knees, facing the stern. He appeared to have vomited, at least once, and from the way his body was convulsing, it appeared he might just do it again.

Something about the scene wasn't right, Kaden thought. Everyone else on the deck was backing away, and silence had replaced the earlier commotion, so that all Kaden heard was the wretching coming from the sailor himself. Why would the others back away? Sailors and vomit were old friends. No matter how salty the sailor, they'd all puked in rough seas more times than they cared to remember. Sure, it was perhaps odd to see one of them throwing up on deck while the ship was at port, but that wasn't anything that couldn't be explained by a bad meal or a little too much ale the previous night.

Then Kaden saw one. It was perhaps a foot or a foot and a half in length, very slender—almost more like a length of string than a length of rope—and it was wriggling around in the dark stain on the deck created by the sailor's vomit. "Is that a gutsnake?"

"It is," Tchinchura said from beside him. "We have to kill them all, and we have to do it now."

Tchinchura slid the blade of his axe along the Zerura wrapped around his bicep and, with a swift motion, threw the axe down at one of the gutsnakes slithering across the deck. The axe struck the slender head of the snake, crushing it utterly. The gutsnake shuddered and lay still, and in a moment, the axe was flying back up through the air to Tchinchura's hand.

The sailor vomited again, and Kaden saw now that there were actually three or four gutsnakes on deck, some having moved away from the sailor in different directions, their slender brown bodies not quite a match against the lighter brown of the deck. Kaden also saw for the first time the tiniest glint of silver on the head of the one closest to them, the tell-tale marking.

Kaden saw the door to the cabin he shared with Nara open below him, and even though he couldn't see Nara herself, he imagined her peeking out from inside. "Close the door, Nara!" he shouted down to her. "Stay inside until I come for you!"

Too late—one of the gutsnakes had noticed the movement of the door and was wriggling that way. Kaden knew the gap between the door and the deck was more than wide enough to allow the gutsnake to slide under, so he raised his arm after rubbing his own axe-blade along the Zerura on his arm and threw.

The axe struck the gutsnake not in the head as he'd intended, but further up the body. The blade severed the head and perhaps one third of the gutsnake's body from the rest. The head and the little bit of the gutsnake attached to it continued to slither toward the cabin, trailing blood from the place where Kaden's axe had severed it from the rest. The section left behind lay still.

"What's happening, Dad?" Deslo asked, watching with fear and disgust. "How can it still move?"

"I have to crush its head," Kaden shouted back as the gutsnake moved relentlessly in the direction of the cabin below them. Kaden tried to reach out through the Arua field and summon his axe back up into his hand, as Tchinchura had done, but though he could feel it, he couldn't call it back. He didn't fully understand why water mediated the Arua field so much differently than land did, but that didn't matter now. His axe was down below, along with the gutsnake, and he needed to kill it before it slipped under the door into his cabin.

The thought of those things growing inside Nara alongside his baby was repugnant beyond words. He would not let that happen.

"Stay here," he said as he glanced sideways at Deslo. Then he placed his hands firmly on the balcony and vaulted over it. His aim was good, and as he fell to the deck below, he saw the gutsnake beneath him. Aiming the heel of his boot at his target, he struck its head with tremendous force. He felt the gutsnake splatter, and moving quickly, he scooped up his axe from the deck nearby as he turned to survey the remainder of the deck.

Tchinchura had struck again, and now there were two gutsnakes dead by the elder Amhuru's hand, to go along with the fragmented one Kaden had just killed. The infected sailor had thrown up again, it appeared for the last time, as he now lay face down in his own vomit, not moving. The deck was clear of all but the hardiest of Captain D'Sarza's men, who held whatever weapons they could find and were standing in something of a makeshift ring, trying to keep the gutsnakes from getting to or past them. D'Sarza was among them, for once in her life so preoccupied that she wasn't barking orders at anyone.

Kaden saw that Marlo and Owenn were also there among the sailors, and he froze when he saw them standing, as they almost always did, barefoot. He felt momentarily torn between standing guard before Nara's door and going to the Devoted to stand with them. He glanced up at the rail above, thinking that if he could ask Tchinchura to watch out for Nara's door, then he would be free to go, when suddenly Tchinchura's axe flashed down right beside him.

He looked down at the place where it hit, just behind his left foot, and sure enough, a gutsnake was quivering its final quiver. It must have been one of the first to emerge, as it had evidently gotten far enough to be out of the sunny part of the main deck, more or less unnoticed. Kaden hadn't seen it at all.

Fear seized Kaden. If one had made it this far unobserved, why not more than one? Maybe one had already penetrated the cabin. He turned, took two quick steps, and flung open the door to the cabin in one swift, desperate motion.

Nara stood just beyond the door, clasping the great big book she had borrowed from the Devoted. Relief flooded her face as she saw Kaden appear.

"Did anything get in?" he asked as he began quickly to survey the small room.

"No," she said, shaking her head violently, "at least I don't think so, but I was sitting at the desk with my back to the door before I heard the commotion."

Kaden nodded. He'd have to search everything, everywhere, just to be sure. A gutsnake could coil itself into a tiny ball to hide almost anywhere, and he couldn't take any chances. He grabbed a cloak draped over the only other chair in the room and tossed it to Nara. "Close the door and shove this up underneath it."

He proceeded to tear the cabin apart, piece by piece. He searched through all the bedding, oh so carefully, even lifting the mattress out of the sturdy frame that was bolted to the wall and standing it up on its side to examine beneath it. When he was convinced nothing was in or under the bed, he searched below the desk and the small chest they used to keep what clothes and possessions they had. At last, when he could think of no place left to search, he breathed a sigh of relief. He'd often missed his expansive quarters in the palace of Barra-Dohn, but today he was glad their cabin was small.

"I need to go back out and help," Kaden said. "Close the door behind me and shove the cloak back underneath."

"Is Deslo safe?" Nara asked as Kaden opened the door.

"As safe as he could be," Kaden replied. "I left him with Tchichura."

He started out and she said, "Be careful."

"I will," he said, closing the door.

The scene on the deck was very different from what it had been a few moments ago. Instead of one large ring around the perimeter, there were three clusters of men standing in tight circles, and Kaden could see in each case they were swinging whatever weapons they were holding, over and over. He could hear the cacophony of sound echoing across the deck, and he could imagine the gutsnakes that must be inside each of those rings, trying desperately to evade the death blow. After only a few moments, it was all over.

The bodies of eleven gutsnakes were gathered and placed inside a sturdy sack, which was in turn weighted down, much more than was necessary, and summarily tossed overboard. The entire crew of *The Sorry Rogue* stood and watched as the sack quickly sank out of sight, and still they stared, until eventually they got tired of watching the ripples of the quiet sea.

As their attention turned to dealing with the body of the dead sailor, Kaden returned wearily to Deslo and Tchinchura, still standing at the rail on the upper stern deck. He'd wanted Deslo's thirteenth birthday to be memorable, but this wasn't what he'd had in mind.

"How . . . ?" Deslo started, looking shaken. "I mean, they came from inside him?"

"Gutsnakes are a very unusual creature," Tchinchura said as he slowly and steadily wiped the guts and blood from his axe. "They like to lie in wait in your bed or under your chair, and they watch for exposed skin on the foot or lower leg to bite, waiting patiently for an opportunity to strike when a simple turn of the head won't reveal them."

"Their bite is like a sharp sting," Kaden said, taking up the explanation where Tchinchura had left off, "but immediately upon biting you, they inject some sort of anesthetic, and the momentary pain from the sting is actually replaced by a kind of foggy sensation, a feeling almost of pleasure."

"If the gutsnake is not found and removed immediately," Tchinchura said, "the foggy feeling spreads and can even make you forget that you were just 'stung' by something. And I do mean immediately, because the more time passes without doing so, the less likely the snake will be found. Well if it's not removed, then the gutsnake begins passing tiny eggs through the puncture wounds into your bloodstream. Eggs that travel through your body until they somehow end up in your stomach, where they grow and develop until they're ready to hatch and come out."

"How many?" Deslo asked, disgust and replulsion evident in his voice.

"Perhaps as many as a dozen," Tchinchura said. "A gutsnake bite doesn't kill you, at least, not right away, but no one survives their coming out."

It took three days for things to return to normal on *The Sorry Rogue* after the gutsnake episode. The sailors subjected the whole ship to an examination much like the one to which Kaden had subjected his cabin. However, with so many dark spaces, nooks, and crannies, especially below decks, there remained a lurking fear that perhaps not all of them had been found.

Time passed, though, and nothing happened. No gutsnakes were found, and eventually the hypervigilance of everyone who lived onboard *The Sorry Rogue* began to disappear. Life slowly returned to normal, and with the diversion behind them, the attention of each person began to drift back to the more mundane matters of their own affairs and responsibilities.

On the evening of the fourth day after Deslo's birthday, the three Amhuru sat together, once more on the raised deck at the stern of the ship. Tchinchura sat cross-legged before the other two, cutting slices of goya fruit with a paring knife and eating them, while the dark juice left stains on his lips and hands. He had told Kaden and Deslo that they needed to consider their next move, since they had already tarried in Brexton longer than planned, and without discovering anything of use to their mission.

"The trail seems to have grown cold," Kaden said, as the elder Amhuru ate.

"It has grown cold before," Tchinchura said, cutting another slice.

"It has," Kaden agreed, "but the last few leads, the ones that led us here, seemed so promising. I thought we'd find something, a clue that would point us in the right direction. Something. Anything."

Tchinchura nodded, chewing. "So did I."

For a while they sat in silence. Deslo, new to their counsels, didn't speak unless spoken to. Kaden looked at his son, wondering if he should bring up what he had been wanting to ask Tchinchura, since Deslo didn't know anything about it. Like the truth about Barra-Dohn, though, he thought that Deslo was now old enough to know. More to the point, as a fellow apprentice to Tchinchura, he probably had a right to know. Still, as a father, Kaden wondered if the boy was ready.

He sighed. It was time to speak.

"Is it time, Tchinchura, to reconsider our decision?" Kaden asked, turning his attention to the elder Amhuru and watching him carefully.

"What is on your mind?" Tchinchura said without looking up from the slice he was cutting. "What do you see?"

"Nothing clearly," Kaden said. Usually when Tchinchura asked Kaden what he saw, the question was to be taken literally; however, from time to time, the elder Amhuru asked the question more metaphorically, as he did now. The question was meant to encourage, to invite Kaden to speak further, that his input might be gathered and considered.

Still, Kaden felt, having broached the subject in the first place, that he needed to justify it. "I am wondering when it is time to choose a new path, if the path chosen does not take us where we want to go."

Tchinchura nodded. "A fair question. Let us consider our options to see if now, perhaps, things have changed and the balance of wisdom points in another direction. Say on."

"In essence," Kaden said, considering his words carefully, "the decision to pursue the Jin Dara and his past rather than to wait for his next move was made out of fear that he might discover the location of Azandalir and attack it, wielding the power of both fragments in overwhelming force."

"That was part of the fear," Tchinchura agreed, "but it was more than that. We also feared the havoc he might wreak in general if he was left to his own devices with two fragments of the Cord. The fragments are our charge, and we bear the weight of responsibility to make sure no man uses their power to do harm."

"True, which is why Zangira led the team charged with searching for the Jin Dara, and you have led us in the search for his past in the hope that we might find something of use, whether it be something that would help us locate him or something that would help us understand and defeat him."

"But we haven't found either," Tchinchura said, setting down both the knife and the goya fruit. He clasped his hands together, looking deep in thought.

"No, we haven't," Kaden said. "And Zangira hasn't found him."

"That we know of," Tchinchura said.

"That we know of," Kaden agreed. "And it's been two years since we fled Barra-Dohn—the Jin Dara's had plenty of time to explore and perhaps even master the use of two fragments."

Tchinchura's eyebrows slipped up more than a little as he gazed at Kaden. "You have been training for a similar amount of time and have learned something of the complexity of using a fragment to manipulate the power of the Arua field. Have you had plenty of time to master its use?"

"No, of course not," Kaden said, perhaps a touch defensively, "but I started as a novice—he did not."

Tchinchura bowed his head slightly, acknowledging the point.

"And I've been at sea much of the time," Kaden added.

"Also true," Tchinchura conceded. "But I suspect that wielding two fragments magnifies the complexity, not just the power. It will take time for him to master it."

"He may not need to master it to pose a dire threat to Azandalir and all the Amhuru of the Southlands."

"He may not, but if he has already grown that strong, how will retreating to Azandalir to wait for his attack help us?" Tchinchura guessed his thoughts.

"It may not," Kaden said, and he hesitated for a moment before going on. He'd known once he started this conversation that it would lead here, and he did not broach this subject lightly. He took a deep breath. "If the Jin Dara is that strong, then it may not matter whether we wait for him in our full strength in one place or keep moving in an attempt to make the third fragment harder for him to find. But are those our only choices?"

"No," Tchinchura said, shaking his head. "But I will not turn from this path to another one unless that which I bear is in imminent danger and there is no other way. And not unless the will of the Council of Elders is convinced it is the only way."

Movement at the top of the stairs caught Kaden's eye, and he turned, welcoming the diversion. Marlo and Owenn emerged from below with a stranger. He was short and wiry, and his wrinkled, olive skin and snow-white hair—hanging in a myriad of braided strands—belied his age even if his step was lively. Kaden deduced from his look and attire that he was a native of one of the many Maril Islands, though he had likely spent the better part of his lifetime at sea.

Tchinchura rose as the Devoted and the other approached, so Kaden and Deslo rose too. As they drew near, Marlo spoke, and though typically even-keeled, his voice betrayed a rare note of excitement. "This is Garjan. We think you'll want to hear what he has to say."

"Very good," Tchinchura said, looking from the Devoted to the sailor, who in turn looked nervously from Tchinchura back to Marlo.

"Go ahead," Marlo urged him gently. "Just tell him what you told us."

"Yes, *saba*," Garjan said, turning to address Tchinchura. "Forgive me . . . When I was a boy, an Honored One helped settle a nasty dispute between my people and a neighboring village. War was averted and lives were saved, perhaps my father's among them. I have spent my life at sea and have seen few men since, so I apologize, Honored One, if I stutter before you like a *fanda* telling his first story."

"It's all right," Tchinchura said with a smile. "The hospitality of your people was ample payment for any service we may have provided, as is your gratitude."

"Yes, Honored One," the islander said, bowing his head to acknowledge Tchinchura's gracious reply before beginning his story. "As I told the *saba,* there is an island, just a little island, not far from my own, which long ago fell under a curse."

"A curse?" Kaden said.

"Yes . . . Honored One," the man replied, seeming to deliberate before noticing the golden band encircling Kaden's bicep that matched Tchinchura's own. "In the days of my grandfather and my father's youth, it was but one of many nameless islands. Its inhabitants had a thriving fishing trade. The *chokra* they caught and traded were second to none.

"But, in the days of my youth, something happened there," Garjan continued. "No longer did fishermen from the island sail to nearby markets to trade their *chokra,* nor did anyone else dare approach it. The village by the coast, visible from the harbor, was abandoned, and strange tales were told of winged nightmares that feared not the light of day and terrorized anyone who ventured ashore, no matter how many or how brave.

"No one goes near the island anymore, not even to fish off its shores. Fisherman or merchant—all avoid it. The island is cursed."

Kaden felt excitement welling up inside as he turned to Tchinchura. "The timeframe fits."

"It does," Tchinchura said. He kept his eyes locked on the sailor. "How far from here to this island?"

Kaden saw Deslo watching them, puzzled. He wanted to explain, but he was too eager to hear the sailor's response to interrupt.

The sailor shrugged, looking about him at *The Sorry Rogue* as though taking its measure for the first time. "On a vessel such as this, you might be able to get there in six to eight weeks, if the winds are good and the sea does not spite you. But, out of respect for the Honored One, I would urge you not to go. This is no tale in order to frighten children. This is truthspeak, I swear."

"I believe you," Tchinchura said, "but it is because I believe you that I will probably have to go. What we seek might be found on this island."

"Then what you seek should not be found, I think."

"That may be," Tchinchura said, "but duty compels me."

For a moment they stood in silence, and then Tchinchura said, "Garjan, would you come with us? We would not . . ."

Garjan shook his head vigorously and waved his hands back and forth in a gesture of strong denial. His eyes were wide, and his lips moved but did not speak.

". . . ask you to go ashore with us," Tchinchura finished, but his words had no effect on Garjan's agitated state.

"Honored One," he stammered out, "I would like to repay our ancient debt, but I cannot go with you."

"I understand, Garjan—and there is no debt," Tchinchura said. "If I have our captain bring her charts, then, would you be able to help us plot a course for this island?"

Garjan considered this. "If you are determined to go, I will help. I would not repay an Honored One with discourtesy, though it troubles me to do so."

"I am grateful," Tchinchura said. "Come, we will prepare you some food while the captain is summoned."

Less than forty-eight hours later, *The Sorry Rogue* left Brexton behind to sink below the horizon in the distance as she sailed for the mysterious island. Kaden did not look back. The hope that they might at last find that elusive something for which they sought compelled him to look forward.

Deslo stood with him by the bow, gazing out over the choppy waters, for clouds were gathering that promised at least a little rain. He fingered the Zerura on his bicep. "Do you think we'll finally find something to help us against the Jin Dara?" he asked.

"I don't know, Deslo," Kaden said, looking down at his son, "but I hope so."

"The sailor seemed pretty scared," Deslo said, turning back to gaze out at the swelling waves. "But I don't believe in curses."

"Me neither."

"Could still be dangerous, though."

"Yes, it could," Kaden agreed. "There are no safe places, Deslo. Not anymore. And as long as our enemy is still out there, there can be no surrender."

4

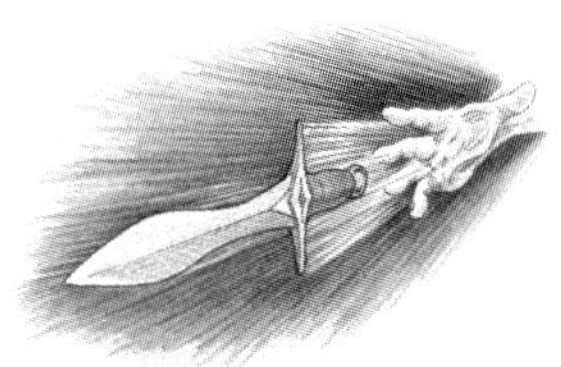

The Island of Dreadful Daylight

Olli sat on the trunk of the fallen tree at the edge of the grove, staring up the grassy slope at the walls that encircled the manor house and its compound. A yellow-orange glow shone above it, coloring a night sky that was illuminated everywhere else by the pale light of the half moon. The glow did not flicker. It was not a fire. It appeared every evening and disappeared every morning—though neither Olli nor anyone else dared risk being on hand at sunset or sunrise to witness its coming or its going.

"Are you going up there or what?" she heard someone whisper at her from the small crowd hiding behind her in the grove. Jann. He liked to goad her. Olli ignored him and sat, still staring up the hill.

"Don't do it, Olli. Let's go back." That was Neren. Olli knew she was petrified that the gorgaal would wake up at any moment and swarm down on them, even though everyone knew they only came out during the day.

"If she's not going up the hill, why'd we come down the mountain?" the first voice said. It was definitely Jann, and Olli heard the annoyance in his voice. "We've wasted hours coming down, and it'll take hours to get back—"

"Not so loud," Neren said.

"They can't hear us from up—"

"You don't know that."

"Well, I'm going back," Jann said. "Anyone else coming?"

Olli stood, and a hush fell on the others. She turned and looked at them huddled among the trees in the shadows. Always huddled. Always hiding. That was life on the island. Well, she didn't want to live that way, and she wasn't going to—not if there was a chance it could be different.

"I'm going up," she said, her voice calmer than she felt.

"Oh, Olli—"

"Jann's right, Neren. It's why we came."

"But the gorgaal . . ."

Neren didn't finish her thought. There was no need. Just the name was enough to give Olli a moment of indecision. She took a deep breath. "I know, Neren. I'll be as careful as I can."

A dozen faces about her age stared back at her in the moonlight. She'd been insistent that none of the younger kids come with them down the mountain. They'd had too far to go, and they would have to move fast on the way back up to get inside the mountain before daybreak. They couldn't risk being slowed down.

Olli and Jann were the oldest of those who'd come. No one older had come, because they didn't know. If word had gotten out among the adults about what Olli intended, she'd have been restrained by the elders from coming herself.

"Anyone coming up with me?" Olli said, and the group was quiet. "As far as the gate?"

"I'll come," Jann said after a moment, and despite their frequent arguments, Olli was relieved she wouldn't be going alone. "As far as the gate."

Jann walked out and joined her just beyond the edge of the grove, his face hard to read in the faint moonlight. Olli could just make out his eyes, watching her. She turned back to face the hill and the manor house at the top. "Thanks," she said softly under her breath.

"You're welcome," he said. "But instead of thanking me, just try not to do something that'll get us both killed."

Olli looked over her shoulder at the others, who clung, if anything, closer together. "Don't wait here too long. If we're not back in half an hour, start back up the mountain. We'll catch up."

Olli started away toward the hill, and Jann followed after.

"Olli . . . Olli!"

She ignored Neren. The grass rustled under her feet as she made her way to the foot of the long, gently sloping hill. There she hesitated, looking up.

"You sure you want to do this?" Jann said quietly. "We can still go back."

"And have you call me a coward for the rest of my life?" Olli said, still staring up the hill. "I don't think so."

"Olli, this is serious," Jann said. "What if you're wrong?"

"I'm not," Olli said, starting forward up the slope. She was right. She knew she was.

As she climbed, Olli tried not to think about what lay beyond the gate. She didn't doubt that once, before the gorgaal, this had been a beautiful place. The manor house—what could be seen of it from below and from the few vantage points on the mountain that looked out over it—was a grand building. People had lived there once, before the gorgaal had come.

That notion, that there had been a time before the gorgaal, was what had fueled her determination to come here. Everyone else accepted that the gorgaal ruled the day, driving the islanders underground in daylight. Everyone else believed the gorgaal were too strong and too numerous to fight, so their meager survival was the best anyone could hope for . . . until they could get off the island.

Get off the island. Ever the dream, only there were no ships and no one had figured out how to build a seaworthy vessel with the restrictions they faced. Getting to the coast took half the night, leaving no time to work on a ship before they had to head back up the mountain. The only alternatives seemed to be to build the ship somehow underground in the caves, only how would they then get it out or down the mountain to the coast? Or, perhaps, they could build an underground barracks near the coast for the shipbuilders, but that posed the same problems as building the ships—it would take time and had to be done at night.

Olli wasn't holding her breath that a way off the island would present itself anytime soon, nor did she accept or believe what everyone else did about the untouchable supremacy of the gorgaal. Too much about them remained unexplained. If there'd been a time before the gorgaal, where had they come from? The oldest among the elders had been children when they first came. They told stories of living above ground. They could remember the terror of the gorgaal before they discovered and extended the network of caves in the mountain for the islanders to take refuge in. Those days had been dark and desperate, no doubt, and Olli didn't question that things were certainly better now. But once, they had been better still. Could they not be again?

Why didn't the gorgaal fly by night? Why would they come no farther into the main cave entrance in the mountains than the sentry rock, even though they knew the islanders lived within? Why did they spend the night at the manor house, and what was the yellow-orange glow that appeared above it every night? Perhaps those questions would lead nowhere. Perhaps they were the key to finding a way to end the gorgaal's reign of terror. Olli intended to find out.

The slope had gotten steeper, momentarily hiding the walls at the top, but as she and Jann crested the rim and the ground started to level out, they could see not only the wall but the manor house rising above it in the distance. The wall was just enough taller than Olli that she couldn't see over it, and it was made of dark stone and lay straight ahead in the distance. Given the orientation of the building beyond the wall and the rumors she'd heard about the manor house, Olli figured the gate was around the corner, some fifty yards or more to their left.

Olli and Jann both dropped to the ground and lay in the grass, looking at the wall and the house beyond it. The glow was above the whole compound, but it did not seem to come from the manor house itself. Rather, Olli thought it emanated from the large space between the walls and the house, in the back of the compound. If that was where the gorgaal were, that meant the gate was on the complete opposite end of the compound.

Olli swallowed. If she got up the nerve to actually approach and enter through the gate, she'd have to find a way through or around the dark manor house to see what made the yellow-orange glow at the back of the compound. Daunting. How could she be sure the gorgaal would be asleep? That even if they stirred, they wouldn't pursue her beyond the compound? Was she so sure of her theory that she would bet her life on it?

"Well?" Olli said, glancing over at Jann.

"Well what?"

"Are you coming with me to the gate?" She stood and brushed off the grass that clung to her.

"I said I was, didn't I?" Jann said. He stood too, but Olli could read hesitation in his body language.

"This isn't a competition," she said. "You've come this far. You don't have to come any farther. This wasn't your idea."

"Just get on with it," Jann said. "If you don't get us killed up here, we'll need time to get back up the mountain. I don't want to die up there any more than I want to die here."

Olli turned away from him and started jogging low along the top of the hill, parallel to the wall. She smiled as she ran, wisps of her blonde hair whipping into her face. Neren was right—Jann definitely liked her. It would be a shame to get him killed before she figured out if she liked him too.

She turned the corner. The moon had passed behind a cloud, and there was very little light, other than the glow rising up from the other side of the compound, which wasn't much help out here. The wall seemed to run a long way in the dark, unbroken, but she thought she could see something that might be the gate. She jogged away from the cusp of the hill, out through the open field of almost waist-high grass that lay around the compound, toward what she thought must be her way in.

Jann kept pace behind her. Olli's heart raced as she drew closer and realized it was a gate. It stood taller than the wall, was closed, but wasn't solid. She could see through it into the darkness beyond, but without the moonlight, she couldn't make out much of what lay there, though she could see the front of the manor house in the distance.

"I hope the hinges aren't rusted," Jann said, leaning over to whisper as they both squatted in the grass opposite the gate.

"Me too," Olli said.

"It probably hasn't been opened in a long, long time."

"Probably not," she agreed. "Good thing for me you came along, I guess. I might need some help with it."

With that, Olli started forward. Staying low, she approached the gate. She drew near, reached up, and took hold of it. It was metal, cool to the touch, and grainy like it was coated with sand. She gave it a tug, and it didn't budge. She pushed and felt a little give.

She turned to whisper to Jann, when the moon emerged from behind the cloud; out the corner of her eye, she saw something large and dark gliding along through the grass, low to the ground, just beyond the gate. Two gleaming eyes stared back into her own. Below them a huge snout rose, revealing row after row of teeth, glinting in the moonlight.

She leapt back from the closed gate, shocked by the sight. She slammed into Jann, and both stumbled to the ground. As she fell, she tried to keep her eye on the creature. The grass beyond the gate was as tall as it was on this side, and whatever the creature was, it stayed largely concealed within it. She heard a rustling sound, saw that there were several more pairs of eyes peering at her from the grass beyond the gate, and did not wait any longer. She leapt up, reached down for Jann's hand to help him up too, and started running back toward the top of the hill.

Only after they'd crested the hill and made their way more than halfway down in the darkness did Olli begin to slow. She reached out for Jann's arm and tugged on him so he would as well. They stopped, and she caught her breath.

"Olli," Jann said, "what . . . ?"

"You saw them?"

He nodded.

"I have no idea," she said. Having put some distance between herself and the gate, the panic Olli had felt was beginning to settle down. A host of thoughts ran through her head. She seized on one of them and looked up at Jann. "Whatever they are, if the gorgaal use them to guard the gate, maybe I'm right: they're vulnerable at night."

"Maybe," Jann said.

"You don't sound so sure."

"Are you?"

"No," Olli conceded. "But they were guarding the gate. There were several, and they must have been nearby before we ever got there. I barely had time to give the gate the merest jingle and they were descending upon it."

"They would have descended upon us if we'd actually pushed it open," Jann said.

"Good thing we didn't."

"Good thing," he agreed. It was a sign of how startled they both were that he left it at that. The Jann who liked to argue with her about everything in the safety of the caves would have happily pointed out that opening the gate had been precisely what she'd brought them all this way to do.

Perhaps it was that thought, or the thought of having to tell the others they'd gotten as far as the gate but no farther, that led Olli to blurt out, "Let's follow the wall around the back."

"Olli—"

"No, wait, hear me out."

Surprisingly, Jann waited. Olli quickly ordered her thoughts. "We've come all this way—down the mountain, up the hill. Worked up the courage to try the gate. We can't go back yet, not when we're this close—"

"Did you not see those things?"

"They're behind the gate," Olli said. "We're safe out here."

"You sure about that?"

"Yes," Olli said, nodding firmly to reinforce her point.

"Really?" Jann said. He almost sounded amused.

"Think about it," Olli said. "The gate's closed. Why? The gorgaal can fly. They don't care if it's open or closed . . ."

"That's why they leave it closed," Jann said. "To keep us out."

"Maybe, or perhaps they leave it closed to keep those things in. They look like a much better deterrent than a rusty old gate. After all, if they are vulnerable at night, as I suspect, the gate wouldn't slow down an attack very much. Those creatures might."

"Olli," Jann said, "you're just guessing, and even if your guesses are correct, why does that mean we're safe out here?"

"I'm not guessing, I'm inferring. That's different," Olli said, but before Jann could say anything in reply, she hastened on. "I think the gate is closed to keep those things inside, Jann, because the gorgaal know they'd wander all over the island if they were let out. They wouldn't offer protection to the gorgaal at night if they weren't locked in there."

"Maybe," Jann said again. "But even if there aren't any of those things out here, why should we go around back? If there's another gate, it's probably guarded by more of them—or something worse. If there isn't a gate, it would be a waste of time."

"No," Olli said, a little indignant that Jann would think she hadn't already reasoned all that out. "In fact, I'm hoping the wall runs all the way around the back. That way we can sneak right up to it, and you can boost me up on your shoulders—"

"No, absolutely not."

"Why not?"

"'Cause you have no idea what's on the other side."

"That's the point, I need to find out!"

"No, you don't," Jann countered. "If you're wrong about the gorgaal and they see you, they could swarm all over both of us before we got ten feet down this hill."

"If I'm wrong—" Olli started.

"That's right," Jann said, "*if* you're wrong, and you could be. I didn't say you are, but you could be. And we're not risking our lives again tonight."

"Don't be dramatic," Olli said.

"I'm not being dramatic. Those gleaming-teeth monsters by the gate could have killed us!"

"Jann, please—"

"Besides," he said, "it's been at least half an hour. We need to get started up the mountain. You know what'll happen to us if we're not back by dawn. We need to go now."

"I'll go on my own," Olli said stubbornly.

"No, you won't," Jann said. "I'll pick you up and carry you back."

"I'd like to see you try."

"Olli," Jann said more gently, "let's go back and think about this. Give it a little time. If you're still convinced you're right—that it'd be safe to approach the compound from the back, and that this is what you want to do—we can come back."

She considered. "You promise you'll come back?"

"No promises, Olli," Jann said. "But I'll think about it."

Olli sighed. That was probably as good a deal as she was going to get, and she didn't especially like the idea of climbing back up the hill, following the wall around to the back, and climbing up to the top to peek over it all on her own. She would never have told Jann this, but she'd felt a good deal of relief when he volunteered to come with her. She'd have come on her own, but she was glad she hadn't had to.

"All right," she said. "We'll go back."

"Good," Jann said, turning around to march down the hill. "And don't act so disappointed."

"Why not? I failed, didn't I?"

"Not at all," he said. "We made it to the gate, we learned that there's something else other than the gorgaal lurking beyond it, and I'm your witness that all this is true. I'd say you made some real progress tonight."

"Doesn't feel like it."

"Maybe not," Jann shrugged as he led the way back down the hill. "But the gorgaal have ruled this island for years and years. You weren't ever going to get rid of them in a night. It'll take time, if it happens at all."

That thought, of the end of the gorgaal's hold on the island, cheered Olli up, and she held onto it as they moved quickly down the hill and then hurried back up the mountain. They caught up to the others about halfway back to the cave, returning just in time to get a good scolding from the sentry on duty for cutting it way too close.

When Olli woke up early the next evening, the caves were abuzz with how much more active the gorgaal had been all day. Apparently, two or three times the normal number had been crawling all over the entrance to the cave, venturing in to the sentry rock repeatedly before moving back out into the sunshine.

Theories about why their activity had increased were flying around the caves, too. Thankfully none of them struck too near what Olli suspected must be the truth—that she had somehow caused this with her nocturnal activities. She stayed out of sight in her room, waiting for a chance, come nightfall, to slip outside to the stream and wash off the black-red rust stain on her hand.

Olli pulled the sled that hovered behind her with furious determination. Her legs swooshed as she walked, the tall grass parting to either side. Jann was a little taller than she was and his stride a little longer, but still he had to work to keep up. "Olli," he said at last, "slow down."

"Keep up," she countered, not slowing a bit. She was still simmering from having to wait until well past First Dark to leave the cave. The sentries treated them like children, always so cautious, even when the sun was clearly down and there was nothing to fear from the gorgaal. She had no idea what she'd find at the manor house or how much time she'd need there, but she hated inefficiency and waste, even if it was only the intangible material of minutes.

"You're not still stewing over the delay, are you?" Jann said as he came alongside her.

"No, of course not, why would I be stewing about the fact it took you almost two weeks to keep your word?"

"Well, I'm here, aren't I?" Jann mumbled, a tad sheepishly.

"Then keep up."

Jann didn't say anymore, leaving Olli alone with her thoughts, and they were many and jumbled. When she was a little girl, she had experienced a revelation, an epiphany—her destiny was to find a way to free her people from the fear that dwelt in the caves, right in their midst, in and around and beside them all the time, every day.

There were only two ways this could happen—she had to find a way to get rid of the gorgaal so she and everyone else could live free right here on the island, or, if that proved beyond her, she had to find a way to get off the island so she could find a place where there were no gorgaal and lead everyone to safety.

What if that place didn't exist?

The old fear echoed in her mind, and she felt the chill from it all the way down in her heart. She could still remember the day the thought, the awful thought, had first occurred to her—that perhaps the gorgaal weren't just here; perhaps they were everywhere. What if she did, somehow, find a way off the island only to find that everywhere she went, that everywhere anyone could go, the people lived in darkness, cowering together for fear of the gorgaal who ruled the day?

The elders said the island hadn't always been like that, so she'd just assumed that other places weren't like that either. What if she was wrong? What if that was just the way the world worked now? What if that was all there was?

She shuddered, dismissing that terrible thought. It couldn't be. It just couldn't. Theirs was a tiny island, but the world was huge and full of mighty nations. The gorgaal could bully a tiny island and the villagers who lived there, a small people content to make a simple living from the sea, but they couldn't bully the mighty nations that existed far, far from here. There, in those realms, people rose in peace and safety, unafraid of the daylight. There, people didn't just exist—they lived. Olli would see the island be like that again, or she would find a way off the island.

And she was willing to die to do it.

That last part was what the others didn't understand—not the adults, not the younger ones, not Neren, not Jann. But Olli believed it as firmly as she believed anything else. There were things worth dying for, and escaping the gorgaal was surely one of them.

At last they reached the top of the run that cut down the mountain more or less in the direction of the manor house. It wasn't the widest of runs, and near the bottom it narrowed considerably, but it was wide enough to accommodate the sled with some room to spare. Olli tossed her small knapsack into the sled and moved around front to get on.

"I'm not sure you should be steering in this mood," Jann said, even though he held the hovering sled steady so she could climb on in front. "I want to reach the bottom in one piece."

"You know I handle these as well as anybody," Olli said. Jann didn't argue, probably because it was true. She might be a little reckless, but her steering was excellent and always had been. Besides, they both knew that it made more sense for Jann to work the anchor-pole than for him to steer. They'd be moving pretty fast, and if they had to slow significantly or stop, he was far more likely to be able to exert the necessary power to do so than she was.

So Jann climbed onboard behind her, holding them stationery as he did so by jamming the hooks of the anchor-pole in the ground. When they were both in position, he said, "Ready?"

"As I'll ever be," Olli said, slipping her feet into the stirrups at the front of the sled and lowering the attached thick rod with wheels at the end until they touched the ground. The sled would glide along above the ground just fine without them, but it would shoot down the mountain in a straight line, careening wildly with almost no means to steer it without the wheels. If you were good with the anchor pole, you could make basic corrections while you flew down, but the wheels provided a means to make corrections these more gently, and by pushing down harder on them, you could slow yourself at least somewhat by pressing the wheels harder into the ground and increasing the friction.

When Jann felt the wheels touch, he unhooked the anchor-pole, deftly flipped it around so the smooth side opposite the trio of hooks rested on the ground, and gave a firm shove. They started to glide down the sled run, and Olli lifted her feet in the stirrups until the wheels barely touched the ground as they picked up speed. Before long they were humming right along in the bright moonlight, the trees whipping by on either side.

Olli loved the feel of racing down the mountain. She always had. When the gorgaal were gone, she'd do this during the day, when the sun shone bright on the mountain, pouring its light down on the open run and even through the thick canopy of leaves on either side, which would illuminate the woods that always seemed so dark and foreboding at night. She'd fly down the mountain without fear. She would do everything without fear. Everything.

But first the gorgaal had to be dealt with.

5

Dangerous Ground

They reached the bottom without incident, and after Jann thanked her for not killing them on the way down, they left the sled at the usual spot beside the big tree near the bottom of the run and headed immediately toward the manor house. They once again climbed the grassy hill that would take them there, and Olli wondered if she was more or less apprehensive this time around.

The first time she had felt the indefinite fear of the unknown, but this time she felt the very real and specific fear of the terrible creatures with the big teeth she had seen gliding through the grass on the other side of the gate. She reminded herself of all the reasons she'd been so sure those things were contained behind the wall and decided she'd been more apprehensive last time. Yes, she told herself again, she had been far more fearful then.

They crested the hill and once more stood looking at the big wall. The moon was up above the horizon, about three quarters full, and it provided excellent light to once more examine the manor house and the wall around it. For a moment, Olli stood and stared, filled suddenly with an even stronger dose of that deep, insatiable curiosity that sometimes threatened to overwhelm her. She might just be moments away from finally knowing what that yellow-orange glow was.

"Olli?" Jann said, and Olli realized as she snapped back out of her momentary daze that it wasn't the first time he'd mentioned her name just now. "I couldn't get you to slow down before, and now I can't get you to move. Let's go, all right?"

"I was just thinking," Olli said with a little huff as she set off at a brisk pace. "You should try it sometime."

"Actually," Jann said as he caught up to her, "I have this marvelous ability to walk and think at the same time. I can walk and talk too; maybe when we get back, I can show you how."

Olli glanced over and caught the wry grin on Jann's face, and she laughed. She couldn't help it. He tended to either sulk or get snappy when she teased him. Giving it back good-naturedly was a pleasant change.

"How are you so calm?" she asked as they continued to walk, now parallel to the outer wall which ran beside them on their left.

"I don't know," Jann said. "I was really nervous last night, could hardly get to sleep, in fact. But for some reason, I'm not feeling it right now."

"Well, maybe that's a sign that all will go well," Olli said. They almost abruptly reached the corner of the wall, and she stopped.

"Wouldn't that be great," Jann said quietly as he stopped beside her for a second, then started along the new length of wall. "Come on, let's do that walking and talking thing."

This was the back, then, Olli thought as they walked. The side where they'd found the gate had definitely been the front, and they were parallel to that now. The yellow-orange glow that had been strong and bright beside them for some time seemed no closer now, but whatever it was that gave rise to it must lie both behind the manor house and perhaps somewhat equidistant from the side and back walls. Would there be another gate here? There had been none on the side.

On they walked, and Olli realized the source of the glow was now not just beside them but also a little behind them, and she wondered if they had passed the midpoint of the back wall. They kept going, quietly examining the solid, unbroken dark of the wall several yards away, and they found no gate or gaps in it of any kind. Then, just as Olli was reluctantly accepting that there would be nothing, they reached the far corner.

They stopped again, and Olli turned to Jann. "No gate."

"No gate," he echoed.

"Well," she said, "let's go back until we're close to the middle and nearer to the glow, and then you can help me scramble up to the top. Then I'll see what I can see."

Jann nodded, and they retraced their steps. They had known it might come to this, and in truth, Olli didn't mind. Being on top of the wall, though perhaps a bit precarious, might provide a better view than trying to peer through the bars of a rusted gate at ground level.

They found a spot that seemed as likely as any, and without discussion or further comment, Jann hoisted Olli up so she could scramble onto the top of the wall. It was wide enough that she could sit fairly comfortably on it with her legs dangling behind her. She thought about swinging one or both over, but the memory of the creatures from her first visit with their long snouts and big teeth kept her from doing so.

The space between the gate and the front of the manor house had been large, but it wasn't nearly so large as the space here in the back. There appeared to be a small grove of trees to her left, and there were other trees scattered in a line along the back wall, but fortunately, she wasn't sitting directly opposite one and could see beyond them fairly well. In the middle of the space between her and the manor house was a large open courtyard, and what she saw there took her breath away.

In the center of the courtyard was the source of the yellow-orange glow—a bright, shining globe of light, perhaps the height of a man. The light it shed on the courtyard was fairly strong, which wasn't surprising, given that the glow that rose from it into the dark sky above the manor house was also visible from the cave entrance on top of the mountain. The globe was mesmerizing in a beautiful way, but what it illuminated was almost equally arresting for its utter repulsiveness.

Lying in what appeared to be a seething mass around the bright globe on the dark paving stones was a sea of pale white bodies—the gorgaal. Olli studied them carefully by the light of the globe, and it didn't take long to realize that they were not perfectly still. Some moved, the occasional twitching and tossing of a restless sleep, and she even thought she could see some of their dark eyes, open and staring. When she saw that, she almost dropped back down off the wall for fear of being spotted, but once she'd gotten used to the initial shock, she steadied herself and remained where she was.

The more she watched them, the more convinced she was that they were sleeping, or at least that they were in a state something like sleep. Their movements were slow and awkward, their pale wings expanding and contracting almost like a reflex, not at all like she'd seen when she'd viewed gorgaal beyond the sentry rock at the entrance to their cave. Why they were all mixed and muddled together around the globe, though, she could not guess.

She scanned the grass that ran along the foot of the wall below her on the inside for evidence of the same long-snouted creatures she'd seen out front, but there were none, and she'd been on top of the wall a good bit longer than she'd been at the gate when they appeared there. It wasn't proof that none would come, but she took it as a good sign.

"Hey," Jann whispered from down below. "What do you see?"

Olli leaned back over the wall and whispered down a quick, basic description of what she had seen. After expressing his own concern over being "seen" by the gorgaal and being reassured by

Olli that they didn't seem to be in a good state to see anything, Jann's curiosity returned to the globe.

"What do you think it is?" he asked.

Olli sat back up and turned to look at it once more, and as she did, she suddenly knew what she had to do. She glanced back down at Jann. "I don't know, but if it is important to them, I'm going to smash it."

"What?" Jann whispered, his voice sharp, indignant even. "Smash it? Are you crazy?"

"No time to argue," Olli said, swinging one leg over the wall so that she now straddled it and could better help Jann climb up. She leaned down, extending her arm. "Take my hand."

Jann did, and Olli pulled as he tried to find at least a little footing on the wall. He made progress before slipping and sliding back down, and Olli felt like her wrist was going to snap. They tried again with more success, and eventually Jann got up far enough that he could reach the top of the wall with his other hand and pull himself up. He released Olli's hand, and they sat on the wall side by side.

When Jann had surveyed the scene himself, he turned back to Olli. "You can't be serious. There's a solid ring of gorgaal around that thing. You won't get near it."

"I will if they're in some kind of deep sleep or hibernation or something. Maybe we don't see them moving around at night because they can't."

"Maybe," Jann said, "or maybe they can move just fine but don't! Or maybe they can't fly or go far but can move a little bit, like just enough to crush a fool who thinks she can tiptoe right through their midst?"

Olli glared at Jann, and then she took a deep breath. "We can keep dancing this little dance of 'maybe,' but we won't know until I go find out."

"Is finding out worth your life?"

"Yes," Olli said. "I told you before that it was. This is what I came for. There they are, our prison guards, lying there, perhaps helpless and vulnerable. Of course, I won't know if they're helpless or vulnerable until I go find out."

"Olli—"

"No, Jann," she cut him off. "Listen to me. I know you think I'm being reckless, but we could go back to the cave and talk about this for weeks and weeks, and in the end, we'd have the same choices we have right now.

"One, we could go to the elders and tell them what we've seen, in the off chance they'd help us investigate. Do you want to do that? Admit we've been down here—twice?!"

Jann didn't look terribly enthusiastic about that prospect, so Olli continued. "Never mind what they would do to us, to make us an example to everyone else about breaking their precious rules. Do you think they'd help? Do you think they'd come?"

"They might come," Jann said, but his voice lacked conviction, and Olli could see that even as he said it, Jann knew it wasn't true.

"No, Jann, they wouldn't. All our lives they've told us stories about the dark days, about what the gorgaal can do . . . They wouldn't come, and what's more, they'd make sure we never came back either."

"No, probably not," Jann said, adding quietly, "and maybe we shouldn't."

"We'd lose our chance to ever investigate what we've found," Olli said, ignoring Jann's last comment. "Which brings us to our other choice. Since we're on our own, we either play it safe and go home, or one of us goes and checks it out. And yes, that's dangerous. But whether it's now, next week, or a year from now, these are our choices, so what good will waiting do? We'll never know more than we do right now—unless I go check it out."

Jann didn't say anything. They both sat, straddling the wall in the dark, looking silently at the strange glowing ball and the muddle of gorgaal around it.

"Then we should both go," he said at last.

"No," Olli objected. "If it isn't safe, if something happens to me, you have to go back and tell them what we've found, tell them what you've see. Maybe you'll learn something that can help someone else find a solution."

"Olli, if those things wake up and attack you, I'm not just going to sit here and watch you get torn to pieces."

"No," Olli said, "you're right. If they wake up, you'll be in danger too. You'll have to drop down and head back, right away."

"That's not what I meant," Jann said, protesting.

"I know, but it's true. If I'm wrong, then I'm lost. Don't wait around to see how it turns out. Get out of here."

Jann ran his hand through his hair and stared at the strange scene that Olli proposed to investigate. "Olli, you may be right about our options, but I still feel like we're rushing, can't we just—Olli!"

It was time to go. So, while Jann was getting warmed up on his little speech, she'd simply shifted her weight, lifted her outside leg over the wall, and dropped down on the inside.

"Olli!" Jann called again, and even though Olli knew his words were not that loud, more of an insistent and determined whisper than anything else, she felt self-conscious about being down off the wall, and didn't want him to make any more noise. What's more, she didn't want to wait. She still hadn't seen one of those creatures from around front by the gate, but lingering here to find out if one was near did not appeal.

"Ssshhh! I'll be back if I can," Olli called up in a whisper, then added, "Don't follow me. You can watch from here, then help me get back up and over the wall when I'm finished."

And with that she started jogging toward the courtyard. She passed between two of the trees that ran more or less along the back wall and then started bending to the right. She didn't want to run straight toward the courtyard with the glowing ball and the gorgaal, but she didn't want to go around it to the left, either, and get too close to the grove of trees on that side. It might be no more dangerous than the other side, but she preferred the seemingly open space on the right where she felt she could more easily detect any lurking danger.

Olli made the decision about which way to go around the courtyard while jogging, but she had already decided as she dropped from the wall that she was going to skirt around the edges of the courtyard altogether and see if there was anything up closer to the manor house that she could use to try to smash the globe. She'd brought various supplies down the mountain, but nothing that might be good for hitting a glowing ball that was bigger than she was. Still, that didn't mean she couldn't improvise.

Olli's heart beat faster as she ran. She could feel herself accelerating as she drew closer to the courtyard. Her eyes were locked on the gorgaal, which hadn't shown any obvious signs of awareness that she was there. And yet she also kept glancing just slightly to the side so she could look out of the corner of her eye at the dark grass between the courtyard and the sidewall on the right, just in case she wasn't alone. She hadn't seen anything moving there yet, but she also couldn't see a wall up ahead beside the manor house that would keep those toothy creatures in the front from coming around back.

She was running parallel to the courtyard now, as far off to the side as she dared. She feared being in the light too much, lest the gorgaal see and attack her, but she also feared being too far from the light, for while nothing was dark, exactly, in the entire walled area behind the manor house, the light from the ball seemed considerably brighter where the gorgaal lay sleeping on the pavement than out here.

The conviction that she was right about the gorgaal grew stronger with each step she took. They were moving—she was sure of that—but her impression from up on the wall that their movements were more like those of a creature asleep, stirring only as one in a dream, seemed confirmed. They were a seething mass, all jumbled up as though huddling together for heat, even though the evening was quite warm. Olli wondered if the glowing ball was casting off heat as well as light, but she didn't think it was any warmer here than it had been on the wall, or beyond it, for that matter.

Up ahead, the manor house loomed closer. If it weren't for trying to watch the gorgaal on her left and the open space on her right simultaneously, she would probably have found staring at the manor house irresistible. The Elders had always told stories of the island before the gorgaal, when its inhabitants had lived in what they called "houses" by the sea. Olli knew a house was a structure built above ground to provide shelter for people, but she'd never seen one before.

The manor house, said the elders, had been on the island, even then. Many generations before the gorgaal had come, went the story, a ship had arrived bearing a large, extended family, who had in turn decided to live on the island and built the manor house. They kept largely to themselves, more or less aloof from the people in the village, though over time the line between the two small, separate communities had been blurred by marriage and commerce.

Now Olli took in the large, dark, sprawling structure in front of her, thinking of her own tiny room in the cave and wondering what it would mean to live in a place like this. She knew from the stories that it had been built as a home not for a single family but for many. Perhaps, had she been born into a family living in a place like this with other families, she might not have had more space at her disposal than she did now.

But, she thought, looking at the places on the second floor of the manor house where the solid wall gave way to periodic openings, she would have had windows, and sunlight. That thought, that every day, sunlight bathed this place, somehow made it feel less foreboding. It might not be entirely rational, Olli thought, since who knew what might lurk inside, but it was good nonetheless. After all, to find something to strike the glowing ball with, she might just have to go in there.

She could see now that even though there was space between the globe and the ring of gorgaal and the manor house, the paved courtyard extended all the way to the building. She would have to leave the grassy area behind, and soon. She slowed a bit as she started angling toward the courtyard and, perhaps a bit reluctantly, stepped onto the pavement.

Olli was now walking parallel to the manor house on her right, with the glowing ball on her left and beyond it the wall where Jann was hopefully still perched, waiting and watching. She looked for him briefly but realized both that from where she was standing the strong glow of the ball made things in the darkness beyond it harder to see, and that the row of trees along the back wall would probably obscure Jann anyway, unless she was directly opposite him.

She had half-hoped that up closer to the house there might be tools or other implements, maybe even furniture or other things left over from before the time of the gorgaal, out of which she might scavenge something that would suit her purposes. She saw now that there was nothing here. The dark paving stones between the gorgaal and the house were completely bare. She saw nothing around her but the tufts of grass that poked up between the stones.

Just ahead, on her right, she noticed a door into the manor house. She hesitated, but only for a moment, before walking quietly over to it. She reached down and gripped the knob. It turned and the door opened a hair, its hinges creaking. The sound of the door shook Olli, and she released the knob, standing before the now slightly open door, motionless.

She glanced back at the gorgaal and the yellow-orange globe. As much as she believed what she'd told Jann earlier, the same clear logic that had suggested now was as good as any other time to investigate this place did not apply to opening this door. She had made it from the wall to the manor house door. The gorgaal had not attacked. The creatures from the front gate had not appeared. These were things she hadn't known five minutes ago, and while she might not be able to presume she could leave and come back just as easily, she might be able to, and perhaps she could come back with something to smash the ball with. She didn't have to go looking inside the manor house.

She didn't have to, she thought, but she was going to.

She still didn't know if she could pass through the midst of the gorgaal and get to the ball without their waking up and ripping her limb from limb, and she might as well find out now. And, as long as she was going to try it, she might as well have something that might reasonably be able to damage the glowing ball when she got there. Since that something wasn't out here, she might as well look inside and see if it was there.

Olli took a deep breath, placed her fingertips lightly on the door, and pushed it gently open.

She stood in the doorway, the light from the glowing ball behind her casting her shadow forward into the room of shadows before her. She stepped over the threshold and into the manor house.

Olli couldn't believe she was actually inside. For all her dreaming and for all her talk, she couldn't believe she was here. She'd scaled the wall—with Jann's help, of course—dropped inside, run past a large glowing ball surrounded by sleeping gorgaal, and now penetrated inside the very heart of the island's mystery. All her life she'd seen the glow from this place, heard stories about its past and been warned of its present, and now she was inside.

As her eyes adjusted to the darkness beyond the small zone of light coming in through the half-open door behind her, she could see that the room she was in was large. It smelled peculiar, too. It was a different smell than the smell she associated with the close quarters of the often damp caves in which she lived, and she wondered what the odor was. She shivered suddenly and hugged herself tight.

She couldn't explain the sensation that swept over her at that moment, but she was instantly and completely convinced that the house was not empty and she was not alone. She hadn't heard anything, seen anything, or noticed anything unusual, but she knew. Glancing up at the ceiling, she wondered if someone or something was up there, in one of the rooms above her. Or perhaps, she thought as she scanned the walls looking for the doors that led out of this room, perhaps there was someone or something in the next room.

She tried to dismiss the feeling as the product of fear, a figment of her imagination, but without much success. She was spooked, and it was all she could do not to turn and run, out the door, out beyond the courtyard, back to the wall where Jann could help her up and over. But she couldn't do that. She couldn't go back without completing her mission, and she couldn't tell Jann she'd been scared by something as vague and insubstantial as a feeling.

She started moving through the room, looking for something that might suit her purpose. There was a table with some chairs nearby, and Olli moved to the table and lifted one side. It was solid but not terribly heavy. She grabbed the leg and took a firm grip. Yes, she thought, it might do very well.

The feeling of dread and fear that had seized her a moment earlier was still very much with her, so when she leaned the table over to rest it on its side, she tried to lower it gently and quietly. It wouldn't do to make too much noise, for even if there wasn't anyone else in the house, there was a sea of gorgaal not far away outside the open door.

Examining the leg nearest her, she realized that there'd be no way to detach it quietly. It hadn't been screwed into the table as she had hoped but was attached much more securely. She tried to work it up and down and side to side, but it didn't really give, and the whole table wanted to move with each tug. She walked down the length of the table to check out the other leg, and the same test produced very different results. The other leg was quite willing to wiggle in both directions, suggesting it was already on its way to breaking off and might just need a little help from her.

Eagerly, Olli worked the loose leg, up and down, back and forth. The give increased and the leg moved further and further each time, while Olli hoped the creaking of the wooden pins that secured the leg, now splintering, weren't echoing too far beyond the room. At last, with a final strong pull, the leg came off the table altogether, and Olli, surprised by the sudden absence of resistance, stumbled back a few steps and collided with a chair.

The chair tipped up on two legs, and Olli watched in horror as it wavered for a second and then proceeded to fall backward. She let go of the table leg with one hand and reached out desperately, catching hold of the chair leg at the very tip. She clasped onto it and took a firm grip, arresting the fall of the chair just a foot before it crashed into the ground. She lowered the chair the rest of the way, as gently as she could, until it lay on the ground. Then she let go, wiped the sweat from her forehead, and took a deep breath. Too close. It was time to get out of here.

Back outside she once more stood on the dark paving stones near the manor house. She didn't want the door behind her open, so she pulled it to, though not far enough so that the latch caught. It was silly, she knew, after the noise she'd made working the table leg free to worry about the noise of the latch, but she didn't see the need to make any sound she didn't have to.

Olli looked at the table leg in her hands. It was a good size, tapered and round at the bottom, with some grooves her hands fit into nicely, and a fair bit larger and square at the top. If she could get through the ring of gorgaal, she'd give that glowing ball a good, strong whack.

Getting through the ring of gorgaal. How to do that? She started walking slowly closer, staring at the writhing mass of pale white bodies. As she drew nearer, she estimated that from the outside of the ring to the ball was a distance of thirty feet or more. What's more, the closer to the inside of the ring she might get, the harder the path looked to be, as the gorgaal seemed to be huddled together in larger numbers in close. Even if she could find places to put her feet down in the outer half of the ring, it looked like it might be a real challenge getting all the way through.

There was no going back now, though. Olli didn't know what the ball was or what it did, but it seemed obvious that the gorgaal needed it. With all of the island before them—lying open in the warm, beautiful night, completely under their dominion—why else would they be lying here, all of them, in a single, muddled heap? It didn't look comfortable or pleasant, and it didn't make any sense, unless there was something in that ball or coming from that ball that the gorgaal had to have. Logic dictated its importance, though not its vulnerability. That was what Olli was trying to discover, and she would, even if it cost her life.

She stepped over the gorgaal nearest her and put her foot down gingerly in a small open space beside it, while she searched out her next step and the one after that. The gorgaal didn't look that much different up close than they looked at a distance—pale white skin, sinewy arms and legs, their wings folded around them as they slept. Their mouths were like thin slits on their faces, with tiny sharp-looking noses and hollow eye sockets.

Some had their eyes open, and those eyes were as black as midnight. Olli had walked a little way around the ring to avoid those eyes and find a place to start her journey toward the center. If the eyes could see her, then the creatures weren't asleep as she believed and she was dead anyway, but whether they could see through those eyes right now or not wasn't the reason she tried to avoid them. Seeing or unseeing, they were just creepy.

Slowly, step by step, she penetrated farther and farther into the ring. Sometimes she had to move sideways when the way up ahead didn't offer a place to put her foot down, and at times she had to backtrack, too. What complicated things was that the gorgaal were moving, twitching, which meant that not only did gaps up ahead start closing with little or no warning, but sometimes the place where she was standing could start to disappear, forcing her to move in whatever direction she could, even if that was backward and not forward.

After one such moment when she'd had to step back to the place she'd just come from, she looked both ahead to the ball and back to the outside of the ring, and she judged that she was only perhaps midway. She'd had some close calls, but so far she hadn't stepped on the head or wing or claw-like hand of a gorgaal. She didn't know how long her luck would hold, but being halfway in meant getting out would be almost as difficult as getting all the way in. She'd known that before she started in, of course, but the fact of it felt a whole lot different now, standing where she was standing.

She saw an opening up ahead and started to lift her foot to step forward. She only started to lift it, because no sooner had she raised her foot off the ground, then a cold, strong hand grabbed her ankle, gripping it tight. She didn't need to turn and look to know what the hand was, so when she turned, it wasn't to look; it was to bring the table leg down on the hand that gripped her with all the force she could muster.

Olli heard a crack as she hit the forearm of the gorgaal that grabbed her, and the hand immediately let go. As it did so, Olli identified its pale face staring up at her from amid the tangle of nearby bodies, those deep black eyes fixed upon her. She watched, helplessly, as the gorgaal retracted its arm from the blow and opened its mouth to let out a high, piercing scream.

They're awake after all, she thought, *and I am lost.*

6

A Voice in the Dark

Olli didn't bother looking for a place to step. She leapt back, toward the outside of the circle, and she didn't care that she came down squarely on the head of a gorgaal. The piercing shriek from the one she had struck was now being echoed by others, and not just from close by—from all around the ring. Claw-like hands rose up out of the seething white mass, and here and there wings extended and retracted, as well.

But none of the gorgaal rose from off the ground, and while they clutched at her as she moved rapidly toward the pavement beyond them—swinging the table leg wildly and viciously at any part of any gorgaal that was near her—their movements still seemed slow and lethargic. Olli neared the edge of the circle. She could see the open dark pavement up ahead, and beyond that, freedom.

I am going to make it, she thought. *They are not entirely awake.*

She was just leaping clear of the ring when another gorgaal reached for her leg, but this time the gorgaal's fingers did not close fast enough to grab hold of her. Still, the talons at the end of the gorgaal's fingers ripped through the light cloth of her pants and dug into her soft skin. Olli's momentum carried her forward, and the clutching fingers tore down her calf and ankle.

When she landed, she was outside the ring, in the open. She winced with pain but did not hesitate. She ran in the most direct line she could take, ignoring the angry shrieks and writhing motion of the gorgaal just a few feet behind her.

Even in her pain and panic, she couldn't help thinking once more that she had been proven right. Alone, surrounded by gorgaal, she had escaped their clutches. They might not be totally incapacitated as they lay around the glowing ball at night, but they were far from the terror they were by daylight. They had a weakness. They could be destroyed.

Limping a little as she ran, Olli left the pavement behind and stepped into the grass beyond the courtyard. She could see the rear wall in the distance, beyond the trees, but she wasn't sure how close she was or wasn't to where she'd dropped in. With the still shrieking gorgaal behind her, she saw no real purpose for silence anymore and called out. "Jann? Jann!"

"Olli?" Jann answered her, and she adjusted her course in the direction of his voice. "I'm coming, Olli!"

"No!" Olli shouted, for just as she heard Jann's voice, she saw movement in the grass and two sets of gleaming teeth like those of the creatures they'd seen near the front gate. Whether they'd been somewhere here in the back the whole time or simply come when the ruckus started, Olli didn't know. But here they were, and unlike the gorgaal, there was no reason to think the darkness incapacitated them.

Jann emerged from between two trees, and seeing Olli, started toward her. Olli knew that he hadn't seen the creatures, so she moved to intercept just as the one closest to them turned toward him. Jann looked puzzled as Olli raised the table leg and veered to the side, but he turned and saw with horror in his eyes what she had seen as she hit the snout of the creature with a firm blow.

The creature let out something like a snort or a grunt as it slid through the grass sideways, and Olli swung the table leg again, striking him a second time before quickly doubling back. She was heading once more toward the pavement and the ring of gorgaal.

"Come on," she said as she passed Jann. "There's more than one coming."

The furor in the ring of gorgaal had not died down, and the teeming mass of limbs and wings and the shouts and shrieks, along with the eerie yellow-orange glow of the globe, provided a surreal backdrop to their mad dash to get to the manor house ahead of the creatures that followed. Olli didn't need to look back to know they were coming; she just hoped she and Jann would reach the door to the manor house in time.

"Olli!" Jann called as she rounded the corner past the circle of gorgaal and angled toward the manor house. "Where are you going?"

Olli's answer was to accelerate, despite her weariness and the sharp pain in her leg, for the door was finally within view, and perhaps also safety. She just hoped her earlier intuition about the manor house not being empty had been wrong.

Reaching the door, she pushed through it, and the door flew open with a bang. Jann came through behind her, and Olli scrambled desperately to grab hold of the door and close it behind them. As she pushed it closed, she saw at least three of the long-snouted creatures closing fast, each of them scurrying across the dark pavement on four short, stumpy legs. The door slammed shut with a crash, and she exhaled with relief when she heard the latch click.

"We're trapped," Jann said as he leaned over, hands on his knees, catching his breath.

"We're alive," Olli answered, walking across the dark room toward one of the doors she'd seen when she was here earlier. It felt like it had been hours ago, but she knew that all told, it had only been ten or fifteen minutes since she'd dropped down off the wall.

"Where are you going?" Jann asked as Olli turned the knob and opened the interior door.

"I'm going to find a way through this house," Olli said, matter-of-factly. "There has to be a front door. We'll go out it and make a run for the gate."

"But those creatures—"

"—are hopefully all here, waiting for us to come back out," Olli said.

"If not?"

"Then we're no worse off out front than we are here," Olli said. "In fact, the distance to the front gate should be shorter than the distance to the back wall, so if we have to fight our way out, we'll stand a better chance there."

"Olli," Jann said, reaching out and taking her arm, "what happened out there?"

"Let's get through the gate first," Olli said. "I'll tell you on the way back up the mountain."

"But your leg . . ." Jann said. "It's bleeding."

"I know," Olli said, glancing down at the back of her leg for the first time. The pants were torn, and a large bloodstain had spread out from the wound. Some of the cloth was matted and stuck to her raw and bleeding leg, and it would hurt like crazy when she had to take it off. She was alive to feel the pain, though, and she would gladly accept that pain when it came—if they could only get out that gate.

"We should go quietly," Olli whispered as she stepped through the doorway into a long, narrow hall. The hall felt much like the smaller tunnels that connected the larger rooms in the caves, except the tunnels were rounded and the hall rectangular. "We don't know who or what might be inside with us."

"It's a bit late for quiet," Jann said. "If anything's in here, it must have heard us come in."

"Then all the more reason to be quiet now, so we're harder to find," Olli said, and Jann did not reply.

They moved quietly down the long hall. Several doors opened off to the side, but Olli bypassed these. She didn't necessarily expect to be able to move from the back to the front of the house in a straight line, but it seemed to make sense to get as far inside as possible along that line before veering off to either side.

They made their way through room after room, as Olli tried all the while to keep her orientation straight so that whatever twists or turns the maze of rooms compelled them to take, she could remember where the front of the house actually lay. At one point, having opened a door and found no way through the room it led to, she turned back to find Jann behind her holding a long, wooden pole in his hands.

"What's that?" she whispered, speaking for the first time since starting on this trek through the house.

"Some kind of broom," Jann answered, holding up the end near the floor, which had a sheaf of stiff bristles sticking out from it.

"Plan on doing some cleaning on your way out?" Olli asked as she slid past him in the dark, moving to the other door that exited the room.

"I'd rather not face those creatures empty-handed," Jann said simply, and they sank once more into silence as they entered the neighboring room.

At long last a small and initially unpromising hallway opened into the back of a very large space, and Olli could see from the much higher ceiling and the appearance of windows along the wall at the back that they must be in the front of the house. Soft moonlight shone brightly enough throughout the room that she didn't need to keep her hand out in front of her.

Then she saw it below one of the larger windows in the middle of the wall—a door.

They moved quickly across to the door, and as they did, Olli noticed that the sloping wall was actually the side of what, at first glance, looked like a wide ramp leading up toward the back of the room. Only, the ramp wasn't smooth—she could see that from the faint moonlight. There were stairs, lots of them. There were a few places in the caves where a stair or two had been carved to get up or down from one room to the next, but she'd never seen anything like this. There must have been twenty or more of them leading up into the darkness above the room.

The sense of not being alone returned in force, and she was glad they were about to leave, even if they might find more of those creatures out front. She turned to Jann and was about to ask him if he was ready, but a voice that belonged to neither of them spoke from the shadows above them.

"Why have you come here?"

Olli jumped and snatched for the doorknob, fumbling in the dark as she took hold of it. She turned and pulled, but the door didn't open. She pushed, and still it did not budge. Panic. They'd made it to the door—why would it not open? She pulled again even harder, glancing over her shoulder to see what was happening behind her. Jann stood, his back to her, holding up the slender wooden handle of the broom as though to defend them both against this voice in the dark.

"Who are you?" Jann called out. "We're going. We mean you no harm. We were just curious about the light, the light outside."

"You should not have come, young ones," the voice said again. It was a firm, baritone voice, and Olli could hear no particular emotion in it. "It is dangerous. You should not have come."

Olli began to search around the knob. Perhaps there was a lock of some sort, some way to secure the door. She found another, smaller knob, only it wasn't really round—it was flatter and more oblong. She turned it and heard something in the door moving, something unlatching, she hoped. She reached for the larger knob again, turned, and pulled. This time the door opened easily. She whirled and grabbed Jann's arm, pulling him out of the door as she dashed out.

They crossed a wide swath of wood planking, and Olli noticed only at the last moment that there were steps leading down on the other side. She leapt over them, since she feared that trying to slow down in order to take the stairs one at a time would mean falling. She landed on a narrow section of paving stone, much like those around back, but the wound in her leg felt torn open anew when she hit the ground. She came up running, though she couldn't help but gasp, and limped as she went.

In the moonlight she could see that the gate was straight ahead, maybe fifty yards. She could also see they were not alone.

The wave of creatures intercepted them some twenty yards in front of the gate. Over and over she and Jann lashed out with the table leg and broom, dodging from side to side to avoid the snapping teeth. The broom was being ripped into splinters by the crushing strength of the creatures' jaws, and Jann had started kicking furiously, which was working better, as his heavy boots seemed both to inflict more damage than the slender broom handle had and to give the creatures more pause in their attacks.

After fighting wildly, whirling and striking and dodging in a frenzy, Olli suddenly realized that the way out to the gate was largely open—they'd somehow broken through.

"Jann, come on!"

She turned and ran, Jann close behind. Olli's heart beat faster as the gate drew near. Perhaps having been here once already would save their lives, for she already knew how to unlatch it and that it opened inward.

She reached the gate, and in a single deft motion unlatched it and pulled it open, passing through and turning to defend against any creature that might try to follow them out. Jann was just about to pass through too when a low, dark form lunged forward through the grass.

He screamed as the long, open mouth with the jagged teeth locked onto his leg. What was left of the broom flew out of his hand. His arms flailed out, reaching for the gatepost across from the gate's hinges. He grabbed hold and held on for dear life as the creature tried vigorously to pull him back into the pack's midst where he would be ripped apart.

Olli leapt into the space between the posts, right beside Jann, who clung to the rusting metal with both hands as he was jerked back repeatedly by the tenacious creature. Olli struck the head of the creature once, twice, and a third time, but still it would not let go. The other creatures were approaching stealthily, eyeing her and the table leg in her hand.

"Just go," Jann somehow said through gritted teeth. The creature gave a particularly strong tug, and he cried out, his grip on the gatepost slackening.

"No!" Olli shouted, and she swung wildly at the other creatures, advancing so that they backed up in the face of her sudden onslaught. Having driven them back for a moment, she turned on the creature that still had hold of her friend and was snarling and ripping its head back and forth as though in a mad attempt to gnaw its way through flesh and muscle, down to the very bone. She raised the table leg and swung with all her might, aiming as carefully as she could a little further up the head in the direction of the place where she thought she'd seen its eyes.

It worked. The creature let go and swung its head to the side before the blow could strike home. She grabbed Jann and all but tossed his bleeding and almost limp body through the open gate. The creatures were regrouping, and she threw the table leg as hard as she could at the foremost among them. As it flew, she reached for the gate and slammed it closed, then fell to the ground beside Jann in utter exhaustion.

7 

No Other Way

The palace of Prince Hadaaya was the grandest building in all of Ben-Salaar, a city with more than a few exotic buildings. As Zangira was led through the opulent rooms and corridors to the room where the prince dined, he couldn't help but feel nostalgic, for Ben-Salaar had been one of the first cities where he had sojourned as a young Amhuru, many years ago.

Two of Prince Hadaaya's servants ushered Zangira into the presence of the prince, who was eating with all six of his wives and all twenty-seven of his children. His first wife, an elegant woman with long dark hair, dined with him at the central table on a small dais, but several smaller tables were scattered around the room on either side of them. Zangira was led past these smaller tables to the main one, where he stood before the prince as the servant offered the proper introduction.

"Amhuru," the prince said, motioning to the chair that one of the servants had just placed in front of Zangira, "Sit, eat, enjoy the hospitality of my table. You are welcome in Ben-Salaar."

"My sincerest thanks, O Prince," Zangira said, bowing deftly as he took his seat. In truth he was very hungry, and when a plate with roasted fowl and warm bread appeared before him, he ate eagerly, and soon a bowl of lush fresh fruit also appeared, and both bowl and plate were replenished liberally.

"Tell me, Amhuru," Prince Hadaaya said after Zangira had finished his second helping, "my soldiers tell me that you are not alone, that while you presented yourself at the gates of Ben-Salaar alone, many Amhuru wait in your camp. I told them this could not be, since Amhuru travel alone and would not come to my city in such numbers, but now I must ask what you would say of this tale?"

"I would say that the prince is very wise, for truly, the Amhuru do travel alone," Zangira said. "And yet your soldiers have also spoken truly, for I have come to Ben-Salaar with several of my brethren."

Prince Hadaaya's eyebrows rose at the mention of the word "several," and he narrowed his eyes as he stared at Zangira. "Amhuru, I must ask for an explanation, for I would almost think the coming of so many Amhuru would constitute a threat to my city."

"Once again the prince displays his great wisdom," Zangira said, nodding, "for assuredly, the presence of so many Amhuru is intended as a threat—but not against Ben-Salaar, for surely the prince must know I love him dearly and would never threaten him."

"Amhuru, do you think that by flattering me over and over with flowery words about my wisdom that you will procure my favor?"

"No, my prince, for I was under the impression that I already had it."

At that, the prince rose suddenly with a beaming smile on his face and came around the table. Zangira rose to receive the prince's embrace, and Hadaaya kissed him on both cheeks affectionately.

"It is so good to see you again, Zangira."

"And it is good to see you, my prince."

"And yet," the prince quickly added, returning to his seat, "how is it that you look no older than you did last time, when I was but a boy of fifteen, while I have grown old like the dog who has sired too many litters and is now too tired to chase his own tail?"

"Truly, O Prince," Zangira said with a wry smile, "you have been quite busy with the siring since last I was here. I do not wonder that you might feel weary, but in truth, you do not look so very old, and even if I also do not look it, I feel much older than I was when last I dined at your table."

"The years have been hard, my friend?"

"The years and the miles," Zangira said. "But such is the life of the Amhuru."

Hadaaya nodded. "Come, you must tell me what brings you and your kin to my city, and I will help you if I can, for do I not guess rightly that you have need of my aid in some way?"

"You do guess rightly, but as for my tale, perhaps after we have dined I will tell you, for I would not wish to bore your wives and children with such a tedious story."

"So be it," Hadaaya said, and when he clapped, the servants waiting at the tables sprung into action, refilling the cups and clearing the plates and bowls before bringing out the next course.

Later, when they were alone on a large and spacious balcony, enjoying a gloriously bright red setting sun, Hadaaya returned to the reason for Zangira's visit. "You have the privacy you desired, my friend. Now tell me, what has happened that such an extraordinary thing as a party of Amhuru traveling together has become necessary? For, indeed, I fear for the man who has incurred your wrath."

"Do not fear for him," Zangira answered quietly. "Fear rather for your wives and children, for Ben-Salaar, and for everything you hold dear."

"Sobering words," Prince Hadaaya said. "I cannot imagine what kind of man could inspire an Amhuru to speak them."

"I do not blame you, for not that long ago I would not have been able to imagine it either."

"We must talk then of heavy things, I see," the prince said. "Now let us speak of the man who causes even Amhuru to fear."

Laughter echoed across the deck, and Marlo saw Kaden and Nara over near their cabin, talking at the rail of the ship, enjoying each other and the clear night under the light of a million stars. Whatever those two had lost when Barra-Dohn fell, Marlo suspected they had found something more important, and he was glad, both for them and for the boy.

He scanned the rest of the deck and saw that he wasn't the only person who had noticed them. Sitting midship on the other side of the deck beside a lamp, feigning interest in a book, was Rika. Marlo watched her watching them, and he knew she wasn't really watching them. She was watching him. Marlo had noticed the growing attention Rika paid Kaden, and he knew Nara had noticed too. He feared that no matter how calm the weather was, a storm was brewing there.

Kaden and Nara went into their cabin, but still Rika's gaze lingered on their door. Marlo watched her, wondering, and not for the first time, if speaking to her would do any good. He doubted it, which is why he hadn't done it. Maybe he should talk instead to Kaden, since Marlo couldn't tell if he could see yet that there was more than mere friendliness in Rika's attentions.

The door to Kaden and Nara's cabin opened again, but only Kaden came out. Marlo glanced back at Rika, and he could see she was already setting the book down and getting up. Almost without thinking about it, he stood himself and moved quickly across the deck to intercept her.

"Rika," he said as she stepped away from the rail in the opposite direction.

She turned toward him at the sound of her name, and irritation flickered across her face when she saw who it was. "Yes?"

"You should leave him alone."

"I beg your pardon?" she said. "What are you talking about?"

"You know what I'm talking about," Marlo said. He had started this, so he would be direct. "They have reforged their marriage bonds. You should leave them alone."

"How dare you!" She practically hissed as she stepped up close to him, glaring at his face. "You have no right to accuse me of anything, especially of interfering with anyone's marriage bonds. We're old friends. I tutored his son for years."

"These things may be true," Marlo said. "But they are not the whole truth. You should leave him alone."

She stared at him, as though really seeing him for the first time. Then she leaned in even closer. "Or else what? What will you do?"

Marlo ignored the question. "Why waste your time? You can see he loves her."

"If he loves her, why are you worried?"

He hesitated. "Perhaps I am worried for you."

"For me?" Rika said, and there was a shift in her voice. "Are you jealous, Kalosene? Lonely? Do you desire the touch of a woman's hand?"

She reached out and brushed his cheek ever so delicately with the back of her hand. Marlo made no move to avoid her; he merely watched her dispassionately, though he couldn't say he was wholly immune to her touch. After that single, light touch, she withdrew her hand.

"You misunderstand me," Marlo said, unmoved. "Your pursuits endanger your own soul. Kaden and Nara can tend to their own affairs."

"Then you should shut up and tend to yours," Rika said, the sharp, angry tone back in earnest. "My soul. You fool, I have no soul, and neither do you."

Rika turned to head toward Kaden, but then she saw, as Marlo did, that Kaden was no longer alone—Tchinchura had joined him during her brief exchange with Marlo. She threw the Kalosene an angry glare and stalked off toward the cabin she shared with Captain D'Sarza.

Marlo watched her go. It was not in his nature to consider anyone a lost cause, but he was not optimistic that she would heed his warning. He would have to consider if there was more to say, and if so, to whom, for even if he didn't think Kaden would return her affection, he feared that if Rika persisted in her pursuit, mischief would still come of it.

Rika seethed. How dare the Kalosene speak to her like that! Who did he think he was?

D'Sarza was not in the cabin, so Rika gave full vent to her rage, sweeping the maps and charts laid across the captain's desk violently from its surface so that they flew and fluttered across the small room. She had once been consort to a king, a respected member of Barra-Dohn's prestigious Academy, and now she was reduced to this, an unwanted member of a lonely band of exiles.

Rika didn't know which was worse: that the Kalosene had possessed the gall to say what he said to her, or that the fool actually believed she wanted Kaden. Kaden was nothing like Eirmon, who, for all his faults, had been a man who knew the value of power. Rika had not come down so far in the world that she would want a man who had so meekly accepted his change in fortune.

And yet, she had been pursuing Kaden, firting with him and ingratiating herself with him. Feeling ashamed, she plumped down on her bunk forlornly. It was not the shame of a woman pursuing another woman's husband, but the shame of a noble who has lost a fortune and finds himself begging for coin in the street.

She hated begging. If she didn't still struggle with the fear that somehow, someway, the exiles from Barra-Dohn would discover what she had been plotting against Eirmon and been imprisoned for, what she had done to Gamalian to get away, and in so discovering these things choose to cast her away, then she would not be forced to show Kaden attention he did not deserve. She loathed herself for doing it, and it was unbearable to think that idiot Kalosene had noticed.

She needed another plan. She needed a way out. She had been looking for an angle, for an opportunity, but none had presented itself; she didn't want to simply go off without a clear purpose or plan.

She had no idea when she would find her chance, but she vowed to herself that this would not be the final chapter in her story. She would rise again from the ruins and the dust and find a place more fitting for her skills and ambitions.

"If I don't find a way out of here soon," she mumbled as she lay back on her bed, "I might just jump overboard."

The shrieking of the gorgaal had at last begun to die down, and as quiet returned, Olli wasn't sure which was more unsettling: the sound of the gorgaal or the knowledge she had gained.

All her life she'd believed that the story of the island boiled down to the struggle between the people in the caves with the gorgaal above ground. It was a story, in essence, of man against monster, and in a single moment, the voice in the dark of the manor house had fundamentally altered that story.

Someone, perhaps even many someones—for if there was one, why not more?—lived in the manor house. Was he the gorgaal's master? The gorgaal's prisoner? Something else she could not imagine? He had not attacked them, or even threatened them—so why had he revealed himself at all? Olli would have to tell the elders about him, about all that she had found. There was no question about this now that Jann was so seriously hurt, but even if he hadn't been, they had learned things they could not keep to themselves, no matter what the price they paid for how they had discovered them.

"I have to stop," Jann said, starting to lower himself so the ground.

"No," Olli said, fighting to keep him upright. "Not yet."

"I have to rest," Jann insisted.

"When I have you on the sled," Olli said. "Then you can rest, all the way up the mountain. Come on."

Jann stopped trying to sit down, and together they hobbled on, their pace slowing almost to a crawl. Olli didn't need to look up and check the position of the moon to know they were digging a hole for themselves—for her in particular—that they might not be able to get them out of.

They did reach the sled, though with considerable effort, and Olli managed to get Jann on it. They had no time to speak and nothing of import to say. They both knew what had to happen if they were going to survive, so Olli set about trying to do it. She took up the coiled rope in the front of the sled and tied it around her waist and, grabbing hold of it with her arms, began walking and pulling up the very same sled run they'd come racing down earlier that evening.

Adrenaline or sheer determination or both kept Olli going, despite the growing pain in her own leg. She tugged and pulled, step after step, until the sweat poured down her face and burned her eyes. Soaked strands of her hair clung to her face and neck. The ground grew steeper, and each step felt more and more precarious. She'd been on firewood detail before, where with the help of another she'd pulled a sled heaped with wood that weighed less than Jann. She'd thought that had been tough work. This was excruciating.

She'd been going up and down this mountain in the dark all her life, and from an early age she'd learned, like everyone else who lived in the caves, how to intuitively calculate time until daybreak based on the season and the position of the moon and stars in the night sky. She'd also learned how to estimate the distance to the cave and how to calculate her rate of travel. And now, as she pulled Jann on the sled, laborious step by laborious step, she had little to do but calculate and recalculate her odds of reaching the top in time. With each new calculation, it was becoming more and more apparent that they weren't going to make it. Morning would come, and with it the gorgaal, and this time there would be no fending them off with a table leg.

"Jann," she said as she stopped and made a futile attempt to wipe the sweat from her eyes. Her arm was as soaked as her face, so all she accomplished, as far as she could tell, was to smear the sweat around. "We aren't going to make it. We have to come up with another plan."

There was no reply from the sled. She could hear his breathing, though, and that allayed her initial fear that perhaps Jann had died while she was pulling him. She felt momentary annoyance at Jann for resting while she was trying to save their lives, but the annoyance immediately prompted a wave of guilt and chagrin. He was seriously wounded, and perhaps dying, and if the loss of blood didn't kill him, come daybreak, the gorgaal would.

Then something happened that hadn't happened to Olli since she was a little girl. She started crying.

It wasn't fair, and it wasn't right. She'd made it to the manor house and halfway to the glowing ball. She'd escaped the ring of gorgaal, and she'd guided Jann to the safety of the house and through it to the other side. They'd even made it out and beyond the swarm of creatures in the front, all the way to the gate. They'd been a few steps away from safety and freedom, and if they'd escaped with nothing worse than her wound, then Jann would be walking beside her right now, much further up the mountain, perhaps even pulling her in the sled because of her injury. They'd almost pulled it off.

She raised her hand to wipe her tears away but gave up, as doing so was as futile as wiping away the sweat. Jann was asleep or unconscious, and they weren't going to make it back. It was up to her to decide what to do now.

She stood, the rope around her waist taut with the weight of the sled at the other end. There had to be something they could do, somewhere they could go. For a moment Olli considered trying to go back to the manor house. Perhaps whoever was there might shelter them. After all, he'd not sounded angry when he spoke.

Neither had he sounded welcoming, Olli conceded, and before they could seek asylum from him, they'd have to navigate the space between the gate and the house again. Olli had no illusions that they could make that distance in their current condition. No, she realized, going back there wasn't an option.

So where could they go? Where might they conceivably find shelter? And then, as soon as the question occurred to her, so did the answer. If going to the manor house had been crazy, though, then this was madness. But madness was all they had left.

She moved closer to the sled and placed her hand on Jann's shoulder, giving him a gentle shake. "Jann? I need to move you a bit so I can get on the front of the sled and steer it."

"Are we back?" Jann mumbled as he stirred from his sleep.

"No, Jann," Olli said. "I'm sorry, but I couldn't do it."

Jann lifted his head up off the sled and looked around them at the trees on either side of the run. "How far up are we?" he asked quietly.

"Not very," Olli answered. "You've not been asleep that long. Just long enough for me to figure out that I can't do it."

"I thought it a long shot," Jann said. He looked up at Olli, a bit puzzled. "Did I hear you say something about getting on the sled?"

"Yes, I need to steer it," Olli said. "I've got a plan."

Jann laughed a laugh that was as much cough and groan as it was a laugh. "A plan. You've always got a plan."

"There's no time for this," Olli said, trying to urge him down the sled a bit with a gentle shove.

"You're right," Jann said before she could continue. "There is no time. No plan can save us now. There's only one thing to do. You have to go on alone."

"Absolutely not," Olli said, stopping to look him in the eyes. "I'm not leaving you here."

"You have to."

"It's my fault you're here," Olli said. "I can't."

"It's not your fault," Jann said. "You told me I had to accept that it might cost me my life, and I did. It was my choice."

"I'm not going to argue about this," Olli said. "Just help me move you over so I can get on and steer."

"Where will you take us?" Jann scoffed.

"To the coast," Olli said.

"Oh good," Jann said. "It'll be much nicer to die by the water."

"Nobody's going to die," Olli said with such conviction she could see the surprise on Jann's face. "Not tonight."

"Olli, I love your determination, but there's nowhere to hide there," Jann said.

"Not the near coast," Olli said, knowing that Jann still didn't understand. "We're going to go all the way to the south coast, to the village."

"The village?" Jann said, looking stunned. "That's crazy."

"There's no other way," Olli said. "Before we moved to the caves, the village was the only place to hide from the gorgaal during the day."

"No one's been there in years," Jann said. "We don't even know if the buildings are still there. We're not even sure how long it'll take."

"That's why we'd better get going."

"Olli, its madness. Leave me and go back."

"I won't!" Olli said. "Now help me move you back in the sled!"

"Olli!" Jann said, reaching out and grabbing the hand she was trying to move him with. "You can't do this. Just think about it!"

"I have."

"Then you've already realized that even if we survive, we might be stuck there for months, until winter when the nights are long enough for us to have enough darkness to get back to the cave in a single night."

"I know, but tonight's problem is finding someplace to survive the day that is coming, someplace we can hide long enough for us both to heal. We'll worry about tomorrow's problem later. Now are you going to move? We have to go!"

Jann didn't look happy about it, but he stopped fighting her. After a moment they'd moved him as far back in the sled as they could, and Olli was about to climb up and take her seat.

"I won't be able to use the anchor-pole."

"I know," Olli said. "There's no time for that, anyway. You better hold on as tight as you can. It's full speed, all the way down."

And with that, Olli oriented the sled so it was pointed straight down the run, climbed up, and they were off, flying down the mountain.

8

Darkness and Light

Olli scanned the horizon carefully. They'd come so far, but the morning was upon them, she knew it, and she still hadn't found the village. If she could but see the outline of a building or something, while they still had some momentum in the sled, she could alter their trajectory and get them as close as possible before having to get out and walk.

"Over there," Jann said, raising his arm weakly and pointing further along the horizon than she'd been looking. "On the right."

Olli swung her head to follow his arm and saw what he had seen. Half a dozen silhouettes of buildings were plainly visible, dark black and clearly contrasted with the shimmering of the water beyond them. She veered sharply in that direction, and Jann dropped his pointing hand to clutch the side of the sled and keep from tumbling off.

"Sorry," Olli muttered as she focused on trying to read the ground and find a gully running more or less in the right direction, a channel she could milk for as much speed as possible.

Eventually the ground would level off, and they'd slow to a standstill. Then she'd have to get out and pull. Glancing up at the sky told her they didn't have a whole lot of time left for that.

Olli didn't wait for the sled to come to a full stop. As soon as she was convinced she could pull it faster than it was coasting, she leapt down, rope in hand. Purpose and energy somewhat renewed, she began to pull. She didn't take the time to tie the rope around her waist, as she'd only waste precious seconds first tying and then untying it.

The nearest of the buildings was close, just a few hundred yards away, and it was easier to pull the hovering sled on roughly level ground than it had been up the mountain. Still, she worried that there just wouldn't be time. The moon had disappeared from the sky, and while the sun had not yet appeared, the sky was growing lighter. Soon the sun would appear above the horizon, and moments after that, the gorgaal would rise from their nightly slumber. If showing up at the manor house gate before had made them active and agitated, Olli could only imagine what their response would be to her appearance in their midst.

Olli had to get Jann inside, and she had to do it now. She ran across the open ground to the front of the building. Leaping up onto the front porch, she almost knocked down the front door before she could turn the rickety knob. It flew open, and she flew inside with it, stumbling to catch her balance. Most of the floor in the large, open room was missing, the bulk of the floorboards having been ripped out. Below, in the darkness, lay a dirt cellar that extended at least as far as the room above it.

Olli knelt beside the opening and peered down into the darkness. The dawn would break any moment now, and she had no doubt that the gorgaal would move with furious purpose. Her intuition told her this was what she would find in most if not all of the other buildings. If her ancestors had survived here for a time, before the caves, they must have created dark places beneath their houses, places where the light of day could not be let in simply by opening a door or window or by ripping a hole in a roof or floor.

She couldn't see through the darkness to know if there was a tunnel or cave dug down, further below the house than this or perhaps off to the side. She knew there had to be some sort of hiding place, though, however large or small. Her eyes, searching for evidence of it, found something else instead—the top of a ladder, jutting out from the darkness on the far side of the opening, extending a few rungs into the light.

Olli jumped up and raced out of the house. This was all she needed to convince her it was worth a shot. The ladder showed that someone had needed a means by which to get out of if not into that dark hole. Someone had once taken refuge there, however long ago. If she and Jann survived the day, she could search every building in the village tomorrow night for a better or more comfortable place. Right now she just needed to get Jann down there, find the most remote, dark corner she could, and hope that this place had not been abandoned precisely because it no longer offered refuge.

Jann lay semiconscious on the sled, groaning. Olli was worn out from pulling, so she got behind and pushed the sled toward the front of the building with all her might. She lined it up with the front door, but it was too wide to pass through. She slipped past it, inside, then dragged Jann off. He gasped with pain when his wounded leg struck some of the few floorboards that remained.

"I'm sorry," Olli said. "There's no time . . . I have to get you down."

She dragged him to the edge of the hole, holding him under his arms, knowing it was going to get worse. She maneuvered him until his legs dangled over the edge of the hole, and she held on as long as she could, trying to lower him gently, but his body grew so heavy and she just wasn't strong enough. She let go, and he dropped into the darkness, collapsing on the hard dirt floor. This time he really screamed.

Olli ran back to the front door, wanting to move the sled away from the building, though she knew that moving it would not throw the gorgaal off their scent for long. As she reached the door, a bright, yellow gleam of sunlight appeared above the horizon and sparkled on the water of the sea. Olli was struck both by its sublime beauty and by a sinking fear. She'd never seen sunlight anywhere but at the entrance to the cave.

She kicked the sled, and it scuttled out across the open space in front of the house, then she turned and ran back to the edge of the hole. Lowering herself, she dropped lightly beside Jann. Madly, she scrambled into the dark, waving her arms in front of her to protect against striking anything she couldn't see there. In this way she fumbled around the perimeter of the room, hoping with all her might that she'd find the opening she sought.

She did. It was not as wide as she would have liked, but it sloped downward, away from the open cellar. She returned for Jann and immediately began to drag him behind her down the long, low tunnel. It ended in a tiny dugout, a bare room no bigger than her room at the cave. A couple of hard objects lay in the dark, but she had no time to examine them, and she swept them to the side. There were also some damp, muddy blankets plastered together and half stuck to the ground where they'd been left for half a century.

Jann's more violent cries had ceased, and Olli struggled to get him comfortable in one corner of the dugout. She extricated one of the muddy blankets and draped the cleaner half over him. She crouched, peering up the long, dark tunnel toward the cellar. She thought she could see the faintest glimmer of daylight beginning to shine through the gaping opening above it. She thought of the door she'd left wide open and cursed herself for not closing it after she'd kicked the sled away from the building. The door wouldn't slow down the gorgaal, not really and not for long, but it had been stupid to leave it open.

And yet, despite her quiet self-reproach, the faint radiance of the half-light beckoned. She leaned forward, on her hands and knees, peering up at it. There were no sentries between her and the daylight, and even if the gorgaal were coming, they were not yet here. She could crawl up there and reach her hand out and feel the warmth of the light. She could stand in the middle of the cellar, for that matter, and feel it upon her upturned face.

She wasn't going to, of course. It would be inordinately foolish. She'd be completely vulnerable if she was in the cellar when the gorgaal came, and she'd not come all the way here to be caught in some childish fantasy. And yet . . . there was nothing to prevent her going up closer to the cellar, to get a closer look, provided she stayed in darkness. It was a simple thing, really—either the sunlight's inability to penetrate all the way down the long tunnel would save them, or it wouldn't. Being closer to the cellar wouldn't change that.

Slowly she started forward.

"Olli?" Jann whispered. "Are you here?"

"Yes, Jann," she said, not looking back, but she stopped. "I'm here. Sleep if you can."

"Has First Light come?"

"Yes."

"They'll be coming."

Olli looked back now. "Sleep, Jann. We're safe here."

She stayed where she was, watching the long tunnel and the steadily growing light at the end. When she could hear Jann's breathing, louder and regular, she started crawling up the tunnel again. Hand over hand she moved, shuffling her knees along through the clinging dirt. The ceiling of the tunnel was high enough that she could have stood, stooping, but she felt somehow safer, crouched low to the ground, as though maybe she would be harder to see or hear that way, though she knew well enough that sight and sound were not the gorgaal's chief tools in the hunt.

The light ahead was growing brighter. Olli thought she was perhaps halfway back through the small tunnel, and she hesitated. She wanted to get close enough to see up through the large opening in the floor, so that perhaps she could see the sun itself through the open door above. That the angle would be right for this she knew was a longshot, but having only ever seen light at a distance, she wanted to see it up close and that from which it came.

As she started moving again, a shadow flickered across the light ahead and she froze. Another flicker. She had not imagined it. She started slowly to retreat without turning, backing on hands and knees down the tunnel, her eyes fixed on the cellar ahead. A gorgaal, wings outstretched, dropped down into the middle of the room. Olli could only see the legs and lower torso and the bottom of those wings. The rest was cut off from her limited view.

The legs moved slowly, but it walked toward the opening to the tunnel. As light as it now was, the gorgaal had undoubtedly seen the tunnel opening from above. Olli didn't know if it could see her, but she knew it could smell her. She retreated as quickly as she could back down the tunnel.

The gorgaal stooped so that it crouched at the tunnel's entrance, and it screamed a high-pitched screech that echoed down past her, filling the dark within and around her. Olli swung around and scrambled desperately the rest of the way down to the dugout. The corner where she'd laid Jann was to the left, and she crawled that way until she was as far back from the tunnel opening as she could be without being right on top of him.

She only had to crane her neck forward the smallest bit to see the gorgaal, who as yet did not appear to have actually entered the tunnel. It remained, stooped at the entrance, silhouetted by the growing light behind it.

"Sounds like they found us," Jann whispered. He reached over and placed his hand on her shoulder.

The gorgaal screamed again. Olli put her hands over her ears and closed her eyes.

Time crawled, and the terrible cries of the gorgaal frequently rent the silence of the long day. Olli slipped from periods of restless sleep to restless wakefulness, as waves of exhaustion fought with the fear and terror inside her for mastery.

The initial gorgaal was not alone for long, and at points during the day, the cellar teemed with them. Sometimes Olli could see dozens of limbs and parts of wings and even two or three or more heads peering down into the tunnel. Once or twice a gorgaal or two would enter and take a few steps toward the dugout, but they never came very far.

The sights were unnerving, but the sounds were worse. There would be periods of relative silence, followed by the shrieking of one or more of the monsters. Sometimes she heard the sound of wood being ripped to splinters, and she hoped with all her heart they were breaking to bits some of the floorboards that remained or even the building walls or door, just so long as they left the ladder alone. She thought she could get out of the cellar without it, but getting Jann out, even with it, would be hard.

Jann seemed able to sleep for longer periods, despite the commotion at the other end of the tunnel. This probably had something to do with the fact he didn't keep peering around the corner like Olli did, so he had only the noises to contend with, not the images that accompanied them. But Olli knew that wasn't the only reason. Jann had lost a lot of blood during the night, and now he was weak and feverish. In addition to searching out the hiding spots that had to be in most if not all of the other buildings in the village when night came, Olli would need to find fresh water and, if possible, something with which to change Jann's bandages.

As Olli lay making plans for what she would do once First Dark came, she fell once more asleep, despite her own leg's throbbing. This time, when she woke, the silence at the other end of the tunnel was deafening. She leaned out so she could take a look, and instead of seeing gorgaal moving about in sunshine, she saw only moonlight and shadow.

First Dark had come and gone.

"Jann?" she said, reaching over and shaking him on the chest gently to see if he was awake.

"Hmmm?"

"I'm going out for a while," she said. "I want to explore the other buildings, see what I can find. If I find fresh water, I'll find a way to bring some back."

"I'm hungry."

"Me too, but water and a safer place for tomorrow are a higher priority right now."

"Safer and more comfortable would be nice."

"It would be," she said, scooting over to the entrance to the tunnel. "Stay put."

He groaned. "So funny."

She smiled as she started up the tunnel. He was lucid and had some humor. She knew this didn't guarantee either health or survival, but she grabbed ahold of them as a good sign and took them with her as she left him behind in the darkness.

The ladder was still there and intact, and she scrambled up and out of the cellar with little difficulty. The hole in the floor did seem bigger than it had been, and the front door to the house was simply gone—she had no idea where. Large pieces of the roof were gone too.

It didn't take long to spot the sled. She doubted that the gorgaal, with their ability to fly, had any concept of how essential the sled was to her ability to cover distance quickly, but she didn't think it wise to leave it out here, untended. They'd really be stuck if she came up one night to find it missing like the door or the other pieces of house the gorgaal had destroyed in their rage and frustration. If time permitted, Olli would need to stow it somewhere safe.

She scanned the other buildings, wondering where to start. She would be meticulous, checking each for the shelter they offered below ground as well as for supplies. She'd keep her eyes open for any places where rain might have collected and where water could be found, though finding a stream emptying into the sea close by would be better and more reliable for the long days ahead. Perhaps she'd have to walk the shoreline a little ways and see what she could find.

The moonlight was bright on the rippling water, as it had been the night before. She'd been to the sea before on the western side of the island, which was closer to the caves. Still, the water drew her, and she walked down through the soft sand to it, kicking off her light boots. She waded in, and the salt stung her wounded calf. It would help cleanse the wound, though, so she waded in further.

The sting receded, and she wondered if she should try to get Jann out here. No, it would be easier to take the sea to Jann than to bring Jann to the sea—she'd just find a container for the salt water. That would be first, before anything else. Wound, water, shelter, and food—she had to keep Jann alive.

That thought, that she needed to keep Jann alive, almost overwhelmed her. She had no idea if she'd be able to find fresh water, no idea if she could take care of his wound or feed him or protect him from the gorgaal—who, if they were a little smarter, or even just a little angrier, might find ways to dig holes down into whatever hiding place their prey took refuge in, and then the darkness would not hide them.

And even if she kept Jann alive long enough for him to recover, how to get back up the mountain?

The people who had lived here once, her ancestors, had made that journey. They'd gotten from here to the caves safely, so Olli knew it could be done. And if it could be done, if they had done it . . . she would too.

Time was wasting. She could tell by the moon that it had been dark a couple of hours already. Even so, the tingle of the water swirling around her legs, the massaging feel of the shifting sand beneath her toes . . . She didn't want to go. She stood, wanting to stay, knowing she had to go. She stared out to sea, wondering if somewhere, out there, beyond the shimmering moonlight, there was still a world worth finding.

9

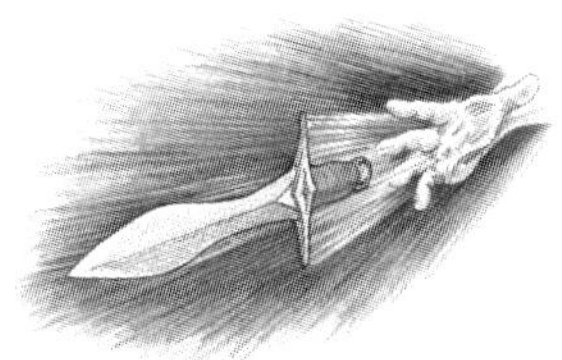

SANTAGO

Rika leaned on the starboard rail of *The Sorry Rogue*. Though the sea was calm now, two days of stormy weather and choppy waves had taken their toll on most of the passengers. Few but the crew were above decks, which Rika didn't mind at all. The peace and quiet were welcome after the tumult of the past few days.

Captain D'Sarza approached and stopped next to her. "Glad to see you up and about."

"I needed the air," Rika said.

"You've come a long way," D'Sarza said. "When you first came aboard, a storm like that would have left you in bed for days, even after it was gone."

"Well, I had to, didn't I?" Rika said. "You would have kicked me out of your cabin long ago if I hadn't."

"I was, perhaps, a little hard on you when you at first."

Rika turned and stared at her. "A little?"

"Hey, sharing my cabin was bad enough, but with someone who whimpered with every wave—"

"I never whimpered," Rika said.

D'Sarza grinned. "Well, the point is, you've come a long way. And I take all the credit. You've even learned to dress with some color and style, thanks to me."

Rika turned back to look out at the moonlight sparkling on the sea. "It took time to let go."

"I know," D'Sarza said, placing her hand on Rika's shoulder. "I know what it is to be a woman in a man's world. If I lost all I'd worked for, I'd probably hold on to whatever I could, too."

Rika exchanged smiles with the captain. She wondered if D'Sarza had any idea that she was articulating in direct and plain language the very hints and suggestions that Rika had used to bypass the captain's gruff defenses when they'd been thrust together by fate. It had taken some trial and error to find a tactic that would work, but once she'd found her opening, Rika had exploited it to the full, until she became D'Sarza's favorite among all the exiles from Barra-Dohn. Whatever obstacles to acceptance she faced with the exiles themselves, she had formed reasonable bonds with their captain, who was capable but not especially clever when it came to the subtler arts of human interaction.

"Are we very much off course?" Rika asked.

"It's not so bad," D'Sarza answered. "If the winds hold, we won't lose too much time."

"I hope they hold," Rika said, reaching up and pulling back her long hair so that it hung over her left shoulder. "I'm curious to see this mysterious island."

"It's a lot of bother about nothing, I'd say," D'Sarza said. "I bet the people on the island fished the *chokra* too heavily and the supply dried up, so they moved on. Over-fishing was probably the only curse involved."

"But why would other sailors be afraid of going ashore there?"

"Who knows?" D'Sarza shrugged. "Islanders are superstitious."

"I guess we'll see," Rika said.

"I guess we will. Good night."

The captain moved on, and Rika remained for a moment, watching her go, then she too moved on, walking over to the water barrel to get a drink. The storm had refilled their supplies with cold, fresh water, and she knew she should savor it while she could. A week from now, if there was no more rain, she'd find herself sipping her warm, stale water ration, longing to have this opportunity back. Her time aboard *The Sorry Rogue* had taught her to take the good with the bad when the waves rose and the winds raged and the heavens opened.

She stood, drinking from the water barrel, lost in her own thoughts, when the door to the Omiirs' cabin opened and Kaden slipped out. He made his way directly to the water barrel, two cups in hand.

"Good evening," she said, smiling as she stepped aside, glancing around to see if the meddlesome Kalosene was nearby.

"Good evening, Rika," Kaden said, focused on his task.

"Is Nara feeling all right after the storm?" Rika asked. "She's been struggling a bit with sickness recently, hasn't she?"

"Yes, a bit," Kaden said, filling the second cup. "She's had trouble adjusting to being back at sea this time for some reason."

Rika noted with curiosity that asking after Nara hadn't set Kaden at ease. Quite the opposite, Kaden's body language and tone betrayed nervousness. She wondered what that was about.

"D'Sarza says the storm didn't put us too far off track."

"Good," Kaden said, and Rika noticed he did relax a bit at this.

"She's also skeptical we'll find anything of use there. If we don't, where to next?"

Kaden held the cups in his hands, but Rika could see him shaking his head, almost imperceptibly in the dark. "I don't know. We haven't looked that far ahead."

Rika wasn't sure she believed that. Several weeks out from Brexton with little to do but sit around and talk, she found it unlikely that Tchinchura and Kaden hadn't discussed their options. "Well, whatever we find, I'm sure you and Tchinchura will come up with something."

"I hope so," Kaden said, turning to head back to his cabin.

"Kaden?" Rika said, and Kaden stopped, turning back to her. "We don't talk much about Barra-Dohn and life before anymore."

"Not much left to say, I guess."

"No, maybe not," Rika said. "Although, I've meant to say something to you, I just never had the nerve to say it." She paused. "I know it must have been hard, being Eirmon's son."

Kaden stood, a few feet away, looking stunned. Rika knew that he was aware she'd been Eirmon's mistress. Nara had known, certainly, and probably most of the palace had, too. They'd never talked about it, though, and so she didn't know if he was stunned just because she had brought Eirmon up, or if he thought maybe she meant to talk about this past they always talked around.

"It was," he said finally. Rika could tell he was waiting to hear where this was going.

"He never made anything easy on anyone around him, did he?" Rika asked, trying to sound as sympathetic as she could. "Except maybe for Deslo."

"Yes," Kaden said. "He had a soft spot for Deslo."

"As a grandfather should."

"Yes," Kaden agreed, still saying little.

He was hard to read in the dark, but Rika knew that would work both ways. "I don't think he'd have handled exile very well. Losing his throne? He wouldn't have coped with that."

"It would have been hard on him," Kaden said. "As it has been for us all."

"And yet you've handled it so well," she said with a slight step forward. "Which, in a way, shows you were really stronger than he was, all along."

She watched him think about that for a moment, then excused herself. Best to plant the seed and then walk away. She could feel his eyes on her as she slipped away into the darkness.

The following morning Captain D'Sarza lowered her looking glass.

"Do you agree, Captain?" Tchinchura asked.

"Yes," she said. "This is not the island we're looking for. That port looks too big to be the place Garjan described, and there are plenty of people out and about."

"So we go on?" Kaden asked.

"No," D'Sarza said, turning away from the rail. "Almost three weeks since Brexton, and no idea what we'll find once we arrive at the right island? I want a chance to trade for supplies. We go ashore."

Two hours later they had pulled one of the longboats up on shore and been greeted by a few locals, who seemed more than happy to welcome them to their town, called Santago. What's more, barely had they had time to hint at the possibility that perhaps some arrangements could be made for trade with *The Sorry Rogue* when D'Sarza and her first mate, Geffen, were marching off to follow the welcoming party. They took along the crew members who'd come ashore with them, leaving Kaden and Tchinchura alone on the beach with the two Kalosenes.

"Think they'll be all right?" Marlo asked as they watched the small party heading off.

"The captain is quite capable," Tchnichura replied. "And she has an escort."

"He wasn't asking about her," Kaden said. "Did you see the look in their eyes? The crew thinks they're going to come out ahead in this exchange. I don't think they know what they're in for."

Tchinchura smiled, his white teeth gleaming in his dark face. "No, I think not. Come, let us go, and we will see what we can see."

They walked up toward the front street of Santago. People walking along the street did little to curb their curiosity as they gawked, and Kaden was not surprised. Even in a larger, more cosmopolitan town like Brexton, an Amhuru like Tchinchura excited a lot of interest. The golden plume of his ponytail falling from his bald, brown head, the bright, penetrating shine of his golden eyes, the wicked axe that hung from his belt—he was quite a sight. And accompanied by two Kalosenes in their long black robes, one of them as big as an ox? In a town like this? Well, there wasn't really much of a chance that they wouldn't be stared at. Word of their arrival would quickly circulate.

They walked along the street, looking at the shops dotted here and there among the houses and other buildings. As they passed one with an open door, they all caught a whiff of the strong scent of freshly baked bread. It stopped them dead in their tracks as surely as if they'd run into a wall and could go no further.

"Bakery" was all that Owenn said as he turned and walked inside. Kaden watched him go, smiling. The big man didn't say very much, and when he did, it was usually about Kalos or food. Today it was food.

Following Owenn inside, Kaden inhaled deeply. Growing up in the palace of Barra-Dohn, he had enjoyed the ability to have almost any food he wanted, whenever he wanted it. Since Barra-Dohn's fall, however, he had learned to savor food—for while it might usually be plentiful on *The Sorry Rogue,* it was not always wonderful.

In the front room of the shop, fresh-baked breads and cakes, with and without icing, sat on tables and countertops all around them. There was no one in the room, and the four men walked around, looking at and taking in the scent of the bakery's various wares. A shuffling sound alerted them to someone's entrance through the door at the back of the shop, and Kaden looked up to see a young girl, no older than Deslo, step through the open door with a tray of small round rolls.

When the girl saw the collection of visitors in the shop, she dropped the tray and all but ran back through the door. Tchinchura, who had been the closest to her, stepped over, squatted down, and gathered up the bread that had fallen to the floor, placing it back on the tray. The sound of voices drifted through the doorway then, and in a moment, a stout woman wearing a large apron covered with flour came bustling through the door, wiping her hands assiduously on the apron, though Kaden suspected from the state of it that there wasn't much a chance that would help.

The woman looked up at Tchinchura, who stood before her holding the tray with the rolls. Her eyes widened. "Honored One, you are most welcome to my shop. Let me take those from you, and please, forgive my foolish girl for her clumsiness."

"We would like to buy all of these from you," Tchinchura said as he handed the tray back to the woman. "We have not had fresh bread in some time, and these are not to be resisted."

"Honored One," the mother said, "I could not sell you these. They have been on the floor and—"

"I insist," Tchinchura said. "But our appetites are large, and they will not be enough. We will also need a large assortment of your other breads and cakes. Would you mind putting that together for us? You would know best what we should not miss."

The woman blinked, then looked from Tchinchura to Kaden and the Devoted, then back to Tchinchura. "Of course, Honored One," she said, and she started immediately to gather samples from among her various wares.

The girl peeked out from the other room at the scene unfolding, and Tchinchura, seeing her face appear in the doorway, winked. At first, the girl's eyes widened like her mother's had, but as she continued to watch the Amhuru, a smile crept across her face.

The assortment of breads and cakes kept growing as Owenn began pointing the baker in the direction of more and more options that she at first had not included, until finally there was more than even the four of them with their substantial appetites would be able to handle. Kaden didn't mind, since Nara and Deslo would enjoy eating some of the leftovers.

After they had settled with the baker, Tchinchura said, "May I impose on your hospitality a little more and ask you a question?"

"Of course, Honored One, you do not impose."

"We would like to talk to some of your sailors or fishermen. Is there somewhere they are likely to be gathered at this hour?"

"Unfortunately, they are all almost certain to be on their boats, fishing as we speak, Honored One. They probably left before dawn and will not return until sunset. It is the busy season."

"Maybe there are some," Tchinchura said, as he tapped the side of the box of baked goods that he held, "who have grown weary from their many years at sea, men who no longer fish the deep waters? Perhaps there are even some that the younger fishermen of Santago consult when times are hard, when weather patterns change and the fish are not where they are supposed to be? Is that so?"

"Yes, Honored One, there are. They will be outside Cantu's shop, where there are tables and they can play their card games in the sun."

"Perhaps your daughter, if you could spare her for a few moments, could show us this place, if it is not far?"

"Yes, yes of course," the baker said, and before she could even turn and summon the girl, she was by her side, almost bouncing on her toes with eagerness.

As the menturned to leave the shop, the baker added one more thing. "You should ask for Daala. If anyone can help you, it will be him."

"Many thanks," Tchinchura said, and they headed back out into the street.

The girl led them up through streets that moved increasingly higher the deeper into the town they got. Finally, she took them around a corner to show them a short street that was a dead end, and the last shop on the right had a wide veranda in front with several wooden tables on it. Around those tables an assortment of older men sat playing cards.

Tchinchura thanked the baker's daughter and handed her a silver coin, which she massaged between her fingers as though unsure if she should really take it. He encouraged her that it was fine, and she smiled and ran back down the hill in the direction from which they had come.

As Kaden watched her go, he noticed a young man on meridium-soled shoes running on the Arua field up the same street. He was moving very quickly and passed them in a blur, continuing farther up the hill. He watched the boy run for a moment and then turned to the others. "Strange," he said. "I would barely have noticed a courier going by in Barra-Dohn, but in a place like this . . ."

"What is common in one place is uncommon in another," Marlo said, suspiciously.

"Indeed," Tchinchura said. "Somehow, I suspect that this young man's haste has something to do with our Captain D'Sarza."

"You still think she's all right?" Kaden asked. Tchinchura sounded amused rather than worried, but Kaden could envision a number of scenarios that might explain why the courier was needed if indeed it did involve D'Sarza, not all of them pleasant.

"Yes," Tchinchura said, nodding. "I think the men who greeted us with talk of trade thought they were sharks encircling their prey. I think that courier means they've realized that they're going to need a bigger shark."

Kaden looked up the hill, watching the courier turn and disappear around a corner, many streets higher up. He closed his eyes and reached out through the Zerura around his left bicep, his replica of the fragment of the Golden Cord that Tchinchura carried. He felt for the Arua field, touching it in a sense, feeling its smooth surface. Sometimes, when he did this, he felt he could almost feel the imprint of the feet or tracks of the sliders that passed by on it. He did not feel that way now, though, and Tchinchura's light touch on his arm ended his attempt.

He let go of the Arua field and opened his eyes. The older Amhuru was looking at him.

"She will be fine. Come, let us find this man Daala and speak with him."

The men playing cards at the wooden tables seemed just as curious about the small band of visitors as the rest of the townspeople had been. Every eye was upon them as they drew closer, though the steady flow of the cards continued in the growing silence.

"We are looking for Daala," Tchinchura said, and several heads swiveled toward a mostly bald man with thin wisps of white hair. Daala was lean, his brown-red skin leathery from years in the sun. He set his cards down and looked up.

"I am Daala, Honored One," he said. If being looked for by Amhuru and Devoted was unexpected for Daala, he did not show it. "Would you and your friends like to pull up some chairs and sit for a while?"

"Yes, thank you," Tchinchura said, and immediately Marlo and Owenn brought two chairs from an empty table for him and Kaden before grabbing two for themselves. In a moment, they were seated in a little arc facing Daala and the rest of the old men.

"How can I be of service?" Daala asked.

"We are looking for an island," Tchinchura said. "It lies a few days west of here, and we have been told that it has been cursed."

The cards stopped flowing. The silence deepened. Kaden could hear gulls from the beach behind them, and the sound of the sea moving ceaselessly in and out.

Daala, at last, nodded. "It is as you say. The island is a few days west of here, and if it can be said that a place is cursed, that one is."

"Can you tell us about it?" Kaden asked.

"You seem to know of it already, Honored One," Daala said, turning from Tchinchura to Kaden, who felt like he was being measured by Daala's penetrating green eyes. "What have you been told?"

Kaden repeated what the sailor Garjan had told them, and when he finished, there was silence again.

"What this man told you is true," Daala said at last. "Though the strange happenings there started before the flying creatures came."

“What happenings?” Kaden asked.

“People started disappearing. Not just from the village but from the vessels that came there to trade or fish. My mother was from that island, and two of my uncles and a few of my cousins were among those who disappeared.”

“And the creatures came after?” Tchinchura asked.

“The creatures came after,” Daala replied. “And when they came, the rest of the village disappeared. And in all the years since then, none have been found.”

“These creatures . . .” Tchichura began. “Have you seen them?”

“Yes, I have,” Daala said. He grimaced, then continued. “We hadn’t seen or heard from anyone in my family or from the village there at all, so I joined a crew that was formed here in Santago to go and investigate. When we arrived, we found all their ships at anchor, the small boats ashore, and nothing seemed to be moving in the village at all.

“Something was wrong, and we knew it, so a landing party was formed. I watched from the deck as they rowed toward shore. The creatures came and attacked just as they were pulling their boat up onto the beach. They tried to fend them off with the oars, but they were ripped into pieces.”

“Can you describe what the creatures looked like?”

Daala seemed to sigh. “They were pale, very pale, and had huge wings, but there were arms and legs too. They were sinewy and strong; that I could see. They caught and crushed some of those oars to splinters with their bare hands, though they were more like claws than hands.”

“Was that the last time you were there?” Tchinchura asked, his words barely audible above the sound of the breeze blowing in off the sea.

“No,” Daala said. He stared at Tchinchura for a moment before continuing. “I have been back many times since, but I only get close enough to survey the village from a distance. I have not been on the island itself, though, not since before.”

Kaden had been watching Daala, engrossed, but he turned now to look at Tchinchura, who appeared deep in thought. Tchinchura glanced at him, and Kaden knew from that glance that the elder Amhuru felt the same way he did. They had been right to come.

"Thank you, Daala," Tchinchura said. "I am sorry for your family's loss. If we find anything there that might answer your questions, we will come back here before we leave."

"You really mean to go ashore there?" Daala asked.

"Yes."

"Why?"

"We seek answers of our own."

Daala frowned. "I answered your questions, Honored One. Is that all the answer I will get to mine?"

It was Tchinchura's turn to examine Daala with his penetrating eyes, gold instead of green, but the elderly fisherman did not wilt under that gaze. Kaden just watched them in stunned silence. At last Tchinchura broke the quiet.

"Long ago, something was stolen, and it might have been taken to the island we speak of, might have been used to make or at least control the creatures you describe. The man who has what we seek is no longer there, but we are seeking his past for clues to his future."

Daala sat, his arms crossed, thinking about this. And then he leaned forward on the wooden table and said, "I would like to come with you."

The rest of the men there, who had listened in fascinated silence to the exchange, now gasped and turned to Daala. He ignored them.

"One of my cousins, Lamya, was the most beautiful girl I have ever known. When she was old enough, I was going to speak to my uncle for her, but I never got the chance. I would like to know what happened there."

"Are you sure?" Tchinchura asked. "We will come back with whatever answers we find."

"I am sure you will, if you survive," Daala said. "I do not have many summers left, Honored One. I would set foot on that island again, even if I never leave it."

"Then you shall come."

Their departure for the island was delayed, as Captain D'Sarza needed to take a few of the local merchants onboard *The Sorry Rogue* to complete a variety of deals. When the last of these merchants had departed for shore with their goods, she welcomed Daala to the ship and listened eagerly as Kaden related the events of their day.

"Sounds like we both did even better than we'd hoped we would," she said, slapping him on the shoulder as she walked off to get the crew moving so they could lift anchor and be away.

Kaden joined Nara and Deslo, sharing with them from among the abundace of the baked goods they'd brought back.

"We've picked up another passenger," Nara said, nodding toward Daala, who was standing with Tchinchura across the deck.

"Yes," Kaden said. "He had family on the island, family who disappeared when the creatures came."

"How awful," Nara said.

"Yes," Kaden said. "He would like to understand what happened there, to get answers. Mostly, though, I think he just wants to see it one more time, whatever the cost."

"In a sense, then, he is an exile also."

"Yes," Kaden agreed, not having thought about it that way. "I guess he is."

10

Another Choice

Olli raked the bottom of the rut with the jagged floorboard, making it deeper. She flung the dirt out onto the growing mound. Her muscles were beyond aching, and weariness did not begin to describe how tired she felt. But she did not slow down. She continued to dig and scrape and pull, flinging the dirt out of the hole with an energy she pulled by sheer willpower from reserves she did not know she had.

She had to finish tonight. She had spent all day yesterday with Jann beside her, cold and lifeless, and most of the day before. She had to get him buried now. She had spent the first part of this night getting him up and out of their hiding place, so there was no going back. And she would not leave his corpse unburied for the gorgaal.

Sweat stung her eyes, but she did not stop to try to wipe it away. She feared that if her arms stopped their digging motion, even for a moment, she'd never get them going again. She closed her eyes, hoping by sheer force to squeeze the sweat out, and kept right on digging, working by feel.

As she closed her eyes, she heard Jann's voice say, "Olli, I love you." That was what he'd said, not long before the end.

Sweat or no sweat, she opened her eyes and kept going. Raking the bottom of the rut, working sideways to scrape the dirt out, hoping more stayed out than slid back in. She was reaching the point where the limits of her tool had been reached, she suspected. The hole was maybe a little more than three feet deep, but that was about as deep as it was going to get without a better shovel.

When she placed Jann in the hole and covered him up, she would be alone in the dark. She hesitated, her arms raised in preparation for another assault on the earth at her feet. She'd only been thinking of Jann's dead body beside her in the dark when she set out to bury him, and how it was starting to creep her out, but she wondered now if being alone would be worse?

She had been right; having stopped, she did not find in herself the will to start again. Her shaking fingers dropped the floorboard on the side of the grave where the dirt wasn't as high, and she climbed out of the grave. She took hold of Jann's ankles, which stuck out a little bit below the blanket she had wrapped him in, and pulled him feet first into the grave. He deserved better, but she had nothing better to give him. She'd gotten him killed, and now she couldn't even give his body a decent burial.

Olli clenched her fists as she looked down at Jann's mortal remains. She didn't have time to linger, but she wanted to look at his face one more time. She stooped down and fumbled for the opening above his head, and when she finally found it, she pulled the blankets apart just enough to expose his head.

In the darkness of their hiding place, she'd not been able to make him out clearly at all, but here, in the moonlight, she could. He didn't look angry or afraid, and he didn't look disappointed or sad. In fact, he looked almost peaceful, like a child that's fallen asleep and left the cares of the day behind.

Her fingers trembled as she wrapped him back up as much from exhaustion as emotion. And as she climbed out and started using the broader end of her floorboard to push dirt from beside the mound into it, she felt the anger that had momentarily disappeared rise inside her again. Peaceful or not, he shouldn't have died. Not down here. Not like this.

The gorgaal had to die. She had to find a way. She didn't remember anymore how long they'd been here, not exactly, anyway. She thought it was a couple weeks, maybe more, but she didn't know. The moon had waned and disappeared, and now it was new again. And still, every day, the gorgaal came back. Even when, on the third day of their being here, they'd moved to the house that had the safest and most comfortable shelter, the gorgaal had followed them and haunted them there.

Olli thought of that day and the promise it had held. The room below that house was larger and more comfortable, and Jann had been in good spirits. His fever had not yet taken a turn for the worst. They'd not yet realized that she wasn't going to be able to find sufficient food for them in her foraging efforts. They'd neither one known that he was already beginning his slow descent into a restless sleep full of fever dreams that would lead to his death.

And so they had laughed and joked and felt their spirits rise. They had spoken of how they'd be received when they went back up the mountain and returned to the caves.

Olli paused from her work of pushing the dirt that had taken two days to remove from this hole, and which now was going so easily back into it. If she was ever going to try for the caves, it would have to be soon. Her leg was healing, but her body was growing weaker. She was so hungry. Thoughts of food preyed on her mind, all the time. Sometimes she could push them away. Sometimes she succumbed and fell into them like falling into a dream. She had to find something to eat, and with whatever strength that provided, she had to try her luck getting back up the mountain. Otherwise, she feared she would never have the strength, and sooner or later she'd die in her sleep, with no one to drag her out and drop her in a hole like this one.

Well, at least if she died and rotted in the room where she hid, the gorgaal wouldn't get her. She laughed at that thought. Perhaps that would be it, her final victory, denying the gorgaal the spoils of their triumph.

And then something occurred to her, something crazy, but it grabbed ahold of her all the same. She had another choice. What if she could poison herself? What if she could poison herself with something as deadly to the gorgaal as it was to her? Then if she died where they could find her, perhaps when they feasted on her dead body she could finally have her revenge? Maybe she could do in her death what she couldn't do in her life?

For a moment just that thought, that she might be able to kill at least some of the gorgaal in such a way, gripped her. Perhaps she could make her death meaningful? Perhaps she could get some revenge for Jann's death?

But the gorgaal hadn't killed Jann, a quiet voice said from some place deep inside her. In fact, the gorgaal had never even touched Jann. Those strange, long-snouted and terrible-jawed creatures at the manor house had wounded him, and it was that wound that had kept them from getting up the mountain and that wound that had led to the infection that had led to the fever that had led to his death. And Jann had gotten that wound because he'd followed Olli into the manor house. Jann had gotten that wound because of her. She'd killed Jann, not the gorgaal.

Well, then, poisoning herself would avenge Jann, and passing that poison on to the gorgaal would be her last desperate act in the lifelong quest that had driven her to set the island free in the first place.

She went back to work, scraping dirt back into the rut. She had it almost filled now. She patted down the dirt that was in there, packing it as hard as she could, and then went back to pushing the loose dirt over top of what she had already packed down.

There were, it seemed, two options before her. She could try to find food to gather strength for the trip back up the mountain, or she could try to find something that would be deadly to herself and the gorgaal. But what? She knew some roots and plants and berries that in small quantities would make someone sick, but would they be potent enough to kill? And if they killed her, would they kill them?

She dropped the floorboard. Where the rut had been a short while ago, a small mound lay now, a little higher than the ground around it. She knelt down and pressed down on the dirt with her hands, packing it as hard as she could with what strength remained. The sky was definitely growing light. She had to go soon, but she would make it as tough for them to smell and find Jann as possible.

I love you, Olli.

He'd been almost incoherent for days, and then that. Just mumbled words in the darkness, but she knew they'd not come from one of his fever dreams. They'd been the last lucid and coherent thought he ever expressed.

And what had she done? Had she told him she loved him too in an attempt to ease his passing? Had she reached over and stroked his hair and said something, anything to lessen the burden he carried? It wasn't true, of course, because she had realized with startling clarity that she didn't love Jann, and this realization, rather than comforting her, had crushed her. For maybe, just maybe, if she'd loved him, then his death wouldn't have been so much her fault. Maybe his coming with her would have been some kind of fate, the result of the growing love that somehow bound them together. But she didn't love him, so it couldn't be blamed on that.

And so what had she done when he made his confession of love his final act? She had done nothing. She could not bring herself, even then, to lie and tell him what he wanted to hear. So she had said, only after an interval of silence, "Sleep now, Jann. Save your strength."

And eventually, he had gone to sleep. At first, it was a restless sleep like so much of his sleep had been of late. He had groaned and thrashed and murmured incoherent nonsense so quietly that Olli had to strain her ears just to hear the sound. And then, his sleep had grown less fitful. His mind had seemed to come through the other side of those dreams, and his mouth stopped working so hard to say nothing. His arms lay still by his side, no longer fighting off the demons in his dreams. His breathing had grown more rhythmic.

And then it had stopped.

Olli stood. She had done all she could do. First Light would be here any moment. She had to get back. She picked up the floorboard, turned, and headed back to her hiding place.

Kaden stood with Deslo, beside Daala, looking at the village on the island.

"I never thought I'd see it again."

"How long has it been?" Kaden asked.

"Eight years."

"Look any different?"

Daala gazed across the water. Kaden wondered how much memory affected what he saw. Kaden saw only the slow decay of time on a rather ordinary, abandoned cluster of buildings. Did Daala see them in their prime, before the wind and rain and long years of neglect had taken their toll? Did Daala see the ghosts of the past walking in their midst? Would he, if this were the ruins of Barra-Dohn?

"It does not," Daala said. "Not that I can see."

Tchinchura approached. "If we are decided, we should not tarry much longer."

Kaden and Deslo turned to face the elder Amhuru. Daala did not. "Do you think we should reconsider?" Kaden asked.

Tchinchura shrugged. "I should have pressed the sailor, Garjan, on just what he meant when he said the 'winged nightmares feared not the light of day.' Did he mean that even the light of day could not stop them, or that they somehow thrived in daylight?"

Kaden laughed. "You sound like me, repeating yourself, self-doubt . . . I'm supposed to be becoming more like you, not the other way around."

Tchinchura smiled. "There has been too much time to think about this plan—to second guess it. Perhaps we just need to act upon it."

"I agree," Kaden said. "We'll go ashore just before sunset, and if we're attacked, we'll keep them at bay until the sun goes down and see if that makes any difference."

"Forgive me, *saba*," Daala said, still facing the island. "And how will you do that? Hold them at bay, I mean?"

He turned now, his bright green eyes searching them. "I mean no disrespect, Honored Ones. I believe you are mighty men, but my memory of these creatures and what they did fills me with fear."

"There is no disrespect, Daala," Tchinchura said. "I will know, fairly quickly, if I am overmatched."

"And even then," Kaden said, "we should be able to hold them back until we can retreat to the ship."

"You do not have to come with the first launch," Tchinchura said. "Why not wait here until we are sure it is all right?"

Daala looked back at the shore. "You misunderstand. I do not fear for myself. My closest friend was among the men who went ashore here, more than half a lifetime ago. He died that day, and I lived. I have always lived. A dozen times the sea could have claimed my life and did not. I do not fear death . . . but I would not take the boy."

Deslo started, but Kaden put his hand on his shoulder. Tchinchura spoke. "The boy is an Amhuru apprentice. He is under my care, and he is ready. All will be well."

Daala glanced back over his shoulder at Deslo, shrugged, and turned back to regarding the village.

Kaden couldn't help but wish he'd been able to alleviate Nara's fears about Deslo's place in the landing party so readily.

He'd had a much more difficult time of it. He understood her point, of course. The reality of the danger that went with being an Amhuru apprentice was far different than just the idea of that danger. And such a strange kind of danger simply heightened her inevitable reluctance.

In the end she had relented, knowing that she didn't have much choice. Deslo was now of age, he was an apprentice Amhuru, and the choice was no longer hers. He would go ashore with Kaden and Tchinchura, with Marlo and Owenn, with Daala, and with a half dozen of D'Sarza's more capable men. They would go armed and ready for a fight, but they would also go knowing that their real hope rested with Tchinchura's—and to a lesser extent Kaden's—ability to manipulate the Arua field.

"Come," Tchinchura said. "It is time to see what we have come all this way to see."

In the longboat D'Sarza's men manned the oars in the middle and back, while the others huddled in the front. Tchinchura was at the very front, his golden eyes studying the shore, bathed in the last light of day. Behind him sat Kaden and Deslo, and both of them had their axes out and in their hands. Kaden knew that Deslo still felt uncomfortable with his, both because Deslo had told him so and also because he remembered how long it had taken him to feel comfortable with his own. Still, he was proud that Deslo had never voiced any doubts about coming with them, even if he could sense the boy's fear.

The Devoted sat with Daala in the rowboat behind them. Daala had only a large fishing knife, while both Marlo and Owenn carried the weapons they had adopted not long after Barra-Dohn's fall. Both men had come to Tchinchura then, asking to be trained to use weapons. Tchinchura had been more surprised at their request than he had been when Kaden asked to become an apprentice, for the Devoted did not usually participate in battles.

"We blew up the Academy of Barra-Dohn when it had become a place of idolatry," Marlo had said when Tchinchura asked if they really meant to do this. "And now this Jin Dara intends a still greater blasphemy, to do what Kalos has forbidden and reunite the fragments of the Golden Cord. We will help you stop him if we can."

And that had been that. Marlo had learned to use throwing knives, quite well Kaden would say, and Owenn . . . Well, he'd learned to use an axe that was as much larger than the axe Kaden carried as Owenn was larger than Kaden, if not more so. The axe was so large that Deslo had barely been able to lift it off the deck of *The Sorry Rogue* when Owenn first started training with it.

That had also been, Kaden supposed, the moment when their odd little fellowship had been solidified. There had never been a formal decision, no vote or council where the exiles from Barra-Dohn had sat down together with Tchinchura and Zangira and said, "We will come with you. We will help you find and stop this man." After that day, it had simply been understood. They had all seen what the Jin Dara was both willing and able to do, and they would stop him if they could.

The shore of the island drew closer, and except for the sound of the oars slapping the water, no other sounds came from the boat. Six men rowed. Six men didn't. All of them watched and waited.

The sound came before the sight. A loud, high-pitched screeching rent the relatively peaceful night. It came from among the buildings, which were off the port side of the longboat; they had made the decision to approach the empty beach well down from the town, so the creatures would have less cover if they decided to attack them. Every head swiveled in the direction of the shrieks, and every eye watched for the first glimpse of the shrieks' source.

Despite the sound, which served as ample warning that the creatures were coming, their appearance still struck Kaden as sudden, and whatever he had imagined they would look like from Daala's descriptions, it did not quite do them justice. They flocked toward them from the town, appearing in the empty spaces between the houses and rising up into the vaster empty space above the town. Even at a distance, they looked big, as big as a man, and their wingspans were extensive. They were just as pale as Daala had suggested, and in the failing light of day, their skin looked to be almost a faintly luminous white against the darker land and sky behind them.

And they were fast. At least a hundred yards of open beach lay between the long boat and the town, but these things covered that distance in what felt like only a heartbeat. One moment they had simply appeared in the distance, and the next moment they were hurtling out over the breakers and the grey sea, on pace to intercept the boat well before it reached the beach.

Kaden gripped his axe and braced for their attack.

11

The Gorgaal

Tchinchura stretched out his hand toward the swarm of flying monstrosities as they drew near, and Kaden felt him reach for the Arua field, felt him take hold of it with a grasp so strong and so powerful that Kaden marveled. The boat was still thirty or forty yards from land, and how Tchinchura could demonstrate such mastery this far out was beyond him. He could not have taken hold so firmly had he been standing in the middle of a vast and empty field.

But Tchinchura did take hold of the Arua, and he bent it up and around the approaching creatures, as though to wrap them up or put a shield between them and the men in the boat, and the attack ground to a halt some ten yards away in midair. It looked as though the flying creatures were tethered to something back in the town and had reached, quite literally, the end of their ropes. They even started moving slowly backward, as Tchinchura pressed them back through the power of the Golden Cord.

The screeches they had heard from a distance they now heard up close, as the creatures opened their long thin mouths to scream, and their eyes raged as they stared at their would-be prey. Several clawed in the open air at nothing, as through trying to slice through the invisible net that had caught them, and they howled and screamed louder and louder in their frustration.

Kaden turned and looked behind him. The longboat had slowed considerably as D'Sarza's men had all but dropped their oars, no doubt thinking they needed to prepare to defend themselves. "Row!" he shouted. "Put us ashore!"

They looked at Kaden like he'd spoken another language, and then snapped to their oars with vigor. They pulled hard, and the longboat lurched ahead. Soon they were in just a few feet of water, and Kaden leapt into the surf, grabbing the prow of the longboat to pull it up on shore. Deslo followed, as did Marlo and Owenn, but Daala sat huddled in the boat behind Tchinchura, seemingly transfixed both by the hovering cloud of creatures a short distance away and by the fact that, to all appearances, the Amhuru could command them to stay back without a word and with nothing but the wave of his outstretched hand.

The longboat ran aground in the sand, and D'Sarza's men leapt out too, drawing their long knives and gathering with the others, gazing up at the hovering creatures. The knives with their long steel blades had seemed strange to Kaden at first, who was used to a world where you either wielded meridium weapons or died in a hurry, but his years on *The Sorry Rogue* had shown him that his was but one of many worlds.

Tchinchura stepped slowly out of the boat, his arm still raised, and he walked up onto the soft sand and stood with them. He glanced at Kaden. "Can you take hold now too?"

"Yes," Kaden said, and he reached out for the Arua and did so, understanding that his task was simply to maintain the shield that Tchinchura had erected.

No sooner had Kaden taken hold, but Tchinchura bent down so he could slide his foot along the fragment of the Golden Cord on his left bicep, and rubbing his feet quickly together, he leapt up onto the Arua field. He ran across it, several feet above the beach's surface, toward the shrieking creatures who continued to writhe in midair.

As he drew near, he threw his axe at the one closest to him, and the blade struck the creature in the forehead, knocking it back and out of the air. It fell with a thud to the beach below, hitting water so shallow it barely made a splash. The axe flew back out the creature's head, rotating backward through the midst of the others, who howled, wings flapping, mad with rage and hatred. Tchinchura caught the axe in his hand, and then, standing on the Arua field and level with the lowest of the creatures, he spread his strong arms out to either side and howled in a deep and rumbling voice.

For a moment the creatures flapping and fluttering out just beyond him were quiet. They hovered and stared, but they did not scream. And then, as though acting in unison according to some unseen cue, they spread out to the side and flew up into the sky, scattering in every direction but the one in which the shield lay. Tchinchura turned immediately and ran back to the huddle of men behind him.

"Are they leaving?" Deslo asked, excited.

"I don't think so," Kaden answered, relaxing his grip on the Arua field, for he feared they would soon have to alter their strategy. "I think they mean to spread out and try us from more than one direction."

"That is exactly what they intend," Tchinchura said, dropping down off the Arua onto the sand. "It was inevitable." He put his hand on Kaden's shoulder. "You saw how I did it?"

"Yes," Kaden answered, telling Tchinchura he could do it, too—not just hold the shield, but make one. At least, he hoped that this was in fact true.

"We will have to work together, to keep them back," Tchinchura said. "Face the sea. I will face inland, ten feet or so behind you. The rest of you stand between us."

Everyone moved quickly, and soon they were clustered together tightly in the formation Tchinchura had suggested. "Watch the sides. They will figure out where the edges to our defenses are."

Kaden spread his arms as though in quiet supplication, an uspoken prayer to this Kalos who still hovered somewhere between myth and reality for him, and he reached out, trying to replicate what he had felt Tchinchura do. He took hold the the Arua field, imposing his will upon it, feeling the Zerura around his bicep pulse with energy and power.

And then he was doing it, bending the Arua up in a curved arc and pulling it back around them. He smiled in pleased surprise.

Then the real struggle began. Tchinchura and Kaden worked together to create as close to a closed sphere of protection as they could. It was hard work, though, and tiring, and the Arua itself pushed back on them, as though seeking to return to its natural form and shape.

Kaden remembered how Tchinchura and Zangira had reached through the Arua field while standing on the walls of Barra-Dohn and broken through the Jin Dara's control of the hookworms and rhino-scorpions. They had directed the creatures, controlling their movement to some degree. He wondered if maybe he could do that now.

He held the shield and reached out to seize hold of one of the flying creatures, to manipulate it through the Arua field and make it attack another of its kind, but he could not. In the end he abandoned the effort and focused all his energy on holding the shield.

One of the flying creatures slipped through a crack in their defenses, and it swooped in to attack, using both wings and claws as weapons. It flew right at Kaden, who reached for his axe, desperate to keep hold of the shield and defend himself. But as it drew near, its outstretched claw ready to strike Kaden's arm as he drew his weapon, Owenn's massive axe severed the creature's limb from its body. It howled in pain and whirled on Owenn, striking the Devoted with a powerful wing, but Marlo and Deslo both swooped in, blades flying, and they hacked the creature to pieces.

Deslo turned to his father, a quizzical look of uncertainty on his face as the blood dripped from his axe. Kaden nodded his approval. The world of Barra-Dohn was far behind them, but the same courage Deslo had taken into the desert when he hunted hookworms there as a boy would serve him well now.

Another gorgaal came, more from above than from the side, and it managed to rip a chunk out of the shoulder of one of D'Sarza's men before the others could fight it off. It drew back a few feet, wounded, but still inside the confines of the shield, and Tchinchura turned enough to have a good angle and put his axe in the middle of the creature's chest. It sank to the sand, dark blood pouring out as Tchinchura's axe flew back into his hand.

A renewed, frenzied flurry of attacks came as the sun dropped low on the horizon, and Kaden found himself staggering back a step or two in the sand, as though driven back by their intensity. He was so tired, and he didn't know how much longer he could hold his side of the shield. He would have to see if Tchinchura could cover them as they returned to the longboat and made for *The Sorry Rogue.*

But the attack did not linger. Almost as abruptly as it had begun, it ended. The creatures flew up above them, shrieking and screeching and looking down at them from above, and then they wheeled off and flew inland. As they moved farther and farther away, they looked like a white wisp of smoke being blown by the wind until it dwindles into a tiny cloud and then disperses altogether. And just like that, the creatures were gone, and they were alone.

Two of D'Sarza's men helped the injured sailor into shallow water to wash out his wound, while the rest stared inland, wondering if the creatures were merely regrouping for another attack. Kaden dropped to one knee in the sand, suddenly aware of the sweat that was pouring off him.

Tchinchura came and bent over before him. He did not speak but simply looked. It took Kaden a moment to realize the elder Amhuru was breathing hard too. Deslo came alongside them both, making sure they were all right.

"I couldn't have lasted much longer," Kaden said when he was able.

"We would have had to find a new strategy anyway," Tchinchura said, panting. "They were starting to exploit the seams in our defenses."

Kaden nodded. "I didn't know we could do that—use the Arua as a shield, I mean."

"It would not normally work," Tchinchura said. "A man or an animal that had not been fundamentally altered as they have been would have passed through it, just as we walk through it all the time.

"But they have been fundamentally altered, and their strength is now their weakness," Tchinchura continued. "Their connection to the Arua allows them to transcend ordinary physical limitations, but to the Arua they are now bound in ways we are not."

"And the one who did this to them?" Kaden asked.

Tchinchura didn't speak. He just nodded.

"Then we have found it at last," Kaden said. "A link to his past."

"I believe we have."

A moan from the sailor who was slumped down in the shallow water drew their attention. Tchinchura stood up straight and said, "Take him back, and when you have put him onboard, meet us at the town."

The sailors hesitated, some looking out at *The Sorry Rogue,* others at the town, but all of them kept stealing glances in the direction that the creatures had flown.

"I do not think they will return, but if they do, and you are alone on the water without me, return to the ship. Now go, quickly."

They did not hesitate now, and lifting the injured man into the longboat, they settled in as Marlo and Owenn, Daala and Deslo pushed them out into the surf. They started pulling hard, backing away from the island eagerly.

"We should go," Tchinchura said, not waiting for the longboat to get very far. "I know we are tired, but let us make haste. If we don't delay, we may be finished by the time they return."

They started down the beach, not quite running but not quite walking either. Kaden was surprised to see Daala hasten past him and come up alongside Tchinchura.

"They came from the village, but they did not go back there," the fisherman said.

"Yes," Tchinchura said. "It is strange."

"If long abandoned, what would draw them there in large numbers?" Daala asked. "If it's their home, why would they not go back?"

His questions hung in the air, unanswered, as the party hurried on through the darkness. The moon ought to have been rising by now, and undoubtedly it was, but clouds filled the sky, and little light penetrated through them. Marlo had grabbed one of the packs with the lanterns out of the longboat before helping to shove it off, but Kaden wasn't sure one pack would have enough for all of them.

They arrived at the nearest of the buildings in the village and gathered around Tchinchura. Without needing to be told, Marlo opened the pack and began to distribute the lanterns. There were only four, but their meridium cores glowed brightly in the dark night. "We will divide into groups to search faster, but only two for safety," Tchinchura said. "Marlo and Daala come with me. Deslo and Owenn, go with Kaden."

"We'll search this side of the street to start with," Kaden said, indicating the side that lay closer to the water.

Tchinchura nodded. "When we get to the end of this street, we'll figure out where to go from there."

"Anything in particular we're looking for?" Marlo asked.

"I don't know," Tchinchura said, "but I think we'll know it when we see it."

Those words echoed in Kaden's head when he stepped through the doorway of the first building on his side of the street. *We'll know it when we see it.* A huge hole opened up before them in the floor. He held out his arm to make sure neither Deslo nor Owenn got near the edge when they entered. He stooped, holding out his lantern over the hole, and all three of them peered into the dank space beneath.

"I'll go," Deslo said. "When I'm down, hand me a lantern, and when I come back, Owenn can lift me out."

Kaden wanted to say no, but he knew this was his test, even as letting Deslo come in the first place had been Nara's. "All right," he said, and he held his lantern lower so Deslo could see the area below as clearly as possible. "Be careful."

Deslo dropped in, and Kaden leaned down and handed him the lantern. Deslo moved quickly, efficiently, sweeping the space and returning to tell Kaden he'd found a sort of tunnel. "I'll check where it leads and be back. Wait here."

Again Kaden bit his tongue, but this time he closed his eyes and did what he knew Nara would do. *If you're really there, Kalos, if you heard me on the beach and strengthened me, then protect my son now. Keep him safe.*

Deslo did return quickly, suggesting that the tunnel was not very long. "It's a dead end. It just leads to a small room. I guess it's a room, at least, tucked away about twenty or thirty yards that way." He pointed in the direction of the street.

They hauled him out, and Kaden said, "Come on, there are lots of buildings to check."

Olli lay in the dark, listless. Even though she was facing the wall with her back to the tunnel and the basement beyond, she could tell that First Dark had come and gone. She didn't move, though, and she had no intention of going out. The mountain in the distance taunted her with the home she had lost, and the sea taunted her with the promise of a wider world she would never lay eyes on.

She closed her eyes and dreamed of the caves, of her own little room there, with its pools of water in which the purple-blue phosphorescent algae grew and provided a gentle glow of pale light. She hadn't appreciated that pale light, wanting rather the bold light of day to illumine her life. And now her folly had caused Jann his life and would soon claim her life, too. She was very hungry, but she had given up going out in search of food. Soon, she'd be too weak, and then the darkness would claim her.

A sound, not unlike a door closing from somewhere outside, echoed through the silence of the morning. Of course, with the gorgaal back at the manor house, there was no one outside to open or close any of the doors of the buildings in the village.

Voices. There were voices outside. She couldn't hear what they were saying, but they were saying something.

Olli sat up. Now she did turn to look up the tunnel at the empty room beneath the house. She opened her mouth, and her lips cracked, they were so dry. How long had it been since she'd climbed out of the hole to get a drink? She couldn't remember if it was last night or the night before. She tried to call out, but she had neither words nor voice.

And then the voices were very near. They entered the building she was in, and a dark figure dropped down through the hole into the basement. A bright light was lowered to the figure, but the light of it hurt Olli's eyes, and then the light was coming down the tunnel toward her. It came into the room and stopped.

"Are you all right?" a voice said, coming from the figure she could not see behind the bright light. It was a beautiful voice—so beautiful that all she could do was close her eyes and weep.

12

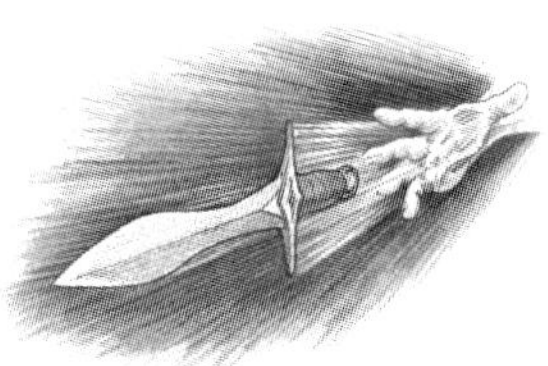

The Light of Day

The gentle hand stroked Olli's hair as she rocked slowly up and down and back and forth. Her first thought was to wonder how her mother had found her down here, in this dingy hole beneath the village where she hid from the gorgaal in darkness. Her second thought was to remember that her mother was dead, which confused her all the more.

She tried to open her eyes, but the dark room wasn't dark anymore. There was light, not a lot, but more than there should have been. The hand stroking her hair stopped, and she wanted to tell it not to stop, but her mouth was still dry and she couldn't form the words. Then the hand was back, but it wasn't stroking her hair, it was dabbing her forehead with a damp, cool cloth.

"It's all right now," a voice said, a different voice than the one that had found her, but a kind voice that had to belong to the gentle hand. "You're safe with us."

Olli licked her lips, trying again to open her eyes and sit up. "Where am I?" she whispered.

"You're aboard *The Sorry Rogue*."

"The sorry what?"

"Rogue. It's the name of our ship."

Ship. That word was familiar, and Olli suspected it had some special meaning for her. If she was just a little clearer in her head, she thought she might know why. And then understanding crashed upon her like a wave. She pushed herself up and forced her eyes open.

"Ship?" she said, trying desperately to focus on the hazy image of a face right in front of her. "This is a . . . I'm on a ship?"

"Easy," the kind voice said, and the gentle hands took hold of her shoulders as she wavered in her upright position. "Lie back down."

Olli felt herself being guided back down into a lying position, and one of the hands that had helped her slid down her arm and took her hand.

"I can't imagine what you've been through."

It was the tone of the words as much as the words themselves that touched Olli and brought the tears. It was not her mother—now that she was awake she knew that, of course—but never since her mother died had anyone talked to her like that. And for a long time, she cried and the gentle hands held and rocked her, though Olli understood now that most of the rocking was coming from the ship and not the hands.

When the tears had run their course, Olli wiped them from her eyes and tried again to see the face that went with the hands and voice. She could make it out now, and it was a lovely face, and smiling, though tears were in the woman's eyes as well.

"I'm Ellenara," she said, "but everyone just calls me Nara."

"Nara," Olli said. "That's pretty."

"Thank you," Nara said, and she leaned over Olli. "I was named for my great grandmother, who I think scared my mother, a lot, so she never could call me by my full name. That's how I became Nara, instead."

Olli smiled, picturing an austere elderly woman as Nara

talked, like one of the elders in the caves, perhaps. "No one calls me by my full name either. I'm just Olli."

"Olli," Nara said, "That's a pretty name too. Are you hungry, Olli?"

"Yes," Olli blurted out, almost before Nara could finish. "I'm starving."

"Well, let me go get you something to eat," Nara said, and she rose to cross the room.

As she did, Olli looked over at the door leading out of the small cabin, saw the light coming in through the cracks around the edges, and she called out to Nara as she sat up in the bed again. "Wait, can I come with you?"

Nara stopped and turned. "Yes, of course you can come if you'd like," she said. "But you don't have to be afraid here. You can stay and rest. I'll be right back."

"No," Olli said, looking past Nara at the door. "You don't understand. I'm not scared. I just want to go outside. I've never been outside in the light of day before."

Nara stood, absolutely still, looking down at her. Olli could see her face tremble. Tears welled up in her eyes. "You've never been outside during the day, Olli?"

Olli shook her head.

"Because of those things."

Olli nodded. "The gorgaal."

"Gorgaal," Nara repeated. She glanced at the door, as though considering what it might mean to never go outside during the day, and then she walked back over to the bed and gave Olli her hand. "Come, let's take you outside. It is a beautiful day today."

Walking through that door for Olli felt like waking up from a long and terrible dream. The blazing sunlight was so bright that it hurt her eyes. She ended up having to squint and hold up her hands to shield her eyes from the piercing brightness, and yet the pain was so deliciously welcome that she couldn't bear the thought of going back into the cabin as Nara suggested. Pain had never been so wonderful.

And then the flood of introductions began. First came the captain of the ship, a boistrous woman in colorful clothing, along with her first mate, and then a whole array of others. Some were in odd clothing, like the two with long dark robes despite the hot weather. One of them was a striking figure with eyes that were completely golden, and another, who Olli gathered was Nara's husband, had tiny gold flecks in his eyes; both men wore similar gold bands around their left bicep. There was a boy with that same armband, but although he seemed always to be nearby, he hung in the background until Nara waved him over to meet her. Then Olli learned he was Nara's son.

"Deslo," Olli said, after he was introduced and said hello. "It was your voice. You found me."

"Yes," the boy said, blushing as she smiled at him.

The introductions continued. There was a third woman onboard, and when she approached, things became odd. With everyone else, Nara smiled and introduced them in an easy, friendly manner, from the gruffest of sailors to her own husband. But when this woman approached, Olli could sense Nara's reluctance. When she mentioned Rika's name, she didn't say it unpleasantly, exactly, but there was a surprising coolness to it. The woman, for her part, acted as though Nara wasn't even there and welcomed Olli to the ship enthusiastically.

Through all of it, Nara never left her side, and when her husband whispered something to her about asking Olli some questions, Nara said she was going to get Olli something to eat and that questions could wait for later. Though Olli had lots of questions of her own, she was glad of this. Eating on the deck of the ship, under the bright, hot sun, was an experience she wanted to savor, and talking about what had happened, which would be inevitable, was not something she was eager to do.

So she did sit in the sun and savor it. She sat with Nara, eating fruit and a little bit of fish, though not much, as her stomach still hurt from eating a few handfuls of those awful berries she had found. She'd been trying to find out if they'd make her sick, really sick, in case she decided to try to poison the gorgaal by poisoning herself. They had made her sick, though she'd not felt any real degree of confidence that even in large quantities they'd kill her, let alone them.

As she sat with Nara, leaning up against the rail of the ship, she could see the mountain rising up above the island in the distance. She remembered being found but little else. It struck her that the ship seemed an awfully long way out for a landing party to have come and found her, and the village was so far off to the left that she could barely make it out. She turned to Nara and said, "We seem a fair way out from the shore."

"Yes," Nara said. "After they brought you onboard, they decided to move out into deeper water, just in case."

"And when the sun came up, did they come?"

"Yes, to the edge of the water but not much further. We've had someone on the upper deck with a looking glass, keeping an eye on them all day."

Olli nodded. "I'm glad someone's watching them. I don't know if they can come out here or not."

Nara took Olli's empty plate and set it on her own. "Would you mind if my husband and a couple others came and asked you a few questions? Would that be all right?"

"I wasn't ready before," she said, hoping Nara would hear her gratitude as well as her willingness. "I'm ready now."

"Good," Nara smiled. "I'll go get them."

"You'll stay with me while we talk?"

"Yes," Nara said. "I'll stay with you as long as you like."

Nara returned with her husband, the dark man with the golden eyes, and an elderly man they said had come from an island not far from this one. They sat down on the deck in front of her.

The man with the golden eyes, who Olli imagined could be a pretty intimidating presence if he wanted to be, smiled at her and asked, "We did not find anyone else in the village, Olli. Were you alone there?"

Olli thought of Jann and the mound of dirt. She wanted to tell them about Jann, but she didn't want Nara to think badly of her. Once she knew that Olli had gotten Jann killed, she feared Nara would. She looked down at her hands. "There was another, but he died. I buried him."

"Were you the only two left on the island?" the man with the golden eyes asked.

She looked up, her head shaking. "Oh no, there are others, many others, but they live in the caves up in the mountain."

There was a choked gasp as she spoke, and to Olli's surprise, she saw that it was the elderly man who had reacted. His hand trembled as he raised it to his mouth.

"There are others?"

"Yes," Olli affirmed.

"Were you born on this island?" the first man asked again.

"Yes," Olli said. "I've lived in the caves all my life."

"How did you come to be down here, in the village?"

"That's a long story," Olli said, looking down again.

"We would like to hear it, if you are willing to tell it."

"I will tell you," Olli said, "if you make me a promise."

"If it is within my power to promise what you ask, I will."

"I know how to get rid of the gorgaal," Olli said, once more looking up. "Promise me you'll help me kill them all."

His golden eyes grew wide, and he looked at her and blinked. "Olli, we'll do whatever we can to help set your island free from their curse. I promise you that."

They brought the longboat in shortly after sunset, or as the girl had called it, "First Dark." Kaden had never heard anyone speak of "First Dark" before Olli, but it struck him that for a people who had to hide in a cave by day and could only come out by night, some such phrase was an inevitable creation. What the rest of the world saw as a kind of end had been for them a beginning.

He wondered if their mission tonight was successful and if the gorgaal were killed how long the phrase would remain among them. How long before they thought of sunset as an ending rather than a beginning?

But that was getting ahead of things. They had first to find this building that Olli spoke of, to deal with the other creatures she had described, and then to see about the gorgaal and this glowing ball.

Kaden and Deslo ran through the darkness, following Olli, who jogged with a limp, the wound on her leg still bothering her. They'd waited two days as she regained her strength, so that this was now the third night since reaching the island. Olli had insisted that she needed to guide them to this place she called "the manor house," and they had quickly realized that it would be foolish to try to find it without her. Not knowing how long it would take to do what was needful once they got there, they could not afford to waste any darkness on the way.

That was why they were following Olli back into the village to the place where she'd hidden her sled. They would put Olli and their supplies upon it, and they would pull it along with them as they climbed to the manor house. She estimated that it would take several hours, as it was all uphill, some of it across fairly steep ground.

They did find the sled, and Olli mumbled something under her breath about "not needing a ride just yet" when Kaden insisted she get on, but she did anyway. Then he and Deslo tied a short length of rope on the sled to go along with the rope that was already attached to it, and they set off at a steady jog, pulling Olli behind them back down the beach to the place where the others waited.

Once there they set out without delay. Olli had told them the first leg of the trip would be across the easiest ground, which sloped upward only gradually, and they hoped to make good time here. They would run, maintaining a good pace and changing out the men who pulled the sled every ten minutes or so, so that fatigue from the pulling wouldn't become an issue. D'Sarza had sent more of her men this time, so there were about twenty of them all told to take turns.

They ran like this for an hour and a half, maybe longer, and were just about to begin their second cycle of shifts pulling the sled, when the ground started to rise in a much steeper fashion. Here, the soft, grassy land underfoot gave way to rocky shale, where a foot misplaced meant sliding on a rock or twisting an ankle. They stopped for a moment and distributed the lanterns to light the way forward more completely, since the difficulty of the terrain meant the moonlight was no longer adequate. For an hour or more they climbed, essentially in pairs, for the pathway up the mountain that Olli called a "run" was fairly narrow here, and the ground to either side of it much rougher.

Kaden and Deslo were climbing near the middle of the pack, when Tchinchura, who was a little bit ahead of them, dropped back to walk beside them. He said to Kaden as he pointed up the slope, off to the right, "Do you see it?"

Kaden peered through the dark, trying to see what Tchinchura was pointing at. And then he did see. In the distance, rising above the ridgeline, a faint yellow-orange glow, just like Olli had described. Kaden nodded. "I see it."

The light became a beacon, and while they did not need to steer by it since the run guided them well enough, it served as encouragement that they were indeed approaching their destination. As Kaden took his third turn with Deslo pulling the sled and his legs complained about the steep ground, he kept glancing over at the glow for inspiration to keep moving.

Eventually Olli had them leave the run behind, and they began to make their way around the side of the mountain rather than up it, moving over to their right in the direction of the light. Here the girl's guidance became invaluable, for the obvious path of the run had been left behind, but she led them surely and without fail, steadily over and gradually upward, until the glow seemed to be right above them, just up a steep, grassy slope that rose from where they came to a stop.

"We walk from here," Olli said, climbing down off the sled. "The manor house is set back just a little way from the top of this hill."

They took their packs off the sled and started up the hill. When they crested the top, Kaden gazed at the wall up ahead in the darkness and the upper portion of the large house beyond it. He had felt goosebumps when Olli told them she'd heard someone speak to her inside this house. It seemed like too much to hope for, that they might find not just clues but someone who actually knew or had known the Jin Dara. But if there was really someone inside, might it not be possible?

Olli led the way around to the gate at the front of the house. Tchinchura and Kaden walked up to it with their lanterns, and there, low to the ground and gliding through the grass, were the nasty creatures with the long snouts and sharp teeth that Olli had described. Kaden thought about the boy she'd mentioned who'd been bitten by one of these things and had his leg ripped open, and he grimaced. He wanted to tell Deslo to hang back, but he knew he couldn't do that. He could keep an eye on him and step in if Deslo seemed in trouble, but he would not damage the boy's confidence by even suggesting he wasn't ready—especially considering that he had told the boy's mother that he was.

They set some of the lanterns down beside the gate and reached up, placing a few more of them on top of the wall on either side. The creatures beyond it continued to gather, as they had hoped and planned they would, and then Tchinchura opened the gate.

There was a rush as the creatures started forward into the bottleneck between the stone wall, and both Kaden and Tchinchura reached out for them through the Arua field. Unlike the gorgaal, whom Kaden had not been able to influence or control directly, he found these creatures easier to manipulate. The Amhuru turned them on each other, and a frenzy of snarling and biting broke out among them.

Some of the creatures pushed through the choked gateway, and these seemed torn between attacking the men they found there and one another. There were not many of these, though, and the scene was becoming a slaughter. Axes and knives struck down the creatures on this side of the gate first and then those clogging it, and the bodies began to pile higher and higher. Finally, a logjam of the dead had the gate entirely blocked for those beyond it, and dark blood seeping out from the mound made the grass slick for several feet in every direction.

"Help us up," Tchinchura said, pointing to the wall, and soon the sailors had raised him and Kaden and Deslo up onto the wall.

Kaden leaned in and said to his son, "If you feel yourself slipping or become unsure of your footing at all, jump down *outside* the wall, Deslo."

Deslo nodded and watched as Tchinchura and his father both threw their axes down, in each case striking one of the creatures cut off from the men beyond the walls by the bodies in the gate. They recalled their axes into their hands, and Tchinchura looked over at him. "You see how it is done. You feel it, do you not?"

"Yes," Deslo said.

"Go ahead. Try it."

Deslo raised the axe in his hand, hesitated for a moment, and with a sudden, swift movement, he threw. The creature he was aiming for moved, and the axe struck the soft earth. He held out his hand, and Kaden could see the look of concentration, replaced by frustration, as the axe simply stayed there, planted in the ground.

"It's all right," Tchinchura said. "Keep watching, keep feeling the power."

Kaden and Tchinchura continued from the wall to strike against the creatures, killing and wounding many who seemed unsure where to go or what to do, though some of them had started to retreat, moving parallel to the gate toward a corner of the large front yard. The Amhuru moved with them along the wall, and they could see that in this corner there was a murky pool of water into which some of the creatures were sliding. The water was deep enough for them to submerge, but only just, and they could still be seen from above, so the slaughter continued.

After a few moments, they could see no more movement in the tall grass or the water. The Amhuru dropped back down outside, and they helped the sailors remove the blockade of bodies from the gate. Taking up the lanterns, they passed inside cautiously.

Just as they stepped through, one of the creatures rose from among several of his dead kin, his mouth open, teeth gleaming in the light of the lanterns. He lunged forward. Kaden reached for the creature through the Zerura on his arm, and taking hold with invisible power, forced it to close its mouth shut. The creature collided with one of the sailors with its hard snout, knocking the man onto the ground, but then several men fell upon it with their knives hacking. Soon it was as dead as it had appeared to be a moment earlier.

Kaden saw Olli looking at him in amazement, and he just smiled as he tapped the Zerura on his bicep. She nodded, for the concept of the Golden Cord and its power had been explained to her, though it was a different then to see with her own eyes what before she had only heard about.

They made a quick search of the ground inside the wall on this side of the house, finishing what few creatures they found still alive, until there were none left. Tchinchura stepped back to the gate and motioned for Olli and the two sailors he'd left behind with her to join them. "The way is clear."

Olli looked grimly at the bodies that littered the ground as she passed through the carnage. "There may be more around back."

"Then we will deal with them as we dealt with these."

"Good, then let's go," Olli said. "It's time to take our island back."

13

Dagin Orlas

Dividing into two parties, one led by Tchinchura and the other by Kaden, they swept through the darkness around the house, making sure both sides were clear of any more of the grass gliders, as Kaden had come to think of them. Once around back, they came together in the paved space right behind the house, and they stood staring at the fantastic sight that greeted them there.

The glowing ball was enormous, every bit as big as Olli had suggested, and the mass of gorgaal lying around it was grotesque and wonderful at the same time. They were there, and they were vulnerable. They would not survive the night.

"I would like to be sure that only the gorgaal remain," Tchinchura said. "Let's sweep the grass and trees within the walls and make sure no more of those other things are here with us, then we will examine this," he pointed at the glowing ball with his axe, "more closely."

Kaden, who had been studying the scene before them, glanced back at the dark house. "What about inside? Shouldn't we check in there too?"

Tchinchura and the others now turned, almost in unison, to study the building looming behind them. Kaden scanned the various windows and wondered if unseen eyes were watching them, even now. "Let's sweep the grounds and make sure they're clear," Tchinchura said, "then we will approach the gorgaal and the orb from the other side, where it might provide some cover from the house."

"And if the owner of the voice that spoke to the girl also has a replica of the missing fragment at his disposal?"

"Then when he uses it, he will reveal himself, and we will be ready."

There was no further discussion, and Kaden led his party around the right side of the grounds, moving between the glowing ball and the far wall, all the way to the back of the manor house grounds. There they turned and swept through the grove of trees, until they met up with Tchinchura's party. Satisfied at last that the grass gliders had all been killed, they moved back toward the globe and the gorgaal.

Tchinchura walked over to Kaden and, grinning, leaned over so he could rub his right foot along the Zerura ring around his left bicep. "Come," he said. "Let's take a closer look."

Kaden followed his lead, and soon both were walking on the Arua field, above the mass of gorgaal. Kaden shivered involuntarily when one of the creatures turned its head, its deep black eyes wide open, as though following him while he walked above it. "I think they are aware of us," he said to Tchinchura.

"I think they are, too," the other replied. "But only perhaps half aware, the way you and I might be right before slipping into a dream or coming out of one."

The flutter of a wing upward, like an involuntary spasm, drew both of their eyes, but when the wing slowly closed again, they turned back to the glowing ball. They had come to within a few feet of it, and Kaden could feel the warmth and light radiating out. Tchinchura started circling, gazing in wonder, and Kaden thought about reminding him that the ball was supposed to be providing cover for them from anyone or anything in the manor house that might wish them harm, but he decided he'd be quiet and just keep an eye out.

"It's remarkable," Tchinchura said, reaching his hand out, not to touch it but to feel the glow. "Ingenious."

"Then you know what it is?"

"I think so," Tchinchura said. Then he added in a voice that made Kaden wonder if he was talking to him or to himself, "He has made a lesser sun, to rule the night."

"I don't understand," Kaden said. "What does that mean?"

Tchinchura pointed at the gorgaal lying below them. "They need sunlight, all the time. I don't know why, but they do. They must. So he made this. He must have mixed meridium with sap or oil from plants that absorb lots of light, so when the real sun is gone, they can be sustained by the lesser sun."

"And since this can't fully replicate the sun," Kaden said, catching on, "the gorgaal are incapacitated. It keeps them alive, but it doesn't give them the energy that full daylight gives them."

Tchinchura nodded. He looked at Kaden. "If we destroy this, I think we destroy them."

"How do we do that?" Kaden said. "If that's one great big meridium core inside that thing, it's solid metal. You'd need some massive explosive like what we used on the walls of Garranmere and what you used on the Academy of Barra-Dohn to destroy this."

Tchinchura reached up and scratched his forehead. "And even if we could destroy this, we don't know that the gorgaal would die immediately. They would die eventually, I'm sure, but we don't know if they'd die before morning, and the rising of the sun might well reinvigorate them."

"We'll have to do this the hard way," Kaden said, gazing around at all the gorgaal intertwined around the globe. "One at a time."

Olli watched as the execution of the gorgaal began. Axes and knives flew, and one by one the men who had found her struck down the vile creatures where they lay. The work had only just begun when the terrible shrieking and screeching screams rent the peaceful night. The gorgaal nearest the killing began to flail, but their hands lacked the unnatural strength they possessed by daylight, and their reflexes, normally quick, were too slow to save or even help them.

The hardest part turned out to be making sure they didn't miss any, as there could be several layers of gorgaal lying intermingled on top of one another. The men Olli had heard called Kalosenes started pulling the dead ones outward from the circle so the others could move in their midst without trampling gorgaal corpses underfoot. Slowly, great mounds of dead gorgaal grew strategically around the bright globe, where one giant man wielded his great axe ruthlessly to make sure all were truly dead. It was not difficult work, but it was messy.

Olli approached the man with the big axe as he was about to finish one of the gorgaal, and she motioned for him to stop. All her life she'd been held hostage by these ghastly monsters, and she wanted to wield a blade herself this night, to represent her people who even now huddled in darkness somewhere up above on the mountain, unaware that their salvation had come.

The man with the axe looked at her for a moment, perhaps unsure of her intent, and then he lowered his axe and nodded toward the gorgaal. Olli fell upon it with ferocity, striking it over and over with the long knife one of the sailors had lent her. She stabbed and stabbed as the dark blood sprayed on her hands and arms, unheeded. She was still stabbing when she felt the strong arms of the Kalosene gently but firmly grip her and lift her up from off her prey.

She looked down at the motionless creature, at its black, staring eyes, and her hands began to tremble. She turned away and took a few steps into the tall grass before collapsing to her knees. She dropped the knife and put her head in her bloody hands.

Kaden looked at Olli as she stepped back from the gorgaal she had been mutilating. He wondered if the images of this night might haunt her in ways she did not expect. He hoped they would not, but as he wiped the dark blood from his own hands, as he saw it running down his axe and his arms, saw it staining not just the ground but also his clothes almost from top to bottom, he thought the memories would linger for some time.

The slaughter seemed to go on and on as they worked first to and then past the meridium ball in the center of the courtyard that had become a killing field. The glow illuminated the work in close so their lanterns weren't necessary, but as they got out toward the edge of the circle again, they did use the lanterns as they separated the gorgaal and checked to make sure each was dead. And then, almost with surprise, Kaden looked up and around and saw that there were no more gorgaal to kill.

All around him the shore party from *The Sorry Rogue* stood, looking at one another, and Kaden knew the weariness he felt was a weariness he shared with each one there. He looked up at the sky. The moon was sinking low. Morning would soon be there. First Light, not First Dark. The world of the island was already changing, even if it would take time for the language to change with it.

From somewhere off to his left, he heard a sob. He turned and saw Olli on her knees, weeping.

By daylight the manor house grounds told a grim tale. By the front gate, the long-snouted creatures lay dark and still, small pools of their blood lying at intervals all around them in the grass. But that was nothing compared with the carnage around back, surrounding the great meridium ball, which by daylight was just a large metallic sphere encased with amber-colored glass. There the pavement would be stained forever with the dried blood, blood that was almost black it was so dark. The stench of death was in the air, and Kaden thought that in a day or two, the smell in this place would be overwhelming.

Kaden looked at his clothes and shook his head. They'd be fit only for burning later. No amount of washing was going to get them clean again, not ever. At least the sun was finally up, and now they could proceed inside and see what they found there. He yawned, covering his mouth with his left hand because it wasn't as bloody as the right. Hopefully they'd finish here soon so he could get some sleep.

He was tired and disliked the delay, but he admitted that the decision to wait until after sunrise to enter the manor house had made sense. Though finished with the gorgaal, they were all weary. It seemed wise to wait, with the day close at hand and what they'd find inside a mystery. So they divided once more into two parties. Kaden's camped outside the front door to prevent anyone leaving the manor house that way, and the other watched the back.

Now the time had come to go in, and Tchinchura directed the sailors from both groups to stay where they were and keep watching the front and back, which they were more than happy to do, as even by daylight the manor house seemed dark and unfriendly. As the Amhuru stood on the porch in front of the house, talking with Daala and the two Devoted, Olli approached, hands on hips, looking determined and a bit annoyed.

"You weren't planning on leaving me out here, were you?" she asked.

They turned to look at her. "Would you like to come in with us?" Tchinchura asked.

"What kind of question is that? You're taking the kid in," she said, pointing at Deslo, "and the old man you picked up from a nearby island. Why would you leave me out? I'm not afraid."

Kaden admired the spirit in the girl, and he tried not to smile since he knew she was in earnest. Daala did smile, apparently not terribly offended by being referred to as "the old man," but Kaden could see Deslo wasn't quite so pleased to be labeled "the kid." A thundercloud of anger swept across his face when she said that.

"No one here doubts your courage," Marlo said, looking at her with sadness in his eyes. "Quite the contrary, we are inspired by it."

Olli did not look quite prepared for that, and the head of steam she'd worked up on the matter dissipated a little. "Then it is all right if I come in with you?"

"You are welcome to come," Tchinchura said. "We did not seek to protect you from anything more than your own painful memories of this place."

Olli glanced toward the front door leading into the manor house. Kaden wondered if she was thinking of the room and the stairs and the voice in the darkness that she had described. Or perhaps just the boy she had been with then. When she spoke again, her voice was softer, less strident. "I need answers. If he has them, I need to hear them."

"Then you will come," Tchinchura said, "and we will seek our answers together."

They entered. The large front room was empty save for an overturned chair along the back wall and a small table next to it. Light from the windows up high above the door and on either side of it fell in shafts into the room, and the wide staircase led up into the darker upper story. Kaden could see a hallway leading directly back from the top of the stairs, and a balcony of sorts running along to either side of it, with doors on either end. He gripped his lantern and followed Tchinchura as he started up the stairs.

At the top of the stair, they paused. A large window let in a pool of sunshine at the far end of the hallway, but between them and the window, the hall was dark with many doors on either side.

"I suppose we should split up," Tchinchura said. "I'll take—"

"There is no need to do that," a voice said from their right, and they turned to see the figure of a man standing in the doorway of the room at that end of the balcony. He was tall but stooped, perhaps with age, though they could not see him clearly in the dusky dark. "Come in, travelers, and let us talk together."

He turned and disappeared back into the room, and Tchinchura led the way along the balcony. The elder Amhuru set one foot in the room, and Kaden felt him reach out through the fragment of the Golden Cord and seize hold of the Arua. Kaden, who was coming in beside him as he did this, looked at the man who stood motionless in the middle of the room. His eyes were golden, and there, around his neck, was the ring that Kaden knew without needing to ask was a replica of a fragment of the Golden Cord.

"You will be wanting this then," the man said, and he reached up, tapping it lightly. It started to uncoil, and the man took it lightly in his fingers, much as you would something delicate that you thought might break if you squeezed it too hard . . . or perhaps as you might pick up a snake that you thought was dead but were afraid to grasp too tightly, lest you turned out to be wrong.

"Kaden." Tchinchura motioned with his head, keeping his eyes on the man and his hold of the Arua. Kaden walked over and took the replica in the man's hand. It felt familiar yet not precisely the same as his own replica. He returned to Tchinchura and offered it, and he took it without comment. Then Tchinchura let go of the Arua, stepping aside so the others could enter the room.

As they filed in, Kaden regarded the man who stood there not far from the large windows on the front side of the house that let plenty of light into the room. He was an older man, perhaps sixty or more, his hair short and golden, like his eyes.

Once the party was all inside the room, the man sat in a large, comfortable chair in front of the window. "I am sorry that I do not have enough chairs for all of you," he said, indicating the smaller chairs placed around the large room. "But please sit, as many as would like to. I know you have had an exhausting night."

Tchinchura looked around at the others. "I will not sit, but please, each of you do as you will."

Kaden walked over and took the chair closest to the man, and Deslo sat in the one closest to him, while Daala and Olli also sat down. Marlo and Owenn remained standing by Tchinchura.

"You are the girl who came before, several weeks ago," the man said as he regarded Olli from across the room. "I am sorry about what happened to your friend when you were leaving. Did he make it back up the mountain all right?"

Olli's face hardened. "No. He died."

The man nodded, not unsympathetically. "It was a bad wound. You were fortunate to make it to the gate at all, let alone get outside it. I thought maybe he had a chance. I am glad that you are all right, at least."

His offered sympathy seemed genuine, but Kaden saw the flash of anger in Olli's eyes and thought it was time to change the subject. "Where did you get the Zerura?"

The man turned toward Kaden. "Must we waste time with questions you already know the answer to?"

"Do I know the answer?"

"No one has come to this island from the outside world in almost thirty years, and yet today, not one Amhuru, but three—if I may include the young apprentice—arrive on my doorstep. I think I may safely conclude that at some point you have encountered *him*, and that this has led you here. So yes, I think you know where I got the Zerura."

"Are you alone?" Marlo asked, looking around at the door, as though uncomfortable having it open behind him.

"I am."

"He left you behind to maintain this place?" Tchinchura asked. "To rule over this island?"

"To rule?" the man laughed. "He left me behind because I disagreed with him, because we argued and he wanted to punish me. This is my prison, not my palace."

"Why would he leave you this," Tchinchura said, holding up the Zerura in his hand, "if he wanted to punish you?"

"Without it, I would be dead. The gorgaal leave me alone so long as I remain inside during the day. Not because they care about me, but because they fear this place—this house is where he lived. If I want to go out at night, I have to use that to get past the creatures that wounded her friend. I would have starved years ago without it."

"Why not leave the gate open and let those things out?" Marlo asked.

"I have thought about it, but I knew I wasn't alone on this island." He looked at Olli. "I couldn't let those things loose knowing the surviving villagers and their children thought the island safe at night."

"So why not do what we just did?" Marlo said, following up. "You could have used the power of the Cord to keep the other things back and killed the gorgaal in their sleep long ago."

"Yes, why not?" Olli said, standing up from her chair. "If you cared about us so much, you could have set us free, and yourself."

The man ignored Marlo, keeping his eyes on Olli. "Even if I could have done, alone, what twenty men did last night, which I find unlikely, I would not have done it."

"You are afraid of him," Tchinchura said.

"Aren't you?"

Tchinchura and the man gazed at one another. Stillness and quiet filled the room, and Kaden became aware of an uneasy feeling in his stomach as he stared at his mentor.

"Let's talk about him," Tchinchura said, breaking the silence. "What is he to you and you to him?"

"He is my cousin," the man said. "My younger cousin."

"What is his name?" Tchinchura asked. "He called himself only the Jin Dara in the place where we encountered him."

"Dagin Orlas," the man said. "And he is descended, through many generations, through many sons and grandsons, daughters and granddaughters, from the widow of a priest who was exiled along with her children from the ancient city of Zeru-Shalim a thousand years ago. Dagin left here many years ago in search of that city. I'm guessing that he found it."

Tchinchura looked at Kaden, and Kaden saw that Tchinchura was deferring to him to reply. He took a deep breath. "That city is now called Barra-Dohn, or was. It is no more. He destroyed it almost three years ago."

The man nodded and looked out the large window, as though he might glimpse the distant ruins of Barra-Dohn and see his cousin's handiwork. "He's not finished, is he?" He turned and surveyed the group in his room. "That's why you're here, isn't it?"

"No," Tchinchura said, "he's not finished."

"He always said his quest would end when Zeru-Shalim lay in ruins," the man said. "But he was his father's son. His hatred ran deep, very deep, and I feared that once he unleashed the full power of the fragment upon the object of his wrath, he would find it impossible to stop there.

"That is why my father felt I should have the original, that I should be the one who led the attack on our ancient enemy. But it was my uncle who killed the Amhuru and took the fragment in the first place. He claimed the right to bequeath it to his eldest son, so he gave it to Dagin.

"And in fairness, Dagin learned much faster with it than I did. He did things that none of the rest of us could do. You have seen what he created, so you understand what I mean."

"And we have seen what he destroyed," Kaden said.

"Yes," the man said. "I can only imagine."

"There is something else," Tchinchura said, and as he spoke, Kaden realized that he was going to tell this man what had happened in the Jin Dara's hour of triumph. "He now has two fragments."

The man sat, staring, as though uncomprehending, and when he spoke, his voice trembled. "Two?"

"Yes."

"He is my cousin," the man repeated, "and I both understand and share his hatred of Zeru-Shalim, but you have to get the fragments back. You cannot let him do elsewhere what he has done here."

"What did he do here, and why did he do it?" Kaden asked. "Why bring those creatures here to terrorize this island?"

"Bring? You don't understand. He made the gorgaal, made them right here."

"Made?" Tchinchura said. "Do you mean altered?"

"What is the difference?"

"When I say altered," Tchinchura said, "I mean to enhance or change or vary a creature that already exists. When you say made, I think of something much more fundamental and at the core."

"Then I mean made," the man said. "I told you he could do things the rest of us could not, because he was willing to try things we would not. When we were still young, he started taking villagers and experimenting on them."

A hush fell on them.

"He experimented on the villagers?" Kaden said.

"Yes, of course, how do you think he made them?"

A gasp from Daala echoed in the room as the awful truth sunk in. "They were human! The gorgaal were once human!"

"Yes, they were most of those who lived here in the village, though some were sailors who came ashore and were captured."

"Then," Olli started, as though just realizing the full, terrible irony, "the gorgaal, when they attacked the village, they might have been attacking their own families?"

"Almost certainly," the man said soberly. "And worse, Dagin said he needed humans who were full grown, so he only took adults, leaving more and more of the children on their own. By the time the villagers moved to the caves, most of the older generation was gone, turned into the creatures that preyed on their own children."

Daala buried his head in his hands. Olli looked stricken. They had come to find answers, but Kaden felt the unbearable weight of those answers and wondered if it would not have been better for them never to know.

The sun was high overhead, and they stood in front of the manor house. The strange man remained inside, and the sailors remained at both doors, watching the entrances. Tchinchura drew Kaden aside. "What did you see?"

"Things too dark to behold," Kaden said, knowing he was being dramatic as he said it.

Tchinchura, though, who normally counseled restraint and simple observation, did not rebuke him. He merely nodded. "But more than that troubles you, I think."

Kaden nodded. "All my life I believed Kalos was a myth as my father told me he was, but you tell me he is real. And yet, how can that be when such dark things as this exist, when such things happen among men?"

"You are right to call such things dark, and the fact that you know they are dark is itself a clue about the answer to your question. There is real right and wrong, and the things that happen in this world matter, because you are more than just a beast. The people who were twisted into those terrible things mattered, and that is why we must not only put right what this Dagin Orlas has done, we must stop what he now intends."

Kaden thought about this, and it raised more questions—but this was not the time, and he knew it. Instead, he redirected the question to Tchinchura. "And what did you see?"

"I saw and learned at least two things that are critical for us to know."

"One of them, at least," Kaden said, "I think I can see for myself."

"Tell me."

"First, we have learned that the Jin Dara's expertise with the Golden Cord is remarkable."

"Far greater than we ever imagined."

"And it isn't just that he made the gorgaal, but the system that sustained them so long after his departure, the manipulation of meridium and creation of the lesser sun."

"Yes, and it is a terrible knowledge," Tchinchura said, "which points to the second thing—he will do anything with his power. He has done things no Amhuru would do, tried things no

Amhuru would try, so I must admit that he must know things no Amhuru would know."

"Then what do we do?"

"First we decide what to do about him," Tchinchura said, nodding at the house with his head. "And then we take Olli back up the mountain so she can tell the others they are free."

"And then?"

"And then," Tchinchura said, "we set sail for Azandalir. The time to reconsider our course has come."

14 

Another Exile

Nara walked toward Olli, who was sitting on the starboard side of *The Sorry Rogue* facing the island, her feet dangling between the rails. She sat down next to the girl and slid forward so that her feet, too, dangled over the side.

"So it is true what I have heard?" Nara said. "Your people have decided to go to Santago?"

"Yes," Olli said. "Daala is bringing a few of them with him, and they will organize ships to come for the rest."

"Is it true one of those who came back with Daala is his cousin?"

"Yes," Olli said. "He found the daughter of a cousin. Apparently, he loved her mother or something. She died in the caves many years ago, but I think Daala is just glad to know she was not made into one of the gorgaal or killed by one."

"It's so awful," Nara said. She'd heard all about the gorgaal and their history from Kaden, and while she didn't doubt that it was true, it seemed somehow too dreadful to be real.

They sat, gazing out at the island. Large, billowing clouds hung high in the sky above. A tiny sliver of the sun was visible above one of them. Even so, the day was bright, and Olli shaded her eyes, still struggling with the light. Nara wondered how long it would be before the girl became used to daylight.

"Do you think anyone will come back?" Nara asked. "Once they've had some time and distance? Do you think they'll return to the village and fix the houses and live in them again?"

"I don't know," Olli said. "Some of them probably will."

"It would seem a shame if they didn't," Nara said. "The island is so beautiful, and now that the creatures are gone, I hope it becomes the peaceful haven I'm sure it was before they came."

"I think," Olli began, "that they will need to not only deal with what happened here and what they endured, but they will eventually have to figure out what to do about the man at the manor house."

"Yes," Nara said, lifting her eyes above the immediate shoreline. She stared further up the mountain in the general direction Kaden had suggested the manor house lay. "Him."

"I know he says he was a prisoner much like we were, and I can kind of see that. I mean, he had to stay inside during the day and could only go out at night," Olli said. "But having that great big house to himself was a whole lot nicer than living in the caves.

"And I've been thinking, even if he couldn't kill the gorgaal on his own, he could have come and found us, you know? He knew there were other people on the island. We could have helped him kill them, and then the gorgaal would have been gone."

"Maybe you're right," Nara said. "I hadn't thought of that. Although," she continued after a moment, "he might have been afraid that you'd blame him for what had happened to them, and to those they had lost."

Olli shrugged. "I guess, but he should have risked it. His cousin did this, and I think he shares some responsibility for not doing more to end it."

"Maybe he does," Nara agreed.

“At any rate, I think the people that eventually go back have the right to determine what they want to do about him. I can’t see them living down there in the village while he lives all alone up in the manor house. If it were me, I’d burn it to the ground.”

Nara heard the anger, knew there was grief wrapped up in layers underneath it, and guilt, too. She wished she could do something to help, but she knew the girl would need time. Going through what she’d gone through . . . well, it would take anyone time to get over that.

“And what about you, Olli?” Nara asked at last. “Why aren’t you going with the rest of your people to Santago?”

“I can’t,” Olli said.

“Why not?”

“Because. Eventually the joy of being freed will begin to wear off, and they’ll realize that even though I was with the Amhuru when they killed the gorgaal, they were the ones, not me, who liberated the island. And that’s when someone will say something like, ‘It’s a shame you were so eager to go down the mountain, Olli. If only you’d waited, then Jann would still be alive.’

“And of course, they’ll be right. They’ll know it, too, and they will blame me for his death. I think some of them already do. I saw how Jann’s family looked at me when Tchinchura told them he was dead.”

“You couldn’t have known, Olli.”

Olli turned to look at Nara. “Couldn’t have known what?”

“That we were coming.”

“That doesn’t matter—”

“Of course it does,” Nara said, uncharacteristically adamant. “Your whole life you’d lived in those caves, and no one ever came. As far as you knew, no one was ever going to come. You found the gorgaal’s secret. You almost got out of there against great odds. Just a little more luck, and you might have gotten back up to the cave, both of you. I think it took a lot of courage to do what you did.”

Olli looked down at her hands, clasping the rails in front of her. “I appreciate what you’re trying to do, but the facts are the facts. It was my idea to go down to the manor house, and going down got Jann killed. And whatever I found, I didn't set the island free—you all did."

Nara put her arm around Olli's shoulder. "Well, don't think I'm trying to talk you out of coming. You are welcome here with us as long as you want to stay. I just wanted to make sure this is really what you want to do, because once we leave Daala and the others at Santago, I suspect our road will take us far, far away from here."

Olli looked up. "Just so long as it leads eventually to the one who did this to us, I don't care how far it leads."

Deslo sat on the deck with his back against his cabin door. He didn't want to be conspicuous when Olli stood and walked away from where she'd been sitting with his mother. He watched her go, watched the stiff breeze blow her shoulder-length blonde hair around her head, and he wondered if she really meant to come with them.

After she'd disappeared into the cabin that she now shared, at least temporarily, with Rika and Captain D'Sarza, he stood and walked over to where his mother still sat. He sat down in the space Olli had just vacated, slipping his own legs through the rails, though they didn't fit as well since the gap between rails was a little tight on his thighs.

"Hello, darling," Nara said, and she raised her hand to stroke the hair on the back of his neck. "I hear you were very brave."

Deslo shrugged. "It wasn't that tough. The gorgaal could barely defend themselves."

"Those other things sounded terrible, though."

Deslo shrugged again. "I don't know. It wasn't that tough."

They sat in silence, and then Deslo said, "Why do you think she's coming? Why leave her own people behind?"

"It's complicated, Deslo."

"We'd never have left Barra-Dohn if we didn't have to," Deslo said. "Why would someone choose to be an exile?"

“I think she’s coming for lots of reasons,” Nara said. “She has no family left. She feels responsible for what happened to her friend Jann. And, perhaps most of all, she knows we’re hunting the one who made the gorgaal.”

Deslo hadn’t thought about that. If he were Olli, and if he’d been through what she had, he’d want to get revenge too. He knew this because even though he’d not been through exactly the same thing, the Jin Dara had destroyed his home, and he was just as determined to see him pay for that.

Perhaps, he thought, she had as much at stake in this as he did.

Dagin Orlas had not thought of himself as Dagin Orlas in a very long time. He had long ago become something much, much more than just a man. He studied his hands carefully, and he could see it even more clearly—the blue-green lines of his veins were definitely starting to shimmer with gold. Just as his tongue, when he stuck it way, way out and looked into a mirror, showed flecks of gold at the base and along the center.

He closed his eyes and felt the fragment of the Golden Cord around his neck and the fragment around his right calf. They both pulsed in harmony with the beating of his heart. They felt like music. They felt like life.

Even before the messenger reached his tent, he sensed him coming. Sensed him hurrying through the camp. He bore replicas of both fragments, just like most of his officers and more trusted men did. Consequently, within a certain radius, the Jin Dara could tell exactly where this man or any of the men wearing the replicas might be. It was but one of many things he had discovered as he had experimented with his new possession and power.

The messenger was near, so he rose and stepped from the tent to meet him. The messenger looked up, startled, and he wondered how long his men would continue to be surprised by his greater power and knowledge.

"What is it?" he asked, eager to have the man's news and then send him on his way.

"They've taken the bait," the messenger said, barely concealing his excitement. "They are on their way here."

The Jin Dara smiled. "How long?"

"A week," the messenger said. "Maybe less."

"And the earlier reports about the Amhuru?"

"Accurate as far as we know," the messenger said. "There appear to be perhaps as many as twenty with the army."

"Twenty," the Jin Dara said. "Excellent."

The messenger, thinking that his master was through with him, turned to go, but the Jin Dara spoke again before he could take a step. "Tell Devaar to bring the pole," he said, "and the thief."

The messenger nodded, and as he walked away, the Jin Dara turned around in the open clearing to survey the large, rocky canyon in which they camped. They were the perfect bait for the perfect trap.

Soon he would have at least one, hopefully more than one, captive Amhuru, and with persistence he would persuade one of these Amhuru to divulge the secret location of Azandalir. There the Jin Dara would find, if not the third southern fragment of the Golden Cord, certainly news, at least, of its whereabouts.

Once he had it, he would cross the Madri and take the rest.

Then the world would be his.

Part 2

The Harder Way

15 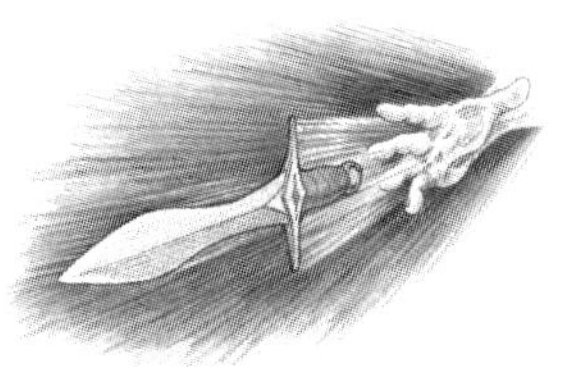

Cat and Mouse

Zangira jogged beside Calamin. The main body of the army lay up ahead. Their scouting mission had turned up nothing of real interest, but Zangira couldn't shake that lurking sense of foreboding all the same.

Below them, on the ground, a brown snake with slender black rings slithered out of the rocks and crossed an open patch of ground before sliding into a hole hidden below a scraggly bush, out of sight. Overhead, a hawk high in the hazy sky wheeled, wings outstretched. Zangira smiled. Clever snake, and bold. It had used the two Amhuru jogging on the Arua field as interference as it returned to its den. It hadn't confused proximity with priority, recognizing where the greater danger truly lay. The hawk flew off to the south, and Zangira and Calamin ran on.

Proximity and priority. Sometimes they were the same. Zangira knew that, for by all reports, the object of his search was close at hand.

In less than an hour, Zangira and Calamin were back among the rear guard. The main contingency was up a good bit further, where the men mounted on the war stallions would be leading the column. Behind them the main body of the infantry marched, almost three thousand men in companies of fifties and hundreds. And here, in the back, the giant Omojen lumbered across the rocky soil, pulling the massive transports loaded with camp gear, army supplies, and heavy weapons.

Zangira had seen much of the Southlands, and few creatures had invoked as much wonder in him as the Omojen. Built like elephants, their shape was not unique, but their size was a wonder to behold. An Omojen next to an ordinary gray or brown elephant would dwarf it the way a horse would dwarf a dog. Their thick hides were a rusty red, their yellow-brown tusks curved ever so slightly outward, and even jogging along on top of the Arua field, Zangira could have passed easily underneath any of the Omojen marching around him with ample clearance above his head and no real worry, save that the Omojen's massive leg might come down upon him like a felled tree.

And yet, large as they were, the Omojen were well-trained and compliant. They pulled their loads from sunrise to sunset, steady and sure, day after day, and yet once roused in battle, they were fearful to behold. Zangira had seen half a dozen Omojen put more than five hundred men to flight, and twenty-two Omojen now accompanied Prince Hadaaya and his army on their hunt for the Jin Dara.

This would have been more comforting to Zangira had he not seen the Jin Dara manipulate the hookworms and rhino-scorpions outside the walls of Barra-Dohn. On the one hand, Zangira had sixteen other Amhuru with him this time to help counter whatever the Jin Dara might try against them, and he and Tchinchura had stood alone before. On the other hand, they had wielded two fragments of the Golden Cord and yet only briefly overwhelmed the Jin Dara then, whereas it was the Jin Dara who would be wielding two fragments now.

The thought that the Jin Dara might somehow be able to interfere with the Omojen in battle and direct them back against their own men was hard to shake. The Amhuru would seek to shield both the horses and the Omojen from interference, of course, but the power of two fragments presented questions that neither he nor any other Amhuru could answer.

The Jin Dara had to be faced, however, and the stolen fragments of the Golden Cord recovered. That was why Zangira had chased him across the Southlands, why an unprecedented concentration of Amhuru had been sent with him, and why he had recruited Prince Hadaaya's army in the first place when the Jin Dara went ashore only fifty miles from Ben-Salaar, his capital city.

And that also troubled Zangira. Why had the Jin Dara come ashore here? And why had he pushed inland, leaving his ships behind, abandoned? The terrain was desolate, the population away from the coastlands sparse and largely nomadic, and Zangira could not see what would induce the Jin Dara to do it.

Maybe that was what troubled Zangira most of all—the inscrutable mind of his adversary. After all the time he'd been hunting the Jin Dara, Zangira still had no clear idea what motivated his enemy. There was no evidence that he'd tried to follow or locate Tchinchura, who bore the third fragment of the Golden Cord below the Madri. He had not destroyed any cities since Barra-Dohn. He had only, as far as Zangira could tell, kept moving with his small fleet of ships, recruiting mercenaries and soldiers here and there along the way.

Zangira looked at the Omojen around him, their powerful legs driving forward as they strained to pull their massive loads, and he sighed. He was grateful. After all, if he was to finally face the Jin Dara again in battle, he would rather have a seasoned army like that of Prince Hadaaya than a lesser force, or worse, none at all. And while he did not understand what motivated his enemy, in the end, he didn't have to. He just needed to recover what the Jin Dara had stolen.

Zangira halted and turned to Calamin. "I think it is time to do as you have suggested."

"Should we leave anyone with you in the camp?" Calamin asked.

"No," Zangira said. "Deploy four on every side, so that two may watch while the other two sleep."

"And you?"

"I will stay and guard the prince," Zangira said, and his gaze strayed inland. "In case he is able to strike at the camp itself."

Calamin nodded. He turned and jogged away, and Zangira watched him for a moment before turning away himself to approach Prince Hadaaya's personal transport.

Unlike the cargo barges pulled by the Omojen, the prince's was two stories. The main level held his private guard, who rode in relative comfort, but Zangira knew their vigilance was not lessened by this. Set back from the outer edge of the platform, four pillars supported a smaller second story, accessible only by a slender stair on the side. In that second story, within the large red tent that stood there, the prince rode not in relative comfort but immersed in complete luxury.

The soldiers on the platform nodded at Zangira to acknowledge him as he stepped up from the Arua. He nodded back as he crossed to the stair and ascended to the prince's tent. "Prince Hadaaya," he said, "it is Zangira."

"Enter," the prince said from within, and Zangira did so.

The prince reclined among a sea of cushions, while one of his wives fanned him, and another massaged his feet. Four of his wives he had left in Ben-Salaar to attend to the palace and children while he was away, while these two had received the dubious honor of being chosen to accompany him. Zangira did not doubt that they saw it as an honor, but the Amhuru had tried to persuade the prince that if they were going to pursue the Jin Dara, they would be safer in Ben-Salaar with the others. The prince evidently couldn't fathom leaving all of his wives behind, and in the end, Zangira had let the matter lie. It was his only to counsel, not to command.

It would be easy for someone who didn't understand the culture of Ben-Salaar or who had only a cursory knowledge of Prince Hadaaya to assume that his presence with the army was merely for the sake of appearances, that the prince could have neither experience nor understanding of anything warlike. But that would be wrong. The prince had been trained in the ways of war since he was old enough to sit in a saddle, and though the grey had only barely begun to touch his hair, he was more than fifty summers old. When the day of battle came, he would descend from his tent and take direct command of his army.

"Zangira," he said as the Amhuru sat cross-legged a few feet away, "you look like the man who walked three days to market to buy a horse only to discover he had left his gold purse at home. Has something happened?"

"As far as I can see, all things are proceeding smoothly."

"Then it is well," the prince said. "And yet, something troubles you?"

"Only that I still can't see what he intends."

"In war we only ever see what a man does, my friend," the prince said. "What he intends is hidden from our view."

"Perhaps," Zangira said, acknowledging his wisdom, "but even so, I would be happier if what the Jin Dara did made more sense to me."

The prince shrugged and motioned with his hand as though he were waving away a fly. "He is a common thief, a murderer."

"He is a thief, Prince Hadaaya, and a murderer, but he is anything but common."

"Bah, he kills women and children," the prince said. "He has no honor."

"Maybe not, but he is clever. I think he wants us to catch him."

The prince withdrew his feet and motioned to his wife to move aside. He sat up and peered at Zangira. "Why do you say this?"

"Because he's done it before. Waited, that is, for the army that was pursuing him to catch up." Zangira thought of Barra-Dohn, of what Kaden had told them about his pursuit of the Jin Dara across Aralyn and how he somehow caught and passed him just in time to place his army outside the city walls. That the Jin Dara had wanted both Barra-Dohn and its army before him, Zangira did not doubt.

"And," he continued, "because I have chased him for almost two years, and up until three months ago, he always covered his tracks extremely well. Finding clues to his whereabouts, despite his many men and ships, was always hard. Always.

"And then, it changed. There'd be a merchant here and a sailor there with a tale to tell, a rumor of a strange fleet with green sails and the insignia of the golden fist. It wasn't so obvious that I knew it was deliberate, but it happened too often, as though he was laying out a trail for me to follow, so that finally, after all this time, I might begin to close the gap."

"But why would he do that?" the prince asked. "You insist he is no fool, so what purpose could he have?"

"I don't know," Zangira said. "And that troubles me."

"Well," the prince said, "he may be laying a trap, but we are looking for a trap, are we not?"

Zangira smiled. "We are."

"Then as long as we are better at looking than he is at laying, it doesn't matter, does it?"

"As always," Zangira said, "the prince speaks with the voice of wisdom." He bowed to the prince, who reclined again.

"Rest here awhile, Zangira, and take my evening meal with me when it comes."

"The prince is most gracious."

Zangira sat, deep in thought. He understood the culture of Ben-Salaar. Showing confidence was necessary, and while you might feel caution and uncertainty, to voice them too strongly or too often would be taken as weakness.

Yet beyond that was a more fundamental issue—it was never a good idea to directly contradict a prince. If he said that looking for the trap the Jin Dara might be laying was enough to protect them, then Zangira would not say otherwise.

But Zangira knew this was not true. They might be better at looking for the trap than the Jin Dara was at laying it, and they might still be lost. If the Jin Dara could spring the trap with power that was beyond them, it wouldn't matter if they saw it coming or not.

The Jin Dara sat on the hard ground, his legs folded beneath him. The sun was low on the horizon would soon drop below it. Still, it was hot. The canyon did provide some shade around the edges of their encampment, but it also felt like it trapped and magnified the heat, especially here in the open center.

Across from the place where the Jin Dara sat, a pole, perhaps seven or eight feet tall, had been driven into the floor of the canyon. Tied to that pole, with his hands above his head, was a man. At least, a creature that had once been a man and still bore a strong resemblance to one, but whether he was a man or not anymore was a question even the Jin Dara would have had trouble answering.

The Jin Dara wasn't even entirely sure if he was still a man himself, but this was different. The being tied to the pole was both more and less than a man now, he supposed, whereas he himself was only more, not less. Whatever the creature before him was, his body hung limp, his head lolling on his chest, and on it a dark shadow of stubble from his recent shave was growing, offering some protection for his badly sunburned scalp.

But would the black stubble become hair or feathers? That was a question that interested the Jin Dara very much indeed.

Also tied to the pole was a large black bird, with a large thick body and a long neck that reminded him of a vulture, although the head made him think of a crow. What the locals called the animal, he did not know, and neither did he care. It was ugly, a scavenger that had feasted on the carcasses of the dead, and it was convenient. So, he had captured it and lashed it to the pole beside the thief.

He didn't know much about the man tied to the pole. He was a local who had attached himself to the Jin Dara's army, offering his services as one familiar with the local terrain as a scout and a guide. He had served in that capacity reasonably well, from what the Jin Dara could gather, until eight days ago he had been found ransacking a tent. Upon further inspection, several missing items from the camp were found in the man's possession. The day after his theft had been discovered, they had set up camp in the canyon, and the Jin Dara had ordered Devaar to place the pole in its center with plenty of open space around it. The thief had been tied to it that very night.

The bird had come later, a day or two, perhaps. And then the experiments had begun. He had started knowing there would not be time to finish, but still, he would see what he could learn in the time that was given to him. He had learned so much already, but it was always the curiosity about what still remained to be learned that drove him to keep coming back to this place within himself where he sat as a student before the power of the Golden Cord.

The Jin Dara closed his eyes. With one fragment, he had always had a vague awareness of the Arua, like a faint melody drifting out the window of a nearby house that you can hear but have to think about and concentrate on to identify and enjoy. Now, with two fragments of the Cord, there was a new kind of effortlessness about it. He was always aware of the Arua. It was more like wading neck deep in the ocean and feeling the water surround you, feeling it lift your arms with each incoming wave and swirl around your legs.

Sometimes he thought that maybe, if he lay back, he would not fall but float, buoyed up on the Arua that emanated from the veins of Zerura that created it. He suspected that if he mastered the Cord and its powers, he could do just that—will himself to float, and then float. But that day had not yet come.

Until such a day, he needed to practice. He needed to continue his work. That was the main reason why he did not feel more impatient about his search. He knew he had time to find the other fragments, because it would take time to master them when he did . . . and master them he would.

He reached out, searching the Arua around him. He thought as he did so of the first time he ever felt the Arua. His father had guided him, talking him through what was happening. He had shown him how to manipulate the Arua, which guided and governed the life cycles of all living things, so that the crops might grow taller or wither, depending on what he did to it and with it. He had shown him also how to manipulate the weather, like summoning the rain or sending it away.

But his father had not taught him how to alter the life cycle of man or beast, how to impose his will upon the rhythms and natural patterns of their growth. He had learned to do that all by himself, and it had largely been an accident.

One day he had been focused on a small flower bud, trying to see if he could manipulate the Arua acting upon it so that it might open before its time, when he had suddenly been aware of the very different feel of the weed growing next to the flower. It occurred to him that the only difference between what was called a flower and what was called a weed was appearance, and he thought the weed would be far more appealing if it too would bud. And that had given him the idea to try to impose upon the weed the life cycle of the flower. Much to his surprise, it had worked. The weed budded, and the blossom that opened was just like the flower next to it.

The Jin Dara had understood intuitively that while the proximity of the flower to the weed had not been necessary, it had been helpful. His ability to see, or rather feel, the different life cycles and the way the Arua acted upon them had allowed him to substitute the one for the other. And that had been the insight that opened the door for almost all of his future experimentation along these lines.

His family had a dog, a small black dog that followed him around wherever he went. One day, just before sunset, he was sitting below a large tree not far from the house when he heard an owl up in its branches. He looked up, saw the owl, and got an idea. He reached through the Arua until he could sense the presence of the owl, and he felt for his dog, who was lying opposite him. He got to work, willing the dog's neck to be able to rotate the way an owl's could, and willing wings to sprout just behind the dog's large front haunches.

The dog whimpered and snarled, growling a low rumbly growl, but it sat transfixed, tense but immobile. The owl, for its part, also remained still, as the boy who would become the Jin Dara studied it through the Arua field and sought to mimic its growth patterns and life cycle and somehow transfer these things to the dog. For hours he sat, as the moon rose and passed overhead, concentrating, reaching out through the fragment around his neck.

And then the dog's head began to turn, and the boy thought he had done it. It turned, and then turned some more, and then cracked as the neck bones snapped. The dog's head fell limp, and the creature dropped dead on the spot. That was the Jin Dara's first lesson in the difficulty of manipulating animals and people, which as it turns out were far more complicated to alter and far more delicate than plants and trees.

But he was not deterred. He continued his experiments with animals he had access to in some abundance so he could compare results. His attempts to mix rats with spiders were the most common. He succeeded in getting some six and eight-legged rats, but usually the extra legs didn't work so well. He tried mixing elements from more than two animals and started having more success, especially when he'd include some traits from plants to help balance or stablize the new combinations he was experimenting with.

His first real success, he felt, came after several years of trying his hand at these transformations. His island had a species of large, low to the ground lizards that liked to sun on the big rocks outside his family's private compoud. They had tiny mouths and ate only bugs and insects and various other small living things and were quite docile. When he tried to approach them, they would scurry away.

At one point, he acquired from a nearby island a very different reptile, a little smaller in the body but a ferocious predator with long and powerful jaws that spent almost all its time in water. He worked hard to give the gentler land lizards those same large and powerful mouths as well as the ferocious nature of the other, and he was successful on both counts.

In fact, he was perhaps a little too successful, as the first prototype of his new breed of reptile liked to cruise along through the grass and take a chunk out of any animal or person that it happened upon. When he wore the fragment of the Golden Cord, of course, he could control the thing, but when he did not, the creature was as happy to attack him as anyone else. In the end, it had to be penned to keep the family safe, but the Jin Dara's father was impressed with his work. He encouraged the boy to continue his experimentation, going so far as to one day bring him a slight and trembling boy from the fishing village on the coast. He encouraged him to start a new project with the boy.

Though that experiment had failed, and he had lost the boy, he had felt a certain obligation to be gentle with him.

He felt no such obligation toward the man tied to the pole in front of him.

He reached out and seized hold of the thief with the nebulous and intangible but nevertheless real and inescapable power of Arua that the Golden Cord laid open before him. The man jerked and spasmed, as though suddenly overwhelmed by a violent and powerful seizure. His head flew up and slammed back against the solid pole, and his coal black eyes opened, and terror emanated from them as vividly as power emanated from the Jin Dara, who neither opened his eyes nor needed to in order to know all that transpired before him.

The face of the man tied to the pole looked human enough from the eyes up—though upon closer inspection, one would see his eyes were a little too black—but from the nose down, he was another matter. His nose had been distorted and manipulated, combined with his mouth until it was beak-like indeed, and his chin had all but disappeared, replaced under the protruding beak-nose-mouth by a fluffy tuft of what very well might be feathers.

The Jin Dara went back to work, bending the physiology of the thief, working on pushing his eyes further back around on the side of his increasingly narrow, bird-like face, all the while keeping before him the image of the actual bird's head, much like a portrait painter might look from time to time from his canvas to the subject of his painting. The Jin Dara exerted his will more and more intently, and he could almost see the thief's face stretch and contort.

The black eyes rolled back in his head, and the beak opened. "Takaa! Takaa," he screamed. "Caw! Caw!"

The thief cocked his head to the side in an unmistakably bird-like gesture, as though straining to hear the sound of his own voice. The Jin Dara, for his part, turned his attention to the bird beside the thief, knowing instinctively after long years of practice the limits of what his subject could and couldn't take and when to pull back as well as when to push on. He had been working on a side experiment with the bird, and he was happy to continue that as well.

He continued working on the bird's beak that was decidedly less pronounced than it had been, and the bird's vocal cords, but when the bird opened its mouth, all that proceeded from it was a low babble, like the mumbling of a man in his sleep, that made no more sense than the thief's squawking. The Jin Dara knew very well that the problem was as much in the bird's brain as its voice box, but he kept probing both, curious as to what it might say if eventually it managed to say anything at all. He had seen in some of the lands he had visited colorful birds that spoke the words of men, but how they did so, he did not fully understand. He would like to understand, but he knew his time here, with this particular experiment, was growing short.

Soon, the army with the Amhuru would arrive, and once the Jin Dara got what he was after, it would be time to move on. He would bring neither the thief nor the bird.

It was unfortunate but unavoidable. The cat approached, and it was time for the mouse to swallow it.

16

Big Brother

Deslo finished scraping the scales from the *chokra* and set down the scaler. He bent over and rinsed the *chokra* off in his bucket and then set it back on his table and went to work gutting it. The incision was quick and precise, his hand moving with practiced mastery, and soon the entrails had been removed, the head chopped off, and the whole mess tossed overboard, where perhaps they would feed a dozen of the fish's near relations.

Though he had spent the first ten and a half years of his life living within walking distance of a beautiful harbor and had in fact caught many fish in his time, he had never cleaned one until coming onboard *The Sorry Rogue.* As it turned out, ignorance was not an excuse in Captain D'Sarza's book, and Deslo had been put to work very early in his nautical career doing just this. It wasn't pretty, but he learned on the job.

The old salt assigned to show him how to clean a fish sat down, picked up a fish, and scaled and cut and gutted so fast

Deslo could barely keep up with what he was doing, let alone see how he was doing it. Then the man stood up, handed the scaler and knife to Deslo, and left him with the remainder of the fish to be cleaned.

Deslo's first fumbling attempts to imitate what he had been shown took a long time and earned only the ire of the cook, who found his handiwork a disgrace beyond all verbal expression, though he had used quite a few words to tell Deslo this. With more practice he had learned the skill tolerably well, been yelled at much less frequently, and then not at all, finally entering into the cook's good graces. Still, the memory of the process was painful, though somewhat mitigated by the fact that he had picked up the skill much faster than his father.

Being a prince, or a prince's son, carried no weight with Captain D'Sarza and excused no one from working while living onboard *The Sorry Rogue.* What's more, no matter how often Deslo or his father tried to explain to Captain D'Sarza that they didn't want to be excused from working, she nevertheless tended to wax eloquent on the matter whenever her dander was up and she thought she could see one of them loafing.

The appearance of loafing had gotten him in trouble with D'Sarza just a few hours earlier, when he had dared to sit down and rest after his training session with Tchinchura had ended. The day was very hot, and sitting for a few moments while he waited for the sweat to stop pouring out of him had seemed, at the time, to be quite a reasonable thing to do. Normally, Captain D'Sarza would have agreed, and normally, she would have noticed the state he was in and realized that he had not been loafing.

But these were not normal times, and D'Sarza was in no mood to notice anything other than the blasted heat and the lack of wind. The ship was becalmed and had been for four days, and while it drifted almost aimlessly in the open sea, the captain's frustration grew more and more evident, and no one was safe from a tongue-lashing, no matter what they were doing. Everyone onboard was hoping for a break in the weather soon, for that was the only thing that might also provide a break in her foul temper.

As a result of his own run-in with the captain, Deslo had offered to clean the *chokra* for supper, even though it was not his turn on the schedule. And while it was not a pleasant job, it did give him something to do, and having something to do when there was a lot on his mind was never a bad thing. He was finished now, at any rate, and setting the long fillet he had just extracted down on the platter with the others, he picked up the whole lot and carried them to the cook's helper, who was waiting for them by the door that led to the galley. The cook might not disdain Deslo's handiwork anymore, might in fact actually like him, but that didn't mean he was allowed in his galley while he prepared the supper.

Deslo washed his hands as best he could, though he knew he wasn't really going to get the smell of fish off them. He was sweating again, though not as badly as before. He settled in below the foredeck, his back against the wall, enjoying its shade.

He removed his replica of the fragment of the Golden Cord that Tchinchura bore, and he watched it as it danced in the air above his hand. He knew he probably shouldn't, that even though everyone onboard knew what he bore and what Tchinchura and his father bore, that drawing undue attention to it wasn't encouraged. He also knew that he was almost invisible to the crew of the ship, a piece of baggage they'd picked up in port a few years back and still carried with them, so Deslo doubted very much that anyone would notice or care.

It wasn't that the crew bore him any particular ill will, but they were sailors on a merchant vessel, and their livelihood was tied to the profitability of Captain D'Sarza's business ventures. While D'Sarza had proven quite resourceful integrating her trading ventures with their travels, Deslo knew that since taking the exiles from Barra-Dohn onboard and agreeing to help Tchinchura and Zangira with the Jin Dara, business for her had not been as good as it might otherwise have been.

For the sailors the dip in their good fortunes, financially, was largely mitigated by the fact that at least one genuine Amhuru and now a couple of his apprentices traveled with them everywhere they went. That presence had a certain business value in it that immediately lent a level of respectability and prestige to *The Sorry Rogue* that set it apart from other merchant vessels. But it had more practical applications as well. With Tchinchura there, few sailors worried about theft or attack, even in the roughest of ports, for who in their right mind would assault a ship with an Amhuru onboard?

But if the crew treated Tchinchura with something even beyond respect, something more akin to reverence, that didn't apply to Deslo. He was just a kid, and not an especially useful one at that. Yes, he had acquired skills along the way that made him useful now, but he had none of those when he first came onboard, and that only reinforced the idea in their minds that he was a spoiled child of privilege, whether that was true or not. And, as he continued to realize from his own experience, first impressions linger long and die hard.

Deslo had harbored hopes that coming of age and joining his father as an apprentice to Tchinchura would change all this. The realization of how much he had hoped for it didn't really hit him until it didn't happen. The day of his birthday had come, and his apprenticeship was made official. His family and the Amhuru and the Kalosenes and Rika had congratulated him, and the cook had even made a special supper for all, but the next day, life onboard the ship had returned to normal, save only for his new training. The sailors who greeted Tchinchura, and even his father, with respect, still walked past him most of the time with little or sometimes even no acknowledgement. To be sure, the day they'd gone to the manor house and faced the grass gliders and the gorgaal had been different, as he had been treated like an equal then, but back onboard things had gradually reverted to normal.

So, he didn't feel especially bad about holding out his hand and watching the Zerura wriggle and dance in the air above it.

It didn't seem to matter how often he watched it do this, the sight mesmerized him. Tchinchura said that the Golden Cord, like the Zerura that ran in veins through the earth far below its surface, echoed the heartbeat and rhythm of all creation and danced to the unheard melody of the eternal music. Deslo didn't know what this meant, exactly, but when he watched the Zerura dance, it sounded just about right.

Across the ship he saw his mother walking with the girl, Olli, and they settled themselves by the port rail. Deslo put the replica back around his bicep and, leaning his head against the wall, closed his eyes.

Neither the immediacy of cleaning fish nor the imponderables of the living matter that governed the life cycles of the world could long distract him from the news his parents had given him the previous night.

He was going to be a big brother.

For years and years, as a boy growing up in the palace of Barra-Dohn, he had longed for little else—a playmate, a friend, someone his own age or close to it that he could romp with in that big palace. Looking back at that now, he could see how crazy that longing had been. As long as he could remember, his parents had hardly even talked to each other, even when they were in the same room, which happened far less often than one would think possible for people living in the same palace.

Since coming onboard *The Sorry Rogue,* though, that had all changed. Slowly at first, but it had changed. Now they laughed and talked, hugged and kissed all the time, and they were finally going to have another baby—now, when he was of age himself and felt too old to be a big brother. He was happy for them, especially when he saw how happy they seemed when they looked at each other after they told him about it, but he also couldn't help but feel a little annoyed. This child wouldn't be a playmate, or a companion, a comfort for his lonely days and nights. It was too late for that.

And it didn't seem entirely fair, either. This baby wouldn't understand what it had been like for him to grow up watching his parents treat each other with cold disregard. And his father . . . he had never shown interest in Deslo back then. He had changed, and Deslo loved that, but this child wouldn't understand what it had been like for him as a kid, dying for his father to talk to him, to take an interest in anything he did, to love him.

He knew he should be glad that his brother or sister wouldn't have to go through the same thing. He sure wished he hadn't had to, and he was genuinely glad that if there was going to be a sibling, he or she was going to be born into a family that was happier and closer than it had ever been before. It just didn't feel fair.

Deslo ran his hand through his hair and propped his elbow on his knee, leaning to the side, head on his hand. Another part of him was worried and a little afraid. He was still having nightmares about the grass gliders and the gorgaal. His father knew about the dreams, for the first night Deslo had them, he had woken to find his father sitting by his bed, having heard him crying out in his sleep. Deslo had seen hard things before, from the destruction of Garranmere to the fall of Barra-Dohn, and this wasn't the first time he'd had a nightmare. But when he woke, he realized that what he really feared was not the creatures, but the one who had made them.

If that one and this Jin Dara they were chasing were the same man, how in the world did a baby fit in? What would they do if they actually found him? Deslo had become an apprentice to Tchinchura because he wanted to help avenge Barra-Dohn, but he didn't want the Jin Dara within a hundred miles of his baby brother or sister—or his pregnant mother, for that matter. And yet, what were they to do now?

Across the deck his mother was still sitting with the girl, who appeared to be fiddling with a length of rope. Probably she was working on her knots; knowing Captain D'Sarza, she had started the girl's nautical education much as she had started Deslo's own, with a mandate to learn to be useful. There wasn't much on a ship like this that didn't involve ropes and knots of some kind, so that wasn't a bad place to start.

His mother was knitting, probably something for the baby, Deslo thought. It seemed oddly incongruous, his mother knitting in the blazing hot sun on the deck of *The Sorry Rogue*. She was the one who had married into the Omiir family from the outside, but to Deslo in many ways, she was the one who seemed most regal, the one who belonged in a palace. She looked happy, though, and Deslo was glad of that.

The girl stood up, and Deslo watched as she rubbed her forearm across her forehead, probably wiping away a trickle of sweat, though Deslo couldn't see for sure from this distance. Then she took the bottom of her shirt, which was hanging loose, pulled it tight behind her, and tied it snugly against her lower back, much the same way Captain D'Sarza and Rika often did, so that her midriff was left bare.

Deslo looked at her flat stomach, at the smooth skin that had been so white when she first came onboard. Now it was red from the sun, and probably painful, though Deslo knew eventually she would brown and grow darker. As she settled back down on the deck of the ship and continued to fiddle with the rope, Deslo looked at the part of her face not obscured by the angle or the blonde hair that hung loose, at her lovely arms and slender hands as they worked with the rope, at the taut shirt now hugging her curves tightly, and at her bare side and stomach.

He turned the other way and looked out over the placid ocean, which lay abnormally still. He looked at the calm blue water, but he saw her in his mind's eye, even there. He leaned over and spat on the deck.

The fact that she was pretty only made her more annoying.

Olli wondered if she should tell Nara about her dreams. Rika and the captain had been friendly and hospitable since she came aboard, but if she was going to tell anyone, it would be Nara. She supposed it was the gentle, motherly way she had about her that made her feel safe. She looked up at Nara, sitting there knitting away, a smile lingering on her lips, and thought maybe this wasn't the time.

Besides, even if she told Nara that she dreamed every night that the gorgaal had stowed away below decks and were now swarming all over *The Sorry Rogue*, tearing it apart plank by plank, there was nothing Nara could do about that. Olli had only two kinds of dreams—bad and worse. In the bad dreams, the gorgaal ran amok and terrorized her and whomever else she was with. In the worse dreams, Jann was there. He was always alive when the dream began, always dead when it ended. Even worse than the dreams, though, was the fact that waking up didn't end the nightmare. He was really dead.

Her fingers fumbled with the rope in her hands. She had hoped practicing her knots would help her not to think about it, but it wasn't. She just couldn't concentrate, and it was so very bright and hot. She stood, wiped the sweat from her brow, and tied back her shirt like Rika had shown her. When she sat back down, Nara looked up and smiled.

"How are your eyes today?" Nara asked.

"They're all right."

"Well, don't push it too long. It'll take time for them to adapt to daylight. We've been out awhile already."

"I know," Olli said. "But I don't want to go back in just yet, and really, they're not hurting."

"Your call," Nara said.

Olli looked at Nara, her fingers working as her knitting needles clacked away, and she changed her mind. "Do you ever have bad dreams?"

Nara stopped knitting. "Are you having nightmares, Olli?"

"Yes." Suddenly she felt very silly, and she wondered why she had opened her mouth.

"I'm so sorry," Nara said, leaning forward so she could reach over and put her hand on one of Olli's hands. "I'm not surprised. After what you've been through . . ."

Olli trembled. She saw Jann, lying dead in the grave she had dug. Jann, who had loved her, and was dead because of that love, was dead because of her.

"It's not forever, Olli," Nara said, and her voice was soft and kind. "The dreams will pass."

"But Jann will still be dead," Olli said.

"Yes," Nara said. "But that's not your fault. You didn't kill him."

"I did—"

"Sweetheart," Nara said, "you are about the bravest person I've ever met, and I can easily see how you inspired Jann to be brave, too, even though I never met him."

Olli looked up at Nara, tears in her eyes, and Nara continued. "And I can see why he'd love you."

Olli was stunned. "How . . . how did you know?"

"I didn't know," Nara said.

"I didn't love him back," Olli said. "I thought I did once, and I think he thought I did, but I didn't."

"So you feel guilty for that too," Nara said. "But that's no more your fault than his death. You are a pretty girl, Olli, and you can't be expected to love any and every boy who fancies you."

Olli looked back at the rope to avoid blushing.

Nara continued. "Be honest and true in what you say, and that's all any man has a right to expect from you."

Olli looked back at Nara, who was smiling warmly, and nodded. Nara squeezed Olli's hand, then took up her knitting again. Olli started half-heartedly working again on learning the knot D'Sarza had shown her that morning, when she saw movement and looked up.

It was Nara's son, Deslo, and he was walking toward them. Olli looked down and hoped like crazy there were no tears still on her face.

"I heard you volunteered to clean the *chokra* for supper," Nara said to her son as she continued knitting, and Olli was grateful that she had spoken first. Olli wouldn't have been surprised if Nara was aware Olli didn't want anyone to notice her at that moment and had deliberately initiated a conversation to offer a buffer.

"Sort of," Deslo said, and there was a pause. Olli felt somehow certain he was looking at her and not his mother.

"How did your training go earlier?" Nara persisted.

"I can help you with that, if you'd like," he said to Olli, as if he didn't hear her question. "I had to learn those knots, too, when I first came onboard."

"Oh, thanks," Olli said, glancing up so briefly she didn't see anything more than his silhouette with the sun overhead, "but I'm fine." Again the pause, and Olli concentrated hard on the rope, hoping very much that Nara would jump in again, or that the boy would get the hint and move along.

"You keep starting off wrong," he said, and she saw his hand reach down and open, as though he wanted her to put the rope in it. "I can show you the steps again."

"I said I was fine, kid," Olli said, trying not to show the annoyance she felt, "just let me—"

"Kid?" he said, and Olli couldn't help but look up when she heard the vehemence in his voice. He looked furious, and he glared at her like he wanted to hit her. "Kids don't wear one of these."

When he moved his right hand to tap the golden ring around his left bicep, Olli jerked back a little. He noticed her movement, and confusion momentarily replaced the anger in his eyes.

"All right," she said, holding out her hand tentatively. "If it's that important to you . . ."

"It's not important to me," he said, looking with disdain at her outstretched arm. "I was just trying to help. I learned how to tie that knot in about thirty minutes, is all, and you've been struggling with it all afternoon."

"Deslo!" Nara said, setting down her knitting. She sounded appalled.

The boy turned without another word to either of them and started walking away. Olli reached out and grabbed Nara's knee before she could speak again, and when Nara looked at her, she shook her head. Olli could see that Nara had seen her mortification, and she let Deslo go.

"I'm so sorry," Nara said. "That wasn't like Deslo. He should never have—"

"It's all right, Nara," Olli said. "Don't worry about it."

"It's not all right," Nara said. "I'll deal with him later."

"Please, don't do that."

Neither of them spoke for a moment, but Nara did not return to her knitting, and Olli did not return to her rope. In the end, Nara sighed, and then she said, "Can you keep a secret, Olli?"

"Sure," Olli said.

"I'm pregnant."

"You're—" She cut herself off before she could finish repeating what Nara had said. Then she added quietly, "Congratulations."

"We're going to make it public soon, but we're not ready yet. Anyway, we just told Deslo last night. He's been an only child so long, you know. I'm not sure how he's taking it."

"I'm sure that's all it was," Olli said, wanting to reassure Nara in the hopes that the subject would go away.

Nara returned to her knitting, but the playful smile had disappeared. Olli directed her attention to the rope, but she wasn't thinking about it. Deslo had kept his distance ever since she first came onboard. Whatever his problem with her was, it hadn't started last night.

17

Guardian of Truth

Marlo fingered the gold pendant that usually hung beneath his shirt and looked at the gleam of the setting sun as it illuminated the water before him. The clear, windless days might be terrible for making headway on their journey, but there could be great beauty in stillness.

"You should talk to the Amhuru," Owenn said.

"You think so?"

"Yes, you know I do. He is our friend, and a true servant of Kalos."

"But not a Kalosene," Marlo added.

"No, but Deras himself sent us to him."

"Well," Marlo said, turning to Owenn, "you could almost say that Kalos brought him to us, the way He told Deras how we'd find him and then directed him past our door at just the right time so you could grab him."

"So you agree. We should tell him."

"I don't disagree, Owenn. I'm just being cautious."

"I thought I was the cautious one," Owenn said.

"Yes, usually, but to claim to be a Guardian of Truth is no small thing."

"I know, but you've had the same dream three nights in a row, so I think we know it's a vision, not a dream."

"Perhaps it is a vision," Marlo said, images from the dream flashing through his mind. "But that doesn't mean we should tell an outsider about the call, if I really have received it, or about the vision."

The normally calm Owenn fidgeted with his hands, and Marlo sensed his agitation. He didn't like to talk, and he so rarely disagreed with Marlo that there often wasn't any need for him to. He simply did what Marlo told him to do. But it would be a mistake to assume from this that Owenn didn't have his own opinions. He just usually kept them to himself, and if he was voicing them now, he felt strongly about it.

"We threw in our lot with them," Owenn said, and Marlo heard a rare note of frustration in his voice. "We left our friends behind, and probably most of them died in Barra-Dohn—"

"Just a moment. When we agreed to go with Tchinchura, we had no idea what the Jin Dara was going to do to Barra-Dohn," Marlo said. "We thought we were the ones who would be making the sacrifice, leaving our homes and friends behind. And so did they."

"I know," Owenn said. "My point is that if we weren't going to trust the Amhuru, why did we come?"

"That's not the same thing," Marlo said. "Of course we trust him, but that doesn't mean we have to tell him everything, does it? Do you think he tells us everything he discusses with Kaden? Do you think he told us everything that passed between him and Zangira while he was here? You think the Amhuru don't keep secrets from us?"

"I'm sure they do," Owenn said, and then hesitated, as though not sure what to say next. "I thought you said you agreed with me?"

"I said I didn't disagree with you."

Owenn stared at him.

"I'm saying I can see your point," Marlo said. "Part of me wants to tell him, too. I'm just not sure yet."

"I know it's a sobering thing," Owenn said, "both receiving the call and talking about it with someone who isn't a Kalosene. But this dream is serious, Marlo. You know it is, and we have no one here to talk to about it."

Marlo nodded. "I know."

"We can trust Tchinchura," Owenn said. "And it isn't like the traditions of the Kalosenes are on the same level as the commands of Kalos, right?"

"No, you're right," Marlo said. "These are somewhat extraordinary circumstances. The usual traditions may not apply.

"And maybe," Marlo continued a moment later, "working with and trusting the Amhuru will start a new tradition of trust between us and them. We do both claim allegiance to Kalos, after all."

Owenn nodded but remained silent, as was his custom when speaking would be merely agreeing with what had already been said.

"I will tell Tchinchura," Marlo said. "I will look for the right time, and I will tell him both of the call and of the vision."

Owenn stood and stretched. "Now that the sun is down, I will go say my evening prayers."

"All right," Marlo said. "I think I'll sit and think here awhile longer."

"He often walks on the deck in the evening. If you see him and decide now is the time, come and get me."

"I will," Marlo said, and Owenn left.

Darkness descended rapidly, and just as rapidly, the light of a million stars twinkled in the nighttime sky. How vast was the universe, Marlo wondered, and how mighty the hand that created it? He did not understand how Kalos could see what had not yet come to pass and send news of it to trouble the minds of men, but Marlo did not doubt that Kalos could see it. Those doubts were greatly diminished the day Tchinchura came around the corner at just the time of day Deras predicted months before it actually happened, and they disappeared when the mighty city, Barra-Dohn, fell before the end of the fortieth day. Again, just as Deras had said it would.

Maybe he could have guessed at one of those things, though Marlo didn't really even believe that. Surely, though, he could not have guessed at both. Yes, Marlo believed Kalos could place glimpses of the future into the dreams of men—but was that what had happened to him? Marlo didn't know—not for sure—but he believed, as Owenn did, that what he had dreamed was no ordinary dream. It was vision of things to come, and if it was, then he had indeed been selected to be a Guardian of Truth.

Tchinchura approached, but Kaden could see he was deep in thought. He was often so, but since leaving the gorgaal island, he had seemed more distracted than ususal. He asked Kaden several times what he had seen during their time there. When Kaden had asked Tchinchura in return what he had seen, Tchinchura had only replied, "Dark things."

Kaden didn't know if Tchinchura had been trying to be deliberately ironic, since of course, "Jin Dara" could be translated either "dark thing" or "dark things." At the time, though, the Amuru had been unwilling to say more, only that the time would come soon when they would need to discuss further what had happened and what it meant. Kaden wondered if that time was now.

"The evening is beautiful," Kaden said, breaking the silence.

"Yes," Tchinchura said, "though I think the captain would like less beauty and more wind."

"I'm sure she would," Kaden said. He glanced out at the tranquil waters and then back at Tchinchura. "Could you do it?"

"Do what?"

"Produce a wind that would carry us on our way."

"Perhaps, if our lives were at stake, and I felt it necessary," Tchinchura said. "How long I could sustain it, I couldn't say."

"It's kind of an inexact thing, isn't it?" Kaden said. "Knowing when and how to use the power that wearing Zerura gives us, and when to refrain?"

"Yes," Tchinchura said. "And no. The principle—not to misuse the power for our own personal gain, not to interfere with the natural cycles of life that Kalos has ordained unless great need presses and your own life or the life of another is at stake—is not terribly hard to understand."

"Maybe, but I can imagine there are times when it doesn't seem so clear," Kaden said. "Take our situation. We're stuck here, becalmed, with information that, arguably, the Amhuru in Azandalir need to hear. Couldn't we say lives might be on the line?"

"Discretion is called for," Tchinchura said, "but lacking immediate danger, we do not interfere with the weather or any other natural cycle. As Amhuru, we trust to the sovereign hand of Kalos first."

Kaden nodded, but he didn't say anything. It was still a strange thing to speak of Kalos as though He were real. He had always liked the Old Stories when Gamalian told them, and so many of them dealt with Kalos. It was easy sometimes to want those stories to be true, to want Kalos to be real, but sometimes the thought of something so big and so powerful was overwhelming.

And he had seen evidence of the reality of Kalos Himself, had he not? How else had the Kalosene his father had executed known that Barra-Dohn would fall? How else had he predicted the timetable so exactly? While Kaden would not have killed the man for his words, he had found them just as unbelievable as Eirmon had at the time. When they had come true, and the Jin Dara had come, Kaden's intellectual world had been just as shaken as the mighty walls of Barra-Dohn.

"What concerns me, Kaden," Tchinchura said, and Kaden put aside his musings, "is that our enemy recognizes no such boundary."

"No, but we knew that already," Kaden said.

"Perhaps," Tchinchura said. "But I do not know if I would have believed that any man would use the power of the Cord this way until I had seen it for myself."

"My father didn't hesitate to use the power of the Cord for personal gain," Kaden said.

"True," Tchinchura agreed, "and over the years, we have dealt with more than a few men like him who saw the Cord as a means to that end. But this man . . . he is a different animal, I think."

"Do you think so?" Kaden asked. "I'm not sure there isn't anything my father wouldn't have done to get what he wanted."

He thought of Garranmere, and of the destruction his father had ordered him to unleash there. Aside from his neglect of Nara and Deslo, it was the great shame of his life. He had destroyed a city, not as fully or as savagely as the Jin Dara, perhaps, but he had destroyed it—all because he had been too weak and too cowardly to say no to Eirmon.

"From what Rika tells us," Tchinchura said, "the Academy of Barra-Dohn was just beginning to suspect that perhaps the growth patterns of children in the city were being affected by the Zerura, as tales of larger, stronger children were becoming common.

"Now, let's say the Academy had gone to Eirmon and told him that experimenting on Zerura in the heart of the city was altering the growth patterns of the city's children—how do you think he would have reacted?"

"Well," Kaden said, "as long as they were still healthy, he probably would have thought that having bigger, stronger children was a good thing. Especially the boys. He would have loved to think his army would be physically larger and stronger than other armies."

"Would he have rounded up the street orphans of Barra-Dohn and locked them in some sunless room deep within the Academy for experimentation? Would he have ordered Rika and the other researchers to see if they could mix the children with a hookworms or rhino-scorpions? See if they could make supersoldiers with hooks protruding from their flesh and the ability to burrow through the sand? See if they could give them a long tail with a deadly blade on the end? Would he have done this regardless of how many died in the process?"

"No," Kaden said in confirmation when the flood of question from Tchinchura finally stopped.

"I don't think so either," Tchinchura said. "He may have been greedy for power or money—"

"—or both."

"Or both, but there are things that would never have occurred to him to do with the Cord, because they are too terrible."

"Dark things," Kaden said.

"Yes," Tchinchura said, nodding. "Wherever this Dagin Orlas picked up his nickname, he is aptly named. What he did to make the gorgaal, what he must have had to do in order to learn how to do it . . . it staggers the mind . . ."

Kaden stood silently, watching Tchinchura struggle for words. The Amhuru rarely showed emotion, but Kaden could see his agitation now. Kaden was struggling with the horror his own imagination presented him. They had come seeking understanding of the man who had destroyed Barra-Dohn, of the man who now possessed two fragments of the Golden Cord, and they had found it, but it was a terrible knowledge.

"He did what he did with one fragment," Kaden found himself saying. "And now he has two."

"Yes, exactly," Tchinchura said. "Now he has two."

"Has had two for almost three years."

"Yes," Tchinchura agreed, his voice barely a whisper.

"He has had a lot of time to make his plans."

"And a lot of time to continue his work, to expermiment further," Tchinchura said, agitated. "I think we know this, Kaden. Whatever his plans, they will be monstrous. *He* is a monster."

"So what do we do?" It was Kaden's turn to whisper.

Tchinchura took in a deep breath. "You asked me a little while ago if it wasn't time to reconsider our options."

"Yes," Kaden said. "When it looked like we weren't going to find what we were looking for."

"Well, now that we have found it," Tchinchura said, "I think it is time. When we reach Azandalir, I will suggest to the elders that we reconsider what, until now, I have considered unthinkable."

The night was warm, the breeze nonexistent, but Kaden felt a chill as it rippled through him. He thought of Nara, and the baby. If this was the road that now lay before him, hard choices lay ahead.

They stood together, looking at the moonlight reflected on the water. They were both lost in their own thoughts when a voice greeted them, and Kaden turned to see Marlo and Owenn standing there.

"Our pardon if we are interrupting something," Marlo said. "But may we speak with you?"

"Only a fool will not listen when one of the Devoted wishes to speak," Tchinchura said.

Marlo bowed his head slightly to acknowledge the compliment. "Owenn and I have conferred, and there is something we need to discuss with you."

"By all means," Tchinchura said. "Let us hear it."

Marlo swallowed and said, "These last three nights, I have had the same dream. It is no ordinary dream. I believe it is a vision, from Kalos. This happens sometimes when one is a Guardian of Truth."

"You believe you have received the call?" Tchinchura asked.

"I do."

"To be a Guardian of Truth is a great honor," Tchinchura said. "I am happy for you. In these times, to have a vision from Kalos is no small thing."

"Yes," Marlo said, "that is why we wish to speak to you. The vision is . . . complex. I do not fully understand it. We would like to share it, and perhaps, discuss it with you. If you would be willing."

"We would be honored," Tchinchura said. "Tell us the vision."

Marlo moved to sit, and the others followed. He closed his eyes, remembering, and then spoke.

18

The Najin

The first image in my dream is no image at all, only a darkness so dark that I feel it will suffocate me. It is not the darkness of night. It is the darkness of the grave.

And then, shining out from that darkness, the yellow-orange light of the strange meridium orb behind the manor house on the island appears. It starts small and then grows larger. But it is not like an object at first viewed from a distance and then seen much closer; it is more like the sun when it breaks through clouds—it is no closer than it was before, only it has triumphed over what concealed it. So also the orb, breaking through the smothering dark in my dream.

Each time in my vision, I feel the same sense of relief, the same hope that something good has come and defeated the dark. But each time, it quickly fades when a man appears, walking out of the bright glowing orb, walking toward me. He stops midway between the orb and me, and that is when I notice that he is a man of gold. His head, his arms and legs, his torso—all are gold. And then I notice that the orb behind him is gold now, too, and the light that comes out of it is gold.

And it is not just from the orb that the light comes. It comes from the man. It comes out of his eyes and mouth, out of his fingertips, out of his toes. It radiates from every part of him, pushing the dark back still further. But it does not comfort me; it terrifies me. I want the darkness to come back so that I may hide from him, so that he will not see me.

The man of gold begins to rise. He lifts up off the ground slowly, steadily. His arms are outstretched as though welcoming into himself some invisible power. The burning glow of light from his body grows still brighter, and now nothing else is visible. The orb from the manor house is gone, or at least, it is lost in the all-consuming light that floods out of the man. He is several feet in the air now, and still he rises. Up. Up. Up.

I am not alone, I see that now. There are many of us, and we stand together on the ground. I am suddenly cold. My heart tells me the incredible, burning light that flows from the man should be hot, should consume me, but it does not. I breathe and see my breath, a frosty mist in the air, as I have heard it does in the far Southlands where it is said frozen rain and wet flakes fall from the sky in winter. I shiver and hold myself, and still the man rises into the air.

He is perhaps twenty or thirty feet in the air, and still he rises until the world is illuminated by his glow. From the mountains to the sea, he brings light as though he were himself the dawning sun. I remember briefly the image of his coming from the orb, and that I was for some reason afraid of him—but he is so beautiful, I can't understand now why I was afraid.

I feel a sudden desire to bow down. I want to fall on my face and worship him, but a voice deep in my heart tells me I am a Kalosene and that I worship no one but Kalos. *But perhaps this is Kalos,* I think, and I look with adoration at the man of gold. I tremble in my confusion, and still he rises.

Then, without warning, the light that is already impossibly bright grows still brighter. It flashes out and sears my eyes so that

I am blinded. I can see nothing, and the world goes from that intense brightness back to the utter darkness where my vision begins. And now I weep because the world is dark again. I weep because I have lost the light.

Time passes, and I know that years are slipping past me, perhaps generations, and when the light returns, it is a paler light than the burning light from the golden man. I do not see him, and I do not see the sun. I am on a plain, but it is a different plain. It is cool, but I am not as cold as I was before, and I seem to be alone.

There is a small campfire in front of me, and I go to it to be near the light as much as to warm my hands beside it. I squat down and extend my hands, and the warmth of the flame is welcome. I draw it in, and I am comforted, though by now I can no longer remember why I was feeling so sad.

A deep rumbling roar echoes above the vast plain, and it terrifies me. I look up from the fire and gaze through the pale light, the light of a sun that has yet to rise above the horizon. In the distance I see the silhouettes of enormous, lumbering shapes. Giant things. Dark things. They walk and the ground shakes, even here, even miles away. The rumbling roar echoes again, and this time another answers it, and another. I fall upon the ground and cover my ears, but I cannot blot out the sound. It fills the plain. It fills the air. It fills my heart with dread. The coming sun will bring no reprieve. It will only illuminate the horrors hidden in the dark.

I lie next to the fire, curled up in a ball, my eyes closed and my hands over my ears. Eventually, I realize that the rumbling roars have disappeared and the world is silent. I sit up. The fire is gone, and so is the plain. I am at the foot of a great mountain, which rises above me. I cannot see the top. It is hidden from view above the clouds. I know that I am supposed to climb. I feel it in my bones. Something is drawing me. I must go up.

But I do not climb the mountain, for as soon as I understand that I must climb, it disappears. In front of me now is neither the mountain nor the plain from before. I am standing by the sea. It is morning still, and at last the sun rises. It rises over a blue sea, and the gentle light of a true dawn whispers peace to my troubled heart. The anxiety of my earlier dream disappears. I know I have reached a turning point in time. The world has pivoted upon some unseen axis, and more than a new day is dawning.

A voice that is mightier than the highest mountain but quieter than the whispering sea speaks. "Turn and see," it says, and I turn.

Behind me is what at first appears to be a vast and useless pile of rubble. Stone, large and small, broken in bits, lies scattered as far as my eyes can see. I gasp. It is the ruin of Barra-Dohn. And then I know—the seventy years that Deras spoke of have come and gone. The price has been paid.

As I stare at the ruin, I hear the voice that told me to turn. It speaks the words of prophecy. It says:

From the many, one. Only he will return.
Dark is the way, and long—
The rest will fall.
He who made the lesser sun will eclipse the greater;
He brings judgement, yet shall he be judged.
The tool of Him he mocks.
Victory will come from defeat, and defeat will come from victory—
My own will betray me.
What was scattered will be brought together, then scattered again,
Beneath the colder moon.
The world will lose what long it had,
That it may find what long was lost.
And in the long dark, two families share one fate,
Two sons bound by hate.
Only one can live.
He will find what has been lost
Restore what was torn apart
Return what was given

Rebuild what was destroyed.
Then the days of judgement will pass,
A new dawn for all shall rise—
A second chance to remember
What should never have been forgotten.

And that is when I awake. I awake with the words of the prophecy in my head and uncertainty in my heart.

When Marlo finished, silence hung over the four men like the stars in the nighttime sky. Kaden knew it would have to be broken eventually, but there seemed to be an unspoken agreement that it should not be yet. And when the time came, it was for Tchinchura to speak, for Kaden knew it was really to him that the Kalosenes had come to take counsel.

"Strange dreams," Tchinchura said at last, "and strange words. Three times you have dreamed this?"

"Yes, three times on three consecutive nights."

Tchinchura nodded. "Then there seems little doubt that it is more than a dream."

He reached up and placed both his large hands on Marlo's shoulders, clasping him tightly. "These are troubled times, Guardian, and your vision does not comfort me, but it is not our place to question the truth you guard; it is our place to learn from it. I welcome you and thank you for your trust."

"These are troubled times, indeed, Amhuru," Marlo said. "Times where all true servants of Kalos must stand together. I would be honored to hear any thoughts you might have on the vision Kalos has shown me, or the words He has spoken."

"It seems clear that the man of gold is the Jin Dara," Tchinchura said after a moment of thought.

"Yes, for in the vision he comes from the meridium orb which we know to be his handiwork," Marlo said.

"And the fact that he is gold is telling too," Tchinchura said. "You see what wearing one fragment of Zerura has done to my eyes and hair. Who knows what wearing two fragments might do to him over time?"

"Or more than two," Kaden said, his voice so quiet that for a moment he almost didn't know if he had spoken the words aloud or only thought them.

"Or more," Tchinchura agreed, almost as quietly. "For who knows if this vision is of things in the near or distant future."

"Then does the vision mean our quest shall fail?" Kaden asked.

"It may," Tchinchura said. "But succeed or fail, it must continue."

For another moment there was silence among them, and when Tchinchura spoke again, his tone was more upbeat. "He may yet acquire more than two fragments and never touch this one," he tapped the gold band on his arm, "so we must take heart that if the vision portends more success for the Jin Dara, it does not necessarily predict failure for us."

"And as Deras used to say," Marlo said, "'Prophecies often raise as many questions as they answer.'"

Kaden frowned. "That doesn't make them sound very helpful."

"It depends what kind of help you're looking for," Marlo said. "While they may not always give specific guidance, like the prophecy that led us to Tchinchura, the main point of prophecy is to remind us that the things about the future we do not understand, Kalos does. The hand that guides the present guides the future."

"So should we even try to guess at what the vision means?" Kaden said. "It all seemed mysterious to me."

"It is wise to be cautious," Tchinchura said, "but it is also wise to consider, lest we miss something that we were meant to see."

"Are there other things beyond the identity of the man of gold that you see?" Marlo asked. "Does it mean something that he rises into the sky?"

"I do not know," Tchinchura said. "Nothing else in the vision seemed as clear as his identity. I do not know what his rising off the ground means, or what either the plain or the mountain might represent."

"Or the lumbering shapes?"

Kaden could hear a note of hope in Marlo's voice as he asked, but Tchinchura shook his head, giving the essence of his reply before he spoke and confirmed it.

"Or them," Tchinchura said. "I assume, though, like you, that the final image of the ruins of Barra-Dohn is indeed Kalos's way of telling us that He will keep His promise. That whatever happens in the meantime, someone will return, and the city will be rebuilt."

"And the words of the prophecy?" Marlo continued. "The part about the Jin Dara again seems clear, about the maker of the lesser sun eclipsing the greater."

"Yes, and probably also the reference to gathering what was scattered," Tchinchura said, and he quickly added, "Though again, we should not necessarily assume that this means the Jin Dara will find all six fragments."

"And it sounded like he must be stopped at some point, if they are to be scattered again," Kaden said, thinking that this part of the prophecy had sounded hopeful, at least.

"That may be," Tchinchura, "but the references to victory and defeat suggest a warning, I think."

"What kind of warning?"

"That whatever happens with the Jin Dara, it may not be the end."

Kaden considered this. It was a sobering thought. Retrieving the stolen fragments already seemed so great a task. What more would have to be done?

"I do not know for sure," Tchinchura said, "but both the vision and the prophecy suggest to me that we cannot yet see the full scope of what lies ahead. And, at this point, it would probably be folly to guess. We know the timetable for the return to

Barra-Dohn, for that was foretold by Deras, and I think this vision does encourage us to trust that Kalos will bring this to pass."

"But in the meantime," Kaden said, "our plans do not change?"

"They do not change," Tchinchura said. "We must resist the Jin Dara in whatever way we may."

"Yes," Marlo said. "Even if a new day will one day dawn for Barra-Dohn, that's more than sixty-seven years away. He can bring a lot of misery to the world in the meantime."

"That he can," Tchinchura agreed.

And then, as though on cue, a gust of wind swept across the deck and buffeted the four men standing by the rail. A cry went up from one of the sailors on the watch, and before long more came pouring out on deck, followed shortly by the captain herself, barking orders to them all as they prepared to unfurl the sails.

The four men exchanged a look, and then Tchinchura smiled and said, "It looks as though it is time for us to be on our way."

The Jin Dara stood with his arms crossed, looking at the mouth of the canyon in the distance. Soon the sun would go down, and he had little doubt that the dawn would bring battle. For all the power at his diposal now, he knew the outcome of that battle was uncertain. He had a plan, he believed it would work, but there could be no guarantees.

And that was just fine with him. The unexpected could be painful or disappointing or even fatal, but it could also be wonderful. He thought of his attack on Barra-Dohn, the city once known as Zeru-Shalim, and how surprised he had been to find and acquire another fragment of the Golden Cord there. Nothing could have been more unexpected than that, and while it was almost his undoing, it had become, in fact, his making. It had given him a new purpose and a greater destiny.

So let the morning bring what it may. An army had gathered outside the canyon all day, with Omojen and warhorses and infantry, and most of all, with an unprecedented number of Amhuru, and yet he would sleep without worry or fear. He faced in the Amhuru a worthy adversary—that he knew. The outcome could be anticipated but not known, so he longed for morning and the answers it would bring.

And, of course, he hoped it would bring him more than answers.

Devaar approached, and the Jin Dara asked, "Are they ready?"

"Yes," Devaar said. "Whenever you are."

"Good." The Jin Dara turned his gaze back toward the canyon's entrance. "We've waited a long time for this moment, Devaar."

"We have, and so have they."

"The Amhuru?"

"Yes. They know what we have and how long we've had them. They may have a surprise of their own for us."

"They do know what I have, and how long I've had them," the Jin Dara said, "Which is precisely why, in this regard at least, they will not surprise us."

"Why?"

"Because they are consumed with getting them back."

"That doesn't mean they'll attack," Devaar said. "They must wonder why we've chosen to come here, to box ourselves in. They may try to wait us out."

"They may," the Jin Dara said, smiling as he turned to Devaar, "but I doubt it. They will be confident in their strength, and probably what they fear more than defeat is losing their chance to reacquire what now seems almost within their grasp."

They stood quietly, and after a moment, the Jin Dara said, "You must remember, Devaar, that they lack what is most necessary for true surprise."

"And what is that?"

"Absolute freedom."

"Freedom?" Devaar said, puzzled. "Are they not free?"

"Freedom inside," the Jin Dara said, tapping his own chest with two fingers. "They are constrained by what they will not do. I am not bound by any such constraints."

Devaar nodded, understanding. "And yet, they may still surprise us, if they prove stronger than we anticipate."

"Come, Devaar," the Jin Dara said as he started walking back toward the camp. "You didn't think we'd take all six fragments without risking all in battle, did you?"

"Of course not."

"And this is but the beginning, is it not? If we cannot win on ground of our choosing, what hope do we have in Azandalir, even if we can find it?"

"True," Devaar said.

"No, it is time to flex our muscles and try our strength."

They walked together toward the camp and began to pass through it. The Jin Dara motioned to the sea of tents and then said to Devaar, "The battles that will matter, including tomorrow's, will not be fought by soldiers such as these. We can lose every soldier and mercenary in these tents and still emerge victorious."

"We'd have to find a new army," Devaar said dryly. "That might slow us down a little."

"Don't miss the point," the Jin Dara said. "Real power lies in the Cord. These are but men."

They passed through the main camp and then across an open stretch of ground toward a second, smaller camp. Beyond it, gathered at the foot of one of the canyon walls, sat a small cluster of men wearing uniforms the color of gold, instead of the green worn elsewhere in the camp. The Jin Dara and Devaar approached, and the men stood, saluting their commander, their master.

The Jin Dara stopped and leaned over, whispering to Devaar. "Here is our true army, eh, Devaar?"

"Indeed."

The men stood quietly, their eyes on the Jin Dara as he paced in front of them, examining them with his golden eyes. "Are you ready?"

In unison the thirty-seven men standing before him raised their right hands in a clenched fist, reminiscent of the golden fist on the green flag that flapped above them. This was all the answer they gave, all the answer that was expected.

The Jin Dara pointed back in the direction from which he had come, toward the main camp, and beyond that, toward the entrance to the canyon. "A small army of Amhuru are out there. They would make the army of any nation tremble, but you will not tremble. Who are you?"

"We are the Najin," they replied.

"You are the Najin," the Jin Dara said. "You are *sons of the dark,* and you will defeat the Amhuru. You will defeat them, not by killing them, but by capturing them. The killing will come later.

"You are the Najin," the Jin Dara repeated. "Everyone has heard of the Amhuru. They are legendary. No one has heard of you." The Jin Dara stopped pacing, surveyed the men before him and smiled. "After tomorrow, they will."

19

The Other Card

The battle, which had begun in the wide mouth to the canyon, had now moved well inside it, with the mouth currently being held by Prince Hadaaya's army. The Omojen had pushed through the Jin Dara's defenses with little difficulty, scattering those soldiers in the mouth that they had not trampled. From where Zangira stood, it appeared that the Omojen were continuing to inflict serious damage. Everywhere they turned, the formations of the enemy broke apart and had to move elsewhere, but in that process they were vulnerable, and many men fell before the lines could be reformed.

The canyon as viewed from its mouth struck Zangira as far larger than the canyon as viewed from above when he had helped to scout it. The walls seemed much higher, and the floor of the canyon far wider. Through it ran the dry wadi, which Zangira had feared might also indicate a way out for the enemy on the far side, even if only a small or narrow way. Their scouting had found no such exit, however, and Zangira now believed that the wadi kept on its way by going under the far canyon wall. And while this would work for the water that coursed through it during the rainy season, it would provide no escape for the Jin Dara and his men.

No, if the Jin Dara was going to leave this canyon, short of sprouting wings like a bird and flying, he would have to come out through the mouth. Consequently, Calamin and Trajax had taken up positions just inside the mouth like watchmen by a gate, and they would go no further under any circumstances, so they might make sure the Jin Dara did not slip away. Zangira had more freedom to move about, but for now he had decided to hover near the prince.

The thought that the Jin Dara might somehow get away was almost unbearable. It was, in truth, more unbearable than the thought that he might fall in battle. Since the fall of Barra-Dohn, Zangira had carried with him the knowledge that both missing fragments of the Golden Cord had been within reach. More than that, they had been well in hand. With Tchinchura's help and the fragment stolen by Eirmon on his calf, they could have managed the Jin Dara. They were managing him, and had they been left to finish what they'd started, this enemy would have been defeated and the Cord recovered.

But Eirmon's treachery had done more than doom his own city; it had perhaps doomed the world, for the Jin Dara might even now be too powerful to stop. Today would be a great test of that, for Zangira knew the Jin Dara had not come here as a cornered animal might, fleeing before his hunter. The Jin Dara had led them here apurpose, and Zangira knew enough to know that whatever that purpose was, an easy victory for Prince Hadaaya and the Amhuru wasn't it.

And yet, so far it had been easy. Too easy. After the Omojen had cleared the mouth to the canyon, one company of Prince Hadaaya's cavalry had pushed in behind them, and together these forces had put the Jin Dara's overmatched infantry to rout. Even men with meridium-soled shoes were not faster than warhorses.

Behind the Omojen and cavalry, Prince Hadaaya's infantry had marched, and they were now engaged with the main contingency of the Jin Dara's army, pressing the attack. The rest of the Amhuru were also in the canyon. They had clear orders to spread out around it, to help as they may but to keep out of the main fighting and wait. If, or more likely when, the Jin Dara revealed himself by using the fragments he bore, then they would know their target and could move on him as they saw fit.

That the Jin Dara had not yet attempted to use the fragments was bewildering to Zangira. He well remembered the way the Jin Dara had guided hookworms and rhino-scorpions outside the walls of Barra-Dohn, and how he had summoned swirling sandstorms to thwart the rotating railguns of Eirmon's army. He didn't doubt that the Jin Dara was waiting for his moment to spring his trap, but how he could wait while his army was being butchered—and why—was beyond him. The battle had already become a rout, and left unchecked, the canyon would soon be little more than a slaughtering pen.

Prince Hadaaya, sitting atop his warhorse, rode up beside Zangira. From the way things were going so far, the Amhuru expected a happier countenance, but the prince scowled as he spoke. "The blood of my fathers runs hot within me, and I love a good battle now and again. But this? This is no battle."

"It may be yet," Zangira said. "So be careful what you wish for."

"I've been waiting for the trap you warned about since the day began and the Omojen pushed into the canyon," the prince replied, "but surely, if this man had another card to play, it would be on the table by now."

At that very moment, Zangira finally felt what he had been waiting for. Somewhere on the far side of the canyon, beyond the thick of the battle, someone had reached out and seized the Arua field. Someone very powerful, and he was moving quickly to seize control of the Omojen and horses. Zangira saw one of the Omojen rear up, its massive forelegs churning the sky, and all around the canyon, the neighing of frightened horses could be heard.

The counterstroke, though, was equally quick and strong. From all over the canyon, the party of Amhuru reached out, place by place and almost animal by animal, to contest the Jin Dara's move. He was very strong, and an individual Amhuru alone would not have been able to contain him, but together they placed blocks and obstacles and wrested the Arua field from him where he sought to seize and control it.

Prince Hadaaya, who had obviously noted both the cries of the animals in the canyon as well as the change in Zangira's face and distracted manner, spoke, "Has something happened?"

"He has made a play for the animals, as we expected."

"And?"

"So far he is rebuffed."

"Then if he is rebuffed, the day is ours."

The prince, who had no wives nearby or underlings to impress with his boasting, said the words as simply as any man might state a plain and obvious fact. Still, Zangira did not accept it as fact, and he did not rejoice. He was sure the Jin Dara had, as the prince had put it, another card to play.

He was equally sure that this was not it.

The Jin Dara continued to hold. He pushed here and there against the restraints the Amhuru had placed between him and his apparent targets, the horses and the Omojen, but he did not push as hard as he might, and he did not focus his strength on any one barrier.

He was disappointed that the Amhuru had not yet taken the bait, for as far as he could tell, the places from which they opposed him were still scattered around the outskirts of the canyon—on the other side of the main lines of battle. They'd been locked in their own silent battle for twenty or thirty minutes, but they had not moved.

It was possible they were just trying to contain him while their armies did their work, which was a wise strategy and more restrained than he had expected. He had thought that their desire to capture him and recover the fragments would be too strong to be resisted. Instead, they remained where they were, content to do no more than hold him back while their army neutralized his own.

Meanwhile, all around him, the battle was going poorly for his army, as he knew it would without his help, and while what he had said to Devaar was true, he didn't really wish to have to replace his entire army. Of course, there was always the possibility that after he was finished here, he might be able to convince whoever was at the head of the army the Amhuru was borrowing if they would like to come with him. Once they had seen what he was going to unleash, they would surely understand that aligning with him was the wisest possible strategy. And if they still resisted, well . . . he could be very persuasive when necessary.

Either way, he could see now that he was going to have to raise the stakes and see if he could force the Amhuru's hand. The obvious choice was the Omojen, and in this case, the obvious choice was also the right one. There were far fewer of them for him to control, and they could do far greater damage than even the whole company of the enemy's cavalry. In fact, using the Omojen to destroy the horses made sense tactically, both for the more obvious battle his men were fighting and for the more important and far more subtle battle that he was fighting.

He took a deep breath. He quieted his mind and heart, picturing the place where he would strike, and with sudden swiftness, he broke through the defenses that sought to keep him from seizing the Arua surrounding the Omojen. He smashed through like a hammer would smash through glass, and when he seized the Omojen, he had them as firmly in his grasp as he had once had the thief tied to the pole or the black bird tied beside him. They were his to command.

It was actually far easier to panic a trained animal so that it ran wild than it was to seize control of a wild animal and manage it. Both were easy for him now, of course, and with the amount of power he wielded with two fragments, there wasn't an animal alive that he could not impose his will upon. Animals were so much simpler than men to work upon, as instinct and the rhythmic cycles of life guided almost all of their "decisions." They acted and reacted in predictable ways, unlike men, who were surprisingly complicated all the way from the cradle to the grave.

For the moment, though, all the Jin Dara wanted to do was to disrupt the Omojen and use their power to inflict damage against the enemy. The more damage the Omojen did, the more incentive he would give the Amhuru to stop holding back, to stop waiting on the sideline and to enter this fight.

He filled the Omojen with terror, both for the men who rode upon them and for the canyon in which they fought. As he did so, all over the battlefield, the Omojen trumpeted their fear and alarm, rearing and stomping and whipping around as though by moving quickly they might be able to seize the men on their backs with their great trunks or gash them with their wicked tusks.

The Jin Dara pushed the Omojen also to see the warhorses around them and the men on their backs as threats intent on their harm. They started lashing out against them, charging into the cavalry clusters around the canyon and dispersing them. The Jin Dara saw one Omojen just across the battlefield lower its great head and skewer a large brown stallion, its tusk pushing straight through the terrified horse's body as the Omojen drove it sideways. The rider who fell off was crushed, trampled first under the horse and then under massive legs of the Omojen.

The Amhuru renewed their efforts to contain them, and their counter was ferocious. Here and there they seized from him control of the Arua around particular Omojen, but they could not take from him his mastery of the main contingency. He could also tell that the Amhuru were closer now, and he rejoiced at that. They had apparently decided it was time to move on him, and he was ready to unleash the Najin. He would give them the sign.

Filling as many of the Omojen as he could with an all-consuming and unreasoning claustrophic terror of being in the canyon, they soon lost all interest in their own riders or the warhorses around them or in anything else except getting out into the open. They moved, almost en masse, back toward the canyon mouth, crushing and destroying anything that got in their way, which meant that they walked over and through their own army with indiscriminant panic and hatred. As they did so, the Jin Dara felt the Najin reach out all over the canyon from their hiding spots for the Arua field and felt them overwhelm the strong but overmatched Amhuru.

He let go of the Arua field.

There was no sense keeping the target on his back now. The Najin had entered the fight, and they would do what must be done.

Zangira picked himself up off the ground of the canyon and brushed the dirt and dust from his body. The Omojen that had almost crushed him was still charging out through the mouth of the canyon and would, no doubt, continue stampeding madly out beyond it as the others had done.

The flight of the Omojen did not worry Zangira, as they had served their main purpose—punching a hole through the enemy so they could enter the canyon in the first place—and they could not be used against Prince Hadaaya's army if they were nowhere to be seen. What did worry Zangira was the remarkable power of their opponent, whose move on the Arua field had been as strong as it was sudden.

If he was this strong, if he could push back the concerted efforts of the Amhuru who surrounded him with such ease, why had he allowed himself to be restrained at all? Why had he allowed his men to be slaughtered? What had he been waiting for?

Zangira had known it would likely come to this, to their axes and not a contest over their ability to seize or control the Arua field. That was a fight he had expected they might not be able to win. No, the Amhuru would have to end the battle by taking the Jin Dara down. They would need to make their way to wherever he was and kill him, the sooner the better.

He could tell that the others had come to the same conclusion, as their counterstrokes against the Jin Dara were coming from places much closer to the far side of the canyon than they had been. For a moment Zangira hesitated, but the prince would have to take care of himself for now, and Calamin and Trajax would have to guard the mouth to the canyon without him. The assault on the Jin Dara might take all that they had, and he would not hang back.

As he approached the thick of the fighting, he saw the Jin Dara's soldier in green, many of them moving on the Arua field, engaged with Prince Hadaaya's men and what was left of his cavalry. Zangira would try to negotiate his way through without having to fight, as his battle lay ahead of him, but he would stop and fight if it was required. He leapt up onto the Arua field with his axe in one hand and his knife in the other.

Then everything changed.

All over the canyon, the Arua was seized and manipulated. It was as if the Jin Dara had multiplied and dispersed himself throughout the battlefield. No sooner had Zangira felt the change then he understood. This—not the Jin Dara's play for the Omojen—was the other card, and it spelled their doom.

He had known, as had the other Amhuru with him, as had Tchinchura and the council of the elders, that it was possible the Jin Dara might disperse duplicates among his men, as the Amhuru did. And of course, it was possible, since he had two originals, that he might disperse replicas of both and train men to use their combined power, even as he did. They had known this, and yet they had believed that two things would likely prevent it from actually happening.

The first had been a dim hope, for it was predicated on something no Amhuru could really believe after the fall of Barra-Dohn: the Jin Dara's ignorance. They had learned from Rika that Eirmon Omiir had not known the replicas he created by dividing his stolen fragment of the Golden Cord could be worn and used in ways much like the original. He had been focused on how the replicas he made could be mixed with meridium to make weapons and technologies that would increase his power and profit, not on how his own fragment actually worked, which, if he had examined and studied more closely, might have opened the door to the undiscovered potential of its replicas.

That the Jin Dara, who had demonstrated far greater understanding and even mastery of the Cord, might not know how to use the duplicates and equip his soldiers with them had been a faint hope. Far more important had been their belief that, while the Jin Dara might be completely different in this way from Eirmon, the two men might have been much more alike in another way—namely, their mistrust of the people around them.

That Eirmon had not explored the power of the Golden Cord as much as he might have was one thing; that he had been mistrustful of anyone else in Barra-Dohn possessing and exploring its uses was another. According to Rika, stringent safeguards had been in place to ensure that the Zerura created through duplication did not leave the Academy in any form other than those that were made by the experiments performed there, and then only in the care of soldiers and researchers from the Academy.

Indeed, that Eirmon's own son had been unaware of the stolen fragment and the process by which the new weapons were made for the army of Barra-Dohn showed just how mistrustful Eirmon was. That Eirmon would have dispersed fragments among his captains to be used freely in battle, if he had known how to activate and use them, seemed impossible given his desire for power, and fear that he would lose it.

So the Amhuru had dared to hope that the Jin Dara, for all his knowledge and understanding of the fragments of the Cord, might also be crippled by mistrust. Maybe, they thought, he would allow some of his men to train with a single replica, but surely he would not trust any of them to have access to the power that came with wearing two. That would be dangerous and risky, and men like the Jin Dara often did not take those kinds of risks or invite that kind of danger.

And yet, as Zangira stood, almost paralyzed in the middle of the battle in the canyon by what he felt going on all around him, he knew that was exactly what the Jin Dara had done. He had trained men—many of them, by the feel of it—in the use of the Zerura and then equipped them with duplicates of not one but both of those fragments that he possessed. That meant that these men had access to all the power the Jin Dara had, for their replicas had almost all the power of the originals, save primarily the ability to be replicated as the originals could be.

The Amhuru, by contrast, would not traditionally wear two replicas nor had they ever even trained in the use of two, for Kalos had forbidden that the originals be brought together, and combining them in any form seemed to violate the very heart of their mission. Now Zangira and the other Amhuru in the canyon were faced with superior numbers wielding superior power. This was the trap, and it had now been sprung.

The battle seemed to slow around Zangira, and he stood for a moment, considering his choices. In the brief interval of time that had elapsed since leaving the mouth of the canyon, the task before him had gone from difficult to near impossible, but he could not go back. Not unless he knew beyond question that getting to the Jin Dara and getting those originals back simply couldn't be done, and he did not know that yet.

He ran forward. A soldier in green saw him and turned toward him, but before he could raise the meridium spear in his hand to throw it, Zangira's axe had struck a fatal blow and was already returning to his grip. Two more soldiers fell by his hand as Zangira now sought engagements rather than avoiding them. He would cut a path to the Jin Dara in blood, letting the battle frenzy take him. If he fell, he fell.

Zangira moved on in his dance with death, and though he moved so fast that the casual observer would have had difficulty tracking his motions, it all seemed to unfold before him slowly, step by inexorable step. With axe and knife, he cut his way through the heaviest section of the battlefield, and he could see he was not the only Amhuru doing so.

And then he caught his first glimpse of the men in gold. One of them appeared, also moving on the Arua, though like an Amhuru, he did not wear meridium shoes to do so and he did not carry a meridium spear. He had two long, nasty knives, and Zangira saw him do the seemingly impossible with them.

He threw a knife at one of Prince Hadaaya's men, and the knife struck the man in the chest. Then the man in gold made a jerking motion with his hand, and the knife pulled back out of the man it had struck. But it did not fly back to the man in gold as it would have done if Zangira had thrown it and then recalled it. Rather, the man made a jerking motion to the side, and the knife—which for the barest of moments had seemed to hover in the air after the man it had killed fell off the Arua field and onto the ground—then flew in the direction the man in gold had indicated with his motion. There, it struck another soldier in the back.

Zangira was startled. The man had redirected the knife without needing to summon it back into his hand. Amhuru could throw their axes and knives and then call them back, more or less on a straight line, but they could not redirect them.

The man in gold looked up and saw Zangira, and the two started across the Arua toward each other. The man threw his other knife, and Zangira used his axe to strike it sideways before it could hit him. Knowing that the man could redirect it saved his life, for he did not assume the weapon had been disabled, and when it came back at him from the side, he ducked as it flew overhead.

As the knife missed him, Zangira noted that the redirecting had taken some velocity off the original throw. That observation, along with the fact that the man in gold was now summoning the knife back into his hand, encouraged him that his enemy could not endlessly redirect the same throw, a fact which lessened his advantage and gave Zangira hope. The Amhuru lifted his hand and threw his own knife.

The throw was true, and the knife sped toward its target, but the man in gold raised his hand, still clenching one of his own knives, and Zangira's knife slowed and came to a halt. And with power that would have shocked Zangira if he had not felt it before, the man pushed through the Arua so that Zangira's own knife flew back in his direction.

The meridium in his knife had been mixed with Zerura from the same fragment that created the replica Zangira wore, however, and he knew that no act of mere force by this man could override the control he could exert over his own knife. So Zangira was not afraid so much as disheartened to see it coming back at him. He would not be taken down this way, but his hope to deliver a fatal blow to his enemy at a distance had diminished. He slowed his knife as it approached and caught it, and rather than throwing again, he ran forward in an attempt to close the gap on his enemy as quickly as he could.

The man in gold, now holding both knives as Zangira held both of his own weapons, made a swiping motion with his right arm, swinging it rapidly across his body and then back again, and before Zangira could wonder what the gesture meant, he slipped and fell off the Arua field.

Even as he felt himself falling to the ground below, he wondered how it had happened. He'd not fallen off the Arua since he was a child and had taken his first faltering steps toward mastery of the Zerura he bore. He hit the ground and rolled so that he was back up on his feet in a flash, his momentum carrying him to the side a little, which also may have saved him.

Another of the men in gold had been approaching from the side, and his knife struck the ground just in front of the place where Zangira had struck it, as though he had anticipated the fall would carry the Amhuru straight ahead. Zangira leapt up as though to regain his footing on the Arua, but it was as slippery to his bare feet as a wet rock in a stream, and he slid along it for a moment before choosing to drop down off it before his enemies engineered another fall.

He now faced two men in gold on an unequal footing, one more or less in front of him and another off to his left, and both were moving his direction more cautiously than he would have expected, since they must have sensed his vulnerability. Between them they had four knives and power he couldn't possibly match, and yet when he glanced at them, he saw immediately in their body language and their manner that they were not coming for the kill.

Now he understood.

They had been lured here, not to be exterminated but to be captured. Toward what end, he didn't know. Perhaps the Jin Dara thought they'd be foolish enough to bring the third Southland fragment, though Zangira doubted it. Perhaps he meant to recover the replicas the Amhuru bore that came from a different original, or perhaps it was for some other purpose that would only occur to him later. Whatever it was, he knew his only real hope was to try to fight his way back out of the canyon. That was the only hope any of them had.

He reached through the Arua, noting that not only was running on it slippery, but grabbing hold of it was becoming slippery for him too, and he called a gust of wind through the canyon, throwing dust and dirt at his enemies. As he did so, he ran in full retreat across the canyon floor. He kept the wind blowing behind him and reached through the Arua for something else, and after a moment a dark cloud came scudding across the sky above the canyon. In its midst flashed a streak of dry lightning, and across the canyon echoed a single peal of thunder.

He had sounded the retreat for the others. He hoped they would heed it and come. He hoped some of them at least would make it out alive.

He hoped he would make it out alive.

20

A Change of Plans

The Jin Dara walked through the canyon in the aftermath of the battle. The dead littered the ground and would soon begin to stink even worse than they already did, given the growing heat of the late afternoon sun. A big part of the stink was the horseflesh, and there was a lot of it. When his Najin had entered the battle, they had seized control of the warhorses and driven them mad with fear so that they impaled themselves on the long spears of the Jin Dara's soldiers stationed on the edges of the canyon for just this purpose. Once the horses had been dealt with, their riders had been easy prey.

As for the Omojen, the Jin Dara thought it entirely possible they might still be running. He almost laughed at the comical thought of those great beasts stampeding across the vast and empty plains, with nothing behind them and nothing in front of them to explain where they were going or what they were running from.

Among the human remains of the battle, perhaps two out of every three bodies wore the bright green colors of his adopted flag of the golden fist on a field of green, but he had expected something like this and was not terribly concerned with it. The real causalties had been the eight Najin who fell in combat with the Amhuru. They were by far the greater loss, and he would need to proceed with recruiting the next wave of Najin and training them so that there would be even more Najin whenever he succeeded in breaking one of the Amhuru and finding the location of their hidden home.

Overall, the Najin had acquitted themselves quite well, and given that their superior strength was somewhat mitigated by the Amhuru's superior experience, he was not disappointed in their performance, even though eight had fallen. Not really, anyway. They had captured five Amhuru alive, a respectable number to be sure, and they had killed nine more. Not bad for their first taste of combat wielding their new weapons, and they would only get better with additional opportunities to hone their skills.

Of course, the killed and captured Amhuru only added up to fourteen, and he had been told that perhaps as many as twenty Amhuru had been traveling with the army that attacked him in the canyon. That meant as many as five or six Amhuru had managed to escape, which was unfortunate, as they would no doubt carry word of their defeat to Azandalir—along with news of the Najin's existence and word that their brothers had been killed or captured. If the Amhuru were smart, and they were, they'd know the time for subuterfuge was over and that he was coming.

How quickly he could arrive there after them was a very real question. He didn't know how much time it would take to break one of his captives and discover the location of Azandalir—though that was a job he could continue while they were on the move even if it was a job he would begin here—nor did he know how long it would take him to replace the men he had lost, though that, he imagined, would be the easier job.

He'd start by riding to this city of Ben-Salaar that he was told had supplied the Amhuru with their army, and he would punish and perhaps plunder it, as he taught this Prince Hadaaya the price of helping the Jin Dara's enemies. Of course, he'd be careful to spare the army of this prince, at least at first, since he fully intended to make the highest ranking military officer he could find an offer of clemency—provided the army agreed to his terms and provided him the help he desired. If they refused, they would be punished fully, of course. It would be inconvenient but not disastrous.

There were many fools out there with armies at their disposal, and he had met several of them in his many years of traveling. Depending on where Azandalir actually was, he was sure he could chart a course that would go more or less directly there and also take him by a city with an army he might "borrow." He wouldn't need it forever, after all.

Once he secured the last Southland fragment, it would be time to cross the Madri, and that was probably a task best left only to himself and his Najin.

He turned and headed to the place where the five captured Amhuru sat cross-legged on the ground, being guarded by half of his remaining Najin. The guard was excessive, perhaps, but he wasn't about to risk losing what he had worked so hard and so long to acquire.

All five were wounded, but only one seriously. He would do what he could to cure those wounds, as he needed them to stay alive long enough to be broken.

As he stood a short distance away, regarding them, Devaar approached. "How does it look, Devaar? How soon can we be on our way?"

Devaar shook his head. "Not until morning, at the earliest."

"If we left all the wounded behind, not just the seriously wounded, could we leave tonight?"

"I don't think it would help," Devaar answered, unfazed by the callousness of the question. "We could barely be packed and ready to move out before sundown under any circumstances. We might as well get a good night's sleep so we can get an early start."

He nodded. "Very well. Do what you need to. And one more thing, Devaar," the Jin Dara said as the other began to withdraw.

"Since we're spending the night, go ahead and have the poles brought to me. I might as well get started."

Zangira jogged along on top of the Arua. Though it was no longer slippery underfoot as it had been in the canyon, he took his steps deliberately, like a man trying to walk across a patch of ice, such as could be found in the distant Southlands. He didn't seem quite able to trust the feel of the Arua beneath his feet.

On his left, Prince Hadaaya rode his horse. On his right ran Calamin and Trajax, the only Amhuru other than himself to escape the canyon, at least so far. That others might still get out, Zangira hoped, but he knew it was an unlikely hope.

The prince's wives rode double on a horse close by, borrowed from one of the cavalrymen in the company that the prince, wisely, had not sent into the canyon once he saw the battle going wrong. He held them back, knowing he might need them to guard their retreat, and that was just what they were doing. The infantry jogged in columns a little ways ahead, and the cavalry rode behind, prepared to wheel and face the enemy should such a maneuver be necessary.

The prince's luxurious transport, like the more practical cargo transports for the army's gear, had been left behind outside the canyon. The prince hated to do so, as much because he didn't want the Jin Dara to have them as because he was loth to lose them. However, without the Omojen to pull them, he'd had no other choice.

Where the Omojen were now was anybody's guess. If they were still spooked by the touch of the Jin Dara, they would still be running and perhaps scattered, too. If so, it would be quite a job to recapture them. On the other hand, if they had regained their right minds and their training kicked in, there was always a chance they would make their own way back to Ben-Salaar. Only time and the prince's return would tell.

Zangira imagined that he would never know, because his road did not take him to Ben-Salaar. They had to be on their way as fast as possible. They did not have time to go all the way to Ben-Salaar at the pace of a tired army. They had only stayed this long because they wanted to help guard the Prince's retreat, though Zangira knew that if the men in gold came now, the three Amhuru could do nothing to stop them. Now that the sun was going down, the army would stop, soon anyway, even if the prince kept going for a while by the light of the quarter moon. It was time for the Amhuru to be on their way. They would not stop this night, and maybe not the next.

Zangira veered just a little closer to the prince so that they could speak without either slowing or shouting. The prince looked down, anticipating the reason for his approach.

"I know you must be on your way," he said, then added, "I am sorry for the loss of your brothers."

"As I am sorry for the loss of your people," Zangira said. "I am sorry I could not protect them."

"Lives are lost in battle, my friend. For all the wisdom and strength of the Amhuru, they cannot change that."

"True," Zangira said, "but I fear I leave you and your people in a dangerous position. The Jin Dara is a vengeful man. He may be primarily concerned with the Amhuru, but that doesn't mean for sure that Ben-Salaar will escape his wrath. Remember what I told you when I first came to you, how he destroyed the great city of Barra-Dohn. He is more powerful now."

"I know," the prince said, "and that is why I came with you. If there was a chance to stop him before he became even stronger, it had to be taken. It was the right decision, and my people and I will live with the consequences."

"Is there anywhere you can take them?" Zangira asked. "Anywhere you can evacuate to? I do not doubt that his ultimate target concerns my people and what they guard, so even a little misdirection may frustrate him enough that he bypasses you entirely."

"There may be possibilities," the prince said, with a look that suggested he had a very specific possibility in mind.

"Then I strongly encourage you to pursue them," Zangira said. "A great storm, not just for your people or mine, but for the entire world is coming. I wish I could tell you how you may weather it, but I cannot."

"When the storm comes and the great winds blow, even the *Balaada* tree must bend or be broken," the prince said. "We will weather it as we may."

"I hope you will be able to bend far enough," Zangira said. "Go in peace, Prince Hadaaya, and may Kalos watch over you."

"Go in peace, Amhuru," the prince said in return.

Zangira, along with Calamin and Trajax, accelerated, veering off to the right so that they would be able to bypass the main contingency of infantrymen up ahead. What's more, their road would take them further south than the army was headed, so they'd have to turn veer right up ahead eventually anyway.

As they ran and left the army behind, Zangira found himself getting lost in his own thoughts. He still wasn't sure why the Jin Dara would have wanted to capture Amhuru, and he had no idea if the Jin Dara actually had. Whether those left behind had been killed or captured, he could not say, and while part of him hoped some had survived, another part of him suspected it would almost be better if they hadn't. Whatever the Jin Dara had planned for any Amhuru taken alive, Zangira doubted that it would end well.

Whatever might lie behind, there was no mystery about what lay ahead. They must get passage to Azandalir, and quickly. The elders had to be warned. The mere fact of the Jin Dara's great power, of the men in gold he had trained to wield the same power, meant that the time to speak in council of fighting and defeating, of finding and recovering had past.

It was time now to speak of hiding and evading. Of surviving.

With the return of the winds came the rain, and for several days it poured and poured, and the seas through which *The Sorry Rogue* sailed grew rough. Much to her surprise, on the fourth day of rough seas, Rika grew quite sick and had to be confined to the cabin.

The captain was quite accommodating, as was the girl from the island, but Rika felt embarrassed. She had fancied herself a seasoned sailor, and growing green with seasickness during a storm was a blow to her pride.

As she lay in her rolling bunk, trying not to think about how much she had vomited that morning and the previous night, and hoping there was nothing left in her stomach to vomit, she found herself unable to forget the bizarre and annoying exchange she had endured with that fool Kalosene way back before they had found the mysterious island. Had she been feeling better, she might have realized that she was obsessing, but curled up in a ball all day in the small cabin feeling like she might die at any moment had limited her ability to be reasonable.

Between groans she cursed the Kalosene for his audacity. How had the man dared to speak to her in such a way? She who had been a member of the prestigious Academy of Barra-Dohn? She who had been the king's consort and therefore powerful, even if indirectly? If she had not realized before that the world had turned completely upside down since their flight from Barra-Dohn, surely she knew it now, for he would never have dared address her at all, let alone speak with such unwarranted familiarity and level such accusations.

She had been careful since that night, and she hoped that would be an end to it—but what if it wasn't? What if the Kalosene decided to go to Nara and Kaden? Rika knew Nara had noticed her flirtations—after all, they wouldn't have been nearly as enjoyable if she hadn't—but Rika didn't know if Kaden had realized what she was up to, or if Nara had said anything to him. If Nara had, and Kaden hadn't figured it out for himself, then he would certainly have denied it. Men were like that with things like this, too slow or too proud or too something to accept what any woman could see unless they first saw it for themselves.

And if Nara could see it and Kaden couldn't, it might be a matter of some friction between them, and that would be just find with Rika.

But if the nosy Kalosene went to Kaden with his suspicions, or to Nara, then Nara would use his testimony as support, and her attempt to secure her position within the group might actually backfire. Her place among them could be at risk.

To be thwarted by a witless Kalosene? How could she have been so careless that he had noticed when others had not? A man so stupid he believed the Old Stories were true? It was bad enough that some, like Gamalian, saw the foolish tales as instructive, but to take them literally? As history? How could such as man as this have seen? It didn't seem quite possible. Perhaps another woman might have noticed, like D'Sarza, or even the sly Amhuru, Tchinchura—he saw much, she thought—but the Kalosene?

The ship lurched, and she almost tumbled out of her bunk. She felt the seizing in her stomach and reached for the bucket. She leaned over it and retched, but they were dry heaves and nothing came out. They were almost worse than the real thing, and she was glad when they subsided and she could lie back down. Her stomach hurt, she was angry, and she felt like crying.

Life was so tedious on this stinking ship. She hated it, and yet what else could she do? What other option did she have? Should she just leave? Walk away at some crowded port in some distant country where she didn't know the customs or the people? A place where she had little money and no friends? Would that be better?

No, she was every bit as much at sea as the ship beneath her. And that was a hard pill to swallow. She thought of those nights, which felt so very long ago, when she had lain in Eirmon's bed after he'd gone to sleep, daydreaming in the dark about slipping away with her stash of Zerura. It was worth a fortune, and she would have been rich beyond even her considerable imagination. It would have been wealth stolen from him, and he would at some point have known it—even if he couldn't have proved it. He would have known that she had bested him.

But she hadn't bested him. He'd found out and imprisoned her, and she had been languishing in a cell awaiting her death when the Jin Dara had come. This man, this Jin Dara that the

Amhuru were in such a lather about, he must have been quite the man if he could defeat Tchinchura and Zangira—with or without Eirmon's untimely interference. To be able to conquer the strongest army in all Aralyn and lay waste to its greatest city, even when two Amhuru were among those opposing you . . .

Rika found herself slipping into a daydream she'd had before, where Gamalian did not come to her cell and let her out. She imagined the Jin Dara finding her there—the image of Barreck in the neighboring cell tried to intrude into her daydream, but she pushed it back—and she imagined that he released and welcomed her with a "the enemy of my enemy is my friend" kind of welcome. He might even have brought her deep into his councils because she was a researcher of the Academy and had learned so much about the properties of Zerura and how it could be used for weaponry.

Rika snapped out of the daydream. She knew what Zangira had reported, that the Jin Dara had killed everyone he found in Barra-Dohn. She knew that would likely have been her fate too, daydream or no, had she not gotten out. It was too bad, though, as it seemed more and more like the Jin Dara's side might just be the winning side in this little war brewing with the Amhuru. They certainly seemed afraid of him.

At any rate she couldn't help but wonder what being in his presence would be like. At first she had been intoxicated by Eirmon's power, but it had grown old over time. But Eirmon was little more than a speck next to this man. What would it be like to be with him?

Rika felt something in her stomach. Not sickness. A flutter. An idea.

In the cells below the palace of Barra-Dohn, she would have had nothing to bargain for her life with, nothing to offer the Jin Dara to persuade him to take her with him. But . . . was she not traveling with the very man the Jin Dara most wanted to find? The very man who possessed the third Southland fragment of the Golden Cord?

What if she could somehow take the fragment? What if she could get it and get away, and then also, somehow, find the Jin Dara? Would she not be welcomed by him then? Would he not have to see in her the ambition and the greatness that he might have missed had he found her in that dingy cell? Perhaps he would make her a partner of sorts. Perhaps he would even make her something more than a partner.

Goosebumps appeared on her skin. She felt a shiver of near ecstasy. She might one day be more than the consort of a king, even as the Jin Dara might one day be so much more than a king. She could help him, and in doing so, she might one day be the Queen of the World.

It was so obvious, so clear. Why had she not seen this before? Fate had cast her in the way of greatness again.

Of course, taking the fragment from Tchinchura would be dangerous, especially since she would be alone in the attempt. She couldn't count on help from anyone on *The Sorry Rogue.* Not that she would want it. She would share none of her power and her spoils with anyone on this ship.

Without help, she thought, the difficulties might prove insurmountable. That didn't mean she was defeated though. There were other options. She would look for a chance to take the fragment, but barring that, she could still accomplish her goal another way. She would listen for information, listen and watch. And maybe, just maybe, she might learn something valuable enough that if she took that knowledge to him, she might gain admission to the Jin Dara's presence, his counsels, and perhaps even his heart.

21

AZANDALIR

As the weeks turned to months, Kaden noticed a number of changes among the females onboard *The Sorry Rogue.* The girl, Olli, grew more and more used to the sunlight, and increasingly she spent as much time as possible on deck. She was like a child making some new and wonderful discovery, and Kaden would catch her staring at the sunlight sparkling on the water or even at far less splendid or remarkable things than that. She would hold up her hand and stare at her fingers or sit cross-legged on the deck, tracing the lines on the decking boards, as though these things took on special qualities when illuminated by the sun.

She gradually seemed to relax, too. At first she seemed so tightly wound, an understandable or even inevitable consequence, Kaden imagined, of all that she had been through. She did not talk about that, about what she had been through, save only with Nara, to whom she had taken wholeheartedly.

For her part Nara seemed only too happy to take Olli under her wing. Kaden wondered how much of this was Nara's natural compassion, which would have been evoked by the girl's plight under any circumstance, and how much was the result of Nara's pregnancy and the growing maternal instinct as the time grew closer. And the time was drawing closer, as evidenced by the second change Kaden had noted.

Nara was beginning to show. It wasn't obvious yet, and Kaden didn't know how many others had picked up on the change, but there was the slightest of bulges in Nara's stomach these days, a slender, outward curve to her belly. Kaden liked to slide his hand along it in anticiption of the day when he would be able to feel the baby moving within, but as yet, there was nothing to feel. Even so, Nara seemed to like it, welcoming the attentions he had not given her the last time.

The third change was with Rika, who had become quite stand-offish since they left the island. In many ways this was a good thing, Kaden thought, since Nara had seemed jealous of their friendly relationship before. Now, Nara seemed hardly to notice Rika or to think of her, and Kaden figured that with the baby coming, it was no doubt for the best that the tension between them over Rika dissipate.

At the same time, the change perplexed him. Kaden had found her friendliness mystifying at first, since Rika had never been especially friendly in Barra-Dohn. She had been courteous but formal in her role as Deslo's tutor, but her attention when she came to the palace had always been clearly directed either to Eirmon or to Deslo. Kaden had never been someone with whom she made small talk. And yet, over the years since the fall of Barra-Dohn, she had become quite friendly—no doubt because he was the adult on the ship with whom she had been best acquainted before—but now that seemed to have disappeared almost overnight, and Kaden couldn't for the life of him figure out why.

In the end he supposed it didn't matter, only he didn't like the idea that he had given offense unintentionally. He had considered approaching Rika to see what he had done and if he needed to apologize, and he had considered asking Nara what she thought, but so far he had done neither. His gut told him to leave it alone, and he had decided in the end that this was exactly what he was going to do.

And as for Captain D'Sarza, well, Kaden figured she hadn't really changed so much, though she had mellowed once the winds had returned and *The Sorry Rogue* was on its way to Azandalir. For someone who had such a tough, even gruff exterior, D'Sarza seemed pretty happy about the prospect of getting to see the hidden home of the Amhuru in the Southlands. She claimed to have been across the Madri before to the Northlands—a trip that was not for the faint of heart, she always said—but she had never been to Azandalir, and the anticipation of seeing it had her in an unusually good mood these days.

They were close now, and Tchinchura had taken an increasingly active role in helping the captain chart her course. He said that her instruments would not help her as they drew closer. The Amhuru had created some natural defenses and deterrents around the island of Azandalir—not exactly like those they had used in the Madri when they had created it, but similar in that they had used their mastery of Arua to alter the natural properties of the sea and sky around the island.

These deterrents were subtle, their goal misdirection. There was perpetual fog that circled the island, obscuring the high cliffs that ringed its exterior until you were almost on top of them. Should you sail into the fog anyway, the currents and winds around the island created natural channels, of sorts, that were difficult to escape and would direct any ship caught in them through the outskirts of the fog and back out into the open water, headed away from Azandalir.

For those ships that found their way through the fog and escaped the channels and penetrated all the way through to within sight of Azandalir, they would see only high cliffs, rocky and forbidding, with no beach or natural harbor to sail into. Circle the island all you wanted, and that was all you would see, for the entrance to the small harbor of Azandalir was hidden, not by special powers but by a cleverly designed rock façade.

The façade was carefully constructed to replicate the jagged walls of the cliffs, and you could sail almost close enough to touch it without seeing the seams where the façade ended and the real cliff face began. It could be raised from the inside by means of heavy chains that would lift it inward so a ship might sail under it, but only after an Amhuru had seized the Arua field nearby and alerted those inside of his presence on the ship.

Once through to the other side, the façade would be lowered as the visiting ship made its way along a short but narrow, enclosed, man-made channel that would eventually dump the ship out into the prettiest lagoon one might ever see.

If an enemy ever, somehow, made it here, the defenses were simpler but no less forbidding—the Amhuru themselves.

Tchinchura had told Kaden that, so far, Azandalir had never been assailed by any outside force. That this day might be coming if they could not recover what the Jin Dara had taken he did not have to say.

For *The Sorry Rogue,* the elaborate defenses of Azandalir posed no problem. Once Tchinchura had located the fog, it served as a beacon, and using his fragment of the Golden Cord, he helped Captain D'Sarza to escape the channel inside the ring of fog and pass through. The tall rocky cliffs loomed suddenly up before them, and the great rock façade was raised and the ship passed inside. For Kaden, this was the most alarming part. The passage through the dark was brief, but it felt so unnatural to be both sailing and enclosed, with rock walls on both sides and a rock ceiling above, that he could hardly express his relief when at last they slipped out into the open again.

The first thought that struck Kaden as *The Sorry Rogue* glided out into the open lagoon was how suddenly the world passed from dark to light. The sky directly above them was wide open, not a cloud in sight, and the sun shone bright and clear. Kaden blinked and had to shield his eyes, thinking not for the first time how glad he was that he hadn't grown up in a cave like Olli.

The second thought that struck him, once his eyes had readjusted to the light, was just how beautiful the lagoon really was. The water was still and dark, not black perhaps, but not the bright blue of the ocean either. The lagoon was also small, for up ahead Kaden could see the entirety of the shore they were headed for, stretched out in a curving arc from one cliff wall to the other. More specifically, what Kaden saw were great trees rising up from the abundant greenery with enormous trunks and no branches until at least fifty feet above the ground, towering over the lagoon.

Kaden marveled at the trees. He'd been an exile from Barra-Dohn long enough now to know that many places were more verdant than the city of his youth. The hot, arid climate of northeastern Aralyn had been better suited to the scraggly sage bushes he was familiar with than any tall or great tree, but even in his sojourn since leaving, he'd never seen trees like this. It looked like it would take three or four men with their arms outspread to ring a single tree, and a dozen or more trunks lined the green shore.

And the shore was green. There was no beach, just grass and bushes lining the ground at the level of the water. Five or six piers extended out from the shore, though only two of them had vessels moored at them, and they appeared to be a good bit smaller than *The Sorry Rogue*. Kaden thought they might be used by the Amhuru for fishing more than transport, for as he understood it, the Amhuru had a pretty regular schedule for their travels, and the outgoing Amhuru generally caught rides on the ships that brought the incoming Amhuru in.

Kaden stood on the deck and turned in a complete circle, twice. The effect was striking. For half or more of the circuit, tall grey cliffs created a boundary between earth and sky, and for the other portion, expansive green canopies from the giant trees served as the marker. But all the way around, there was something looming high above him that created the feeling of being tightly hemmed in, even in the open lagoon.

Soon, the scurrying of D'Sarza's sailors as *The Sorry Rogue* made ready to dock interrupted Kaden's peaceful observations, and he put his arm around Nara's shoulders and said, "What a lovely place this is."

"Yes, it is," she said smiling. She touched her stomach gently. "It wouldn't be the worst thing in the world if we ended up staying awhile, would it?"

"It would be great," Kaden said. They had had this conversation before, and Nara knew Kaden couldn't guarantee how long they'd be in Azandalir. Still, in a world that felt like it was becoming less secure by the day, and the future less certain along with it, they both knew this might be as close to safe as a place could be.

And then Kaden noticed the activity on the shore. Coming out onto the more open ground from further back amongst the trees were several people. Men, women, and children, all with golden hair and those same striking, golden eyes that Tchinchura and Zangira possessed. The golden hair and golden eyes that Kaden himself would have if he lived long enough, and Deslo too.

It was odd, though, perhaps even a little eerie, to see those eyes in the faces of women and children. What's more, as the Amhuru coming toward the ship drew closer, Kaden could see the axes and knives he was used to seeing on Tchinchura and now Deslo hanging from all of their belts. They were all armed like warriors, even down to the very young, for some of the children Kaden could see were likely only six or seven years old.

And yet, if the appearance of the Amhuru was intimidating, their welcome to Azandalir could not have been warmer. D'Sarza welcomed them all onboard, and Kaden thought that for the first time since he had met her, the captain seemed overmatched by the situation and more than a little at loss for words. Still, Tchinchura stepped forward and was greeted warmly by all the Amhuru, who then moved quickly past him to greet the rest of them too, treating all men and women alike with courtesy and respect, down to the youngest member of D'Sarza's crew.

Kaden and Deslo received special honor from every Amhuru who greeted them, for as Tchinchura had told them, in those instances when apprentices were brought in from the outside world, the first visit to Azandalir was regarded as a significant occasion. Yes, there would be grave councils and difficult decisions ahead, but tonight would be a night of feasting, for not only had one of the original fragments of the Golden Cord returned to Azandalir, but two new apprentices had come home with it.

"All things in their season," Tchinchura had said a few days before when he explained this to Kaden. "Especially in dark times, we must celebrate when we have cause, or else we will be tempted to forget that Kalos is always good, even if we are not."

As the party from *The Sorry Rogue* disembarked and followed their Amhuru hosts across the soft, grassy ground toward the giant trees, Kaden, Nara, and Deslo fell in alongside Tchinchura as they walked. Passing beneath the great canopy of leaves of the nearest tree, Deslo couldn't contain his wonder. "It's so big."

"And very old," Tchinchura said. "These are Talathorne Trees, and they are as old as Azandalir itself."

Kaden felt stunned. "These trees are almost a thousand years old?"

"Yes," Tchinchura said.

"Remarkable," Kaden whispered, and they walked on for a moment in silence.

When at last Nara broke that silence, it was not about the trees that she spoke. "Do only the male Amhuru roam, offering their services to the places they visit, or do the women do that too sometimes?"

"Only the men," Tchinchura said. "Keeping the original fragments apart is our burden to bear."

"It must be very hard," Nara said. "Being apart, I mean, the husbands and the wives. Can they not roam together?"

"When Amhuru are married, they are excused from their other duties among us for a year and a day," Tchinchura answered. "When that year is up, the men take up again their place in the rotation of our travels, and though they are gone a long time when it is their turn, they can also be home for a long time when they return.

"As for the women, they have an equally important job to do—they protect Azandalir and provide stability for our children. Many wives would indeed travel with their husbands if they could, but it is better for the children not to be scattered from all others of our kind."

"But isn't it hard?" Nara persisted.

"Yes," Tchinchura said, "it is hard. But it is the sacrifice we make to honor the charge that Kalos gave us. It is an imperfect system, but we have created something of an enduring home without becoming entirely nomadic, something of a family and community without becoming entirely disconnected."

"What about you, Tchinchura," Kaden said, "and the others who bear original fragments? You can't all be home at the same time, and it seems like from the tales you tell, you are rarely here."

"Usually, those who bear the original fragments are not married," Tchinchura said. "They are chosen from among the older, seasoned Amhuru, and they are generally either men whose children have grown or widowers who have lost their wives, like me."

Tchinchura glanced up at the majestic Talathorne tree above them, at the thick blanket of leaves that shaded them from the bright sunlight, and then continued on without a word. Kaden reached over and took Nara's hand as they followed him through the wood in silence.

Beyond the Talathorne trees an open grassland lay, and from what Tchinchura had told Kaden, he knew much of the interior of Azandalir was dominated by this plain. The grass was almost waist high and bent in the steady breeze blowing through it, and the party of Amhuru and their visitors moved along, heading farther into the island.

Before long, they could make out the outline of buildings ahead, and as they drew nearer, Kaden noticed that most of them were quite peculiar. The first thing he noticed was that they all seemed to be built on stilts, so that the bottom of each were some four or more feet up off the ground and had to be accessed by stairs or ladders. The next thing Kaden noticed was that the walls of most of houses seemed to be made of a material not unlike the thick canvas of the sails on *The Sorry Rogue.* Some of these walls were in fact rolled up and tied at the top, so that the large room inside was open to the world.

Kaden could see the appeal of the canvas walls. On the one hand, it was a temperate climate and a close community, and during the day in good weather, opening the house to air it out would be quite advantageous. On the other, the walls could always be let down at night for privacy or in a storm for shelter from rain. It seemed somehow appropriate, and Kaden smiled to himself at the thought of half a dozen Amhuru sitting cross-legged on the floor in one of these open houses as the sun was setting, saying things like, "Tell, me, what did you see?" to one another as they discussed their day.

The stilts, though, were not as easy for him to understand. Such a device would make sense for a village by a river or water source that had a tendency to flood, but they were a good distance from the lagoon, and Kaden saw no evidence of a river or stream whose rising tide would threaten this place. As the tall grass thinned out and gave way to the large, open clearing in which the houses were built, Kaden asked Tchinchura about the stilts.

"The whole island inside the cliffs and high places that ring it forms a basin that lies just a few feet above sea level," Tchinchura said. "When the heavy rains come, the waters can fill the basin, but rarely more than a foot or two, until the water seeps back into the sea."

Walking among the houses, Kaden was struck by their simplicity. Inside were mats for sleeping and implements for working and cooking, but few other possessions. As they passed buildings that were constructed without the canvas walls, Tchinchura would explain their purposes, and many of them were essentially storage units for the things the Amhuru held in common, like their farming implements and the larger tools they used for construction and so forth.

The settlement extended further than Kaden had first thought, and as they made their way through it, more and more Amhuru came out of their houses to join the crowd, until at last they found themselves in a large open circle at the heart of it. There, the crowd that had been gathering began almost immediately to set to work preparing for the feast. Tables were produced from somewhere, and lots of them, strong and sturdy and placed in long rows side by side. The tables were soon covered not only with platters of fruits and vegetables and loaves of bread but with bunches of wildflowers to provide splashes of color and fragrant scents.

Not one but two great fires were started, and over both large boars were soon roasting, and soon the more subtle smells of the flowers and fruits and breads were superseded by that one, stronger scent of the cooking boars. Kaden inhaled deeply, thinking of the dried meats, fish, and other rations that were standard on *The Sorry Rogue*. He was going to enjoy this meal.

And then the music began. It started with the drums, deep and rhythmic, pounding out a beat that was at first slow and steady, but which grew more complicated and louder. To the deep drums was added a higher percussion, and when Kaden looked, it seemed that this sound came from a few Amhuru drumming on long cylinders that might have been hollowed logs polished or painted with some shiny coat. And then over these beats, the other instruments joined in, playing a melody that made even Kaden's feet want to move.

Kaden wasn't sure how to describe that melody. It was festive, even joyful, and yet there was something in it, a current beneath the surface, that seemed wistful, perhaps even sad. He decided, in the end, that the best word for it was longing—the music was full of longing.

And as the meat cooked, the people danced. The Amhuru danced, the crew and passengers of *The Sorry Rogue* danced, even—and perhaps especially—the children danced. Kaden and Nara laughed as they watched Deslo and Olli get pulled into a cluster of teenage Amhuru. Kaden didn't think Deslo had ever danced in his life, unless perhaps he had done so as a child at some festive occasion Kaden could not remember. Whether he had or not, he danced now. And he and Nara exchanged looks full of knowing when they noticed he seemed often to be dancing near a pretty Amhuru girl, perhaps a year or two older than Deslo, with long golden hair and those clear, striking golden eyes.

The sun was setting when the meal was at last ready, and the sound of music was replaced by the sound of talking and laughing, as the tables filled and the feast was eaten. It was then that Tchinchura introduced Kaden and Nara to Zangira's wife, Alayna, and they learned that she and Zangira had two children, a boy a little younger than Deslo named Trabor, and a girl a few years older, Shaline—the same girl Deslo had been dancing with just before supper.

As they sat together and ate, they talked quite naturally of Zangira and of meeting him in Barra-Dohn, but when things drifted toward the difficult things that had happened there and since, even Kaden and Nara instinctively steered away. It was as Tchinchura had said it would be, a time for celebrating and for remembering that Kalos was good, and that life was good. The time for darker things, for harder things, would come. The time for facing and discussing those things would also come, but it wasn't now.

After the dinner had been eaten, as the firelight from the two great fires illuminated the darkness, the music returned. This time, though, the dancing gave way to singing, and now the melodies, though equally full of longing, had somehow become inverted. They were not the festive, uptempo songs with an undercurrent of sadness to which they had danced; they were slower, sadder tunes with an undercurrent of joy.

Kaden did not know the songs, but he listened with pleasure as the Amhuru sang. It struck him as they sang that he was listening not to music that was sad so much as he was listening to music that was true. They were the songs of a hard people who had been given a hard task that they had faithfully performed for a thousand years. They were songs born of difficulty, laced with hope and trust.

The evening grew late, and the fires and the music died down, and eventually they were led to houses where they could sleep. It didn't take long for Deslo to fall asleep, for soon Kaden could hear the boy's rhythmic breathing become soft half-snores across the room. Nara was not asleep, though, and Kaden thought he could almost hear the silent wheels turning in her mind.

"What is it?" he whispered as he stroked her hair in the dark.

"It's a hard life," she said. "Isn't it?"

"Yes."

"And yet they seem so happy," Nara said. "Or perhaps content, more than happy."

"Maybe difficulty can be endured when you know you have been called to a high and noble calling," Kaden suggested.

"Maybe so."

They lay in silence for a moment, and then Kaden added, "We may have our own difficult choice to make before long."

"I know," Nara said. She put her arm across him and leaned her head on his chest. Kaden understood. Tonight was not the night for that, either. It, also, could wait.

22

A Place to Belong

Olli sat on one of the long tables around which they had feasted the night before, her legs drawn up under her chin as she hugged them tight. It was no longer dark, but the morning sun had not yet risen above the high ridges that circled the island. She wasn't the only one up, as she'd seen a handful of Amhuru going here and there about their business, but the morning was quiet and she was enjoying the peace.

For her the celebration of the night before—the food and the singing and the dancing—had been a thing of wide-eyed wonder almost as much as standing out in the light and heat of the afternoon sun without fear of the gorgaal. She had never seen something like that before, let alone been a part of it. So much mirth and so much joy—it was almost incomprehensible.

She understood, of course, and did not blame her people. They had lived a hard life in the caves, where reasons to celebrate, not to mention adequate provisions for it, were in short supply. She wondered if they had been a people of feasting and dancing before the gorgaal came. Had they known this kind of happiness? And if they had, what had it been like to lose it?

"Good morning."

She turned to see Tchinchura walking quietly toward her, and said, "Good morning, Tchinchura."

"I hope you slept well," he said.

"Like the dead—once I got used to not rocking back and forth in my bed."

He smiled. "Yes, welcome ashore, sailor. May I sit?"

"Of course," she said. "Please do."

"You looked deep in thought," he said, sitting down next to her. "I did not want to interrupt you if you desired to be left alone, but on the other hand, I thought I might offer you my company, since it is early yet and I suspect many of our companions will not be up for some time after last night's festivities."

"Your offer is welcome," she said, and for a moment they sat in the quiet morning in silence. Then a bird with an unfamiliar but pretty call that Olli did not recognize sang in the distance, as though from somewhere amid the high grass that surrounded the large clearing in all directions. As that call died down, another took it up, and then another.

"I always know I'm home when I wake up on my first morning back and hear the call of the *mirimae.* They're a little bit of a nuisance, really, but I love how they sing." Tchinchura had a twinkle in his eye as he listened.

"Is it hard to be away so much?" Olli asked.

"It is very hard," Tchinchura said, and though Olli knew him to be candid, the frankness of this admission surprised her somewhat.

"Can you at least stay awhile, now that you're here?"

"That will be decided soon, I think," Tchinchura said, "but I think not. Indeed, I suspect that I am soon to begin a journey from which I will not return."

Again his frankness took her aback, and when she glanced sideways at him, she did not see an expression to match the dour prophecy he had just uttered. Instead, he sat still and upright, gazing thoughtfully into the distance. She didn't know what to say in response, so she just gazed ahead thoughtfully too.

She wasn't completely oblivious to her surroundings, and she had realized over time that something serious was up amongst the Amhuru, even though they didn't share their councils with her. Even Nara, who seemed happy to discuss almost anything with her quite freely, shied away from the deeper matters that concerned her husband and Tchinchura. She knew, of course, that it involved this Jin Dara person who had somehow created the gorgaal, who was responsible for the deep suffering of her people. She knew this, and it was enough of a cord to tie her to them for as long as they would have her.

And suddenly, it was there, not the tease of an idea as yet cloudy and unformed as it had been the previous night, but a startling revelation, whole and complete. She turned to Tchinchura and blurted out, "There are female Amhuru."

That interrupted his reverie, and Tchinchura laughed as he turned to face Olli. "Yes, there are."

She felt self-conscious and wondered if she was blushing, but she was committed now. No turning back. She pressed on. "I hadn't realized that women could be Amhuru. I didn't even really know about Amhuru until I met you."

"Perfectly understandable," Tchinchura said, with another twinkle in his eye. Those golden eyes sometimes felt so searching, and she was finding it harder to say what she wanted to say than she had thought it would be.

"Speak freely, Olli," he went on. "You are safe and among friends here."

It was all the encouragement she needed. "I want to be an Amhuru. I mean, I know Kaden and Deslo are apprentices, and I was wondering how I can become one, too."

Now that she'd said it out loud to Tchinchura, she was full of misgivings. Not about her desire to be an apprentice, but it felt so presumptuous just to say it, as though she was somehow worthy of it. She wondered what Tchinchura must think. For his part, he sat looking at her, and she thought that maybe she saw in those golden eyes a hint of the sadness that she had looked for earlier when he was talking about his possible fate. She was on the verge of apologizing or even backtracking when Tchinchura spoke.

"It is a difficult, even if an honorable choice, Olli. You should know that, first and foremost. It always has been, and in these days, it is even more so."

"I am used to difficult things," Olli said, regaining her confidence a bit.

He nodded in agreement. "I know. And it may be that no matter what we do, a difficult future lies ahead for everyone. But whatever uncertainty there is for the world, I think I can guarantee that this road will be difficult, even beyond what you have so far endured."

"I am not afraid."

"I have seen your courage firsthand, so I believe you." He had been watching her as they spoke, but now he turned back to the houses that surrounded them and said, "You want vengeance against the one who made the gorgaal."

"Is that wrong?" Olli said, wincing a bit at the defensiveness in her voice. "Isn't it all right to want justice? To want wrongs to be righted?"

"Seeking justice is indeed a noble pursuit," Tchinchura said, "but justice and vengeance are not quite the same thing, and we are all capable of self-deception when it comes to what we really want and why we want it."

"Is that a no?" Olli said, feeling like she was losing a dream that she had only just realized she had.

"It is not," Tchinchura said.

"So you'll consider it?"

"I will consider it," he said, "although it isn't entirely up to me. I am suggesting, though, that you need to consider it. For instance, do you understand that traditionally, our women have dedicated themselves to training our young and defending Azandalir?"

Olli thought about this. "You mean they don't travel like you do? I couldn't go with you when you leave?"

It was Tchinchura's turn to think. He leaned forward, appearing to study the ground before them. "We are entering an unprecedented time, Olli. I can't be sure of what will be required of any Amhuru. I think I see my own road, but even that is unclear. I just wanted you to see that this is a decision you are not yet ready to make. There is more to know and consider."

"But we can talk about it? And maybe figure out if I can come with you before I have to decide?"

"We can talk about it," Tchinchura said. "And, perhaps, we may figure out what becoming an Amhuru apprentice might mean specifically for you."

Olli started to nod in appreciation, but Tchinchura hastened on, raising his hand as though to forestall her. "If you decide to become an Amhuru, Olli, you will have to do so knowing that every Amhuru accepts a higher authority than her own desires."

He did not say this harshly, but the words stung, and for a moment she considered defending herself. She caught herself, though, and did not. Instead, she added, "There's another reason why I want to be an apprentice, Tchinchura."

"What is that?"

"I've left my home and my people. I no longer have a place where I belong. I thought maybe *The Sorry Rogue* and the people on it could be that place."

"And maybe they will be, though again, the road ahead is unclear to me. They may have a different path than I do, so even if you became an apprentice and were granted permission to leave Azandalir, you might have to make a difficult choice."

"I understand," she said.

Tchinchura rose and stretched. "I cannot say when we will have a chance to speak further about this, Olli, but we will. I won't forget what you have said."

"Thanks," Olli said. "And not just for this, Tchinchura. For everything."

"You are welcome," he said, and as he did, the song of the *mirimae* broke out once more in the still quiet morning.

They both smiled at the sound, and she suddenly stood and gave Tchinchura a big hug and a gentle kiss on his cheek.

For the first time since she had met him, he looked surprised.

She smiled and said, "Welcome home."

Deslo approached Kaden slowly, glancing back over his shoulder at Shaline and Trabor. Shaline's long golden hair framed her light brown face, and her golden eyes studied him as he walked. He wished he could read her expression more clearly, but when she broke into a wide and beautiful smile, he smiled too and turned back toward his father.

"Good morning, Deslo," Kaden said, smiling himself as he glanced over Deslo's shoulder at Zangira's children.

"Morning," Deslo said, and he looked around for his mother, thinking maybe it would be better to talk to her.

"She's with some of the Amhuru women, helping them make bread or something," Kaden said, seeming to read Deslo's mind.

"Oh," Deslo said. He resisted the temptation to look back over his shoulder at Shaline and Trabor. There was nothing for it; he'd need to ask his father. "Shaline and Trabor want to show me around the island. We might be gone all day. Is that all right?"

"I don't see why not," Kaden said.

"Really?" Deslo said. "You don't need me to hang around, in case Tchinchura wants to talk about stuff?"

"It's all right, Deslo," Kaden said, placing his hand on his son's shoulder. "Remember, everyone's an Amhuru here, so things are a little different than on *The Sorry Rogue*. In other words, it's not just Tchinchura conferring with us."

"I know," Deslo said, though admittedly, he hadn't quite considered this fact.

"Anyway," Kaden said, "even if this council of elders that Tchinchura talks about meets today, I'm not sure either of us will be included, so that shouldn't keep you from going with your friends. Go, have fun."

"Thanks," Deslo said. "Shaline said we should be back around supper, so I'll see you later."

Kaden smiled again and waved as Deslo turned and walked back to Shaline and Trabor.

Trabor was a thin, wiry boy, just a month younger than Deslo, as Deslo had discovered while they were talking last night. Even though it had been a while since he had last seen Zangira, Deslo thought Trabor bore a strong resemblance to his father.

Shaline, who to Deslo looked nothing like Zangira, was almost two years older than he was, having recently celebrated her fifteenth birthday. But, unlike Olli, who obviously thought of him as a "kid," Shaline had been friendly and warm from the first moment they had met. So, Deslo was excited, both about exploring Azandalir and about spending time with two Amhuru his own age who treated him like a peer.

"He says it's fine," Deslo said as he approached them.

"Good, then we're set," Shaline said. "Though perhaps we should see if your friend Olli wants to come with us?"

"Oh," Deslo said, "I doubt she'd be interested."

Shaline looked at him, perhaps a little curiously. "Really? Why not?"

Deslo scratched his head and searched for a compelling answer, but failing to find one, he simply offered, "She spent most of her time onboard our ship with my mother and the other, older women. She'll probably want to spend the day with them."

"I see," Shaline said, and for a moment Deslo thought that might be the end of that, but then she said, "Still, we should at least ask, shouldn't we? She can always say no, and I'd hate for her to feel left out."

"Yes, of course," Deslo agreed, since he didn't see what else he could do.

They did not have to look long before they found her, and Deslo felt somewhat vindicated that she was indeed, with his mother and some of the other Amhuru women, working alongside them. He hung back with Trabor as Shaline approached and leaned down to speak to Olli. He could not hear the exchange, but he didn't need to. He could see Olli's reaction, and Nara's smile as she shooed her away. He could imagine his mother insisting they'd be fine without her, that she should go have fun. And so he was not surprised when both Shaline and Olli returned. Shaline flashed him a terrific smile, which helped him not to feel too glum about it. Perhaps having Olli along wouldn't be all bad.

As they left the circle of Amhuru women behind, moving out once more into the grasslands, Shaline explained that the island of Azandalir, though not a perfect circle, was nevertheless pretty close. What's more, the considerable power of the fragments of the Golden Cord had been brought to bear in shaping and structuring certain elements of the island, which helped account for its oddly symmetrical nature. The Amhuru lived almost exactly in the island's center, and equidistant from their dwellings there, at the four points of the compass around the island's edge, lay the other places worth seeing.

To the east lay the lagoon and the tunnel through which ships entered and exited it, but since they had seen this already, it was the one side of the island they wouldn't be seeing today. Instead, they would head due north, to a place that Shaline referred to as the Temple, and from there they would move southwest around the outside, stopping to see the Seat of Judgement on the west side on their way to the Springs to the south. Deslo wasn't sure how exciting any of these places would actually be, but if going to see them meant spending the day with Shaline, that was all right with him.

As they walked through the thick grassland, Deslo suddenly wondered why they should bother to push through it, when they could walk over it. He stopped, bent over, and rubbed his feet on the Zerura on his left bicep and leapt up onto the Arua. "Come on," he called to the others as he jogged above the top of the tall grass. "Let's run!"

"Hold on, Deslo," Shaline called back to him, and her tone, though not angry or emotional, was strangely insistent. He stopped.

Turning, he saw Shaline and Trabor standing on either side of Olli, and Deslo knew without being told why Shaline had called to him. Of course, that didn't stop her from telling him anyway.

"Since we have no meridium-soled shoes for Olli, I think we should stick to the ground, don't you?"

"Yes, of course," Deslo said, stepping down off the Arua, trying hard not to sound sheepish or look stupid but fearing he failed miserably at both.

Even though no more was said about it, Deslo fell silent and gradually dropped back a little behind the group as they continued on their way. Trabor, noticing he was lagging a bit, dropped back too, so before long the two girls were moving together up ahead while the two boys followed some ten or fifteen yards behind.

As they passed through the grasslands, heading north, Deslo noticed Trabor glancing back and forth between Olli and the bright blue sky above her. Trabor saw Deslo watching him and smiled, but it wasn't the wide, happy smile he shared with his sister. It was restrained, subdued.

"It must have been very hard for her," Trabor said, and then he added, as though he thought perhaps his words needed clarification, "Living in caves and only being able to come out at night."

"Yes, I'm sure it was," Deslo said, and he glanced up at the clear blue sky too, almost despite himself.

"I wonder what this feels like for her, walking out in the open. As much as I'm sure she loves to be free, it could be overwhelming. So much space, after so little."

"She's been outside a lot on the ship," Deslo said. "I bet she's fine."

"True," Trabor said, "but a ship is itself confined. She's on land somewhere other than her island for the first time, surrounded by colors and space and all kinds of things she's either never seen at all or only in the dark. I am glad for her, but I feel for her too."

Deslo didn't have anything to say to that, so he nodded, feeling he had to acknowledge Trabor in some way. Trabor might have a point, but Deslo didn't quite feel ready to give Olli a pass for her aloofness and condescension on the journey here. So, he searched for a way to change the subject. Trabor, though, spoke first.

"It must be nice for you to have her along, anyhow," he said. "I bet it was lonely before she showed up."

"It wasn't too bad," Deslo shrugged. "Besides, though we are close in age, she doesn't really see it that way."

"I understand. Neither does Shaline," Trabor said, slapping Deslo on the back. "It doesn't matter that I'm of age now—I'm still just her little brother."

Trabor smiled, and now it was the face splitting, ear-to-ear smile that made Deslo think of Shaline. He looked at her, walking beside Olli, her shoulder-length, golden hair shining in the sun. He didn't want to be walking behind her; he wanted to be walking with her.

"Let's catch up to the girls," Deslo said, and he quickened his step.

When they did, Deslo fell in beside Shaline, and Trabor fell in beside Olli, and Deslo quietly blessed him for that, for as Trabor talked steadily to Olli, Shaline was now free to converse with Deslo. Unfortunately, Deslo suddenly found himself almost completely unable to think of anything interesting to say. He offered various remarks about the pleasantness of the day and the scratchiness of the grass and so forth, and Shaline entertained every observation, no matter how innocuous or vapid, quite seriously, until Deslo was torn between shutting up to save himself further embarrassment and wanting to say anything that came to mind just to hear her continue to respond with such warmth, patience, and kindness.

Just when Deslo had decided that perhaps shutting up would be his best bet, Shaline stopped and pointed excitedly. "Do you see?"

Deslo, who had been so absorbed with his conversational struggles, looked up and surveyed the world around him for the first time in quite a while. When he did he saw that the towering ridge that rimmed the entire island was not very far off, but obscuring the portion directly ahead were some more of those enormous talathorne trees.

At first it looked like there were just two of them, a little bit apart, but as Deslo looked more closely, he realized there were actually several, but they had been planted in two lines, parallel to each other, running toward the great wall of rock. Their enormous branches high off the ground created a canopy over a wide and resplendent avenue, but the wall of rock at the far end of the avenue was out of Deslo's sight.

"It's beautiful, isn't it?" Shaline said, grinning at him.

"The trees?" Deslo said, a little uncertain.

"No, the Temple," Shaline replied, then she turned to him and put her hand on his upper arm. "I'm sorry, Deslo, I forgot for a moment that you have only worn your fragment a short while. Of course you cannot see the Temple yet. That was thoughtless of me."

"Really, don't worry about it, Shaline, it's not important," Deslo murmured. "I did the same thing with Olli and the Arua field earlier. No harm done."

"The good news is," Shaline said, letting go of Deslo's arm and turning back toward the avenue of talathorne trees ahead, "that we are almost there, and when you do get your first glimpse, I assure you, it will be worth it."

"I'm sure it will," Deslo said, and they started walking again. Shaline's excitement had sparked Deslo's curiosity, and for the first time since setting out, he found that he was looking forward to more than just spending time with Shaline.

And yet the memory of her recent touch lingered, and as he walked beside her, eager to see what lay at the other end of the majestic avenue of talathorne trees, he found a different curiosity at work inside him, just as strong, if not stronger. He wondered what it would feel like to reach over and take hold of her hand, and to feel those fingers in his.

Maybe, if they stayed in Azalandir long enough, he'd have a chance to find out.

23

The Temple

Shaline was right. Deslo's first glimpse of the Temple was worth it.

Stepping from the open grasslands into the avenue that ran beneath the talathorne trees, they had stepped from sunlight into shadow, and whether the temperature actually changed or it was just a trick of the mind, Deslo thought it felt cooler. The tall grass disappeared here, too, so their way had become easier as they walked on the soft, springy turf that lined the avenue.

For Deslo, though, his attention was fixed not on the avenue of trees but on what lay beyond it. He knew he couldn't expect his senses to match those of someone who had worn Zerura almost since birth, after only a few months of bearing it himself, but he felt as though Shaline was waiting for his reaction to the Temple, and as much as anything else, he didn't want to disappoint her.

And yet, for all that, when he actually did catch his first glimpse of the Temple, all thought of Shaline and what she might be thinking slipped away. He had been looking for a building at the end of the avenue, but all he could make out at first was open space beyond the last of the talathorne trees, where the bright sunshine illuminated the ground in stark contrast to the shade they were walking in. And then, as he looked further ahead, beyond the empty space, he saw and understood.

The wall of stone that rose to form the high ridge running in a ring all the way round the island had itself been carefully and meticulously carved like the front of a great building. As they drew closer, Deslo began to appreciate the magnitude of the project. The carving didn't go all the way up to the very top of the ridge. In fact, a very clear delineation between the front façade of the Temple and the rest of the stone wall had been made around both edges and the top, and the contrast of the rough, natural stone and the smooth, ornate carvings was striking.

As they moved out beyond the end of the avenue into the open space between the trees and the Temple, Deslo turned to Shaline. "You're right. It's pretty fantastic."

"It sure is," Olli said, and Deslo could hear the awe in her voice.

He glanced over at her as she stood, gazing in wonder at the Temple, and he thought about all the great buildings of Barra-Dohn that he had known as a child, and about how she'd never seen anything like them. So if this towering wall of carved rock was visually striking to him, what must it be like for her, who had never seen the Palace, or the Academy, or . . .

That was it. The Academy. Deslo turned back to look at the Temple. The front of the Temple looked a lot like the Academy, though of course there were differences since the Academy was—or had been, anyway—a free-standing building. The columns and steps and so forth had created a certain depth, or three-dimensional feel, at the Academy that was lacking here, though whoever had carved this had worked hard to create, if not real steps and columns and so on, at least the illusion of them. Still, the resemblance was uncanny, right down to the enormous doors in the center at the base.

"It looks just like the Academy of Barra-Dohn," Deslo said, turning from Olli to Shaline. "A building from my home."

"Does it surprise you, Deslo," Shaline asked, "that this place would remind you of your home? After all, the Amhuru are originally from your city, even if it was called Zeru-Shalim back then."

"That's it," Deslo said as he looked back at the massive frontpiece carved into the side of the great wall of stone. "When I was a kid in Barra-Dohn, the building at home that looks like this wasn't a Temple at all. It was called the Academy and was used for scientific experiments and stuff. I didn't go there much. Rika, one of our party, would know more. She worked there."

Shaline didn't say anything to this, nor did Trabor, though a look full of meaning Deslo did not understand passed between them. Shaline saw Deslo watching them, and she said, "We do not wish to offend, but you see, it seems to us like a bold and not altogether wise move to use the great Temple of Kalos for such things."

"I can't say for sure the building I'm thinking of—"

"You are describing the Temple of Kalos, Deslo. My father said he saw the inside of it when he was in Barra-Dohn."

"Then it must have been," Deslo said, looking back at the wonder before him. "So, when the first Amhuru came here, they did this to remind them of home."

"They did," Shaline said, "and from an early age, we are brought here to be instructed both in our own personal history and also in the worship of Kalos."

"Maybe going inside will be a bit like going into your past too," Trabor said.

"Maybe so," Deslo agreed.

"Let's go take a look," Shaline said as they started walking toward the entrance to the Temple.

They approached the enormous front doors, though Deslo supposed it was more accurately a front doorway, since upon closer inspection there were no doors—just a large open space. Trabor took up a large pitcher and stepped inside into the dark, and a moment later light sprang out from two large lamps on either side of the doorway, inside. Shaline led Deslo and Olli in after him.

Deslo glanced at the lamps Trabor had lit with the pitcher and tried again to catch the scent of the oil he had used. He had been so used to the smell of sage oil back home that he had associated it with all lamps like these, and yet through his travels he had come to realize that different places used different plant oils and saps to mix with meridium and make both light and heat. But, when this oil had been produced to light the lamps the previous night at the feast, he had been unable to place the slight scent of this particular oil, and he still couldn't.

"What is that oil that you are using, Trabor?" he asked.

"It's a wild olive oil," Trabor said. "We have a large olive vineyard between the center of the island and the Seat of Judgement."

Deslo had eaten olives before, though he didn't especially like them. It seemed strange to him that the oil that fueled the lights of the Amhuru could come from such things, but he supposed the Amhuru might think the same about the scraggly sage bushes that had grown in the desert near Barra-Dohn.

Trabor, meanwhile, had produced handheld lamps they could carry with them, and so Shaline had started moving forward again. As they walked, Deslo was struck by the vast, openness of the space they were in. The light of their lamps cast shadows for some distance, but he could not clearly make out the wall ahead, only those on either side, and the echoes of their footsteps reinforced the idea that this main chamber was substantial.

Other than those footsteps, though, they walked in silence. Shaline had not said they couldn't talk here, and her comment about coming to learn about both Kalos and their past suggested the Amhuru had classes of a sort in the Temple. And yet Deslo felt somehow that he ought to keep silence and let Shaline or Trabor be the first to speak. It just seemed right to do so. He didn't know if Olli felt the same way, but she was silent too, and together they walked further into the cavernous room.

The far wall soon came into view, and Deslo was struck by the fact that there was an enormous figure painted on it. It was a picture of a man, as vast in proportion as the Temple itself, standing in the picture on a slightly raised dais of some kind. Deslo craned his neck up toward the roof of the great room to see the man's face, but he couldn't. He could only make out the picture from the man's feet up to his shoulders.

And then he saw why. The place where the man's neck would have begun was also the place where the wall joined the ceiling of the Temple. He could not see the man's neck or head because none had been painted. The figure merely stood on the dais, his enormous arms outstretched as though to welcome to the Temple whomever might enter and approach—but with what look upon his face? The absence was curious, but still Deslo waited for someone else to speak first.

Shaline came to a stop at the foot of some stairs that led up to a real dais, not a painted one, and she turned to Deslo and Olli and said, "Welcome to the Temple of Kalos."

"Is that Kalos?" Deslo asked, pointing to the picture of the man on the wall before them.

"It is symbolic of Kalos," Shaline said, "since Kalos is often described with words that picture him as a man, although of course, he isn't."

"What do you mean?" Olli spoke for the first time, and Deslo heard in her voice the same puzzlement that would have been in his own had he asked first.

"I mean, we might speak of the mighty hand of Kalos or of the long reach of His arm, even though we do not really believe He has a body with arms and hands."

"That's kind of strange," Deslo said.

"Is it?" Shaline said. "It is so natural for me to do so that I hadn't considered it might be odd to say so. I think it fairly understandable that men would describe Kalos with terms that are familiar to them."

"I guess," Deslo said. "But if they were trying to picture Kalos in a way that was familiar, why didn't they give Him a head? That's kind of strange, too."

"Ah yes," Shaline said. "Again, I am so used to it that it isn't odd to me."

"The headless guy isn't weird to you?"

The sound of Olli saying something that essentially agreed with what he had already said caught Deslo somewhat off guard, and he looked at her. She was holding her lamp up in front of her, peering up at the picture of Kalos, oblivious to the fact that all three of the others were now looking at her. Whatever Shaline thought about what Olli had just said, she answered her as patiently as she had answered Deslo.

"No, the picture isn't strange to me," she said, "because I have been taught from an early age that this picture is only meant to be a symbol. We do not picture His face and head, as a reminder that while He is a person, He is not a man."

"Though it is said," Trabor added, jumping in, "that in the days of peace, men will behold the face of Kalos."

"Yes," Shaline agreed, "that is true. But the days of peace have not yet come, and so we do not try to portray a face that no man has seen."

"The days of peace," Deslo said. "It doesn't seem like there will ever be peace."

"Sometimes it doesn't," Shaline agreed, "but we believe the days of peace will come. In fact, the word for peace in the old tongue is *shalim,* and our hope for it is so important to us that my parents named me Shaline for that reason."

"*Shalim* means peace?" Deslo said.

"Yes."

"Barra-Dohn was once Zeru-Shalim?"

"Yes," Shaline said. "The City of Life and Peace."

"Such a beautiful name," Olli said. "I wonder why they changed it."

They looked at Deslo, but he shrugged his shoulders. "I have no idea. That happened a long, long time before I was born."

But even as he said that, he had a memory of something his old tutor, Gamalian, had said to him once, only he couldn't quite recall it. He searched his mind, but it was no use. Whatever memory the name had evoked, it was gone, and left behind there was only a feeling of sadness for Gamalian, whose body had been left behind like so many others in the rubble of Barra-Dohn.

"Come," Shaline said, moving off toward one side of the Temple. "There is something else I'd like to show you before we head out for the Seat of Judgement."

Shaline headed toward the east side of the main room of the Temple, and Deslo was able to see as they walked another open doorway ahead of them—this one far more ordinary than the enormous doorway that led in from the outside—and beyond it, a smaller side chamber. At first glance this side chamber seemed quite ordinary and empty, but as they reached the open doorway, Deslo saw that it was neither.

Floating in the air, in the center of the room, moving rhythmically to a silent music that Deslo longed to hear but could not, were three strands of Zerura.

"Those aren't . . ." Deslo said, looking at Shaline and pointing through the open doorway. "They're not originals, are they?"

"No," Shaline said with a smile. "They are the only three duplicates of the three Northland fragments of the Golden Cord on this side of the Madri."

Deslo's head swiveled back to stare at the slender strands of Zerura dancing their ceaseless dance. "What are they here for? What is this place?"

"This is a replica of the Room of Life, the room in the great Temple of Kalos in Zeru-Shalim where the Golden Cord was kept after Kalos gave it as a gift to the king of that city. For centuries it stayed there, and Kalos blessed the city through it."

Shaline paused and Deslo glanced at her. She seemed to be deliberating.

"What is it, Shaline?"

Shaline's eyes darted quickly to Olli, so quickly that Deslo almost didn't notice. He didn't think Olli had seen, but even if she hadn't, Deslo had understood. He was an apprentice to the

Amhuru, while Olli was not. Although a friend, she was as yet an outsider. Perhaps they were straying near territory that Shaline was less comfortable talking about in front of her. But if Shaline had reservations about continuing her answer in front of Olli, it didn't show when she spoke.

"It's nothing," she said. "Only your first question, what are they here for, is a little more complicated than your second."

"You don't have to explain it," Deslo said. "I was just curious."

"Really, I don't mind," Shaline said. "But maybe we should start on our way to the Seat of Judgement, and I can explain as we walk?"

"Are we finished here?" Olli asked.

"There are other rooms," Trabor said. "But you have seen the main things."

They returned their handheld lamps to the place they were stored beside the front doorway, where the larger lamps were already beginning to fade, and then proceeded back outside into the midmorning sun. As they walked across the open space between the Temple and the avenue, Deslo looked back at the magnificent structure.

"I see now, Shaline, maybe a little better," he said, "about what you said before."

"What's that?" Shaline said, walking again beside him.

"Oh, just that to take a place—that place—after using it to house the Golden Cord and worship Kalos, and, you know, use it for something else . . ." Deslo searched for the right words. "I see how it would feel wrong, and maybe even be wrong."

"Yes," Shaline said, nodding gravely. "I am glad you can see that."

For the second time since coming to the Temple, Deslo had a sudden flash of memory, but this one wasn't partial or incomplete or elusive like the memory of Gamalian. This was full and complete and almost stopped him in his tracks.

He remembered the elderly Kalosene who had dared to interrupt his grandfather on the day of the anniversary celebration back home, the one that Marlo and Owenn said they had known and followed. He had come out of the crowd, right up to the giant statue of the craftsman who had discovered meridium, and he had spoken words that, as a boy, Deslo had not truly understood. In retrospect, as they fled as fugitives and exiles from Barra-Dohn, at least one part of that prophecy had made perfect sense to Deslo—the man's assertion that for the various failings of the city and its kings, a price must be paid.

Deslo didn't remember exactly how the Kalosene had put it that day, but as they left Barra-Dohn for the wider world, the failing of his city and its kings that had most concerned the young Deslo had been its treatment of Garranmere. He wouldn't have understood that the Kalosene would have also had in mind things like the transformation of the Temple of Kalos into the Academy. He wouldn't have understood the seriousness of such a thing, or that this also was something for which a price must be paid. He did see now.

"Well," he said as they approached the avenue, "the price for that, and for its many other failings, has been paid. The Academy, or Temple, lies in ruins now. Just like everything else in Barra-Dohn."

Shaline drew closer, and again he felt her hand on him as she reached up and gently squeezed his shoulder. He looked at her, and for a moment they walked along together, looking at one another, her hand lingering on his shoulder. There was sadness in her golden eyes, and sympathy, but Deslo thought maybe there was something more there, too, though he didn't know if he was just seeing it because he wanted to.

She dropped her hand and looked away as they passed under the Talathorne trees. "You asked what the replicas of the Northland fragments were doing in there," she said. "I'll give you the brief version."

"You? Be brief?" Trabor teased.

"There's no need to be brief," Olli said, sticking up for Shaline. "I'm sure we have plenty of time."

"We do," Shaline said, "but I'll be brief nonetheless. When the decision was made to divide the six fragments geographically, so that three would remain in the Northlands permanently, and three would remain in the Southlands, the Amhuru created the Madri."

"Created the Madri," Deslo said, echoing the words out loud. He knew this from stories Gamalian had told him and that Tchinchura had confirmed, but he never ceased to marvel at it.

"I'm sorry," Olli said, "I know this might seem stupid, but in my defense, remember what my life was like up until a few months ago . . ."

"Go on," Shaline said, trying to encourage Olli when she stopped, as though she was secondguessing her decision to speak.

"I've heard this Madri mentioned before, but I have no idea what it is. Could you explain it?"

"That makes perfect sense," Shaline said, as though Olli hadn't just asked a question that was for Deslo almost as strange as asking what meridium was or where one might find snow. It was a question a child might ask.

"The Madri is an invisible line," Shaline said, "that runs all the way around the world, dividing the Northlands and the Southlands. Anyone who crosses it gets very sick, for several days."

"And anyone crossing it wearing Zerura," Trabor said, "would get very, very sick—how sick no one really seems to know for sure."

"Why would anyone make that?" Olli asked, looking horrified. "It sounds terrible."

"It is meant to be."

"What my brother means," Shaline said, "is that the Madri was made to discourage travel, not all between the Northlands and Southlands necessarily, but certainly the travel of anyone bearing a fragment of the Golden Cord."

"Because Kalos said the six original fragments were supposed to be separated," Deslo added.

"And if crossing the Madri makes one deathly ill," Olli said, seeing the logic, "then hopefully that will help keep the fragments apart. The ones in the Northlands would stay in the Northlands, the ones in the Southlands in the Southlands."

"That's right," Shaline said. "The three replicas you just saw are a kind of warning system. Before the Madri was created, a single replica of each Southland fragment was given to the Amhuru charged with keeping the Northland three, and vice versa. I don't know exactly how it works, but if any of the Northland originals are brought across the Madri into the Southlands, then the corresponding replica in our Temple will cease moving and fall to the ground, inert. Then we would know that someone has done what is forbidden, and we could take whatever steps we would need to take if that happened."

"What steps are those?" Deslo asked.

"I don't know," Shaline said. "It has never happened."

24 

The Seat of Judgement

Almaren, the oldest Amhuru in Azandalir, and therefore the ranking elder, made his slow way toward Tchinchura. Though many of the signs of advanced age that plagued other people, like grey hair and wrinkled skin, did not show among the older Amhuru, Almaren's step had slowed since Tchinchura was here last. He took each step deliberately as he approached, as though desiring to be sure of each placement before lifting his other foot and moving it.

"Give me your arm, Tchinchura," he said as Tchinchura turned to walk beside him, "that I may lean upon you on the way."

Tchinchura extended his arm, and Almaren seized it firmly. Measured by that grasp, the strength in his hands was still there, whatever the situation with his feet.

"Tell me, Tchinchura," Almaren finally began, and he proceeded with the traditional question for an Amhuru who had just returned, "what have you seen?"

Tchinchura proceeded to tell his tale about their effort to track the Jin Dara's past, and how those efforts had finally led to the island where he had been born and raised under the name Dagin Orlas. He told about the island and its inhabitants, both the people who lived there in the caves and the creatures that had tormented them. He told of the manor house and the Jin Dara's cousin they had found there, of the replica of the stolen fragment they had recovered from him and now returned to Azandalir, and of the stories they had heard about young Dagin. And he spoke of what he had come to believe they must do in the wake of what he had learned.

When Tchinchura stopped speaking, there was silence and stillness, for Almaren had stopped walking, and Tchinchura stopped too. The elder Amhuru gazed out on the land ahead, where the tall, wild grassland gave way to the carefully cultivated olive vineyard. When at last he spoke, he still looked straight ahead.

"What you suggest is forbidden." His words were soft but firm, and he added, "But you know this already, of course."

"I do."

"And it does not give you pause?"

"Of course it does, Elder," Tchinchura said. "It troubles me greatly. Nevertheless, it is what I have come to you to recommend."

"You would ask the Council to violate its own law?"

"I would ask the Council to remember that it is *their* law," Tchinchura said. "This is not the law of Kalos, who neither made the Madri nor gave commands concerning it. We did. May we not violate the law we made when the same desire to keep the Golden Cord safe drives us, as it drove us to create the Madri and the law in the first place?"

"There is truth in what you say," Almaren said, as he turned at last and looked at Tchinchura. Tchinchura could see that Almaren was wrestling with his own heart. "It is ever the temptation of man to take his own word as law, and to replace, if not forget entirely, the laws of Kalos. We must remember the difference.

"And yet," Almaren continued, as he also started walking

again, "though our laws are not divine and therefore lack the same force, they reflect the best wisdom of our forefathers, and they should not be set aside lightly."

"I would never suggest it lightly—"

Tchinchura cut off when Almaren squeezed his arm and turned once more to look at him.

"I chose the wrong word, Tchinchura. I know you would never suggest this unless you firmly believed it was the only way. I only meant it is a very, very serious thing to suggest, and I know you are aware of that. I was speaking out loud to myself more than to you."

"Yes, Elder," Tchinchura said, and they started forward again. They were drawing near to the olive trees now, and the high grass gave way to the carefully cultivated soil in which they grew.

"You must rememeber, Tchinchura," Almaren said as they passed among the trees, "while you and your mission have been much on our minds, of course, we have not been wrestling with the situation as you have. The Council might need time to accept what you are suggesting, as indeed I imagine it took you some time to accept it as well."

"It is true that I resisted the idea as long as I could see other choices," Tchinchura said. "But once I knew all that I know now, it did not take me long to reach this conclusion."

"Still, the steps by which you reached this destination were gradual, as indeed they must be for the wise when they stand before momentous decisions."

"And if there is no time for gradual steps, Elder?" Tchinchura said, a tone of uncharacteristic doubt in his voice. "What do the wise do then?"

"They do what all men must do in such times, both the wise and the fool alike," Almaren said with a sigh. "The best that they can."

They walked for a while silently among the trees, and Almaren stopped beside one and with his free hand reached up and plucked a ripe olive, which he popped into his mouth. They stood, and Tchinchura waited, for he knew the elder was still considering what he had said, otherwise he would have suggested they head back already.

"And if the Council says yes, Tchinchura?" Almaren said. "You are prepared to undertake this journey?"

"Prepared?" Tchinchura said. "I cannot say that I am prepared. But I am willing."

Almaren patted Tchinchura's arm and nodded. "Let us turn back, Tchinchura. I have walked enough for now."

They turned and headed back the way they had come, and as they left the vineyard behind, Almaren gazed up into the clear blue sky. "If the Council agrees with you, and if you go, and if you surive the crossing . . . every Amhuru in the Northlands will know the ancient law has been broken."

"I know."

"They will almost certainly take up defensive positions to protect the three Northland fragments, and they will attack you on sight."

"I know."

"They will not ask why you have come, even though you are their brother, and you may never get a chance to explain. I know of no way to stop this."

"All these things I have considered, Elder," Tchinchura said, "and I would not do it if I could see a better way."

Almaren nodded, and they kept walking.

"If I can make contact and explain why I have come, without getting myself killed," Tchinchura said, "then, of course, I will do so. But even if I fall at the hands of my brothers, as long as the fragment I bear reaches them safely, then I will not have failed."

"But what if you fall without having a chance to explain why you have come? They will think you stole the fragment and betrayed your people. They would almost certainly try to bring it back here, back into danger."

"I will need to be ready for this," Tchinchura acknowledged. "Perhaps I should bear a letter from the Council that explains why

I have come, so that if I fall at their hands, they can find and read it and understand what I have done."

"We will consider it," Almaren said, "if, of course, we decide that you should go."

"Whatever the Council decides, and whatever happens to me," Tchinchura said, his voice hardening, "the Jin Dara—this Dagin Orlas—he must not get a third fragment. Having seen what I have seen, having been granted a glimpse into his heart by what he has made, I see that there is nothing he will not do."

"And he already has two fragments," Almaren muttered.

"Yes," Tchinchura said. "Kalos help us all."

Deslo and the others walked with the high rock wall on their right. It had been on their right the whole way from the Temple, of course, but now it loomed very close. For some reason, as he contemplated its magnitude, the rock wall suddenly reminded Deslo of the great walls of Garranmere. Sadness washed over him.

He didn't talk about it, and he wouldn't have admitted it to anyone, but sometimes in the dark, as he lay in bed, he still shed silent tears for Garranmere and for the girl he'd seen crushed in the streets there. In fact there had been a number of nights where he had dreamed of her. The dream was never exactly the same, but it was nevertheless the same dream. She was always buried, sometimes under rubble, sometimes in the earth, and even one time beneath a mountain of sand. Always he found himself desperate to get her out, to save her before she was crushed to death, before she suffocated, but he could never get there in time.

He had often wondered what her name had been, and what her life had been like before the army of Barra-Dohn came and sacked her city without cause or provocation. He didn't know, and he would never know—but something good had come from even that terrible day. As his father had taken his hand and led him away from her dead body, Deslo had pressed him that when he was king he would never do such a thing again. Kaden had agreed. He had made the promise, and Deslo had seen that he was serious. Even though Deslo had been young, he had known at that moment that his father was not like his grandfather, and that he would not rule like him.

Of course, Deslo had not known that the promise was unnecessary. Even as Kaden had made it, the Jin Dara had been within a few weeks of crushing Barra-Dohn. Neither his father nor he would ever rule it. The House of Omiir might have survived when they escaped the city's collapse, but Eirmon had been the last king of Barra-Dohn, and for all intents and purposes, the royal line had died with him. Deslo missed his home and often longed to see it again, but sometimes he wondered if it wasn't for the best that they had been cast out into the world. As a family they had lost their throne, but in the process, they had found each other and been spared the horrors of ruling from a throne.

Shaline veered inland, saying that the Seat of Judgement was best approached from the east, rather than the north. So they traveled in a long, gentle arc, at first away from the high rock wall and then gradually back toward it. As they did so, Deslo saw first the Seat of Judgement, but shortly thereafter the enormous painting on the rock face above and beyond it.

"I see why you wanted us to come from this direction," he said as they drew closer.

The Seat of Judgement was itself a fairly simple structure. A few stone steps led up to a dais of dressed stone, not unlike the one at the front of the main room of the Temple, except this one was larger, and a sizeable stone table sat in the center. Slender stone pillars ran around the dais, but there were no walls or roof. Even so, Deslo could see what looked to be large canvas curtains tied up at the top of the pillars and running along the stone beams the pillars supported.

Assuming this structure worked much like the open houses of the Amhuru themselves, Deslo imagined the canvas could be lowered to provide a break on the wind or to keep a driving rain out of the dais. He also imagined there must be a similar canvas covering that could be pulled across the top to serve as a roof, but he couldn't see from where they were standing just how it might work.

These things Deslo took in at a glance, but what truly mesmerized him was not the Seat of Judgement itself but the remarkable image visible above it. Six Amhuru men stood shoulder to shoulder, painted on the great rock wall. Their figures were almost as huge as the headless symbol of Kalos in the Temple, but not quite. Each of them had the golden eyes of an Amhuru, and each bore a piece of Zerura, though every one of them bore it in a different place.

One Amhuru bore the fragment on the left bicep, as Deslo did. Another bore it on the right forearm. Another on the right calf. Another on the left leg, just above the knee. One had it around the neck, like a collar, and the sixth wore it as a circlet on the brow, like a crown. All together, they were an impressive picture, their stern faces and penetrating gazes looking down upon the stone pavilion and the four life-sized figures who stood before it, looking up at them.

"They are the six brothers," Shaline said, "who fled Zeru-Shalim bearing the six fragments of the Golden Cord."

"Did they really wear their fragments in separate places like that?" Deslo asked.

"Yes, indeed," Shaline said. "As their descendants still do. You wear your fragment on the left bicep, as my father does and we do, because it was cut from the fragment that Tchinchura bears, which is and has always been worn there."

"Why?" Deslo asked.

"I cannot say," Shaline answered. "All I know is that it is so and has been from the first moment the Cord was divided. Each fragment chose its own home on the body of the brother who bore it. So it was, and so it is."

"Are the brothers grouped in any special way?" Olli asked, raising her hand to point toward the painting as she talked.

"The gap between the two in the middle seems a little larger than the gap between the others."

"You have a keen eye," Shaline said, but she turned toward Deslo, not Olli. "Can you figure out this mystery, Deslo?"

Deslo had been looking at Shaline, but he looked back up at the painting now. He could still her searching eyes upon him, though, and he very much didn't want to disappoint her.

"Tell me," Shaline added, "what do you see?"

"The Madri," Deslo said, giving his answer out loud even as it came to him. "We're facing due west. The three on the right, to the north, represent the three brothers who went to the Northlands, and the three on the left represent the three who stayed in the Southlands."

"Very good," Shaline said. "That is correct."

Deslo scanned the three brothers on the left. They bore fragments on the left bicep, right calf, and around the neck. He knew the fragment his grandfather had stolen had been worn around the right calf. That meant the fragment that the Jin Dara had worn when he came to Barra-Dohn had been the one around the neck. Now he had both, of course, and Deslo imagine a shadowy figure in his mind with a glowing band around both neck and calf, approaching through the darkness. He shuddered.

"Why is this place called the Seat of Judgement?" Olli asked, and at the sound of her voice, the image dissolved and the sudden shiver of terror that had swept over Deslo passed with it.

"This is where the Council meets," Trabor spoke up, "where they weigh all matters of significance and pass judgement."

"And the painting?" Olli said. "I mean, it's impressive, truly, but what's the connection to what happens here?"

"It is there as a reminder," Shaline said, "that the Council may bear in mind who we are and why we exist in the first place, in all that they decide and do."

"That's a serious reminder," Olli said.

"Yes it is," Shaline said. "We have been given a serious task, have we not?"

"I guess so," Olli agreed gravely.

They lingered on just a few moments before Shaline encouraged them that they should move on. The sun was high overhead, and they had some serious walking to do if they were to see the Springs and get back to the center of the island by nightfall.

The Springs, like the Temple and the Seat of Judgement, did not disappoint. The Springs themselves were an intricate series of terraced shelves and channels carved into the rocks on the southern wall of rock that protected Azandalir. The shelves were cut like long shallow bowls to catch water and the channels designed to guide the flow when the shelves overflowed. Gradually the whole system funneled down and fed a large basin of stone that the Amhuru had created to serve as an enormous cistern to store the water.

Though there was water in the cistern, the water level was several feet below the top of the basin and the shelves and channels above it were dry, as it had not rained in some time. Still, the rains were often very heavy when they came, and in a matter of hours, the Springs could be full to overflowing, filling the basin with ease. Shaline said she could remember a handful of times of drought when the Amhuru had been forced to ration water for a few days, but never a time of any serious concern about it, in large measure because the Amhuru possessed the ability and the means to summon rain if their lives were threatened by thirst.

On the rock walls to either side of the system of shelves and channels, a large assortment of scenes had been painted on the rock wall. Unlike the six brothers above the Seat of Judgement or the image of Kalos in the Temple, they were numerous and much smaller, so that the eye was pulled here and there from one to another. They were colorful and fascinating, as well as diverse in what they portrayed.

Though Deslo did not recognize all of the images, one grabbed his attention and held it for quite a while. There were grotesque and distorted creatures of great size lumbering beneath a crescent moon, and Deslo thought immediately of the Old Stories Gamalian had told him of the world before Kalos had placed Zerura in veins beneath the earth to create the Arua field, of a world where *jin dara*, or "dark things" had roamed the land. Gamalian had not believed the stories that he taught, of course, but the Amhuru did.

"Are these pictures taken from the Old Stories?"

"Yes," Shaline said. "We have painted these over the years to proclaim the truth of what Kalos has done, even as the world seems less and less willing to acknowledge it."

Deslo stood and stared, and he could have gone on staring for a long time, but Shaline and Trabor were moving down toward the basin, where a large number of empty water jars were clustered by its edge. He followed them down and helped Trabor to fill four of them. Shaline had mentioned that the responsibility for keeping the heart of Azandalir supplied with water fell to the young among the Amhuru, and that they'd be carrying water back from the Springs, so the task was not a surprise.

What was a surprise was the way Shaline and Trabor carried the water jars, balanced easily upon their heads. They both walked, one hand resting lightly on the side of the jar they each bore, and while Deslo waited for the jars to jostle and spill water over the sides and splash upon them, it didn't happen. He looked at Olli, who was carrying her jar like he was with both arms wrapped around it to hold it up, and when she looked at him, she did something he'd never seen her do before when she looked at him. She smiled.

"I don't think we'd better try that," she said softly, nodding toward the others.

"No, I guess not," he answered, thinking that Olli's smile was almost as nice as Shaline's.

Almost.

25

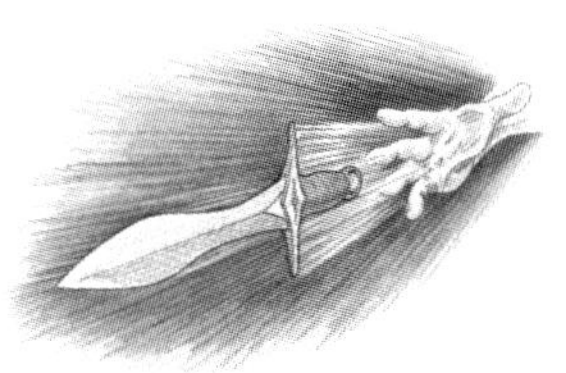

Reprieve and Return

Kaden stared at Tchinchura in disbelief. They were standing in the pale moonlight, well beyond the edge of the village, out in the tall grass. "That can't be right, Tchinchura. That can't be their answer."

For a moment Tchinchura did not speak. He stood, shoulders slumped, looking down at nothing in particular. "I am afraid it is."

"But . . . how?" was all Kaden could muster.

"You knew this was a possibility," Tchinchura said. "The laws of our ancestors are not easily set aside."

"I understand that, but never before have two fragments of the Golden Cord been in the same person's hands—someone who is perfectly willing to destroy a city to fulfill a vendetta that's a thousand years old." Kaden struggled to keep his voice down. "Do they not understand the danger he poses?"

"Do any of us really understand the danger he poses?" Tchinchura said, looking up at last. "Can we really fathom what things might be possible? What he might do?"

"That's what I'm saying," Kaden said. "This isn't at all like my father taking one. Eirmon could pose no threat to you, to this place, or to the Amhuru all over the world. The Jin Dara can."

"I know," Tchinchura replied. "You do not need to convince me. I could not, however, convince the elders, and that is what matters."

"I don't see how they could refuse you. Do they not believe us?"

"Of course they do."

"Then what?"

"They understand the challenge he presents," Tchinchura said. "They do not yet agree about how to deal with it. They don't believe that the time has come for such a dramatic and risky step."

"When exactly will it be time?" Kaden asked, frustrated. "He's had two fragments for almost three years. Even if, as you say, it takes him time to learn his new capabilities, he will learn, and he will use that knowledge against us."

"I know," Tchinchura said, "but unfortunately, the fact that it has been so long since he took the second fragment has worked against us. It is hard for the Council to see why now, all of a sudden, the third fragment isn't safe, when it has been safe all this time."

"So they won't believe it until he comes for it himself? Or until he destroys another city? Another empire? Or perhaps until he comes here and does to Azandalir what he did to Barra-Dohn?"

"And what if taking this fragment across the Madri removes the Southlands' only defense against the Jin Dara's power?" Tchinchura's shoulders were no longer slumped. He stood tall in the moonlight, and he motioned with his arms expansively. He paced in the tall grass. "What if all the Jin Dara wants is to build his own empire," Tchinchura continued, "perhaps to rule the Southlands? What if he's not even after the third fragment? After all, we've only ever surmised this. We don't know for sure. What if he makes his move to conquer an empire for himself, and there's no one here to stop him because we've fled?"

"Is this you talking or the Council?" Kaden asked. "I thought you believed going north was the best plan?"

"I do, I'm just trying to show you how the Council saw things," Tchinchura said. "We must always remember that there's more than one way to think, even among the wise, and if we are humble, we must be open to the possibility we are wrong. And if we are wrong about something like this, the ramifications could be enormous."

"Doesn't that work both ways?"

"It does," Tchinchura said. "If the Council is wrong, the consequences could also be dire."

Tchinchura's tone, as much as his words, stifled the restless unease that Kaden had been trying to express. He could hear that the elder Amhuru was fully aware of every misgiving, every fear that he felt. In fact Kaden knew that Tchinchura understood them better than he ever could. There was no point in Kaden taking his frustration out on him. The decision wasn't theirs, and it had been made.

"So what now?" Kaden asked.

"For now," Tchinchura said, sighing, "we wait."

"What do we wait for?"

"Either for the Council to have second thoughts and reconsider my proposal or for Zangira to come with news—either of the Jin Dara's fall, which would, of course, bring much rejoicing and render all this moot—or of news that confirms our fears."

"That would sway the Council, you believe?"

"I do," Tchinchura said. "It is on Zangira that they appear to have hung their hopes. They were not willing to give their consent for me to go as long as there is still a chance that Zangira might find the Jin Dara and recover the other fragments."

"And if Zangira falls? Or is unable to bring word?" Kaden spoke softly, almost unwilling to voice these fears out loud.

"Then what will come will come," Tchinchura said. He reached over and set his large, powerful hand on Kaden's shoulder. "You must remember that we are not alone. A greater hand than ours guides the fates of men."

"Does that mean everything will work out all right, no matter what we do?" Kaden asked, trying not to let the doubt and suspicion he felt whenever Tchinchura said such things show through.

"In the very longest of runs, all will be well," Tchinchura said. "But I think you mean something quite different, and I cannot guarantee that the plans of Kalos match our desires."

"Then I'm not sure how much better that makes me feel."

"I understand, but to me, the weight of difficulty, of hardship and suffering, is easier to bear when I remember that I do not bear it alone."

Kaden didn't know what to say to that, so he simply nodded, acknowledging that he had heard and understood. They stood together in the moonlight a little longer, but they had spoken their piece. Before long they returned to the village, passing silently through a darkness that felt opaque to Kaden, despite the moonlight.

Although the morning did not bring a complete reprieve from the heavy mood of the previous evening, Kaden had to admit—to himself, at least—that it was hard to be downhearted in Azandalir. Especially since he could tell that the news of their delay was encouraging to Nara.

To be sure, Nara had commiserated with him in every way possible, but Kaden could tell that part of her could not help but rejoice. And fair enough—the prospect of crossing the Madri in flight from the Jin Dara was a difficult and foreboding thing under any circumstances, and the prospect of doing it with Nara pregnant was so overwhelming that they had acknowledged the possibility that she might have to stay behind. It was just a possibility, but they knew it might come to that.

For the time being, though, neither of them was going anywhere. And in that Kaden did find consolation. What's more, as the sun rose high and hot overhead, he found himself thinking that perhaps the Council had been right. Zangira had a small army of Amhuru with him, and if they could find the Jin Dara and recover the missing fragments, then the matter would be settled.

He tried to resist getting his hopes up, but the prospect was so enticing he couldn't help but let the thought linger. By the late afternoon, he had already daydreamed twenty years into the future, a future based right here in Azandalir. He envisioned traveling the world, doing the work of an Amhuru, coming home to spend long periods of rest and enjoyment with Nara and the kids—though he knew Deslo would have his own travels and work to do. It would be a more difficult life than being king of Barra-Dohn, perhaps, but he thought most likely a happier one, too.

In the days and weeks that followed, Kaden found himself settling into a place somewhere between the despair of that first night when he heard the Council's verdict and the muted euphoria of the day after when he envisioned a peaceful life in a world where a defeated Jin Dara did not trouble him or anyone else anymore. It was a place of resigned uncertainy, where he accepted that for better or for worse, their hands were tied.

And yet, the waiting was not as unbearable as he had initially thought it would be. He worked, helping the Amhuru in whatever ways he could. He trained, especially with Deslo, enjoying the chance to show him how to work with Arua in ways they simply could not on the water. Deslo was a quick study, and soon his ability to manipulate the Arua field was not much less sophisticated than his own.

What's more, a new apprentice joined them in some of their training. For Kaden it came as something of a surprise because he had been unaware of any interest on her part, but Tchinchura brought Olli to them one day, having already received her replica of the Golden Cord around her bicep, ready to begin. Tchinchura had led her through the vows in private, as Olli desired, though Tchinchura indicated she would be a guest of honor at the evening meal. He entrusted her to Kaden and Deslo, charging them to begin her training, and promising that he would help himself whenever he could.

Kaden had some misgivings about how that would go. He had noticed Deslo's attitude toward Olli, and in talking with Nara, he had gathered that the two of them had gotten off to a poor start. And yet whatever issue had existed previously didn't seem to affect them now, as Olli was eager to learn, and deferential to both he and Kaden. Deslo, as well, appeared perfectly happy to show Olli what he knew and help her practice the things Kaden or Tchinchura had already shown her.

He couldn't be sure, but Kaden wondered if Zangira's daughter, Shaline, wasn't the main reason for Deslo's change of heart and better moods these days. Both he and Nara could see his interest in that direction, and it was no surprise, as Shaline was a sweet and pretty girl. What they couldn't tell was whether Shaline returned Deslo's interest or not. She and Trabor embraced both Deslo and Olli from the first, and the four of them spent a great deal of time together. But whether Shaline's interest in Deslo went beyond mere friendliness was hard to know, even for Nara, and she was normally very good at figuring these things out.

But what eased the burden of waiting for Zangira's return for Kaden, even more than these distractions, was the fact that Nara seemed to be showing more and more each day. Having been essentially absent for her first pregnancy, even though he had been living in the same palace, he was fascinated by her second one. He was as solicitous as he could be, apparently to the point of annoyance, as sometimes Nara would send him away, laughing that she needed a break from his questions and attentions.

Even so, he knew that Nara was enjoying this new problem of hers, and every night he lay down beside her and placed his head beside her growing belly so that he might talk to the child, for Nara insisted that by now, the baby could hear what he said. At first this had felt strange, but as the weeks went on, he grew so used to it that he would sometimes stop in midconversation with Nara, out in broad daylight, and bend over to address her stomach as though asking the baby to weigh in on the matter being discussed.

And so life took on an odd, disjointed quality of basic happiness, though periodically interrupted by various reminders of the possible storm brewing in the outside world. The clouds of that storm could not and did not completely overshadow their other joys, but Kaden found as time went on that his brief flirtation with the hope that maybe, just maybe, this might all be settled by Zangira and the others with him, did not last. He felt somehow sure that the Jin Dara was going to live to fight another day. He hoped the same was true for Zangira.

More to the point, he hoped it was true for all of them.

And then, just like that, after almost six weeks, Zangira returned.

Deslo never forgot the day Zangira returned to Azandalir. Even long after the Collapse, in the dark days, it remained with him—one of those days from youth that forms a distinct and permanent groove in the field of memory.

He spent the morning helping to water the swineherd that the Amhuru grazed not far from the Springs. They didn't let the pigs near the basin of the Springs for sanitary reasons, which meant daily trips from the Springs to the pig troughs during drier months to replenish their water supply.

Afterward, though, he ended up staying behind to take the empty water jars back to the Springs with Shaline, while the others who had been helping headed straight back to the village. That job complete, they sat and watched the sun sparkle on the placid waters. Large white clouds drifted lazily overhead, and as Shaline seemed content to sit and chat rather than return, Deslo happily settled in too.

In all their conversations since Deslo came to Azandalir, he had talked only in general terms of her father. To speak of his specific memories of Zangira would be to open the door to things Deslo was ashamed to discuss—the sack of Garranmere and Eirmon's betrayal of the Amhuru chief among them.

And yet, on this day, Shaline opened up about how much she was worried about him, about the danger of the mission he'd been given, about how much she missed him. Before he knew it, Deslo was sharing his own memories of Zangira, about how much kindness Zangira had shown him before, during, and after the destruction of Garranmere, and about how he had wished at the time that his own father had been as caring and as kind.

From there it was a short step to speaking of things he'd never shared with anyone. The fractures in his family from his earliest memories, the unspoken and seemingly insurmountable barrier between his mother and father, and the near miraculous resurrection of their long dead marriage while in exile after the destruction of Barra-Dohn. The dam, once breached, could no longer hold back all the emotions built up within him. With Shaline's gentle encourgement, out it came, all of it—the happiness about the change, the fear that it wouldn't last, the anger that his parents hadn't figured things out sooner and that he'd had to deal with it at all. When he was finished, he pulled out the red marble figurine his father had given him, and he showed it to Shaline, telling her what it was and what it represented—a piece of home he could carry in his pocket and hold in his hand.

Shaline examined the figurine appreciatively and listened to all of Deslo's tale attentatively, and when the flood finally slowed to a trickle, she reached over and took his hand in hers. The touch of her fingers was electric, and his heart stirred. The strength of his own desire surprised him, and he clasped her hand tightly in his own, thinking in that moment that he would never let it go.

That was the same moment they heard Trabor calling to them as he ran toward the Springs. Instinctively, Deslo relaxed his grip, and he felt her fingers slip away. In that same, deep place inside him that had responded to her touch a moment ago, a pang of loss replaced it.

And that pang, also, like the day itself, he never forgot.

But there was no time when it happened to analyze or to understand, for the closer Trabor came, the clearer his words were. Word had come from the lagoon. Zangira was back, as were a couple of the others, but the rest were lost. Their mission had failed, it seemed, though the details were still sketchy. Come, he called. They must come.

Soon Shaline and Deslo were running with Trabor, and all that had passed between them felt lost and washed out to sea by the wave that had crashed over them.

Chaos, or something very near it, reigned in the village. Kaden wondered if in the thousand years since Azandalir had been settled, if anything like the current scene had transpired here. Had it looked like this the first time the Amhuru realized one of the fragments of the Golden Cord was no longer in their possession?

The sound of wives grieving for lost husbands and of mothers grieving lost sons echoed from many of the houses around them. Kaden didn't know where Nara had gotten to in the confusion, but he would be very much surprised if she wasn't sitting somewhere among the mourning women right now, offering the comfort of her quiet presence.

Here, in the heart of the village, the normally staid Amhuru were struggling to impose order on the confusion. Some called for an accounting from Zangira, others were calling for the matter to be discussed before the Council at the Seat of Judgement, and all the while Zangira and the two with him stood wearily in their midst, flanked by their family and loved ones. Olli appeared—from where, Kaden did not know—and she slid up close to him and said, "Can I wait here with you?"

"Sure," Kaden said, and then he added, "Have you seen Deslo?"

Olli shook her head. Kaden glanced around, but he saw no sign of him. He glanced back at where Zangira stood with Alayna, his wife, and he realized neither Trabor nor Shaline were with them. He suspected that wherever they were on the island, Deslo was there too.

And then he saw Shaline, making her way through the crowd. She ran the last few steps and threw her arms around Zangira.

Trabor came through the crowd as well, and when Shaline released him, Zangira stepped over to Trabor and slipped his arm around the boy's shoulder and kissed him softly on the head, holding him close.

"Dad?"

Kaden turned to see Deslo approaching. He was flushed and sweating, and Kaden could see that, wherever they had all been, they'd run to get here.

"What's going on?"

"I don't know, exactly," Kaden said. "Zangira is home, with two others. The rest are dead."

"Killed by the Jin Dara?"

"It looks that way," Kaden said, nodding. He motioned toward the cluster of Amhuru elders around Zangira, where Almaren stood with his hand raised, trying to settle and silence the crowd. "I think we're going to find out."

"The time for formality has passed," Almaren said, when there was finally enough quiet for him to be heard. "Whatever matters there may be for the Council to discuss later at the Seat of Judgement, Zangira will tell his story here. It affects us all, and all must know the truth of it."

And so the crowd grew quiet, and Zangira told his tale, oddly punctuated by the sounds of mourning that echoed across the village. He told of their pursuit of the Jin Dara, of the battle in the canyon, and of the gold-clad men who joined the fight there, all equipped with and trained in the use of two replicas of fragments of the Golden Cord.

He painted a picture that was quite vivid, and Kaden could almost see the canyon filled with ordinary soldiers on both sides fighting with the tools of war at their disposal, all of them equally irrelevant to the outcome. He could almost see these men in gold that Zangira described, hunting the Amhuru to kill or, as Zangira was claiming, more likely to capture them, and he felt a shiver run down his back. The Jin Dara was forging—had indeed already forged—an army to counter and surpass the strength of the Amhuru.

As Zangira paused in the telling of the tale, Calamin, who had also survived the battle and returned with him, said of these men in gold, “They call themselves the Najin. As one of them lay dying, he told me this with pride as he boasted that the Najin would sweep away the Amhuru as the wind sweeps away the dust.”

There was quiet then as an eerie silence fell over the entire community. Even the sounds of mourning seemed to dissipate, and in the end it was Zangira who spoke into the silence and carried on the story he had begun of their return journey home. As he finished, Tchinchura stepped out from among the elders, approached, and embraced Zangira. He turned then and addressed the gathering.

“If the Jin Dara comes here, with these Najin,” Tchinchura said, “he must not find me or what I bear. I must go—the only question that remains is where. Will the Council now give me leave to cross the Madri?”

Kaden held his breath, wondering if Tchinchura’s question would spark renewed debate among the elders, but before any of them could say a word, Zangira spoke up in support. “It is the only way,” he said. “Whether it is Tchinchura’s burden to bear is actually the only question. But whether he goes or . . . another, the fragment must be sent north. Perhaps there is strength enough there to protect and defend it, but we can no longer hope that we are sufficient to win this war.”

And then the chatter of the elders did begin again in earnest, but Kaden knew the most important matter had been decided. He could see that Zangira was going to try to argue, to take the burden from Tchinchura, but Kaden knew Tchinchura would never consent to that. Who would be going with Tchinchura was likely the only real matter left to decide.

As for himself, he also knew that his season of reprieve had passed. The choice he had known was coming and long avoided was upon him. It would have to be made now, and soon, for Kaden was sure Tchinchura would seek to leave as soon as possible.

He glanced around at this place, still so beautiful despite the sadness and fear that hung almost palpably over it like a veil. He looked and knew that he could not stay.

As surely as he stood here, his father had contributed to this catastrophe. Eirmon had incurred a debt that Kaden would have to help pay.

Though no roads were safe now, for him, as for Tchinchura, the road forward would involve a harder way.

26

Hide and Hope

Deslo ran across the surface of the Arua field as fast as his feet would carry him, beneath the majestic talathorne trees. He had been back and forth to the lagoon on several occasions during his time in Azandalir and knew the way without needing to be guided. Ahead, the talathornes opened up to reveal not one but two large ships moored in the lagoon.

Captain D'Sarza and her crew had slept onboard *The Sorry Rogue* during their stay, which seemed kind of odd to Deslo. He'd been in enough ports to know it was common practice for D'Sarza and her crew to stay in their cabins when in port, both to guard the ship and to save the expense of renting rooms, but he figured Azandalir was different. Why stay on the ship at the lagoon and have to travel back and forth to the village if you didn't have to?

Whatever Captain D'Sarza's reasons, it didn't matter anymore. *The Sorry Rogue* was to make ready to sail as soon as possible. That was Deslo's mission, to let the captain know Tchinchura and those who were going with him would be coming soon.

Deslo did not know who that meant, precisely, and his father had been evasive when Deslo had asked. He didn't even know if it included himself.

Deslo tried not to think about that. Six weeks ago he'd have been adamant that whatever happened, he was going to go wherever Tchinchura went. But now he felt torn. He wanted to go, to cross the Madri and see the Northlands, no matter how dangerous it was. And maybe, if all worked out right, Zangira would come too and bring his family. If he didn't, or if they didn't, well, then leaving would be a lot harder.

Deslo raced up the gangway onto *The Sorry Rogue,* barely stopping to acknowledge the sailor who greeted him. He found D'Sarza with Geffen, her first mate, and before he could catch his breath and pass along his message, she took one look at him and said, "Get your wind and save your breath, Deslo, I know why you've come. We're already preparing to sail."

He nodded and did what she suggested. Then he stood straight and said, "When should I tell Tchinchura you'll be ready?"

"I doubt they could pack and be here before I'm ready," D'Sarza said, "so just tell him we'll go whenever he gets here."

"I will," Deslo said, and then he added, "He wanted you to know something about where we're going."

D'Sarza had been about to turn away, but his words caught her off guard, and she turned back to him. "What do you mean?"

"He said that you might not be able to go where he has to go, and that if you can't, that it is all right. It will be enough to take him where he can hire—"

"What are you babbling about, boy? Out with it? Where could he possibly mean to go that I—" D'Sarza stopped midsentence and peered at him with narrowed eyes. "You can't be serious?"

She turned to Geffen. "Have you ever heard of an Amhuru crossing the Madri?"

"No, Captain," Geffen said quietly. "Amhuru don't cross the Madri. Every sailor knows that."

"Speak up, Deslo," the captain said. "Is that what you were going to say? He means to cross the Madri?"

"Yes," Deslo said. "He does."

The captain stared at Geffen, who stared back, and neither one of them spoke for a long while. Then D'Sarza turned away from them both and stepped toward the starboard rail that was only a few feet away.

"Captain, I—"

D'Sarza waved for Geffen to be quiet without turning around to look at either of them, and Geffen looked at Deslo a little sheepishly. Deslo shrugged his shoulders as though to say, "What can you do?" Both of them waited, until Deslo figured he should at least finish saying what Tchinchura had told him to.

"He says that if you can't go, he would like you to take him wherever he can hire someone who will be able to get him safely across, and if you know someone you trust, all the better."

"Someone I trust," D'Sarza snorted, still without turning around and looking back. "An Amhuru, looking to hire passage across the Madri. Absurd. Who would I trust with that madness?" She glanced around at them as though they were the ones who were mad, then she turned back around as she kept talking. "They'd either assume he had something incredibly valuable, which he does, and kill him once they had recovered on the other side and while he was still incapacitated, or they'd assume he was desperate, which he is, and simply refuse him knowing no good could come of it, which of course it won't. Someone I trust, indeed."

Deslo opened his mouth to speak, and Geffen quickly motioned to him, shaking his head and wagging his finger insistently. Deslo bit his tongue, and Geffen nodded, approving. Together they waited, until eventually D'Sarza turned back around.

"I want you to take a message back to Tchinchura," she said. "Do you hear me?"

"Yes, Captain."

"You tell him that when I said I was willing to take him wherever he needed to go, that I meant that."

"But, Captain!" Geffen started.

"O hush, Geffen," D'Sarza snapped. "We've crossed the Madri before."

"I know we have, but that was—"

"That was what, for trade?" D'Sarza stared him down. "And this isn't, is that it? Don't see where the profit lies, eh?"

Geffen didn't answer right away, and D'Sarza didn't wait very long to see if he was going to.

"If Tchinchura is asking to cross the Madri, then he must be pretty desperate. He knows better than we do what crossing will do to him. And if Tchinchura needs to go, then someone needs to take him, and that someone is going to be me."

D'Sarza planted her fists on her hips and stared them both down, even though Deslo wasn't about to say anything and didn't think Geffen was going to either. "I've always said there wasn't a run too dangerous for me to make if the price was right, and I stand by that. If Tchinchura is asking for this, then I'm guessing the price of failure will be pretty high. That's good enough for me."

She turned on Deslo and snapped her fingers in his face. "Now off with you, boy. It'll be a fine moon for sailing, and the sea calls to me."

She wheeled away, barking orders to the sailors who were already scrambling about getting the ship ready, and they scrambled even faster. Deslo followed their example and raced back down the gangway even faster than he'd raced up it.

Kaden sat cross-legged on the floor of the small house that Marlo had shared with Owenn since arriving in Azandalir. The Devoted were both there, along with Olli and Rika, and he had just explained their situation and options.

"So, if you want to leave with the ship that brought Zangira here, you can. It will probably sail in the morning."

"And if we want to go with Tchinchura?" Marlo asked.

"Then you may come," Kaden said. "Tchinchura said he would welcome you, but he wanted me to be sure to say to each of you that you do not owe him this."

"We understand," Marlo said, and Owenn bowed his head in acquiescence. "Nevertheless, we will come."

"Where is Tchinchura?" Rika asked.

"He is with the elders, but anyone who means to go with him needs to pack now and be ready."

"You're going with him also, I take it?" Rika asked.

"Yes."

"And Nara?"

"I am going to her now," Kaden said, knowing this didn't answer the question. "You don't have to come, Rika."

"So you've said," she said, curtly. "I will think about it while you consult with your wife—if that's all right with you."

"Do as you please," Kaden said, as he rose to go, "only be sure you decide quickly."

"I intend to," Rika said, and she turned to Olli. "Are you going too, my dear?"

Olli nodded. "That's why I became an apprentice."

Rika smiled, but in the fading daylight, her smile looked to be more smirk than smile. But, if she was mocking Olli, the girl took no note of it, and Kaden didn't have time to wait and see if there was more to come. He took his leave of them and headed out into the village. He had done what Tchinchura asked, and now he needed to find Nara to decide what was next. And, if need be, to say goodbye.

When he found Nara, she was sitting with the head of a little Amhuru boy in her lap, as the child's mother rocked back and forth, racked with grief and shaking with silent sobs over the news that had reached her just hours before. News that confirmed she was a widow and her son, fatherless.

Nara looked up at him and understood. She asked no questions; she simply lifted the head of the boy and slid aside so she could gently place it down on the soft cloak that she placed beneath him to serve as as pillow. She rose to follow Kaden, and all the while the mother did not speak. She just rocked, back and forth, back and forth.

They walked together through the camp, and Nara said, "He's leaving? Tonight?"

"Yes."

"You mean to go with him?"

"Yes," he said again. "I have to."

"I know," she said. "I suppose I always have."

"You can't stay here," Kaden said. "If the Jin Dara comes, there will be no stopping him. You need to get as far away as you can. We should pick a destination, now, tonight. You can take the other ship and when you get to the first port, find passage—"

"Kaden. Stop."

She had probably just meant for him to stop talking, but he stopped walking as well. Nara stopped too.

"I'm not going to do that. I'm going with you and Deslo."

"No, Nara, you need to take Deslo with you—"

"Kaden," Nara said, her tone firm, "you can't send him away from you. Not now. Not after all this. Besides, he's of age, and an apprentice. He has the right to make his own decision."

"But I'm trying to save his life, your lives." Kaden stared at her, desperate for her to understand. There wasn't time for argument tonight.

"I know," Nara said, and she smiled. "But there are more important things than that."

"More important than your life?"

"Kaden, sweetheart, if you knew you could save my life, and that one day you would find me again and we would share the rest of our days together, that would be one thing, but you know no such thing."

"How could I?"

"Exactly," Nara said. "Which means the real choice before us is whether I will send my son and husband into danger alone, or if I will go with them. And I want to come with you. I don't want to be alone, and I don't want you to be alone."

He stared into her eyes, wishing it could be so. "But the baby?"

"The baby will share our fate, whatever it will be."

"What if the crossing hurts you, or the baby?"

"The crossing will be risky for us all."

"Nara," Kaden said, "I appreciate what you're saying, but you need to think about this—"

"I have, and this is what I know—even if I find some quiet corner of the world, I won't know for sure that I am safe, and that you know well. What's more, I won't know if you're safe; I'll have no idea. Even if you're successful, it could take a long time. You could spend years trying to evade the Jin Dara, or even fighting him. How would I know you were still alive? How would I know you hadn't failed and weren't already dead?"

Nara reached up and brushed his face with her hand. "Have you thought of that? Of what it would be like for me? I would be alone, with our child, and with no way of knowing anything about the two people in this world I care most about. I'm sorry—I'm just not going to do it. Whatever the future holds for us out there, we'll face it together. I'd rather die together than live without you."

Nara stood with her arms crossed, staring at him in the gathering twilight. He looked at her and knew, both that he wasn't going to convince her to go and that he didn't want to convince her to go. Even though he'd been telling himself she couldn't come, he'd been hoping she would override him and insist on coming, even as she had just done. He closed the distance between them and wrapped his arms around her, kissing her lightly on the forehead.

"Thank you," he whispered as he held her close.

"For what?"

"For not questioning my need to go. For being willing to come too. For just being you."

She clasped him tight and kissed him with a passion that made him wish they were alone. They weren't, though, and there were things that needed taking care of.

"Come," he said, "let's go pack. We go as soon as Tchinchura is ready."

Rika leaned against the rail of *The Sorry Rogue,* watching the talathorne trees around the lagoon and the lagoon itself disappear as the ship sailed into the tunnel toward the hidden entrance and exit to Azandalir. She heard a bird call, one of those awful *mirimae* birds that had woken her every morning they'd been here, it felt like, and she was glad to be saying goodbye to them, even if part of her wondered if she was making the right decision. In the end she knew she was making the safer decision, and that was enough.

As long as Tchichura bore an original fragment of the Golden Cord, and as long as she stayed near him, she would have a chance to make her play. The Jin Dara would come for it eventually, and she would have to be watching and be ready. Perhaps she would get a chance to take it herself and give it to him, though most likely she would have to take a more indirect role in delivering it to him.

It was exactly that possibility which had made her consider staying in Azandalir. If he came, as she could see the Amhuru clearly feared he would, then she might have gotten her chance to tell him about Tchinchura, about *The Sorry Rogue,* and about the plan to cross the Madri. But that plan had a couple flaws.

First, and most obviously, he might not come. If he did, she would still have to figure out how to get word to him that she wanted to help him, before he killed her and everyone else. She knew perfectly well what he'd done to Barra-Dohn, and she knew she'd couldn't guarantee, with the power he wielded, that he'd allow anyone on Azandalir to get anywhere close to him before killing them, so there would be difficulties even if he did come.

And, not least of all, there was the problem of the second ship sitting in the lagoon, and the obvious expectation that those who had come with Tchinchura would either be leaving again with him or leaving on that ship. It seemed the Amhuru were hunkering down for a fight, and she wasn't at all sure how she could convince them that she didn't want to leave on either ship.

So, in the end, she had accepted the offer to keep traveling with Tchinchura and company on *The Sorry Rogue*, and she had resigned herself easily enough to that fact. She had been patient before when the stakes were high, and she would be patient again. Her time would come, and she would be ready.

They passed out from the tunnel into the sea, out into the bright, clear moonlight. Rika glanced over at the Amhuru, for there were several of them now that the two who had returned with Zangira had joined them. Those two and Tchinchura stood with the Kalosenes and the three apprentices, Kaden, Deslo, and Olli.

They were a small and pitiful band compared to the power and strength of the one who was pursuing them, and the thought of their being caught by him, and what he would do to them, almost made her laugh.

The Amhuru who had gone to the lagoon to see off the ship that had brought Zangira back returned to the village, and preparations for their journey to the caves began immediately. Zangira found the thought of retreating there with no knowledge of the Jin Dara's exact intentions or whereabouts unfortunate, but he could see no other way, and neither could the Council.

They could not fight him, and they could not run. They had no way to evacuate the island, having only a few fishing boats, and even if they did, they couldn't be responsible for drawing the Jin Dara after them to whatever country they took refuge in, as they would inevitably do. Their only choice was to hide and hope.

The existence of the caves was a secret all Amhuru kept to themselves, on or off the island. Even the apprentices who had come with Tchinchura had been kept in the dark, since some in their party were not Amhuru. The caves had been conceived and built as a line of last defense, and now it looked as though, for the first time in the long history of Azandalir, their use would actually be necessary.

The entrance to the caves was as carefully concealed as the entrance to Azandalir itself, and there was good reason to suspect that even if the Jin Dara had tortured the captured Amhuru into giving away the island's location that he still would not have knowledge of the caves. And, if it did come to fighting, there were natural defenses inside that could be turned to the advantage of whatever force defended them. Not that Zangira held out much hope that these would save them should it come to that.

Of course, the only way the caves might truly save them would be for the Jin Dara to find Azandalir and believe they had fled the island, and that was why they had to go to the caves now. They couldn't wait for him to come first and then go, for there would be signs of recent habitation for the Jin Dara to see. They had to go, and they had to pray that he believed the evidence of his eyes when he came—that Azandalir had been long deserted.

"We will have to ration the olive oil," Almaren said as he walked with Zangira through the village. "We can only use the supplies we already have. He may not examine them carefully, but he should find the vineyard untended and the olives unharvested."

"Yes," Zangira said. "I have already spoken to the elders about this."

"Of course," Almaren said, nodding as he shuffled along. "And the swineherd?"

"Several of the boys should be letting them out of the corral even as we speak," Zangira said. "And they should be helping them to scatter about the island, too."

"Good. They will make a mess of things, of course, trampling here, there, and everywhere."

"Yes," Zangira said, "let us hope so."

They walked on in silence, and Zangira caught sight of Alayna with some of the other women, helping to pack up food for removal to the caves. He was glad he'd made it here ahead of the

Jin Dara. If he was coming, and Zangira was sure he was, whatever happened, his family wouldn't face it alone.

He had offered to take Tchinchura's burden for him, to cross the Madri bearing the last Southland fragment, but he knew that his place was here—and so had Tchinchura. Zangira would do all he could to help Azandalir survive the Jin Dara's coming, if it could be survived, and then there might be a chance to follow after Tchinchura and the others and help as he may. And, if Kalos willed it, maybe the whole family would come with him.

If he could keep them together, he would. The world had changed, the situation had changed, and as much sense as the old way of doing things had made, for the immediate future, at least, it no longer seemed necessary. Once Tchinchura crossed the Madri, there would no longer be any Southland fragments in their possession for the Amhuru of Azandalir to safeguard.

"The replicas of the Northland fragments in the Temple . . ." Almaren said. "They have been sent for?"

"Yes."

"And what will we do with them if the Jin Dara gets into the caves?"

That the elder himself did not have an answer for this dilemma did nothing to ease Zangira's churning thoughts.

"I don't know, Almaren."

"Then that is our first priority once we have gathered safely inside."

"I agree," Zangira said. "It is a problem we must solve. He cannot be allowed to have them, under any circumstances."

27

FAREWELL, AZANDALIR

Rain lashed *The Sorry Rogue,* but fortunately, the ship had stopped rolling as much as it had been earlier. Deslo didn't get seasick very often anymore, but he'd been feeling a little queasy earlier. He wasn't feeling queasy now, and that was good since he wanted to be able to concentrate on the conversation.

D'Sarza had gathered the three Amhuru and the three apprentices, along with the Devoted and her first mate to talk about the crossing. She had laid out a chart across the table they were sitting around and was explaining to Tchinchura where they were headed, though Deslo didn't know the reference points she was mentioning or fully grasp how to read the chart in front of him.

"How long do you think?" Tchinchura asked.

"Maybe three weeks," D'Sarza said.

Tchinchura nodded as Kaden said, "We'll find Runners at this port? This . . . what did you call it?"

"Dengai," D'Sarza said. "And yes, we'll find Runners there. The Asa, specifically—the Runners I've used before. They run Dengai."

"And you trust them?" Tchinchura asked.

"Runners are dangerous men who do a dangerous job," D'Sarza said. "It wouldn't be wise to get too comfortable or be too trusting of any of them, but yes, on the whole, I trust the Asa."

"So," Marlo said, "this may be a silly question, but how does the crossing work? What do the Runners do?"

"Runners provide an armed escort to the Madri," D'Sarza explained, "but more than that, they provide colors to fly that identify your vessel as under their protection. That way, when you come through the Madri on the other side, Runners from the same organization can provide protection while you are defenseless."

"And what if another group of Runners or some other random ship comes upon us first?" Marlo asked.

"That's the thing," D'Sarza said. "There are pirates, of course, and others that specialize in preying on people who've come through. That's why crossing the Madri is so dangerous. It will incapacitate us all, and as for them—"

D'Sarza broke off for a moment, as she indicated just about everyone else in the room, all who bore a piece of Zerura. Deslo swallowed as she scanned them with her eyes. He knew the crossing would be tougher for him, but he didn't really understand just what that meant.

"—well, for them, it will be worse."

"How long will the effects last for you and for those who do not bear Zerura on their bodies?" Tchinchura asked.

"Hard to say, but at least a few days."

"Last time we went through," Geffen said, piping up, "I didn't know who I was or where I was for a week."

"A week!" Kaden said. "That's a long time to just float there, defenseless."

"We won't," D'Sarza said, emphatically. "Listen, the Runners know what they're doing. Given that we have Amhuru onboard, they'll drive a hard bargain, of course. This crossing will get very pricey. And since we will only pay half up front, they'll put a man onboard to confirm the amount we owe once we're safely through on the other side, so the Runners on the Northland side will know just how much they still need to collect.

"They'll lead us to waters that they patrol with regularity, and, while nothing's completely safe, we'll be as safe as we can be. Once we get far enough into the Madri, and the effects take over, the ship will keep drifting ahead until it comes through, and Asa on the other side will see their colors flying and take over.

"They will board us, and a crew will sail *The Sorry Rogue* to their port on the other side. They'll dock the ship, take us ashore, and watch over us until at least most of us are on our feet."

"Most of us?"

"Yes," D'Sarza said. "No one really knows, I don't think, how severe the effects of the crossing are for Amhuru. Do you have any idea, Tchinchura?"

"No. All I know is that for Calamin, Trajax, and myself, they will be severe. For Deslo and Olli, they will hopefully be comparatively mild, and for Kaden, it will be somewhere in between."

"And since 'severe' could mean months and months—or worse?—with you boys weak or unconscious, we won't stay with the Runners until you're all better," D'Sarza continued. "As soon as the rest of us are able to travel, we will. I'd say we'll be safer on the sea than in any port, though I guess we have some time to figure out our specific plan."

"Yes, we'll have time to plan, but we all need to understand that the danger of the crossing is just half of the problem," Tchinchura said. "The other half is that as soon as I cross the Madri, the Northland Amhuru will know. They'll know, and though I don't know exactly how they'll react, we should assume two things: they'll hide the Northland fragments of the Golden Cord, and they'll send teams of Amhuru to find and kill me."

The table grew quiet, and Deslo felt a chill inside, way down deep, in his bones. And even though in meetings like this he normally kept quiet, he couldn't help saying, "I don't understand that. You're one of them."

"Not anymore, I won't be," Tchinchura said. "At least, not as far as they're concerned. Crossing the Madri with a piece of the Golden Cord is one thing no Amhuru would ever do. They'll assume the worst—that I've come to make a play for the Northland fragments, to try to reunite the Golden Cord, and they will take whatever steps they deem necessary to stop that."

"But when they find us, we can explain, right?" Olli spoke up.

"I'll try, Olli," Tchinchura said. "But I can't guarantee I'll get the chance. I'll do everything I can to get word to them somehow, to convince them that crossing the Madri was necessary, that we're not a threat. But they will take no risks, even if that means killing me and anyone helping me, and that means all of you."

Again silence fell on the table, but it was D'Sarza this time who broke it. "I think we're getting ahead of ourselves. Crossing the Madri is quite enough to focus on right now. How to survive the dangers on the other side is a different conversation, and while we'll of course be more vulnerable to attack while Tchinchura and the rest of you are still dealing with the effects of the crossing, we have some time to plan for that."

"That's right," Geffen said. "In our experience, Southland Amhuru give the Madri a wide berth, so I'd expect Northland Amhuru do the same. Even if they mobilize against us, they'll still need to find us, and we won't make that easy."

"No, we won't," D'Sarza agreed. "Which brings us to one of the things Geffen and I wanted to communicate today. We're going to have to adapt to the Northlands quickly. They use words differently, have different customs and rituals, and so on, and we'll have to pick these things up and practice them as much as possible. With Amhuru teams on our trail, news that a ship of Southlanders has recently been in port will, unfortunately, be very memorable, obviously making covering our trail difficult."

"Great," Olli said, and Deslo could hear the discouragement that he felt in her tone. "So every word we say and everything we do, even things we don't know we're saying or doing, will betray us and make it easy for these men that have been sent to find and kill us to do just that."

"We'll start teaching you some things that will help minimize the learning curve on the other side," D'Sarza said, "and, more to the point, we won't let you off the ship while in port unless we're confident you won't do or say something really stupid."

"Well, then I guess I'll never be allowed off the ship once we're on the other side," Olli said. Everyone laughed at that, even Deslo.

Deslo sat with his bare feet dangling over the side of *The Sorry Rogue*. The storm from the previous day was long gone, and an oppressively humid heat had replaced it. He was leaning forward with his forehead against the wooden rail, trying not to think about anything, but mostly, trying not to think about Shaline.

Things had been so rushed, so confusing, on the night that they left Azandalir. He had only really known for sure that Zangira and his family weren't coming a short while before they had to head out for *The Sorry Rogue,* and there had been no time to seek her out and say goodbye. In the end he hadn't needed to, as Shaline and Trabor had come to find him.

He'd been glad to see them, glad to say farewell, but with Trabor there, he'd felt unable to say the things he wanted to say to Shaline. Of course, Deslo knew well enough that even if Trabor hadn't have been there, he might not have had the courage to say them anyway. So, in the end, he'd shaken Trabor's hand, given Shaline a quick hug, and waved goodbye as he followed his parents and the others out of the village.

"Hey."

Deslo had noticed the shadow of someone approaching, and he recognized Olli's voice, of course, so there was no need to look up to know who it was. "Hey," he said in return.

"Mind if I join you?"

"Sure."

Olli settled in, slipping her legs through openings in the rail, too, but not right next to him; she left a little cushion space between them. Deslo kept staring down at his feet, and beyond them, at the water.

"That was weird, this morning, wasn't it?" Olli said.

"What, the lesson?"

"Sa, sa," Olli said.

Deslo turned and looked at her now, blankly. She was smiling, knowingly, like they'd just shared a huge joke.

"Oh, come on, Deslo," she said after a moment, looking surprised more than exasperated. "Don't tell me you've forgotten already."

"Oh, sure," Deslo said after a moment, feeling a little stupid. "Sorry, I'm a bit distracted."

"That's all right," she said, surprisingly kindly. "It'll take some getting used to, using 'sa' for 'yes,' and 'na' for 'no.'"

"Sa, it will."

"Very good," Olli said, laughing.

"Na, na, it was nothing."

They both laughed for a moment, but Deslo found the good humor the moment created hard to hold onto, and it slipped away like mist between his fingers.

"And just think," Olli said, "your little brother or sister will grow up calling your mother, 'Noni,' and your father, 'Yadi.' That will definitely be strange."

"I'll have to call them that, too," Deslo said, "at least on land, in front of Northlanders."

"Sa, you will."

Deslo looked at Olli and gave her a weak smile. Their time at Azandalir, with Shaline and Trabor as buffers, had bridged the gap between them, at least mostly, and Deslo could see Olli was trying to keep that connection alive, now that they were gone, and now that they had no buffer. Deslo didn't mind—he just couldn't muster much energy to play along at the moment.

And then, just as Deslo had turned back to face forward,

staring down, head against the rail, Olli reached over and placed her hand gently on his shoulder. Her touch was unexpected, but he didn't pull away from it as he might have done before.

"It gets easier, you know," she whispered.

"What does?"

"The ache from missing someone you care about."

He turned and looked at Olli again, and he saw that there were tears in her eyes. He didn't speak, only waited.

"There was a boy on my island, a boy named Jann, and he loved me," she said, very matter-of-factly.

"Did you love him?" Deslo asked.

"In a way," she said. "Though not the way he loved me. It would have been a hard thing for him to accept, had he survived our trip down the mountain."

Deslo stared, understanding at last. "He was the one you had to bury. By the beach?"

Olli nodded.

"I'm sorry," Deslo said.

"It's all right. You don't need to be."

"No, I mean, I'm sorry I wasn't very nice to you when you first joined us. I was being stupid."

"You were being stupid," Olli said, smiling through her tears and giving Deslo a playful shove. "But I forgive you."

"Thanks."

"And I mean it," she said as she rose to go. "It does get easier. And at least with Shaline, there's hope you'll see her again."

"It doesn't feel like there's hope," he said. "The Crossing, the Northland Amhuru, not to mention the Jin Dara. What chance do we have?"

"Maybe not much," Olli said, standing over him. "But you know, I used to lie in my room, in the caves at home, and think there wasn't any hope I'd ever get off the island, no hope I'd ever even get to feel the sunlight on my face. But here I am, right? Sometimes even hopeless and impossible things happen, don't they?"

Deslo thought about that, thought for the first time in a long time about the gorgaal and Olli's island, and about how he had helped to set the island free from the winged nightmares that ruled it.

He nodded, looking up at her. "Sa, I guess they do."

Squatting beside a table in the open middle area of the large cluster of houses he had found near the center of Azandalir, the Jin Dara found himself thinking of the island where he had been born and raised. He had been Dagin Orlas then, just a little boy, raised among an ancient and bitter family. But he was so much more than little Dagin Orlas now.

A handful of pigs had been grazing on the short grass here when he found this place, and now one of them had strayed to within a few feet of him, a sign of the animal's domestication that it didn't fear him. Also, a sign of its stupidity.

He reached out and seized the creature through the Arua field. A frightened squeal broke the silence of the warm afternoon, until it suddenly broke off as the Jin Dara crushed the animal's vocal chords from within. The pig made a stifled gurgling sound as it spit up some blood, shuddered and spasmed, then tilted over onto its side, where it lay motionless in the grass.

Ham for dinner.

Devaar jogged over, and the Jin Dara stood to meet him. Devaar shook his head and sighed. He said, "No sign, then?"

"No sign," Devaar said.

"What have the scouts reported?"

"There's fresh water to the south, and that seems to be where the pigs were once kept, as there's an open corral there. The water trough is dry as a bone, which I guess is why they let the pigs out, so they didn't die of thirst penned in there."

"No doubt, Devaar," the Jin Dara said, "but as you can see, I don't care about pigs. What else have the scouts found?"

"To the west, there's a big table and a painting on the rock you might find interesting, of six Amhuru, all wearing a fragment in a different place."

The Jin Dara perked up at this, and facing west, pictured the mural Devaar described. "The six brothers," he whispered, almost under his breath. "It has to be."

Devaar didn't say anything. He'd been with the Jin Dara long enough to know when keeping his mouth shut was the best course of action.

Still staring west, the Jin Dara said, "And what else?"

"The place you described to us, the place like the Temple at Barra-Dohn—it is north of here, but there's nothing inside, or at least, there's no Zerura. There's another painting of a headless man, but nothing else."

"A headless man?" the Jin Dara said, turning to look at Devaar again.

"Yes, a giant man with no head."

"How strange," the Jin Dara said, wondering what that was about. He felt pretty confident that he knew what the other painting was, but he had no idea about this one. It didn't matter, he supposed, since what he really wanted from there appeared to be gone. He wasn't surprised, though, as he imagined wherever the Amhuru had gone, they had taken the replicas too. They wouldn't have left them behind.

"And no one has found any signs of people? Or even any signs of people being here recently? Embers of fires? Food that looks only a few days old? Anything?"

"Nothing. The bread here is moldy, the firepits cold with nothing but ash in them. There are signs of pigs across much of the island, trampled grass, and even droppings that aren't fresh. Looks like this place has been empty, maybe ten days or even a few weeks."

"Or that's what they want us to think," the Jin Dara said.

"Do you want us to keep looking?"

"Yes, send everyone out again and have them meet me here at nightfall."

But when they reported back at nightfall, there was nothing different to report. There simply were no signs of recent habitation to be found. It appeared that Azandalir had been deserted. What he sought was not here.

He had known that this was a possibility, but rage boiled in him. All around him, his men—his Najin anyway, the rest were on the ships—sat eating their roasted pig, but his anger was rising like a storm swell in a raging sea. He called out to Devaar and the Najin, saying, "Take your food and go to the ships. Go now!"

Devaar hesitated, looking puzzled, but only for a moment. Soon he and the Najin were running on the Arua back east, toward the place where the ships were moored.

The Jin Dara concentrated very hard, and the clear, warm evening started to change. A stiff wind picked up, blowing in steadily from the south, and it started blowing harder and harder until the roar of the wind filled his ears. Storm clouds were now rolling on that wind, and the roaring wasn't just the roaring of the wind, as lightning and thunder rolled in those clouds.

Suddenly, all around the perimeter of the island, lightning fell from the sky, striking the high ridges of stone, over and over. He could hear the cracking of stone as large pieces of the ridges toppled off and fell into the sea. Perhaps the Amhuru thought to evade him and one day come home to this place. Well, he would leave them a very different island to return to.

He made sure the lightning didn't fall directly to the east, lest he collapse the tunnel that was the only way out of here, but after summoning the lightning to strike the rest of the high ridge around the island, he directed the strikes ever inward. He would set every last flammable thing on this island on fire, from the tall, dry grasslands that would flare up in a moment and burn fast as could be, to the tall, ancient trees that would simmer and burn, hotter and hotter, most likely for days or even weeks, until they toppled to the ground and lay smoking long after he was gone.

And of course, these dwellings would burn, every last one of them, until only ember and ash remained across every square foot of this island. He stood where he was, directing the strikes, and as the fires started around the edges of the island, he saw part of the pig herd running in the tall grass not far away. He reached out through the Arua and, instead of killing them, he drove them mad so that they reversed course and started running toward the fire they had been fleeing from. They ran straight into it, and he could feel the smoking of their singed flesh.

A flock of colorful birds likewise flew overhead, and he reached up for them. Despite the dissipating power of Arua that far above ground, he had more than enough strength with the two fragments he bore to likewise manipulate them, and they wheeled together like they were one bird and flew straight for the place to the north where the fire appeared to be burning hottest and most vigorously.

The Jin Dara then jogged back toward the ships, for the fires were truly raging all around him. He summoned the wind now and again to blow his way clear, but he could feel the heat on his face and skin as the glow from the crackling flames lit up the darkening sky.

The great trees around the lagoon burned like massive candles in the night, and as much as he enjoyed looking at them burn, he couldn't help but reach out for some of those nearest to him to crack them until they toppled over, falling with a mighty crash to the waiting earth. He smiled at the flames that raced up and down the surface of the fallen trees as he headed on to his waiting ship.

When he reached the edge of the water, he could see the faces of his men illuminated in the firelight, standing safely onboard the ships, watching in awe at the destruction he had created.

It was true he had not found what he was after, but it was only a matter of time. They could run, and they could hide, but they could not win.

Nothing in the world was stronger than he.

28

Crossing the Madri

The Sorry Rogue maintained her course, running parallel to the Madri, which was marked by a line of visible haze off the starboard bow. Kaden looked behind them, and sure enough, the haze lay like a thin, gauzy, low-level cloud hanging upon the ocean for as far as the eye could see.

He could feel it too. As they'd approached it that morning, following the Asa scout ship that was still running ahead of them, he'd noticed the queasy tingling even before the haze became clear. The tension onboard had already been papable, but the appearance of that haze and the fear of the passage before them had deepened that tension so that it wrapped them all in its firm embrace just like the haze would soon do.

Running on their port side, a second ship flying the colors of the Asa was shadowing them. It was a larger vessel than the small, sleek scout ship running out in front, but both of them had the purple and yellow standard that was also flying from the main mast of *The Sorry Rogue*. The three ships had left Dengai the previous morning, and if Kaden understood the plan accurately, they would be approaching the place where they would make the crossing soon.

Nara slipped her arm around him and leaned in, resting her head on his shoulders. He held her, knowing that the anxiety they all felt was heightened in Nara, since the baby's time was not far away. Tchinchura didn't think the Madri would affect the child in any permanent way, not any more than it should affect Nara permanently, but that didn't mean she wasn't worried. He could feel the child kick, sometimes, but she could feel the baby all the time: kicking, yawning, stretching, and rolling over. It was something he could only imagine, but it was very real to Nara, and so was the fear.

"Do you want to go to the cabin?" he asked.

"There will be time when D'Sarza gives the sign."

"True," he said, and he kissed her gently on the head. "We'll be all right. Baby will be all right."

She took the hand he had placed on her belly in her own hands by way of the reply and held it tightly. "I know. It's you I'm worried about."

"I'll be all right too," Kaden said, though he admitted to himself that of that statement, he felt less certain.

"I still don't understand why you can't just take it off," Nara said. "All of you—we should lock them in a box until we're across, and—"

"It wouldn't work," Kaden said. "The Zerura's effects are inside us, in our blood and in our bones. You see the flecks in my eyes and hair. It's there and it won't go away just because I take off the fragment.

"And besides, you know that even if we could spare ourselves or lessen the effect, we can't. Amhuru swear to protect their fragments with their lives, to die for them, and to put them in a box and leave them ripe for the taking? It won't happen."

"They'll be ripe for the taking anyway, won't they?"

"Tchinchura doesn't think so," Kaden said. "Admittedly, he doesn't know, but there's a process when you get your Zerura, a ritual of sorts—you know what I described to you when I got my replica—and it kind of syncs with your heart. That's the best I can explain it, anyway. Tchinchura thinks that his fragment and our replicas will be affected by the passage too . . . that while we're incapacitated, they will be too."

"I don't understand what that means," Nara said, sounding confused and anxious.

"I'm not sure either," Kaden said, "but I think part of what it means is that it will remain just a solid, metal ring around my arm. It won't respond to the touch like it does when active, won't unwrap itself or hang in the air and pulsate, or any of those things."

"But couldn't someone still slide it off and take it?"

"That's unclear," Kaden said. "Tchinchura doesn't think someone could slide it off, though he admits that perhaps they could cut it off."

Nara turned and looked at Kaden. "That isn't terribly comforting."

"Nara," Kaden said, bending over so that his forehead touched hers lightly. "Marlo and Owenn will stand guard once they've recovered, as will D'Sarza's men. They'll protect us until we're able to protect ourselves."

"They'll be incapacitated themselves," Nara said. "For a while."

"I know. But aren't you the one who usually tells me we have to trust in Kalos?"

"Yes," Nara said, "only you usually give me a look when I do that says you don't believe me. Are you saying you do?"

"I'm saying that being in Azandalir, among the Amhuru—it changed me. I realized that even though I've distanced myself from Eirmon and the kind of man he was, I've been holding onto the way he saw the world. I think I need to give the beliefs of the Amhuru and the Devoted a chance."

Nara smiled, and she stood up on her tiptoes and kissed Kaden. "I'm so glad to hear that."

As Kaden held Nara, a cry from the crow's nest high above

them broke the relative silence of the day, and both Kaden and Nara craned their heads back to peer upward and see what the ruckus was about. The sailor above them was calling and gesturing wildly, and when Kaden looked off the port side of the bow, it took him a moment, but he did see what the sailor was pointing at.

The Asa scout ship that had been sailing ahead of them was turning to port, and Kaden could see why. A handful of sails were visible on the horizon there, coming their way, and it looked like the scout ship was turning to cut them off. Kaden glanced at the larger vessel immediately off their port side, and he could see a lot of movement on their deck as the heavily armed ship prepared for engagement.

D'Sarza was motioning with hand gestures to the captain of that vessel, and after a moment she strode away from the rail, calling to the crew to come about. Soon, *The Sorry Rogue* was turning hard to starboard.

"That's our signal," Kaden said.

"Those ships are coming for us, aren't they?" Nara said.

"They're probably pirates patrolling the Madri, looking for fools who attempt the crossing without Runners," Kaden said. "The Asa will handle them, and we'll be through before they can get here."

"And if there are more on the other side?"

"Go to the cabin, Nara," Kaden said, gently but firmly. "I'll be there in a moment. I'm just going to corral Deslo."

Nara hesitated, but then she nodded and walked across the deck to their cabin. Kaden glanced around the deck, and he saw Deslo standing by the port rail, watching the Asa ships moving off to intercept the ships sailing their way. Kaden walked over to him quickly.

"We need to go to our cabins, Deslo," he said. "D'Sarza warned us that when the darkness comes, it will come suddenly."

Deslo turned away from the rail, reluctantly, but he did turn. He looked up at Kaden's face. "Can you feel it? Inside you?"

"I can."

"I'm afraid," Deslo said simply. "What if we don't wake up?"

"We'll wake up," Kaden said, putting his hand on Deslo's shoulder. "Come on, let's go take our nap. By the time we wake up, the hard part will be over."

"If only," Deslo said, but he started across the deck with Kaden. They paused at the door to Deslo's cabin, and Deslo looked back at him. "See you on the other side."

Kaden smiled. "See you on the other side."

Inside his own cabin, Nara sat expectantly on the side of their bed, her hands clasped in her lap. "So what do we do now? Just lie down and wait to pass out?"

Kaden listened by the door. "I can still hear the crew moving about out there. I think if we were moving into the Madri, or if we were close to the place where it would take effect on us, they'd be going to their cabins too. I think we're all right for a little while longer."

And so Kaden paced, up and down the cabin, as Nara sat on the side of the bed, watching him. He could feel the tingling nausea growing, but he felt oddly restless.

Desperate images and thoughts flooded his mind. The cabin whirled around him. This was madness. They shouldn't be here. It was crazy, reckless, foolish. They needed to get as far from the Madri as possible. He thought maybe he should run to Tchinchura. Perhaps he could convince him to turn around. Maybe it wasn't too late.

"Kaden? What is it, Kaden?"

He could hear Nara's voice, but it sounded muffled, as though it was coming from a long, long way away. He tried to focus on her, to hear her, but suddenly all he could hear was the pounding of his own heartbeat. He clutched at his chest, but as he did, a sharp, stabbing pain radiated from his arm, where the replica seemed to seize and contract, squeezing his bicep unbelievably hard as if to crush it.

He staggered, starting to fall, when suddenly soft hands grabbed him. They didn't so much hold him up as guide his fall toward the bed.

He tumbled into darkness.

Maarta ran as fast as he could run on the Arua, sucking the crisp, cool air into his lungs. He had to find Telsiin, immediately.

He had run all the way to the village, and there, the men he had asked had said Telsiin had gone for a walk along the river, beneath the pines, so he had run through the village, out the other side, and along the river. He had news that even he could not believe, and until he found the chief elder, he would not stop. He had to run.

At last he saw him, Telsiin, up ahead, sitting on a large rock. As Maarta approached, he realized the chief elder was not gazing out over the river as he had supposed. His eyes were closed, and his head was slumped a little to the side as he snored.

Maarta stopped and stepped down from the Arua. He reached over and touched Telsiin softly on the shoulder, shaking him. "Elder, Elder."

Telsiin's eyes fluttered open, and he looked up at Maarta. Maarta could see Telsiin react to what he saw, and concern appeared in the older man's face as he said, "What is it, child? What news do you bring?"

Now that the moment had come for explaining, Maarta felt his mouth dry up, his words failing him. Telsiin lifted one gnarled hand and placed it on his arm.

"Whatever it is, all will be well, my son. Just tell me."

"I think one of the Southland fragments just crossed the Madri," Maarta said at last, blurting it out.

Telsiin's hand fell from Maarta's shoulder. The chief elder stared at him, and when he spoke, his voice trembled. "The replica fell? It is inert?"

"Yes, Chief Elder."

Telsiin nodded. "Then it is so. Someone has done what is forbidden."

The chief elder stood, and now he did gaze out over the river. "You will need to head back ahead of me, Maarta. Summon the Council. We must meet, immediately."

"Yes, Chief Elder," Maarta said, but he lingered. "What are we going to do?"

Telsiin did not turn from the river, but stood, watching the water roll on. "I have no idea. That's why I need you to summon the Council." Telsiin turned and peered at him. "Now go, my child. Go. I am coming."

Part 3

The Sharper Blade

29

The Northlands

Draagan shouldered his pack as he stepped out of the small boat. It contained the few items he'd brought with him, the only things he owned of any use: clothes, weapons, some metallurgical tools, and various supplies. He paid the driver for his labors and their passage, and he waited for the rest of his party to gather their things so they could continue upriver.

He knew they weren't altogether happy about his choice of hideouts. After all the jungle in the interior was inhospitable land. As far up as the stronghold was—even beyond the most remote village outposts of the local tribesmen—it was downright deadly. But even so Draagan had spent a good deal of time here over the years, enough that he felt somewhat at home, and as long as he was being sent into hiding, he wanted to go somewhere not completely unfamiliar. This was no small matter, for if the one who had crossed the Madri with a fragment of the Golden Cord was seeking what he wore, he wanted to be on familiar ground when he came.

Besides all that the stronghold itself was ideal. It was big enough to house a considerable company of Amhuru, and since things had been a little confused when Telsiin sent word of what had happened, Draagan didn't know how many more might be coming to join him. What's more, it was a strong place, easy to defend, and remotely located. All these things made it a solid choice, no matter how much the others might quietly grumble about its location.

With any luck, though, they wouldn't be here too long. It sounded like Telsiin was going to send quite a few kill squads out in search of the Southlander who had made the crossing. How many, Telsiin hadn't yet decided, which was why Draagan didn't know how many more mouths he would have to feed at the stronghold. Overall, Draagan supported a pretty aggressive policy and hoped Telsiin sent as many as possible. He felt they should move fast while the Madri's effects incapacitated the violator. He should be found and killed, and the Southland fragment recovered, as soon as possible.

If this reduced the defense he could be given, he wasn't especially worried. He could defend himself quite well.

But he thought that in the end Telsiin would seek a more moderate course. Rather than dedicating the bulk of their resources to pursuing the violator, he would probably try to divide their strength pretty evenly, boosting the defenses of the three Keepers and using the rest to attempt the recovery. Perhaps that was just as well, Draagan thought, for the move to cross the Madri was audacious, and they still had no real idea just who would be that bold or what they were up against.

There was a splash on the far side of the river, and Draagan turned to see the long, fat body of a large crocodile gliding downstream. It had probably been sunning itself on the bank and then decided it was time to move along, perhaps because of the activity on this side of the river. The others were ready now, so they started on their way going in the opposite direction, up rather than downstream.

Whatever it was they were up against, Draagan thought as he returned to his musings, he just hoped it wasn't a Southland Keeper gone rogue, making a play for more original fragments. It was true the power of the Cord could be overwhelming, almost intoxicating, but the thought that one of their own would betray their very purpose made him uncomfortable. Uncomfortable and angry.

If it was a Keeper who had come, and if the kill squads found him, then they would have no mercy—and that was as it should be, for the violator, whoever it was, would deserve none.

The morning was crisp, just like every other morning for the past month or so. The trees Deslo jogged beneath on the Arua field were more of those pine trees that had also become more common as the band moved north, and the ground beneath him was littered with the brownish needles they dropped. They looked sharp, but when he picked them up, they were surprisingly soft—most of the time. There were also odd, brown objects like small cobs of corn that fell from these trees, though trying to eat them did not seem like a good idea, as they were often hard and sharp. Deslo thought the Northlanders called them "cones," but he wasn't sure exactly why.

Olli jogged quietly off to his left, running parallel to him. He motioned quietly to her that he was going to turn a little to the right, and she motioned that she understood and would come too. They'd seen the deer bounding through the trees a little while ago, but they'd lost sight of him and had hoped to pick up his trail again. If they didn't see him soon, though, Deslo would turn back. It was unfamiliar country, and he didn't want to stray too far from the beach.

Deer were odd creatures, Deslo thought, with their great big eyes, spindly legs, and furry hides, often with pretty white spots. He thought about the rhino-scorpions and the hookworms he'd seen and even hunted in his boyhood near Barra-Dohn, and wondered about how strangely delicate these deer were for this colder world he now inhabited. He would have thought that the cold would breed tougher creatures than the heat, but Marlo had said the opposite was true when Deslo made this observation to him.

Marlo said that the hot, somewhat unforgiving environment that surrounded Barra-Dohn had required both men and animals to be tough in order to survive, but that here, in a more temperate part of the world, more delicate plants and animals could flourish. When Deslo had questioned Marlo's use of the word "temperate," saying instead that it was very cold here, Marlo had laughed.

"If we get far enough north," Marlo had said, "you will see true cold."

Deslo wasn't sure he liked the sound of that. He knew that the far northern reaches of the Northlands, like Golina and other parts of the southernmost Southlands, could be very cold—he just thought that *this* was very cold. The idea that it might actually get colder, a lot colder, made him shiver and dream of home. Their journey to uncover the past of the Jin Dara, which had eventually taken them to Olli's island, had never veered very far south—and consequently had never involved going anywhere terribly cold. Now, in their attempt to flee the Jin Dara, it looked like they just might, and Deslo wondered if at long last, he might actually see this strange stuff called snow that he'd heard about but never seen.

Movement ahead through the trees caught Deslo's eye—the antlered head of the deer, he thought. He slowed, moving a little to the side to duck behind the trunk of one of the pines. It was thin and not nearly wide enough to hide him entirely, but Deslo didn't think the deer had seen him yet and wanted to do what he could to make sure it didn't.

He glanced over at Olli, who had likewise stopped and moved behind a tree. She was watching him, though, which probably meant she hadn't seen the deer yet. He pointed toward it, and she turned to see if she could see it too. After a moment she must have caught a glimpse, because she looked back at him and nodded.

Deslo peered around the tree. The deer was definitely stopped, head erect, looking at something Deslo couldn't see. Maybe it was looking for them in a different direction, or maybe it was distracted by something else. Either way, Deslo thought they had a pretty good chance to get it. The deer he'd hunted before were fast, but they ran through the Arua while he ran on top of it, and that made a difference.

Perhaps it was because he'd been thinking about Barra-Dohn already, missing the warmth, but the thought of running on Arua rather than through it made Deslo think of that day when Rika had taken him to the waterfront to illustrate her point that Arua was a real thing even though he couldn't see it, and that this was why movement on top of it was faster than movement through it. This fact was still something he didn't fully understand, but he didn't question it anymore. He could move so much faster on it himself that he didn't see the point of worrying about why.

Still, starting a foot race with a deer from this far away seemed foolish. He would try to get as close as possible without the creature seeing or smelling him, but the wind wasn't exactly cooperating, and he figured that as close as possible wasn't going to be terribly close. He started out from behind the tree, moving in a bit of an arc so as not to approach the deer in a direct line. That meant moving away from Olli, but he knew she'd understand and follow. They'd hunted together more than a few times in the last few months, and they worked better as a team each time.

Deslo kept his eyes trained on the deer, which still hadn't moved as it stared in a different direction. He kept arcing toward the deer, increasingly surprised at his good fortune. He hadn't expected to be able to get this close undetected, but he wasn't going to complain. He felt pretty confident that he was close enough already, that even if the deer caught wind of him, he would be able to track the deer down, close the gap, and use the slender throwing knife that he was carrying.

And then the deer did something completely unexpected. It turned and bolted almost straight toward Deslo.

Olli saw Deslo hesitate for a moment, standing still on the Arua as the deer zigzagged through the pine trees, moving his way. He readied his knife, while Olli wondered if the creature meant possibly to attack him with its antlers, or if perhaps it had just gone crazy. Then the deer seemed at last to look at Deslo, to actually see him, but instead of doubling back the way it had come, it veered to his right, heading in a new direction altogether.

The bolt in his direction had been strange, Olli thought, and this turn of events just made it feel stranger. Then she understood. The deer wasn't worried about Deslo. It was running from something else.

She turned away from the deer as it ran along its new path to look back in the direction it had come from, and she saw it.

The deer was a graceful creature, running lightly along the ground with strong but precise leaps as it wove in and out among the various trees in its path, and what Olli saw now looked nothing like that. It was large, with plush, deep brown fur, and its great front claws ripped up the ground as it tore ahead in as much of a straight line as the trees allowed. What's more, she could see that the dark eyes set above the snout on the creature's great, round head were looking not at the deer but at Deslo.

Deslo turned and ran, sprinting as fast as his legs could carry him. Olli hoped he could perhaps go a little faster, because running through the Arua didn't look to be slowing down the large brown creature any; it was doing just fine. Just then Deslo turned and looked at her, and from the look on his face and his widened eyes, she could see he was genuinely afraid. He screamed as he drew nearer to her, "Run!"

His scream was drowned out by the growl that erupted behind them, and she turned and ran without need of any further prompting. As Deslo drew up behind her, she glanced back over her shoulder to see if the creature was still coming, or if perhaps, with any luck, the growl was a parting shot as it kept after the deer. They had not been lucky. The thing was still coming, and it was coming fast.

Deslo drew alongside Olli. She wasn't sure how far they were exactly from the beach or their longboat or any help they might get from the others who'd come ashore from *The Sorry Rogue,* and she figured that they would probably have to deal with this problem themselves.

"We need to split up," Deslo shouted, just before he had to veer to the right to go around a pine tree that she was bypassing on its left.

"What?" she shouted as they drew together on the other side. She hoped Deslo would hear in her voice not a question about what he had said but a question about the sanity of what he had proposed.

"It can't follow us both," Deslo said. "The other can circle around, maybe get a good angle on it."

"Can we take it down?"

"We have to try," Deslo said, and then she saw a look on his face, like he was getting an idea or recalling a memory, and he added, "If you get a chance, go for an eye. Maybe we can wound it enough for it to decide we're not worth the risk."

Olli nodded. She had lived to see the gorgaal destroyed and her island liberated. She had left it far behind and crossed the Madri. She wasn't going to die today. Not here, not like this.

Deslo peeled off to the right, turning sharply and dodging between a couple pine trees that lay that way. Olli turned the other way, looking over her shoulder to see if the creature had turned her way or his, and saw that it had followed her, so she continued ahead. She had to trust that Deslo would notice and cut back to come after her. For now she just needed to keep running, since turning had given the thing a chance to take a new angle and gain some ground. In fact she could see the great brown beast out of the corner of her eye now without needing to turn her head. That wasn't good.

She veered back right, not enough that she was heading back in their original direction, but she knew she needed to buy Deslo some time. She needed to buy herself some time, and she couldn't wait until the thing got a whole lot closer. She deliberated. She could turn, throw her knife, and still have time to take evasive maneuvers, as long as the thing was far enough behind her. If she waited too long, and if the knife didn't slow the thing down—well, she imagined those claws could rip her right open, given a chance.

And then Olli got another idea. Maybe fifty yards ahead was a pine with solid branches not much higher off the ground than her head. She thought maybe she could grab ahold and pull herself up. It would be risky, since if she misplayed the maneuver it might only succeed in knocking her off the Arua, but if it worked, she might be out of the creature's reach.

Before she had any more time to contemplate that possibility, though, she heard another growl from the thing behind her, but a different kind of growl. She heard pain as well as rage in this one, and she turned to see the knife Deslo had been carrying sticking out of the creature's shoulder. He had probably been throwing for the head, and Olli knew that the miss meant her decision had been made for her. She had to take her shot.

The creature slowed, distracted as much by Deslo's reappearance, Olli figured, as by the knife in its shoulder. She readied her knife and started to run back at the thing, which seemed taken aback by this brazen move by its prey. And then, when Olli raised her arm with knife in hand, the creature suddenly wheeled around as though to flee.

Olli threw, but she was just a moment too late. The creature's head swung out of view, and the knife hit the same shoulder that Deslo's had, just a little bit further back. Deslo had almost reached her by now, and she saw him reach and slip his axe from his belt. He must be wondering too if even two knives sticking out of the thing's shoulder would be enough to stop it if it decided it wanted another crack at them.

But it didn't turn back, and as it disappeared from view, Deslo lowered the axe in his hand. Olli approached and stopped beside him. They both stood still, panting for breath.

"What was that?" Olli asked, wiping the sweat from her brow.

"I don't know," Deslo said, "but I guess we've just been warned."

"Warned about what?"

"Not to underestimate the Northlands."

"I see," Olli said. "Were we doing that?"

"I might have been," Deslo said, "underestimating the wildlife, at least. I won't anymore, though. That was terrifying."

"Sa," Olli said.

Deslo frowned. "Can't we say 'yes' when we're alone?"

"Na," Olli said. "Or we might say it when we're not. You know that."

"Sa, I guess I do," Deslo said. He glanced back through the pines. "Our deer is long gone, and I'm not really in a hunting mood anymore. Head back?"

"Sa, let's," Olli said as they turned to head back to the beach. "Those knives are gone for good, Deslo."

"I know. Let's hope Tchinchura's not too mad that we borrowed them."

"I don't know if he'll care that we borrowed them," Olli said, "I'm just worried he'll be upset that we lost them."

"We couldn't lose them without borrowing them first," Deslo said. "And anyway, they aren't technically lost. We know that thing has them, we just don't know where he's taking them."

"Why do I put up with you?" Olli murmured, smiling.

"Because you have no choice?" Deslo suggested, helpfully. "Just like why I put up with you?"

Olli gave Deslo one of her looks, one of her "you-should-really-stop-talking-now" looks. They'd come a long way since she'd first joined the wanderers aboard *The Sorry Rogue,* and even though they teased each other good-naturedly now, there were limits to what she would take, and Deslo was starting to be better about recognizing when he was approaching one of those. He seemed to be getting the hint now.

“Thanks for moving so quickly back there, Deslo,” she said after a moment. “I was getting a little nervous. That thing was fast.”

“You’re welcome, Olli,” Deslo said.

“See, being nice isn’t so hard, is it?” she asked after his polite reply.

“Sa, it is, but I’m working on it.”

30

The Land of Broken Dreams

Back at the longboat, Marlo and Owenn were setting casks of fresh water filled from the nearby stream in the boat. Actually, Owenn was setting them in the boat, and Marlo was watching. They'd carried them back from the stream together, but Owenn was strong enough to lift them one at a time and set them gently in the bottom of the boat on his own, which he was doing.

Marlo explained that the sailors who'd come ashore with them had found a grove of apple trees, and that they had returned to the grove after bringing their water cask back to collect some. Deslo wasn't eager to wait, as his adventure with the creature in the wood had made him more than anxious to leave this place behind, but the thought of fresh apples was appealing. He'd never had an apple before coming north of the Madri—though his mother and D'Sarza both said they'd encountered them in the Southlands—and he liked them a lot.

Olli sat by the longboat, and before long she was recounting their adventure in the wood with the two Kalosenes. Deslo, though, drifted away from the longboat, walking restlessly along the pebbly beach. He didn't mind Olli telling the story, but he didn't especially want to relive it, and he didn't feel like sitting still and waiting for the sailors to come back.

He picked up a handful of the smooth pebbles beneath his feet and started slinging them, one at a time, into the water out beyond the waves that were rolling in. He could still hear Olli, now answering questions, describing the great brown creature, and he kept walking, farther and farther away.

He didn't mean to be difficult with Olli, and he knew his inability to stand or sit still had become noticeable with her and the others. He couldn't help acting antsy. He felt antsy. He didn't know if it was the fact that he'd been unconscious for almost a month after passing through the Madri, but ever since he'd woken up, he hadn't been able to shake this nervous feeling.

Olli had been out almost that long too, but she seemed to have adjusted better, and that made him think it wasn't really physical. He was worried about his father, his "yadi"—the word was still awkward, even in his mind—who was still unconscious, just like the Amhuru, even though they had crossed the Madri almost four months ago. Deslo suspected that was the real reason, that maybe what he felt each day was just a deep-seated anxiety that Kaden wouldn't wake up again.

Deslo knew his fear wasn't entirely rational. After all, he had woken up, and that was evidence that the effects of the Madri on someone wearing Zerura weren't necessarily fatal. What's more, Tchinchura had warned that the amount of time each of them was unconscious would be different, depending on how long they had worn their fragment and how deeply the effects of the Zerura had touched them.

Still, his experience of passing through the Madri had been terrible, far worse than he had expected. He had understood it wouldn't be pleasant, but in the end he figured that just meant he would feel pretty sick when he woke up. He hadn't thought that the experience of being unconscious would itself be unpleasant. Quite the contrary, he figured he would fall asleep, the time would pass while he was unaware, and then he would simply wake up. He assumed the time would pass in a blink, just like it always did when asleep.

He had been wrong. Very, very wrong.

He wouldn't exactly say that he had been aware of the passage of time while he was out, not accurately and not completely, but he had been aware of something like that, and that something had been nightmarish. He had seemed to pass from troubled dream to troubled dream, each worse than the next, and in all of them, there was the shared, vivid experience of feeling trapped with no way out.

The dreams weren't nightmares, not in the traditional sense. There were no monsters, no catastophes, and no violent deaths, but there were oddities. There were bends in the nature of things, some slight, some more significant, and unlike most dreams where you don't realize these things until after you wake up, he saw and understood the "off-ness" of each and every new dream into which he wandered.

In one of them, the sky was not quite right. It was blue, but blue with a trace of purple, and there were far too many birds flying above his head. The strange sky and the abundance of birds creeped him out, and while he tried not to look up, he couldn't help it. He kept shutting his eyes, hoping that the dream would end—he knew, even as it was happening, that it was a dream—but he kept opening his eyes to find the sky the same, the birds still there, and no way out.

In another dream, Deslo was on a ship like *The Sorry Rogue*, only it wasn't *The Sorry Rogue*, and Deslo knew he wasn't supposed to be on it. He was alone, the ship was perhaps a few hundred yards away from land, and he kept going below decks in search of someone to help him get the ship to port. Each time he went below, he found no one, and when he came back up on deck, he was on a different ship. Over and over, the same cycle repeated. Every time he came up, he felt a glimmer of hope that on this ship, there might be help below decks, but there never was, and on and on it went, until he thought he would go mad.

What Deslo could't remember, what perhaps he didn't want to remember, was how he had transitioned from nightmare to nightmare. He could remember all the places, the awful succession of places, the vivid feeling that he would never escape them, the tedium of going over and over through some repetitive process in each one, but not how he left any of them or arrived at the next.

Waking up from that long and troubled sleep had been a relief, but Deslo still felt its effects. The antsiness was just a part of it. He was anxious about going to sleep, fearful of even ordinary dreams, and constantly wondering if the situation he was in was real or not. He was constantly worried if he wasn't still somehow trapped in the land of broken dreams—as he had come to think of that place he had gone during his long and miserable sleep.

Curiously, the terrifying brown beast in the pines reassured him that his adventure today had been quite real. The nightmarish landscapes he'd wandered through hadn't been so overtly hostile, so directly threatening. That gave the episode he had just endured a feeling of reality that he treasured. Those things that reminded him he was awake and that the world around him was real were good, even if, like the creature, they terrified him.

The challenge, of course, was that the Northlands were much like the Southlands, though with real if sometimes subtle differences. For someone who'd passed through the Madri, spending as much time wandering through the broken dreamscapes as Deslo had, it was disconcerting to wake up in a world that was much the same but a little different—all the time, every day.

Life on *The Sorry Rogue* felt much like it always had, only with people all around him saying "sa" and na," and with the expectation that he'd refer to his mother as "Noni" and to his father as "Yadi." Meals were similar but with slight changes, like the apples now often used to garnish them, and going ashore always brought him face to face with more of these slight changes. He didn't want to stay onboard, as the waiting for the others to wake up was driving him crazy, but going ashore too often felt like falling into another seemingly inescapable dream.

Deslo was standing still now, just staring out to sea, so wrapped up in his own thoughts that he didn't notice Olli until she was almost upon him. He reacted, a little startled, when she said his name.

"I'm sorry," she said. "I didn't mean to sneak up on you."

"It's all right," Deslo said, giving Olli a weak smile. "I was just preoccupied."

"Yes, I can see that," Olli said. She reached up and placed her hand gently on his shoulder. "You're not alone, Deslo. I understand what you're going through."

Deslo looked at Olli, looked and knew that this was true. He didn't know how she knew what he'd been thinking about, but she did. He nodded. "I know you do."

They stood, side by side, staring out to sea, and Deslo added, "What if he gets stuck in that awful place? What if he never wakes up?"

"He will," Olli said. "They all will."

"When? It's been almost four months. Can you imagine that? Almost four months? There?"

Olli shook her head. "No."

"And he only became an apprentice three years ago. If he's still . . . out, then how long will the Amhuru be stuck there?"

Olli didn't answer. She didn't know any more than he did, and Deslo knew there was nothing either of them could say that would change that.

"Hey," Olli said a moment later, turning away from the water and looking at Deslo. "The sailors have returned, and we can head back whenever you want. Let's go see Kita. She'll cheer us both up."

Kita, Deslo's baby sister, had been born just days before he woke and returned from the land of broken dreams. Olli was right.

She was one of the few things that could take his mind off the memories and doubts and fears that plagued him. He couldn't believe he'd ever been anything less than completely enthusiastic about having a sibling. He'd only known her for three months, and already he couldn't imagine life without her.

And yet his yadi had never met her, had never held her in his arms, and kissed her soft head. Deslo's fourteenth birthday was just a few months away, and while he didn't want his yadi to miss it, it somehow seemed worse that he had missed so many "ordinary" days in Kita's life. She changed so much, so quickly, and Kaden had missed all of it so far.

"Yes," he said, sighing as he turned to Olli, "let's go back."

The sailors and the Devoted were waiting, and they rowed back to *The Sorry Rogue* with their haul of apples and fresh water. Deslo was sorry they didn't have fresh meat to go with it, but there would be more chances to hunt the next time.

Back onboard, Deslo prepared to help stow the casks of water, when Captain D'Sarza came and pulled him back, away from the others. She whispered quietly in his ear. "Come with me, Deslo. Your father is awake."

Kaden gripped the lamp tightly in his hand, the familiar, sweet smell of sage oil somehow out of place. Of course the lamp should smell like that—they all did, didn't they?

The dark stairs kept going, on and on, down and down, and he kept going too. Just when he started to wonder if he should turn around and go back up, he saw the bottom. Once there, he saw the open door on his left, passed through it, and noticed the jar of sage oil and the lamp on the floor, much like the one in his hand.

Kaden stared at the jar and lamp. He already had a lamp, but for some reason, he thought he should take up this one. He set down the one he was holding, picked up the jar, and filled the new lamp. The sage oil reacted with the meridium core of the new lamp, and it emitted a strong light as he picked it up. He turned, surveying the tomb, and walked over toward the large, marble sarcophagus.

Examining it, he was surprised to see the lid propped open a little bit. Who had been here? Why had they opened the sarcophagus? What was inside it? He pried the lid open further, and he saw to his surprise that inside there were stairs, descending down into darkness. He leaned over, holding the lamp so he could see below, but the bottom of the stairs lay beyond his view. He hesitated, but only briefly, knowing instinctively he needed to go down there. He climbed over the edge of the sarcophagus, dropped lightly onto the top stair, and started down.

Kaden gripped the lamp tightly in his hand, the familiar, sweet smell of sage oil somehow out of place. Of course the lamp should smell like that—they all did, didn't they?

The dark stairs kept going, on and on, down and down, and he kept going too. Just when he started to wonder if he should turn around and go back up, he saw the bottom. Once there, he saw the open door on his left, passed through it, and noticed the jar of sage oil and the lamp on the floor, much like the one in his hand.

Kaden stared at the jar and lamp. He already had a lamp, but for some reason, he thought he should take up this one. He set down the one he was holding, picked up the jar, and filled the new lamp. The sage oil reacted with the meridium core of the new lamp, and it emitted a strong light as he picked it up. He turned, surveying the tomb, and walked over toward the large, marble sarcophagus.

A voice, from somewhere far away, or maybe from deep down in Kaden's mind, called to him. It said his name, softly, distracting him from the sarcophagus. He thought, vaguely, that the voice was familiar, as was the sarcophagus. He knew he'd been here before, many times in fact, maybe hundreds of times. He was lost and alone, wandering in the dark. He couldn't remember a time before he had come here, but that voice . . . it was a voice from somewhere else.

Kaden opened his eyes.

Nara was sitting beside him, running her fingers through his hair, softly stroking him. When his eyes opened, though, her fingers stopped. "Kaden? Are you really awake?"

He tried to say her name, but his mouth was so dry, nothing came out. She noticed his lips moving, heard the croak of his failed words, and lifted a cup of water to his lips. He drank, eagerly, not minding the small rivulet of water than ran over his chin down his neck.

"Nara . . ." he said at last. "Am I really here?"

"Yes, darling," Nara said, tears forming in her eyes. "At last. I've sat by your side calling you back to me every day for the last four months. You're finally back."

Four months. Kaden heard what she said, but he had difficulty comprehending it. On the one hand, it seemed a staggeringly long time to have been unconscious, but that wasn't the real reason he struggled with what she said. He had felt lost in that dark place for so long, he couldn't believe it had only been four months. He would not have been surprised to wake and find himself an old man, to find that years had slipped away from him. He felt relief wash over him that this was not the case, and tears came to his own eyes to match the ones in hers.

"And Deslo?"

Nara nodded, smiling. "He woke months ago."

Kaden nodded, acknowledging the news, then, as though afraid he would forget, he added, "The baby?"

"Beautiful," Nara said. "She's sleeping right now, but I'll bring her in after I've gotten you something to eat. Are you hungry?"

"She," Kaden said. He had a daughter.

"Yes, she," Nara said, and laughed. It was a beautiful sound. "You have an adorable little girl. Are you hungry?"

"Yes," Kaden said, suddenly realizing that he wasn't just hungry, he was famished.

Nara brought food, but despite how hungry he was, Kaden didn't eat much more than some soup and bread, with a little fruit.

Nara said Olli and Deslo had been the same, that they'd taken a few days before they could eat in a manner consistent with their appetites. It seemed to be something to do with the aftereffects of passing through the Madri, and it would take him a while before he regained his strength. He might even, she thought, have to stay in bed for a while.

He didn't like that idea at all. Being in bed made him think of sleeping, and the thought of going back to sleep was as unappealing as anything he could think of. And yet he felt his weakness and knew she was right. He had little business doing anything but lying down at the moment.

Nara took the tray she had brought his food on and left, returning a moment later with a small bundle in her arms. She sat beside him and pulled back the blanket just enough to reveal the face of their sleeping baby. Tiny blonde curls peeked out from under the blanket on top of her head, and a little ball of a fist lay against her red cheek. She yawned, opening her mouth wide, but her eyes remained closed, and she seemed to settle herself again, nestling against her mother.

Kaden stared in wonder, felt his heart go out to this tiny little thing, and knew that he was truly back. Whatever doubt had plagued him that perhaps, just maybe, this was but another dream, disappeared. "Kita?"

"Yes," Nara said. "Sonakita."

They had discussed names before the crossing, and agreed on Andira if they had a boy—a name out of a popular story they both liked—and Kita if they had a girl. Sonakita had been Nara's mother's name, but everyone had called her Kita, much like everyone called her daughter Nara rather than Ellenara. Sonakita wouldn't have been Kaden's first choice, but he knew how much Nara missed her mother and how much she wanted her little girl to be named after her, so he had agreed And now that he saw her, he thought Kita somehow seemed just right.

"I . . ." Kaden started. "I want to hold her, but I don't think I should."

"I know," Nara said. "It's all right. You'll be strong enough soon."

There was a knock on the door, and Nara rose with Kita in her arms and went to answer it. She opened the door, disappeared momentarily from sight as she stepped through it to speak to whoever was there, and then the door opened wider to reveal Deslo standing in the doorway, staring. Then, in a single swift motion, he crossed the room, sat down on the bed, and bent over to give Kaden a hug so strong that it hurt.

Kaden grunted a little with pain, and Deslo let go, sitting back up. "I'm sorry, I didn't mean to—"

"It's all right," Kaden said. "I'm glad to see you too. Glad to be back."

"It's . . ." Deslo started, looking into Kaden's eyes with understanding and fear. "It's terrible there."

"Yes," Kaden said. "But we're back. We made it."

Deslo nodded. He didn't want to talk about the land of broken dreams right now, and he doubted that his father did either. There would be time later for that, he supposed. "You'll need help at first, when you try to walk. I can help you, if you'd like."

"That would be good," Kaden said. "Maybe it's only been four months, but I feel like an old man."

"It'll pass," Deslo said. "Maybe Tchinchura and Calamin and Trajax will wake soon."

"Still out, then?" Kaden said.

"Yes."

"Tchinchura did say it would hit them harder," Kaden said.

That sat for a little while, and then Deslo said, "Would you like me to go and get Noni, or do you maybe want a little rest?"

"Noni?" Kaden said, confused at first.

"Yes, Yadi," Deslo said. "I've been getting used to saying 'yadi' and 'noni,' but even Captain D'Sarza said 'father' to me a little while ago, so it's not completely ingrained yet."

"Oh, yes, that's right," Kaden said. "No, I don't even want to think about sleep, I've had all the rest I want for a while, thank you very much. Stay with me a little while? Tell me what's been going on."

"Had a little episode today," Deslo said.

"Oh? Tell me."

Deslo recounted the story, and Kaden asked him questions, specifically about what the creature looked like. The more Deslo described him, the more Kaden thought that perhaps he knew what it was that his son had encountered among these strange "pine trees" Deslo spoke of.

"I think the animal is called a bear," Kaden said. "When Gamalian taught me about the flora and fauna of the deeper Southlands, he described an animal much like the one you are describing."

"We have them in the Southlands?" Deslo said, eyes growing wide.

"I think so," Kaden said. "Just far south of Barra-Dohn, where it's colder. I think that heavy fur you described would be tough for the desert near home, don't you?"

"It would be awful," Deslo agreed. After a moment he added, more soberly, "I miss Gamalian, Yadi."

"So do I," Kaden said. "I think he would have been very pleased to see the Northlands with us, don't you?"

"Yes," Deslo said. "I think so. He loved learning."

"He did indeed." After a moment Kaden started again. "So, if we're off the coast of land that has woods like those and a creature like that, D'Sarza must be far, far north of the Madri."

"That's right," Deslo said. "We've been working steadily north almost the whole time."

"Interesting," Kaden said. "I thought we'd stay in the more tropical regions closer to the Madri while we waited for the Amhuru to wake up."

"Yes, well, D'Sarza says Tchinchura gave her freedom to do what she thought was best," Deslo explained, "and that he didn't really know where the Amhuru would be on this side, so any direction was as good as another as far as he knew."

"I see," Kaden said. "So why north, then, if any direction was as good as another?"

"The captain says that as rare as Southlanders north of the Madri might be, the one place that's even remotely familiar with them are the ports closer to the Madri. She thought that the farther north we went, the more our accents and habits might be chalked up to being travelers from a distant port, and that the more northern Northlanders might not pick us out as Southlanders as easily."

"Ah, yes," Kaden said, thinking about that. "I see her point. Clever. I hope she's right."

"Me too," Deslo said. "Especially if the Amhuru are going to be out a lot longer. We'd be in real trouble if they found us before they wake up. We might be in real trouble, anyway."

"Perhaps," Kaden said. "But let's not think about that. Not today."

"All right," Deslo said. "Not today."

"The Northlands," Kaden said, a moment later. "I never thought I'd see the Northlands. Never once, in all my years as a prince in Barra-Dohn. I can't believe we're really here."

"We're here," Deslo said. "When you're feeling better, I'll take you ashore to see it."

"I'd like that," Kaden said. "Though I'm not sure I'm ready to see a bear, not up close, anyway. Not yet."

"No," Deslo said, with a sheepish grin. "I can wait awhile before I see another one too."

31

Picking up the Trail

Amintuu sat in the dark corner booth, a steaming cup of jonda in front of him. The cup was hot to the touch, the jonda scalding, and he blew on the dark surface to cool it a little before sipping again. The first sip had burned his tongue, and he didn't want to do that again. The serving girl told him it was very hot, but Amintuu thought that was just something serving girls say and hadn't anticipated quite how true the statement would turn out to be.

The jonda was good, a little bitter, but good. The door opened, and Amintuu turned to see a couple of bushy-bearded guardsman walk in. One of them looked his way, saw his eyes, and looked nervously away again. They walked over to a table across the room and sat down.

Maarta had gone to roust out the merchant he'd been so eager to tell Amintuu about the night before, and even if the man was reluctant, it shouldn't have taken this long. Merchants didn't normally refuse the requests of Amhuru, even young ones like Maarta.

Amintuu hadn't been happy when Telsiin had told him to take Maarta along as part of his kill squad, but after traveling together for a year, Amintuu had come to see he was wrong about the lad. Maarta certainly did things his own way, but Amintuu had figured out this was not out of rebellion or a desire to avoid the rules but because Maarta just didn't see the world the way most people did. Originality and creativity weren't traits that the Amhuru discouraged necessarily, but they weren't their most common attribute, either.

Yes, there were times when Amintuu had to rein in Maarta's meandering mind, and at times he had to just say "enough" to the flood of questions that always seemed about to overwhelm him. At the same time, there had definitely been moments when Maarta's questions had revealed that the boy saw things the others did not, that he could imagine things that they could not. Indeed, it was fair to say that Amintuu would not trade Maarta for any of the others he had pleaded with Telsiin to send in his place—yet another sign that Telsiin saw a larger picture and understood things that Amintuu just didn't. Not yet, anyway.

The door opened again, and this time it was Maarta, followed by another man who was very tall, taller than Maarta, and perhaps even taller than Amintuu himself. The man was broad-chested, with a shock of white hair and a matching white goatee, and a scar across his left cheek. Maarta located Amintuu in the corner booth, and he made his way over with the merchant in tow.

"Good morning, Keeper," the merchant said, tipping his head in a deferential gesture as he slid into the booth opposite Amintuu. Amintuu observed the term of respect and the man's general demeanor with satisfaction. He would help if he could, Amintuu thought.

"Good morning, thanks for meeting with us so early," Amintuu said. "Please, have some jonda." Amintuu raised his arm and motioned to the serving girl, who nodded and went to fetch the jonda according to the arrangement he had made with her.

"It is not necessary, Keeper," the merchant said.

"It is nothing, I insist," Amintuu said.

"Thank you," the merchant said as the serving girl came, setting fresh cups of jonda before the merchant and Maarta.

"Na, it is nothing," Amintuu said. "But I warn you, it is very hot."

The merchant sipped the jonda carefully, and smiled. "Sa, it is."

Amintuu sipped his own. "I trust Maarta has told you what we are seeking?"

"Sa. You seek news of Southlanders traveling the Northlands."

"Sa, sa," Amintuu said and nodded. Then he gambled. "Especially Southlanders keeping company with other Keepers."

Amintuu kept his eyes on the merchant, but he could sense Maarta's reaction. Maarta would not have told the man this, for he knew Amintuu would have been furious if he had. Even Amintuu had never said anything like this to any of the others that they had spoken with during their search. Sometimes, though, risks had to be taken.

The merchant considered Amintuu for a moment, as though reappraising him, and then he said, "I have news of Southlanders, Keeper, but I cannot say if they had other Keepers with them."

"It is well," Amintuu said. "Please, tell me your news."

"Like I told the young one," the merchant said, indicating Maarta with a nod, "it was about six weeks ago, at Dreesen. I had business with a captain there."

"Maarta mentioned her," Amintuu said. "She acknowledged she was a Southlander?"

"Na," the merchant said. "That's the thing. She didn't, and all Southlander merchants who cross the Madri do."

"To brag?"

"To brag," the merchant said, "but mostly to haggle. They know having Southland goods will raise the price and give them a better deal simply because they're from the other side. Especially this far north."

"And she traded with you without doing this? Without pushing her claim?"

"Sa, she did."

"Then how did you know she was a Southlander?"

"Keeper, my father was a merchant and his father before him," the merchant said. "I've served beneath the mast my whole life. I have met more than a few Southland merchants in my time, and talked with them, and though she tried to sound like a Northlander, I could tell she was not."

"She tried to sound like a Northlander?" Amintuu asked. He kept his rising excitement under control, but it was difficult. After so long, to finally be picking up the trail instead of hunting in the dark . . .

"Sa, she did, and she was pretty good," the merchant said. "I think she would fool most people, but I have been across the Madri, Keeper. I have spent time in the Southlands. She was a Southlander, I would wager my ship on it."

Amintuu looked at Maarta for the first time during the conversation. The young Amhuru nodded. He had been excited the previous evening when he had reported to Amintuu that he thought he had found something that would help them at last. Amintuu hadn't wanted to hope, not until he spoke with the man himself, but he understood Maarta's excitement now and shared it.

Amintuu looked back at the merchant, who was taking another sip of his jonda. "Do you remember the name of the ship?"

"Sa, it was called *The Sorry Rogue.*"

Amintuu nodded, taking his own drink in turn. "I don't suppose this captain gave any indication where she was headed next, did she?"

"Na, she did not," the merchant said, shaking his head. "I can'na say where she was headed."

"Or where she had just come from?"

"I am sorry, Keeper, I can'na say."

"It is well," Amintuu said. He drummed his fingers on the table next to his cup of jonda. It was time to consider an even larger gamble, and he looked at the merchant, who sat waiting patiently for any further questions he might ask.

"Have you given transport to Keepers before, merchant?"

"Sa, I have," the merchant said. "My father taught me it was ill fortune to refuse a Keeper."

Amintuu nodded slightly to acknowledge the merchant's past service to his people. Though the Amhuru worked hard to communicate to the ship captains they sought passage from that they were free to say "sa" or "na" as they willed, there were many who felt that the choice was not as free as the Amhuru said it was. Some feared reprisal, but most were simply superstitious and feared, as this man did, ill fortune.

Amintuu leaned forward, setting his elbows on the table, his hands clasped. "Merchant, I have a proposal for you, but only if you assure me that you understand you are free to say 'na.' I can'na ask unless I know you understand this."

The merchant watched Amintuu, and the Amhuru could see the struggle inside him. The man had seen more than sixty winters, Amintuu was sure. It would not be easy for him to accept what Amintuu was saying. Nonetheless, Amintuu could not ask unless he believed the merchant understood.

"Keeper, I would be happy to give you and the young one passage if you desire it. We are at your—"

"Na," Amintuu said, shaking his head. "That is not what I asked, merchant, and you know it. Are you telling me you are not free in your heart to say 'na'?"

"It would be difficult, Keeper," the merchant said at last, acknowledging the truth of it. "It is not what I was taught."

"I appreciate your faithfulness to your fathers," Amintuu said. "Perhaps it would help to see what they taught you as counsel not for all requests from Amhuru but only as counsel for the typical Amhuru requests for passage. This is different, and you may say 'na' without breaking their precept."

The merchant considered this thoughtfully, and at last he nodded. "You have a point, Keeper. The tradition was about Keepers who sought passage, and if that is not what you ask, then to say 'na' would not be to break it."

"I do seek passage," Amintuu admitted, "but it is not all I seek."

"A fine line," the merchant said.

"Indeed, but not the first fine line you've encountered in life, I'm sure."

"Na, to be sure." The merchant gazed down at his jonda, then nodded, slowly at first, then more strongly. "I am ready for your proposal, Keeper, and I will say 'na' if I feel I must."

"It is well," Amintuu said. "We need you to take us to Dreesen. There we will seek news about where this ship has gone. And, whether we find that news in Dreesen or not, we must seek it until we find it. Wherever it takes us. However long it takes. *The Sorry Rogue*—and those it carries—must be found."

The merchant had not said "na," and Amintuu had negotiated a price with him to hire his ship, *The Lion's Mane,* to take them to Dreesen and beyond, though to be sure, the merchant didn't try to negotiate very much, accepting almost immediately all the terms that Amintuu proposed. The merchant's name was Kanns, and Amintuu was hopeful he might dissuade him during their time traveling together to abandon his misgivings about dealing with Amhuru as he must with other men.

Kanns had been more than a little surprised that his cargo was to be not two Amhuru but six. He acknowledged that he had never encountered two traveling together, let alone more, but he accepted Amintuu's proffered compensation for the extra men and said he would figure out how to free up two cabins for them, though that was probably the best he could do. Amintuu assured him it would be enough.

Amintuu and the rest of his kill squad were to meet Kanns at the dock just before dawn, so he was headed with Maarta back to their camp outside of town. Amhuru caused a bit of a stir wherever they went, even when alone, and traveling in such large numbers tended to draw far more attention than Amintuu wanted. So they had gotten used to camping well outside of whatever town or city they were investigating and taking turns to be the ones who went in and enjoyed the hospitality of each new location.

"Amintuu?" Maarta said as they turned from the main road onto the rough, smaller road that led to the clearing where the other four in the kill squad were camped. The young Amhuru had been uncharacteristically quiet most of the way from their meeting with Kanns, but with their time alone on the road running out, Amintuu was not surprised that he had decided it was now or never to ask his questions.

"Yes, Maarta."

Maarta did not speak right away. He gazed ahead as he walked on the Arua beside Amintuu. "Why did you ask Kanns if he had seen Keepers with the Southlanders?"

"I wanted to know if he had."

Maarta glanced over, frowning. "Do you really think an Amhuru would cross the Madri with a fragment?"

"I would not have thought so," Amintuu said. "But whoever did has evaded us for a year. It's almost as though they knew we'd be looking. Who but an Amhuru would know that we would know?"

"Kanns said he hadn't seen an Amhuru with this captain."

"True, he did not see one," Amintuu agreed. "Though we both know that doesn't mean much."

They walked on a ways, and then Maarta asked another question. "He had only just arrived when you asked. What did you see that made you trust him?"

"Respect," Amintuu said, shrugging, and then he added, "And a look of honesty."

"But wasn't it risky?"

"A year, Maarta," Amintuu said. "We've been searching a year, with no luck. I wanted him to understand this was serious. What's more, I knew that if the news he gave us was valuable, then I would ask him for passage, and I wanted to establish the gravity of our task before I did so."

"You didn't answer my question, Amintuu," Maarta said, with the bluntness that other, older Amhuru like Amintuu sometimes took as disrespect, but which was really just Maarta's candor unchecked. "Wasn't it risky?"

"Sa, it was risky."

"Then why?"

"Because I deemed Kanns trustworthy and the risk to be worth it. I thought that if I showed faith in him, he might later be willing to put faith in me."

Maarta nodded. "We have cast our lot with him now."

"And he with us."

The rest of the kill squad heard their news with subdued expectation. Maarta's news the night before had encouraged them all, but now Amintuu confirmed that it was true. They had indeed, at long last, found news that brought hope. They might soon be within reach of their journey's end.

The six Amhuru squatted together in the clearing, heads bowed low, and together they gave thanks to Kalos for this day, and for what He had provided for them on it. Then, as they struck the hard earth with their knives and the long sharp blades sank deep, they asked that they might be able to complete the task they had been sent to perform—to recover the Southland fragment and kill the one who had taken it.

After, Amintuu sought out privacy a fair distance away in the wood, where the voices of his kin would not intrude on what he must do. He found a small cluster of trees and squatted within it. Reaching down, he tapped the band on his right forearm and it began immediately to pulse and unwind, until at last it danced in the air above his hand, still pulsing rhythmically.

He tapped it again and whispered to it, and it formed a circle in the air where it rotated, still pulsating. He leaned in close, but did not yet speak through it.

Of the various kill squads that Telsiin had sent to find the missing fragment, only four, he thought, would be close enough for their leader to receive his message. All the same, he would call them and see if any of the others could spread the word still further.

The message would be simple and clear—Southlanders had been spotted in Dreesen. Not just Southlanders, Amintuu thought, but Southlanders trying to pass themselves off as Northlanders.

He leaned in still closer and whispered into the circle created by his Zerura. The words would be transported across the miles; the members of the other squads that were in direct communication with him would feel a vibration in their Zerura, and when they had a chance, they would listen to his message.

Then they would come, and together they would draw the net tight around the Southlanders who had dared to cross the Madri.

It saddened Amintuu to think that behind this whole thing, there might be a rogue Amhuru—making the name of the Southland ship a sorry pun indeed—but even if it was, there was no room for pity. He would find whoever it was, whatever it took.

And then his kill squad, or one of the others, would do what must be done.

32

Sar Komen

Not long after Kita's first birthday, after more than a year in the strange dream state that Kaden had also come to think of as the land of broken dreams, the three Amhuru on *The Sorry Rogue* woke up.

Physically they were very weak, and it took more than a month for them to get up on their feet and to be strong enough to move about without help. Even then, they moved with care, and Kaden knew that it would be some time still before they had completely recovered. Even so, the physical effects of their missing year were not what worried Kaden the most.

For Kaden, his return to reality had been one of joy, greeted by his wife and children, and of course being released from the terrible dreams that had haunted him. And yet he had found sleep difficult for some time thereafter. He tensed when it was time for bed, felt internal resistance as his mind and body struggled not to sleep, and when he awoke, he found a need to check his surroundings for signs of their reality, always afraid that he might somehow have fallen back into the world that had held him captive for so long.

And he had only been their four months.

For the Amhuru the effect was magnified. Curiously, Tchinchura had seemed most like his old self on the day he first awoke. He smiled, talked quietly with them, and expressed his gratitude that Kalos had kept them safe during the year he had been unconscious. He talked with Calamin and Trajax, who had been awake for a week or so already, and Kaden could see the good effect his return had on their spirits. Kaden had hoped that day that all would be well.

But as the days went on, Tchinchura started showing signs of the same lingering effects that had plagued them all to differing degrees. He grew quiet, pensive, often staring around as though trying to tell if what he saw was real. Kaden would come up alongside him and gently touch him and say, "This is real. You are free."

Tchinchura would nod, would acknowledge Kaden's words, but Kaden knew he could only help so much. He knew that Tchinchura couldn't really know if those words were true, that they too weren't part of a dream world where every day he woke up on a ship wondering if he was real and the world around him was real and every day he was comforted by a friend as though he was out of it when he might, in fact, not be out.

The only thing that could help Tchinchura and the others now was what had helped Olli and Deslo, and Kaden too, and that was time. They would need time, and likely plenty of it, which meant that a choice would have to be made about Captain D'Sarza's plan without having the Amhuru quite all the way back, physically or emotionally.

For a year they had been winding their way from small port to small port, slowly working their way north, away from the Madri. Sometimes they'd drop anchor off a pretty piece of land with no nearby habitation and stay there a few weeks, hunting and fishing to restock their supplies, before moving on when it seemed opportune to do so. This had been working pretty well, but D'Sarza had pointed out that their second winter in the Northlands was approaching soon, and this time it would find them much farther from the temperate middle latitudes than it had the first time. So, some time after the Amhuru had awoken, D'Sarza and Geffen met with them and the three Amhuru apprentices to discuss the captain's thoughts on this.

"We should go to Sar Komen," D'Sarza said.

"Sar Komen?" Kaden said, frowning. "I thought we were trying to avoid big cities?"

"We are, but we need to find a harbor that the *Rogue* can winter in. Ships need maintenance, and it has been too long since we've had any. We can get it in Sar Komen while we winter there."

While Kaden and the others were still considering this, D'Sarza added, "And there is another reason to do this."

She hesitated, looking around the table at them, but Tchinchura encouraged her to continue. "Say what's on your mind, Captain."

"I have almost run out of things to trade," D'Sarza said at last. "I thought that perhaps I could stay with the ship and the crew and oversee the repairs, and that you might consider doing some trapping for furs and pelts. They are a common commodity in these parts. They won't fetch a lot of money in the spring markets, but at least they're something."

"Wait, hold on," Kaden said. "Trapping? Furs and pelts? Sar Komen is a large city—how would we do that?"

"You'd have to go inland, beyond the mountains that ring the city," D'Sarza said. "We'd have to split up, at least for the winter."

"No, absolutely not," Kaden said. "I couldn't take Nara and Kita over mountains in winter on an extended hunting expedition. That's ludicrous!"

"They would stay with us, as would Rika, I imagine," D'Sarza said. "You all could go with the two Kalosenes."

Kaden sat back, shaking his head. "We shouldn't split up, Tchinchura. I don't want to leave Nara or the ship unguarded."

"The *Rogue* would not be unguarded," D'Sarza said, glaring at Kaden across the table. "I have taken care of my ship for some time before you were my passenger, Omiir, and I will do so again when you are no longer my passenger."

"The men who are seeking us and this ship are Amhuru," Kaden said, annoyed at the condescending way D'Sarza had used his last name, as though he were a spoiled princeling. "So it seems reasonable that I would think Amhuru a necessary part of its defense."

D'Sarza rolled her eyes. "In case you've forgotten, it is Tchinchura and not my ship that those Amhuru want. Going inland with him and leaving Nara with me might be the safest thing you could do for her."

There was some sense in this, Kaden realized, but still he resisted. He turned to Tchinchura and would have pleaded his case with him, but the Amhuru did not give him a chance. He raised his hand and said, "Peace, Kaden. We are not ready for a decision. We are only talking, and should consider all reasonable possibilities." The Amhuru rubbed his brow, and Kaden saw the weariness in his face.

He held his tongue, forcing himself to sit back and try to relax. He looked at Deslo and Olli, who were listening with interest and concern, but who were unlikely to speak unless directly addressed by the captain or one of the Amhuru.

"If the ship needs repair," Tchinchura said at last, looking at D'Sarza, "then we should go to Sar Komen and get it. The issue really is how we should pass the winter there."

The Amhuru turned from D'Sarza and scanned the others at the table. As he did, Kaden saw something in his face that made him think that D'Sarza wasn't the only one who had a plan for their winter, but he had no idea what the Amhuru was thinking.

Tchinchura continued, "We could spend the winter trying to replace the cargo we have sold to stay alive here, and getting pelts and furs would be one way to do this, though I am also leery about splitting up. I am not entirely sure the danger will leave with me if I go, though the captain has a point there."

The Amhuru paused, considering, and he looked at Calamin and Trajax, and when both of them nodded, Kaden knew that something unexpected was indeed up. Curiosity almost overwhelmed him, but thankfully, he didn't have to wait long to hear what Tchinchura was thinking.

"On the other hand, we could spend the winter trying to make contact with the Northland Amhuru—something a large city might facilitate."

Every face in the room, save only the other two Amhuru, mirrored the astonishment that Kaden felt, and for some time all he could do was stare around the room at the others in stunned silence. D'Sarza's plan almost sounded sensible compared with this. To seek out those from whom they had been hiding for over a year seemed like madness.

That the others were thinking this, Tchinchura very clearly understood, for he did not wait for any of them to say so. He went ahead and defended his suggestion against the unstated objection they all shared.

"They will find us eventually. We might as well try to make sure that they find us on terms as close to our own choosing as possible."

D'Sarza, who sat almost directly opposite Kaden, visibly paled at that, and whatever difference Kaden had with her, he knew she was a woman who did not frighten easily. She said in a voice barely louder than a whisper, "How would you do it?"

Tchinchura shook his head. "That I do not know. We would need to go there, gather as much information in the city as we could, and then we would decide how to proceed.

"Either way," Tchinchura concluded, "I think our path leads to Sar Komen."

And that was where the matter had been left. D'Sarza set a course for Sar Komen, and the conversations and arguments continued with each passing day. Kaden did not like either D'Sarza's plan or Tchinchura's, and he had no idea if he was forced to choose which one he would support. Perhaps more troubling, he thought it entirely possible that Tchinchura and the other Amhuru would make a decision without consulting him—or anyone.

He knew it was their right to do so, but given that they still showed the aftereffects of the land of broken dreams, he worried that they were not in a frame of mind to think clearly. They needed time, but they didn't have much. They were only a week out of Sar Komen, so whatever the decision would be, they would know soon.

Sar Komen was a city unlike any Kaden had ever seen. True, it was the only Northland city he had ever seen, since they had avoided every other one in their path so far, but the point remained that it was unlike any of the other big cities in Aralyn that he had known in his previous life as the heir to the throne of Barra-Dohn. And, even as his horizons had expanded during their wanderings, he'd never seen anything like this.

It seemed to Kaden that Sar Komen was both larger and smaller than Barra-Dohn, as paradoxical as that sounded. The city proper of Sar Komen was probably not as big as Barra-Dohn, though this wasn't easy to know since the city had no walls—something which Kaden found almost impossible to fathom—and so the line between the city and the outlying houses and estates and farms was less than clear. So, while the city center felt smaller, if you included these outlying areas, it stretched much, much farther than Barra-Dohn did. Outside Barra-Dohn's walls there had been little but desert and sage bushes. Here, fertile land stretched as far as the eye could see between the heart of the city and the mountains that rose around it.

Kaden assumed it was those mountains that served Sar Komen as a wall of protection. Even if an enemy possessed the same weapons Barra-Dohn had at its disposal before its collapse, crossing those mountains with an army to attack Sar Komen would be challenging, if not impossible. He didn't know if that was the reason for the lack of walls, but it was all he could come up with on his own without actual knowledge of the city's history.

Sar Komen was impressive beyond its sheer size. There were things in the city that he had never seen anywhere else. One was a system for public transport that greatly intrigued him. Teams of horses pulled large meridium platforms fitted with benches, and these stopped at regular intervals throughout the city. When they did, people already onboard would often hop off, while other people would hand the driver money to get on, and then he would move along down the street toward the next stop. The transports must have operated on some sort of regular schedule and stopped at predetermined places, since people would somehow simply congregate in a place before the transport was even in sight, and then the transport would without fail come around a corner and stop, and people got on and off with great efficiency. In addition, some of these transports ran quite a distance beyond the center of the city out into the surrounding country as well, further connecting the outlying areas to the city itself.

Also of interest to Kaden were the pedestrian footpaths beside the road. Sar Komen certainly wasn't the only city to have lanes designated both for pedestrians with meridium-soled shoes as well as for those walking on the ground, but the ones for people on the ground were strange. They were gravel, with slanted rails of meridium running underneath. The design was certainly perplexing until a sailor from a merchant vessel explained to Kaden that the meridium rails generated low-level heat all year round—not enough to burn feet, but enough to prevent snow and ice from accumulating on the gravel.

Given where he had grown up, the idea of snow and ice making travel difficult was almost entirely new, but Kaden could imagine that walking either through or on either could be risky. At a minimum enough snow or ice would slow people down, but with the meridium rails warming the gravel, the snow and ice that fell there melted and ran away as water. This sometimes created large snow and ice formations on either side of the footpaths and in low-lying places where the water pooled, but the paths themselves stayed pretty clear all winter long.

Yes, Sar Komen was a city full of many wonders, but it was also, in a way, a city just like any other, with all the expected sights and sounds of a place that is home to so many different people. Of course, the first few days that *The Sorry Rogue* was anchored there, Kaden was unable to see the city up close for himself. As had been the case in every other Northland port, the Amhuru and their apprentices had been limited to their ship, so their golden eyes—or golden-flecked eyes, in Kaden's case—and their other Amhuru features could not be seen or noted by anyone at those ports.

However, when Tchinchura had made his decision that they would indeed spend the winter making themselves bait for the Northland Amhuru, this had changed, and Kaden had been free to wander the city with relative freedom. The freedom part Kaden liked; the bait part not so much. Still, Kaden could think of no other, better plan, admitting, even if reluctantly, that sailing endlessly through the Northlands, avoiding notice or detection with no larger plan in view, wasn't a longterm strategy.

Tchinchura's rationale was simple. Their hope for making contact with the Northland Amhuru without bloodshed hinged on their ability to communicate in a simple and effective way—should they live long enough to get the chance—that their motive for doing what a thousand years of Amhuru law forbade was good. This would be, he thought, increasingly difficult as time passed. The Northland Amhuru would be skeptical of their intent already, perhaps irreconcilably so, and the longer their band succeeded in hiding from them, the more the Northland Amhuru would likely be convinced that they had come to do precisely what the Jin Dara was trying to do and which they were trying to prevent.

Consequently, they were going to stay. Here they would succeed or fail, and here they would live or die. It was that simple.

They found a small farm on the outskirts of Sar Komen, near the base of the mountains west of the city, and rented it. The idea was for the Amhuru and their apprentices to move in, while the rest stayed on the ship—though the Devoted were more often with them on the farm than on the ship. That way, with any luck, if the plan failed and they were attacked by the Northland Amhuru, any blood that was spilled wouldn't involve the others. Kaden still didn't like being separated from Nara and Kita, but there would be opportunities to see each other, and he knew this was safer for them.

The dangling of the bait started very simply. Geffen went to one of Sar Komen's fancier inns, a place frequented by captains and first mates and other crewman of note on their respective ships, a place where news of the world was swapped, where merchant captains made connections and many deals had their genesis. Geffen spent an evening there making it look like he was drinking far more ale than he actually was, watching for the right moment to let it slip that his ship had crossed the Madri more than a year ago with no less than three Southland Amhuru and their apprentices onboard.

He found his moment and seized it, and the remark elicited just the right response—lots and lots of laughter, to which, Geffen responded by protesting in loud and strident tones that it was true, which in turn only encouraged his mockers to deride him all the more. Soon the whole place was enjoying a laugh at his expense, and in feigned anger and embarrassment, Geffen left, shaking his fists at his most vocal critics and swearing oaths at them that would make most sailors blush as he stumbled out of the inn.

Within a week, though, sightings of Amhuru in Sar Komen began to occur—never all three at once, but always one with an apprentice. They were seen here or there making inquiries and seeking information about the last time any other Amhuru had been in Sar Komen. The reports began to circulate, and it became clear that even if they might all involve the same Amhuru—a tall, dark man with golden eyes and golden hair—the apprentices certainly seemed to be different. Some accounts spoke of a man, some of a teenage boy, and still others of a girl.

Soon those reports reached the ears of some of the same men and women who had laughed Geffen out of the inn, and they put two and two together. Rumors flew around the docks that Southland Amhuru had crossed the Madri, perhaps in large numbers, and some of those were hovering around Sar Komen for some reason. The seed had been planted, the flag raised.

The only question was how long it would be before Northland Amhuru descended upon Sar Komen to kill them.

Rika pulled her scarf tighter as she gazed out at the city and tried to ignore the two women talking on the bench beside her. Nara was talking to D'Sarza, and little Kita was sound asleep in Nara's lap, wrapped tight in a thick blanket. That was well enough, as the girl had wriggled incessantly all the way out to the inn where they'd met Kaden and Trajax. She might be a cute little thing, Rika thought, but as far as she was concerned, Kita was cuter when asleep.

Rika shivered and one more time silently cursed this frigid place and her own ill fortune that had brought her here in such dull company. If she thought the year of wandering and waiting for the Amhuru to wake up had been awful, the two months they'd spent in Sar Komen waiting like idiots—as she understood the plan—for the Northland Amhuru to come and most likely kill Tchinchura, if not all of them, and take his fragment of the Golden Cord away, well, these two months had been even worse.

To be sure, Sar Komen, like all large cities, offered diversions, and she had been happy to take advantage of that and to begin to make friends and connections in case a sudden change of plans became necessary. Still, the memory of her failure to take the fragment haunted her like a ghost. She closed her eyes as the transport stopped again, and the specter of that memory rose inside her.

It was early in the morning, midsummer, perhaps a couple months after Kaden had woken up. The three Amhuru were still unconcious, and the ship was spending its third day at a small port, preparing to leave the following day. Rika had scouted out the town, had prepared a plan of escape, and had been working up the nerve to finally make her attempt.

The two Kalosenes had given themselves the job of providing security for the three Amhuru in general, and the one that had challenged her on Kaden, Marlo, had been keeping his eye on her in particular—not that Rika thought he had any idea what she planned. He just didn't trust her, and they both knew it. So, she always felt keenly aware that she was under surveillance when he was near, and she knew that he was especially alert to her comings and goings.

Still, half a year above the Madri without incident had lessened their diligence somewhat, and as the crew always provided around the clock security for the ship when they were in port so no one could board without permission, Rika found the deck almost empty at this early hour, no Kalosenes to be seen. She took a deep breath, crossed to the door that opened on the cabin where the Amhuru were sleeping, and entered.

She would try to remove the fragment without disturbing the sleeping Amhuru, but she had no idea what effect this might have on Tchinchura—if taking it might waken him from his long slumber. She had a knife tucked into her belt under her cloak if she should need it, and she would have to be fast if she did. She would be in serious trouble if the alarm was raised before she could get off the ship, and she would silence Tchinchura permanently if that was her only way to keep him quiet.

She stood over Tchinchura. The arm that bore the fragment was out on top of the blanket, and even in the dark cabin, the Zerura gleamed in her eyes. She wouldn't have to try to move or maneuver Tchinchura at all; it was there, within reach, his body in perfect position for her to slide it off. She hesitated, but only for a moment, steeling herself, then she reached down and took hold of the fragment.

The moment her fingers touched the warm metal, a dark fog descended upon her, and the room disappeared from view. She felt herself falling, and the next thing she knew, she was on the floor. It wasn't the wooden plank floor of the ship, however; it was the cool stone floor of her cell beneath the palace of Barra-Dohn. She remembered it well. Too well.

She saw the bars of her cell just a foot or so away, and as she lifted her head from the floor, she heard . . . singing. Two men were singing a song that sounded like a child's lullabye, only it sounded somehow wrong to her ears.

Falling darkness, fading light,
Rising moon greets the night,
Sleeping baby, dream of stars,
Wake and feel the iron bars.

The voices laughed, a cruel and mocking laugh, and then they sang their stupid little song again. She was looking straight ahead, afraid to turn her head to either side, afraid to see what she knew she would see, but as the singing and the laughing continued, unabated, round after round, she eventually dared to look.

Sure enough, Barreck was on one side and Gamalian on the other, their grinning faces barely visible through the dark.

Then Gamalian turned sideways, so Rika could see him in profile, and she saw the knife sticking out of his back. He reached around and grabbed it, wrenching it out. Then he turned back to her, still grinning, and tossed it into her cell.

"Care to take another stab?" he said. He slapped the floor with his open hand, making a loud smack, and he and Barreck laughed even harder.

Rika opened her mouth to scream, only she discovered as she tried to do so that it wouldn't open. She reached up and felt stitches. It had been sewn shut.

The lullabye continued, and she lay down on the floor in a ball, her hands over her ears, trying unsuccessfully to drown out the voices and the laughter. There she had been lying when Owenn found and tried to wake her. She did not wake, though, until he carried her from the room, out into the sun on the main deck, and when she did wake, it was midday. She had no memory of Owenn finding her, of his picking her up and carrying her out. Fortunately, her knife—her real knife, not the dream knife—had been securely tucked away, and though a small crowd had gathered around her, no one had found it.

Most of the crowd dissipated as she woke, and D'Sarza helped her up off the deck. Still, the Kalosenes and Kaden hung nearby as D'Sarza sought to find out what happened. Rika, like all good liars, knew that the closer she could keep her story to the truth, the more likely she could sell it, and in her groggy state, only one idea popped into her head when the captain asked her question.

"I must have been sleepwalking," Rika said, shaking her head as though she too was mystified by how she had ended up in that cabin. "The dream, it was so vivid. I was in the palace of Barra-Dohn. I haven't dreamed of that place in years, but I was there, I was really there . . ."

She allowed her voice to trail off, and she rubbed her eyes as though to drive the sleep from them, but mostly, it was just to avoid the searching gazes of the others. When she opened them, she added, "I was wandering the palace freely, but then I opened a door and ended up somehow back in the dungeon where Eirmon locked me away."

She looked at D'Sarza then, hoping to read how convincing the other woman found her tale, and after a moment, the captain nodded.

"You are lucky you didn't start down the gangway and tumble off into the water. I've heard of sleepwalking sailors doing that before."

That had been it, essentially, since once the captain bought it, the matter was effectively settled. Only it wasn't. She might have imagined the skepticism she saw in the Kalosenes' eyes the rest of that day, but she didn't imagine their increased attention to the Amhuru's room. From that point on, one of them or Kaden was always on deck, always within view of the door, except for the rare times when Olli and Deslo would stand watch for them, but that was only ever in the middle of the day when the deck was busy anyway. Rika knew her chance to grab the fragment while Tchinchura was asleep had been missed.

And yet she wasn't sure what else she could have done. She'd heard enough of the chatter among the three apprentices to have an idea what had happened. Whatever dream state they had been in after passing through the Madri, it was connected to wearing Zerura, and somehow, when she'd touched Tchinchura's fragment, some portion of that effect had hit her immediately. She couldn't have known this would happen, nor did she necessarily see how she could have removed the fragment without touching it. Perhaps using a glove or strip of cloth to keep it from touching her skin directly would have helped, but somehow she doubted it.

The situation now seemed almost hopeless. Either the Northland Amhuru would kill Tchinchura and take it, or they would make contact successfully and the fragment would be more closely guarded than ever. Rika had to acknowledge that whatever hopes she had harbored of being the one to take it and give it to the Jin Dara, they were just about gone now.

Still, there was always the possibility that she had started with, that maybe she would be able to lead him to it. To do that, though, she needed their attempt to connect with the Northland Amhuru to succeed. If it didn't, if the Northland Amhuru killed them and took it, then the fragment would disappear, and she would never know where it had gone. She'd have nothing to tell the Jin Dara. She'd have come all this way for nothing.

No, she needed this crazy plan of Tchinchura's to work. The memory of that dream from more than half a year ago was still vivid, and it still made her shiver almost as much as this terrible weather. But, in a strange way, it was almost a comfort to her now. It reminded her that she had escaped her almost certain execution in Eirmon Omiir's prison cell, and it gave her hope that she might turn around her fortunes yet.

33

Out of the Mist

Spring had come to Sar Komen a couple weeks ago, and Deslo had been overjoyed to see it. He'd been fascinated by his first snow, thrilled even. Dipping his hands into it and feeling the soft, delicate coldness was something he would never forget. After four months of bitterly cold weather, though, much of it without the diversion of snow to blanket the landscape a picturesque white, he was more than ready to say hello to spring, to hints of new life everywhere, to the smell of budding things on the air, to muddy fields and to longer, warmer days.

His fifteenth birthday was only a few months away, and he was eager for it. Olli had turned nineteen during their winter, and when Deslo had brought her a small present from the Sar Komen market, she had thanked him and kissed him on his cheek. It had been the kiss of a friend, but Deslo couldn't help but wonder if when he was a little older, Olli might not consider him as something more than that. He didn't dare to hope that she did now. After all, he might be of age, but he wasn't even fifteen yet.

Perhaps one day she would, though, and that thought on a spring morning like today was hard to repress.

It was spring, and through all the long winter they had watched and waited, and still the Northland Amhuru had not come. Tchinchura had deliberated with Calamin and Trajax, and they had decided to stay here and wait. They had gathered a small stash of hides and pelts during the winter by hunting in the mountains, and by trading them over the last week, they had made enough money to pay the docking fees for *The Sorry Rogue* to stay a little longer and to purchase seed for the farm.

In fact Deslo and Calamin were on their way back from the market with the seed now, two large sacks slung over their shoulders. The sacks were full of wheat, the grain their neighbors told them had been grown on their farm with some success by the previous tenants. The weather today was brisk, and they would likely wait to make sure a surprise frost wasn't coming before plowing, but if all went well, they'd be turning the soil before the week was out. After so much time, both before and after crossing the Madri where they had little to do but wait, Deslo was excited for his hands to have meaningful work to do.

The farm was not far now, and Calamin turned away from the road to cut across the field to shorten the way—walking on the Arua, they didn't need to worry about the sloshy ground that would be a little harder given today's chill but still soft. He adjusted the sack on his shoulder and leaned over to Deslo. "Doing all right?"

"I'm fine," Deslo said. His shoulder was sore, and his arm ached, but he wanted the Amhuru to know he wasn't just a man in terms of age, but that he could do a man's work and carry a man's load.

A thick, curling, grey mist lay above the ground but beneath their feet striding on the Arua, and it was odd for Deslo to look down. It felt a bit like they were walking on a cloud. Deslo smiled at the thought, glad of something to divert his attention away from his sore body—and his thoughts of Olli. For some reason his sack felt heavier since Calamin drew his attention to it. He heard a familiar sound and turned to look at the glider zooming along above the road, coming their way.

It had taken a little getting used to, thinking glider instead of slider, but as these machines were a little different than the sliders he'd grown up with in Barra-Dohn, it hadn't been too bad. Sliders ran on sage oil—like just about every other meridium-based technology from home—and they had been things you straddled with your legs as you rode them, like a smaller, faster, metallic horse. Gliders were different, as you sat in them and leaned back, working pedals with your feet, and they ran on liquid pressed from corn, something the locals in Sar Komen called "corness."

They were noisier than sliders too, which was why the hum of the glider had caught Deslo's attention, echoing across the fields in the quiet afternoon. He turned to look, wondering if it was the same, mysterious woman who had taken to riding up and down their road a couple times a day the last month or so. She was always bundled up with a hat and a pair of goggles on, so he couldn't tell if she was one of their neighbors or not, but as they'd met most of them over the winter, he didn't think it was.

And, sure enough, it was the same glider and the same woman. Deslo wondered, and not for the first time, where it was that this woman went and what her story was. Maybe one day she would run out of corness and come to the farm asking for some, and perhaps then the mystery would be revealed, but in the meantime Deslo guessed he'd have to live with it.

He started to turn back around as the woman passed them by when something in the distance in a field across the road caught his eye. He paused, wondering what it had been. He peered into the grey mist to find it, but he couldn't see anything. He felt an odd, sinking feeling in the pit of his stomach, a curious tremble of fear. He knew without knowing how that it had not been nothing, that something was very much amiss.

He reached for Calamin with his other hand to try to get his attention without looking away from the field, but he missed and his hand grabbed at nothing in the air. He glanced instinctively to correct his poor aim, and when he turned back, he saw multiple, grey-cloaked figures rise out of the mist and leap onto the Arua field.

Everything started to happen at once. The men started running toward them across the Arua field, even as Deslo felt Calamin reach out for the field to manipulate it. The mist seemed to thicken and rise off the ground all around them so that it swirled around their legs. Calamin dropped his sack of grain, as did Deslo, and they started running for the farm. As they ran Deslo could feel the men chasing them reach for the Arua field too, to try to disperse the mist Calamin was trying to use to hide them, and a struggle for control ensued.

The struggle was intense but short-lived, as Calamin was overwhelmed by the collective strength of the men pursuing them. Deslo risked another look, and there were more men than he'd thought, perhaps ten all told, and they were coming from multiple directions. His heart sank at their numbers, at the golden eyes focused on them both beneath their grey hoods, and at how far they still needed to go to reach the farm.

"Keep going!" Calamin shouted at Deslo as he drew his axe and turned to face the men in grey.

Despite this admonition, Deslo hesitated, wondering why Calamin had turned back. He saw why immediately when he also turned and Calamin's axe flashed to the side, intercepting a knife one of the men had thrown. As quickly as it had moved to intercept the knife, Calamin whirled to strike another. This one he only barely hit, and it was deflected down and hit his leg. Fortunately, it was rotating awkwardly because of the deflection, and only the handle hit him.

"We wish to surrender!" Calamin called, even as another knife came hurtling toward him. He knocked that one away too, but he made no attempt to use his axe against the men who were closing the gap on them quickly. At the same time, he shouted once more at Deslo, "I said run, Deslo!"

Then the first knife struck Calamin, hitting him from the side in the thigh, spinning him around, but he managed to keep his footing on the Arua field. The second knife, though, hit him in the back, and he pitched forward off the Arua field, falling into the mist.

"We surrender!" Deslo shouted, just as Tchinchura had instructed him to should something like this happen. He also pulled out his axe and ran over to stand above Calamin's fallen body. Tchinchura had not told him to draw his axe if threatened; in fact he'd been quite clear that this was the last thing he should do, but Deslo couldn't stand defenseless over Calamin.

The knife that hit Deslo struck him in his right shoulder. Pain shot down his arm, and Deslo felt his hand spasm and his axe fall out of it. He also slipped, pitching sideways off the Arua field and down into the mist. Perhaps this was what saved him.

He could see Calamin struggling on his hands and knees not far away, trying to rise, the knife still sticking out of his back. Deslo pulled the knife out of his own shoulder and dropped it to the ground as he scrambled across the soggy field to assist the Amhuru. The mist surrounded them, and he was torn between shouting their surrender one more time and keeping his mouth shut in case the men pursuing them had lost their bearings, though this felt like a vain hope.

He had just about decided to try to surrender one more time, but he had not yet done so when the hum of the glider suddenly echoed across the open field to him again, and he could hear that it was moving very fast and coming right for them. The woman must have returned and must also be riding out off the road, directly across the field. She was a lunatic if she was, for surely if she was coming here, she had seen what the grey-cloaked men had done. And, if she had seen, what in the name of the six brothers was she doing?

Deslo reached Calamin, who was still struggling to rise. The blood from the knife in his back had soaked the back of his shirt, and Deslo could see the Amhuru was in no condition to fight.

He wasn't sure if he should pull the knife out for him, or if that would do more harm than good, and in the end he simply put his hand on Calamin's shoulder and whispered, "Stay down. We can't fight them."

A shadow suddenly appeared overhead, and Deslo saw the glider pass almost directly above them. It came to an immediate stop, and the woman sitting in the glider leapt out into the mist just a few feet away. She stood, arms raised, between Deslo and Calamin and the approaching men. Then she shouted. "Put your weapons away. They are friends, and one is only a boy!"

Deslo's heart thumped. The voice was familiar. He'd known it his whole life. What was Rika doing here? He wanted to raise his head and see what was going on more than ever, but he resisted the urge.

"Stand aside," a man's voice said to Rika from somewhere very close. "Or we will cut you down too."

"Are the Amhuru of the Northlands butchers then?" Rika said, her voice full of the boldness that sometimes made her sound insolent to Deslo. She didn't sound insolent to him now, but wonderful, full of righteous indignation.

"They have done what is forbidden," the voice answered her. "Their lives are forfeit, and if you know them or helped them, then I imagine you know it too."

"While you are imagining things, try imagining why men as committed to protecting the Golden Cord as you are would cross the Madri with a fragment—knowing, mind you, that their own kin would come and try to kill them. Or are you too stupid to do that?"

Deslo cringed. Maybe insolent was the right word for her after all. Still, the men had not yet found and killed him or Calamin hiding in the mist, and they were talking rather than throwing knives, so he would forgive her everything if she could pull this off and save their lives. He couldn't imagine, though, that insulting the men sent to kill them and recover the Cord was a great strategy, as he figured they were probably already angry enough.

And yet, when the voice spoke again, there was a hint of uncertainty in it that hadn't been there before, so maybe she had managed to convey the righteous indignation along with the insolence. "If they had reason to cross the Madri with a fragment of the Cord, why not bring it to us?"

"You idiot," Rika said. "What do you think they're doing? They picked a spot and made certain word got out that they were here. They've waited all winter for you to come. Why do you think—"

Rika stopped midsentence, and even though Deslo could not see her well through the mist, he could well enough to see her turn and look back toward the farm. He couldn't see what she was looking at, but he knew all the same.

"Brothers," Tchinchura called from across the field, "I have what you seek and will surrender it into your hand. I only ask that you wait to hear our full story before deciding what to do with us."

Deslo dared to raise his head now. There was Rika, a few feet away, and beyond her, in a wide arc, stood the Northland Amhuru, one of which was only a few feet away from Rika herself—the spokesman, Deslo assumed. He turned and looked back toward the house, and there was Tchinchura, his hand outstretched and the original fragment dancing rhythmically in the air above it. Behind him came Trajax, Olli, and Kaden, along with Marlo and Owenn.

"Is this all of you?" the Northland Amhuru in front of Rika asked as Tchinchura and the others approached, their hands out and empty. Deslo scanned the rest of the Northland Amhuru, and every one of them had a knife in hand, and each of them seemed tensed to strike at any moment.

"The Southland ship that brought us here is in the harbor," Tchinchura said, "as I am sure you know. There are no more Amhuru or apprentices on it, and we are all that are here at this farm."

"This woman," the man said, indicating Rika with his knife, "she is in your company?"

"She is," Tchinchura said, "though it is a surprise that she is here. She was told to keep her distance."

"Well, Tchinchura, old friend," Rika said, "it is a good thing for you that I didn't listen, and for Deslo and Calamin, too."

"You need to learn some respect," the Northland Amhuru said, jabbing the knife at her in the air.

"Sure, I'll get right on that," Rika said, before saying to Tchinchura, "Are we going to stand and argue while Deslo and Calamin bleed to death?"

"Do we have a deal?" Tchinchura said, ignoring Rika and extending the hand with the Zerura dancing above it as he fixed his gaze on his Northland counterpart.

"You will give me the fragment of the Golden Cord?"

"I have said so, and I do not lie," Tchinchura answered. "So long as I have your word you will not hurt anyone in our party until I have told you my story."

"You have done what is forbidden," the other said. "You will forgive me if I am skeptical about your word."

"I will," Tchinchura said. "Do we have a deal?"

Deslo waited for the answer to this question, but he never heard it. Without warning, a wave of pain from his injured shoulder radiated through his body, a rush of lightheadedness flooded him, and everything went black as he fell back down into the mist.

34

He Will Come

Kaden stooped down through the mist to pick up his son. He had not seen the ambush, but Trajax had been watching from his post by the upstairs window and had seen it all. So, as they'd gathered to come out together and surrender—just as they had discussed and planned that they would when this day came—Trajax told them of Calamin and Deslo's fall.

Consequently, even before Rika's remark about bleeding to death, Kaden had been anxiously awaiting the end to the verbal standoff between Tchinchura and the leader of the Northland Amhuru so he could see to his son. Finally the arrangement was made, and even as Marlo and Owenn took up Calamin to carry him back to the house as quickly as they could, he stooped down and checked Deslo.

It took a moment to locate the place where the knife had struck him, but Kaden found the bloody shoulder and the cut in his shirt and was relieved. The wound was clean, if deep, and Kaden knew Deslo would live. As Deslo weighed almost as much as he did these days, Kaden had no choice but to hoist him up by the waist and drape him over his shoulder.

As he stood up, Rika offered him the glider—they could set Deslo there and walk both it and him across the field to the house—but now that Kaden had Deslo up on his shoulder, he would not let him go. He could not have explained why this was so important to Rika or anyone but Nara, but it was.

As he jogged across the field, his eyes fixed on the Kalosenes in front of him and the farm beyond them, he remembered a day back in Barra-Dohn when Deslo had been a little boy. He had been leaving the palace to go somewhere with Eirmon—where exactly, he could no longer remember. No doubt Eirmon had been in a hurry to get there, as Kaden could remember being hustled out of the palace without regard for anything or anyone else, as he so often was when Eirmon was involved.

At any rate Kaden and Eirmon had just gone down the stairs that led from the palace into the open square beyond it, and Deslo came tearing out of the palace calling out to Kaden to wait, that Deslo needed to give him a hug before he left. Kaden had stopped to turn back—probably to tell Deslo to go back inside to his mother—when Deslo had lost his footing at the top of the stairs and flown down, through the air, splitting his chin open on the bottom stair.

As Deslo rose from the stair, sobbing great big tears that came as much from the shock of falling as from the blood and pain, Kaden had scooped him up and carried him back inside. Deslo's arms shot immediately around Kaden's neck, and his little hands took hold and clenched him tight, so that even when Kaden had found Nara, Deslo had been unwilling to let go.

Deslo had been a very little boy then, so little he did not yet know that he didn't have a very good father . . . so little that the gulf that yawned between Kaden and Nara had not yet opened up and swallowed him whole.

And so he had clung to Kaden like he was clinging to life itself, completely unaware of all his father's deficiencies, and for one of the few times in Deslo's childhood, Kaden had not pushed him away. On that day, despite the blood and the screaming and the inconvenience, he had been a real father, and he had offered his sobbing son what comfort his words and his arms could provide.

There had been times, throughout the lost years, when Kaden had remembered that day, often with guilt and embarrassment. He did not feel any of that now as he made his way through the mist with Deslo over his shoulder. Now, he only felt love and gratitude that he could be here for Deslo to take care of him, that the wound wasn't worse and that his son would live. That perhaps, despite the gamble they had taken by staying in Sar Komen, they might all live.

Once inside the farm, there was a flurry of activity. Marlo and Owenn took Calamin to the main floor bedroom where they normally stayed when they spent the night at the farm, putting him down in one of the beds there. Tchinchura and Trajax went in after them to see to his wounds, and Kaden set Deslo down on the mat in the corner of the main room where the Amhuru on watch downstairs at night would rest when the morning came and his watch was over.

Rika and Olli both stayed with Kaden and hovered over Deslo, trying to make him comfortable. He'd started to come around by then, and they got him a pillow and blankets. Olli said she was going out back to get water from the well for both of the injured men, and one of the Northland Amhuru who had come in with them—the one who was much younger than the others—offered to help her. At first Olli just looked at him, as though unsure if he was an enemy or a friend, but in the end she shrugged and said "Fine," and he followed her down the hall and out the back door.

They returned just a few moments later with lots of water, and Kaden peeled off Deslo's bloody shirt and washed his wound. With Rika's help he tore the shirt into strips, taking the part that wasn't already bloody to make bandages. Before long the wound was clean and dressed, and there wasn't much more to do other than to sit beside Deslo as he lay there, looking up uncertainly at the men who had attacked him.

Kaden noticed then that only half a dozen of the Northland Amhuru had come inside, and peering out the window, he saw several more milling around the house. In fact, unless he was mistaken, there looked to be more outside than in; he didn't remember seeing that many a few moments ago in the field. He wondered how many they had brought on this quest to find the fragment Tchinchura bore and to kill those who had dared to bring it north, and he reflected once more on how fortunate they all were—Deslo especially—to still be alive at this moment.

The Kalosenes emerged from the main floor bedroom and stood at the entrance to the hall that led there as though to guard it, but none of the Northland Amhuru made any attempt to do anything but wait. In fact, now that the younger one had rejoined the others, they merely stood in a cluster near the main door. Kaden found the situation somewhat amusing, as both clusters seemed to be guarding different things. Eventually, Tchinchura returned with a comment to no one in particular about having done all that could be done for Calamin. Trajax did not come with him.

Tchinchura offered the Northland Amhuru who had done the speaking so far a formal greeting, which the Northland Amhuru acknowledged, though he did not return it. When Tchinchura offered his name as well, the man did give his: Amintuu. Then, Tchinchura and he sat at the main table, and between them—dancing in the air above the table—hovered the original fragment of the Golden Cord. The rest of both groups remained standing or sitting elsewhere. And there they remained while Tchinchura told his entire story.

It was a long story, and it took quite a long time, for Tchinchura went all the way back to his search for the missing fragment that Eirmon had taken. He explained how two had been missing, how he'd been searching for the one taken more recently, and how it had led him to the king of Barra-Dohn. He also explained that Barra-Dohn was the name of the city that had once been known as Zeru-Shalim, and all the Northland Amhuru reacted at the mention of that name, although they reacted to little else.

Tchinchura then explained the twist of fate that brought Dagin Orlas, the Jin Dara, to Barra-Dohn at the same time as he. He explained how he and his traveling partner, Zangira, almost recovered both missing fragments, and how Eirmon's betrayal cost them their success. He then explained how they fled, barely escaping, and all that they had done since to both learn about the Jin Dara and find and kill him if they could.

Kaden listened to the whole sad history again, but the shame he felt at the mention of his father was surprisingly less than he would have thought. He kept looking down at Deslo while Tchinchura told this part of the story, grateful that Tchinchura at no point indicated the connection between Deslo and himself and Eirmon. It occurred to him that they had finally escaped Eirmon's shadow. They were free of him and free of the fracture he'd been at least partially responsible for in their family. Consequently, Kaden realized he was, at long last, free of the shame over the things Eirmon had done. It had been a long, bewildering but rewarding journey.

Tchinchura, meanwhile, explained how he had gone to Azandalir to seek permission to cross the Madri, explained how permission had been refused until Zangira came. Tchinchura spoke of the Najin, an army equipped with and trained to use two separate fragments of Zerura, and for the second time since Tchinchura started his tale, there was a visible reaction from the Northland Amhuru.

That brought Tchinchura to the night of their departure from Azandalir, to the decision to send them to take the last Southland fragment across the Madri in the hope that they could keep it safe. He spoke of the letter the elders had given him for the Northland Amhuru—and he pulled the letter out to give them—and he spoke of the explanation it contained of his actions. Tchinchura also spoke of something in the letter that Kaden had not known was in there—words of forgiveness from the Southland elders in case the letter was found by the Northland Amhuru only after they had killed the bearer of the fragment.

At that point in the story, Tchinchura paused while Amintuu read the letter and then handed it to the others to read and pass around. Amintuu did not wait for them to finish reading but turned back to Tchinchura and bade him to continue.

Tchinchura did, explaining that for a year after crossing the Madri, he had been unconscious. He said little about the effects of the crossing, moving on quickly to the decisions that had faced them shortly after he awoke. He explained why they had come to Sar Komen and stayed here, how they had hoped to draw the Northland Amhuru's attention and make this connection so their story could be told, but also to get the Southland fragment into Amhuru hands as soon as possible.

The story, once finished, left everyone in the room in silence, and the fragment, still dancing above the table, drew all eyes. There was much to consider to be sure, but there was also the awful weight of what the story revealed to the Northland Amhuru for the first time—namely, that two of the six original fragments had been seized by a malevolent power, a power who was bent on taking more. Kaden had lived with this knowledge for some time, but as he watched the Northland Amhuru try to come to grips with what Tchinchura was saying, he felt anew the force of their predicament. They were, and the world as a whole was, in serious trouble.

Amintuu eventually broke the silence by asking Tchinchura questions, mostly to fill in gaps in the story. Even in the brief exchange, Kaden was impressed by how much the other Amhuru had observed and surmised based on things omitted, as well as things included in the story. When at last Amintuu had no more questions, he told Tchinchura that he would withdraw and discuss what to do with the others. He rose, taking the fragment with him. He didn't need to tell the Southlanders to stay put; they all knew the house was surrounded.

When the Northland Amhuru had all stepped outside, the silence inside hung heavy for a while. In the end it was Olli, of all people, who spoke first. "Surely, we will be safe now," she said. "They can't punish us, not now that they know why we've come."

"Assuming that they believe me," Tchinchura said, "I think we will be all right. But do not be too quick to assume we will not be punished. We have done what we judged to be best, but they were not there. They have not seen the Jin Dara or what he has done. They may not support our judgement, even if they understand it."

The silence returned but not for long, as Tchinchura turned to Rika and said, "So you are the one who has been going up and down this road on a glider for many weeks now. I would hear why, if you would tell."

"I'm happy to tell," Rika said. "I understand that by coming here to this farm and telling the rest of us to stay onboard the *Rogue* that you were trying to keep us safe. At the same time, we were a resource, I thought, that you should have been using. After all, my theory turns out to have been correct."

"And what was your theory?" Tchinchura asked, and Kaden thought he sounded a little bit amused.

"That the Northland Amhuru would be less willing to kill someone who wasn't wearing Zerura than someone who was."

"You think that was what saved you?"

"I think they hesitated because of it, at least," Rika said. "That, and my insolent mouth keeping them off guard long enough to plant a seed of doubt."

"You may be right," Tchinchura said. "But it was risky. Why not run this plan by me? By any of us? Were you worried I'd say no?"

Rika shrugged. "I am not your apprentice. I didn't think I had to run things by you."

"Are you sure that's it?" Tchinchura asked, his tone now unreadable.

"You can just say thanks, you know," Rika said.

"What you did was very brave," Tchinchura said. "I thank you for it."

"As do I," Kaden said from the corner, reaching down to take and squeeze Deslo's hand. "Thank you for protecting my son."

Rika looked at Kaden for a moment, and he wasn't sure what was in her eyes. Then she nodded. "I have served the house of Omiir for many years. I am glad I could help."

The door opened then, and the same six Northland Amhuru returned. When they entered, though, Amintuu did not return to the table. He stayed in front of the others, and when he spoke, it was clear that he addressed them all, even though he kept his eyes on Tchinchura.

"You will come with us," he said. "We will take you to Telsiin, our chief elder. He will make a final decision. For our part, though, we believe you have done only what you had to do."

Kaden didn't realize until he heard Amintuu say these words that he had been holding his breath. But, as he exhaled, he felt relief wash over him. It had worked. They would live.

"And the fragment?"

Amintuu handed it back to Tchinchura. "I believe you are my brother, a man of honor. You may have it back, if I have your word that you will surrender it to Telsiin if he requires it of you."

"Sa," Tchinchura said, taking the fragment back and putting it on his left bicep. "I will."

Amintuu extended his hand then, and Tchinchura took it. Amintuu said, still clasping Tchinchura's hand and staring him in the eye, "I admire your courage, brother. This could have gone very differently."

It was Tchinchura's turn to nod and acknowledge the words that Amintuu spoke. "We will all have need of our courage, I think, before this is over."

"This man, this Jin Dara . . ." Amintuu said. "You think he means to come across the Madri, too?"

"I was going to ask you if he already had," Tchinchura said by way of reply.

"Two winters now I have been looking for you," Amintuu said. "I have not been home in all that time. The last I knew, he had not crossed."

"It is well," Tchinchura said, "but it will not last. He will come."

Dagin Orlas woke, sweating. It was just a dream, he thought, relieved. He sat up, wiping the sweat off his brow with his silk sheets. On either side of his bed, lamps sat atop tall iron braziers, giving off a faint green glow. He got out of bed to add oil, and they glowed much brighter, illuminating the room.

He crossed to the little dressing table and chair and picked up his robe. It was green with gold trim, and embroidered on the shoulder was his golden fist insignia. He slipped the robe on and left his bedroom.

The hall was empty and dim. He didn't know what time it was exactly, but it felt like it might still be well before dawn. Entering the spacious, open room at the end of the hall, a large fire was burning in the enormous fireplace opposite the main door. As big and as bright as the fire was, it still wasn't enough to illuminate the room it was so vast. Even so, only one piece of furniture was inside—the ornate, plush chair that sat about midway between the door and the fireplace.

Dagin crossed to the chair and sat down. The heat from the fire brought beads of sweat back to his forehead, but this sweat he didn't mind so much. He liked the fire, liked the heat, and he welcomed it. For a long time he sat, thinking of nothing in particular, simply gazing at the dancing flames, mesmerized.

He closed his eyes, and the images that rose before him were images of himself and his great triumph. He had become so much more than he had ever thought possible, accomplished so much more than what he had originally set out to accomplish. He had set out on that darker road which fate had placed before him, and he had succeeded. He had mastered the Golden Cord, and now he was the master of all things.

He could feel each fragment against his bare skin, each one playing a separate part in their common song, combining to make one grand melody out of all living things, himself included. He could feel the fragment around his forehead and the fragment around his neck, the fragment around his left bicep and the fragment around his right forearm, the fragment around his right calf and the fragment above his left knee. They were all there; they were all singing.

Dagin smelled smoke, and he opened his eyes. Something had clogged the chimney, for smoke was now billowing out of the fireplace instead of up into it. And then, remarkably, something appeared out of the smoke at the top of the fireplace. It was a man actually climbing out of the chimney, apparently impervious to the smoke and flames. His head appeared, and then his arms as he pushed his way clear of the smoke and swung out beyond the actual fire. He stepped forward onto the expansive hearth.

The obstruction now clear, the smoke dissipated, once more rising as it should through the flue. The man, for his part, was curiously free of soot. His skin was bronze, his eyes and hair a brilliant gold, and he carried in one hand a long-handled axe with a golden axehead that gleamed in the bright firelight. The man walked casually forward until he stood in front of Dagin.

For his part, Dagin watched the man without concern, all the way up until the moment he swung his axe and chopped off Dagin's left arm. The pain was sharp and intense. Confusion and panic flooded him. Who was this? What was he doing? And what's more, why couldn't he doing anything about it?

"You really shouldn't have taken these," the man said as he bent over and picked up Dagin's arm off the floor. He slid the fragment of the Golden Cord off Dagin's detached limb, dropping the Zerura into a large pocket in his cloak. Then he turned and tossed the arm into the fireplace, like just another log. It caught fire, and soon the room was full of the unpleasant smell of burning flesh.

The man turned back to Dagin, and with another vicious chop, cut off Dagin's right arm. "Even a legitimate grievance has to be handled the right way," he said, as he picked up the second arm, stripped it of its Zerura, and tossed it also into the fire.

"Your family had a right to be upset over how it was treated," the man said, now proceeding to chop off Dagin's left leg. The third fragment reclaimed, he tossed the leg into the fire.

"Still, destroying a whole city? Stealing all six fragments? Conquering the world?"

His right leg was gone—the man hadn't stopped his work while he talked—and it was now burning with the rest of his severed limbs. All four fragments from his four limbs were in the man's pocket, and now he faced Dagin again, the blade of his golden axed dyed deep crimson.

"Did you think you could defy Kalos and get away with it?" the man said, leaning near Dagin's face now, his bright golden eyes peering into Dagin's own.

"I'm sorry, about this, I really am," the man said, moving back in order to have room to swing. "But you know what I have to do."

The man pulled his axe back. Dagin watched the blade fly.

Dagin Orlas woke, sweating. It was just a dream, he thought, relieved. He sat up, wiping the sweat off his brow with his silk sheets. On either side of his bed, lamps sat atop tall iron braziers, giving off a faint green glow. He got out of bed to add oil, and they glowed much brighter, illuminating the room . . .

35

Opportunity and Responsibility

The docks of Sar Komen were abuzz. The rumor that multiple Southland Amhuru were in the city was old news, but the sudden appearance of almost thirty Amhuru, walking out in the open on the quay, was not. Sar Komen was reeling. Captains and crewmen alike gave up all pretense of working, and they simply gathered along the rails of their ships or stood on the docks and stared. Shopkeeps and street vendors also found their way down to see it for themselves, for this was a story they would tell one another as they sat by the fire with hot jonda in their hands for many winters.

Tchinchura felt a tinge of sadness as he looked at the onlookers gawking at the preparations being made for the three ships that would carry them away to sail (the four kills squads of the Northland Amhuru had needed two vessels to transport them all here). He knew that their departure might not be enough to spare the city. The flag they had raised here to draw the Northland Amhuru might draw the Jin Dara too, which was why they were being even more conspicuous in their departure than they had been in their arrival and residence.

If word of three ships carrying a large number of Amhuru leaving Sar Komen reached his ears, perhaps the Jin Dara wouldn't come, or perhaps he would come in secret to try to learn news about where they were heading. Tchinchura had known when he came and when he decided to make sure word of their presence got out that they might attract the attention of more than the Northland Amhuru. His hope, and the hope for Sar Komen, was that the Jin Dara hadn't yet crossed the Madri, or if he had, that the Madri's effects on him, given the two fragments he bore, might incapacitate him long enough that their presence here would be old news by the time he woke up and learned of it.

And yet, Tchinchura knew that the stakes of his gamble had been far larger than the safety and well-being of Sar Komen. The remaining fragments of the Golden Cord had to be kept out of the Jin Dara's hands, and it was very possible that to succeed at this, there would be casualties. If it was true that Tchinchura had brought danger to Sar Komen when he came, it was also true that the world—and Sar Komen by extension—was already in danger, and the success of his mission here might just as easily save as destroy it.

Tchinchura met Amintuu on the dock by the gangway onto *The Lion's Mane*, and they boarded the ship together. Amintuu took him to meet the captain, a merchant named Kanns. As it turned out, it had been Kanns who had first put Amintuu and his kill squad onto the trail of *The Sorry Rogue,* as he had done business with D'Sarza at a small port named Dreesen.

Kanns welcomed Tchinchura aboard, and Tchinchura quickly realized that this merchant captain was about as different from D'Sarza as could be. Slow to speak and softly spoken when he did, he came across so seriously as to be almost somber. And yet he was friendly in his own way, and the welcome he extended to Tchinchura felt genuine.

"It is an honor to have a Southland Amhuru onboard," Kanns said after they had exchanged their greetings.

"Thank you for providing passage," Tchinchura said. As they walked across the deck, he added, "Have you been across the Madri, Captain?"

"Sa, I have," Kanns said. "Once when I was a boy, with my father, and once myself, a few years back."

"I hope it was a profitable trip," Tchinchura said, "and that you enjoyed the hospitality of the Southlands."

"I can'na say so," Kanns said, shaking his head with a rueful smile. "I'm afraid I made some unfortunate deals there, and I have not been back. I have come to accept in time that I'm not as adventuresome as my father. I have a decent trade, nonetheless."

"It is well, Captain," Tchinchura said, smiling. "To stand on his own two feet and build a good life is what most fathers want for their sons."

"Sa, it is so," Kanns agreed. "Be welcome on *The Lion's Mane,* Keeper."

The captain moved on, and Amintuu showed Tchinchura the cabin they would be sharing with a few other Amhuru, and Tchinchura stowed his few possessions. When they came back on deck, Tchinchura asked Amintuu, "I gather 'Keeper' is a term of respect for Amhuru among Northlanders?"

"Sa, it is," Amintuu said. "Among us, though, the term Keeper is used only for the three who bear the original fragments, but Northlanders either don't understand the distinction or don't care and call us all Keepers. Kanns probably has no idea that you really are a Keeper, and that I am not."

They walked across the busy deck, finding a somewhat quiet corner out of the way of the busy crew and their preparations. There, Amintuu said to Tchinchura, "You are, of course, welcome to sail with me on *The Lion's Mane,* Tchinchura, but you don't have to do this. You are free to follow on your own ship with the rest of your group."

Tchinchura nodded and smiled. "I thank you for your trust, but I understand that you have a great deal at stake. Your chief elder might not be pleased that you let me keep what I bear, and letting me travel as well on a separate ship might be seen as a serious lapse in judgement."

"It would not be the first time my judgement was questioned," Amintuu said, and it was his turn to smile. "As long as I bring you back, and what you bear, all will be well."

"There is another reason for us to take this journey together," Tchinchura continued. "We are the sons of brothers who have been estranged by circumstances and duty for a thousand years. I would like to know what you see, and what your fathers have seen."

"Know what I see?" Amintuu asked, looking at Tchinchura curiously. "Is that a Southland expression?"

"Na, not as such. It is an expression of Southland Amhuru," Tchinchura said, and again he smiled. "Already we bridge the divide of time. We are taught from an early age to ask each other what we see—an exercise in learning from one another and sharpening our powers of observation."

"Ah, it is well," Amintuu said. "And I agree. It will be good to speak of our different customs and ways. We are each lost tribes to the other, are we not?"

"Sa, we are, which is all the more reason for me to come with you," Tchinchura said. "And for a few of yours to take my place on *The Sorry Rogue.* Crossing the Madri was a measure of last resort, undertaken in grim times, but perhaps some good may come of it—getting to know one another and our respective histories, not least of all."

Rika sat cross-legged near the bow of the ship, gazing out at the water and the spray that looked like it might splash her face at any moment as the *Rogue* bounced up and down across the large swells in the open sea. It felt surprisingly good to be back under sail, heading for parts unknown. The sky was clear and bright, for the stars were out in force this evening.

How odd the last few days had been. She had gone from being an exile even among the exiles of Barra-Dohn to being a hero among all onboard. She was treated with respect and even deference by the captain and crew, by the Amhuru from both the Southlands and the Northlands—at least by all but Amintuu, who still seemed affronted by how she had spoken to him—and even by those who had long disliked and mistrusted her.

Nara, of all people, had hugged her when she returned to *The Sorry Rogue* and learned what she had done to save Deslo. It was as though at that moment the years of cold indifference and icy glares had simply disappeared, and Rika had stood there, arms at her side, being clasped by Nara like she was a long lost sister. She almost shuddered to think of it. She detested Nara, but she had borne it as best she could.

Even Marlo had reached out to her, even if not immediately. He had approached her quietly after dinner, just a few hours ago. When he did, he not only thanked her for her intervention with the Amhuru kill squads, but he apologized for his previous mistrust. At least Rika thought he had; he had been so awkward and mumbly during that part that she had been forced to guess at what he was getting at.

And yet, even if odd, Rika knew her newfound celebrity might well have saved her and her ambitions. Not only had the Northland Amhuru not proceeded to kill Tchinchura and take his fragment of the Golden Cord, but in a single moment, their suspicions of her had been allayed. She had gained their trust, and that trust might just be the key to her success and their downfall.

It was funny how the world worked. If you wanted to take something from someone, you first had to give. It was always this way. You gained trust when you gave, so the more you gave, the more trust you gained. Then, when the moment was right, you cashed in on all of that trust and took the thing you wanted.

She had almost forgotten this after being humiliated and imprisoned by Eirmon. The failure of her plan to take the stolen Zerura and make her fortune with it had damaged her confidence in general and blinded her to this one inescapable reality of all schemes and betrayals.

To succeed as the villain, you must first play the hero.

A few days ago, in that misty field, she had played the hero with stunning effectiveness. Tchinchura had called it risky, which, of course, it was. But risks had to be taken when you played for high stakes, and the battle for the power of the Golden Cord was the biggest stake of all. She had survived that gamble, and with any luck, it would set her up to take the next one.

And so, while everone aboard *The Sorry Rogue* treated her like a hero, she would look for her opportunity to betray them into the Jin Dara's hands, to hand over the last Southland fragment of the Golden Cord. And now, since everyone loved her, they might help her to do this willingly. In their eyes she had been transformed from a disgraced mistress of a fallen king to a selfless savior by a single, desperate act.

And that, Rika thought, was why the world was full of idiots. People didn't change, not really, and they should have known that. To be wise in a world of fools was a gift beyond measure, and she looked forward to the day when she would reap her reward.

And the rest of them? They would get what they had coming.

Draagan stooped on the riverbank. The track in the mud was hard to read clearly. It was old and partial, and other smaller tracks had since been left there, too. But, if he was reading it right, if the complete print he thought he was seeing was as big as it looked, then there could be no question. It was a *salandra*.

The rumors had started in the winter, spread up and down the river by the hunters who ventured deep into the jungle in search of hides and pelts for the spring markets. The hunting had been poor, and the discovery of more than one carcass in close proximity to the river had confirmed that even the big cats who ruled the jungle were being hunted by something else—something not human, something capable of ripping jaguars and cougars and even tigers into pieces.

The big cats weren't the only carcasses the hunters had found; the remains of some of the larger species of monkey and even other large reptiles had been found, too. Many of those remains were almost unidentifiable, often just bits of bone and skin. Only the *salandra* was a predator with both the capacity and the appetite to put all the larger animals of the jungle habitat on notice at the same time. And so, the rumors and the whispers had started, drifting downriver all winter. A great croc had returned.

Draagan had been watching for the signs that the *salandra* was moving toward the coast ever since, and it was with resignation but not surprise today that he examined the track in the mud, the first concrete evidence he had seen that the *salandra* had been in this area. As its prey fled before it, the great croc's insatiable appetite would drive it where the food was plentiful, and that usually meant it would head downriver until it was turned back or stopped. Draagan and the brothers were a long way from the coast here and the big populations that lived there, but only a few days farther downriver was a small village, the first of many that dotted the landscape all the way to the larger towns near the coast.

The villages had heard the rumors too, and they would be watching for signs of the *salandra* also, but unfortunately their tribal rivalries would prevent them from working together until they absolutely had to, and by then the great croc would have a taste for humans, making it almost impossible to drive it back into the heart of the jungle. To be sure, killing the *salandra* was a permanent solution to their problem and turning it back inland was not, but killing a great croc was even harder than turning one around, which would prove hard enough.

What complicated the situation even more was the fact that Draagan and his brothers were supposed to be in hiding, in virtual if not actual seclusion. That was why Draagan had retreated to the Amhuru's jungle stronghold. But the stronghold was even closer than the nearest village, so it wasn't just the villages along the river that were in danger.

Draagan felt pretty confident that he and the other Amhuru with him could protect the stronghold from the *salandra*, but if they merely encouraged it to bypass them, the villages and towns would still lie in its path. If they wanted to protect the people who lived downriver as well as themselves, they'd have to do more than just shoo the creature away. This meant they'd have to convince the great croc to turn back inland, which meant in turn that they'd have to work in concert with the nearest villages and jungle tribesmen.

That meant Draagan would probably not be able to stay hidden.

Draagan looked out across the river at the crocodile that was sunning itself on the far bank. The river was wide here, and the creature hadn't even stirred when Draagan emerged out of the cover of the jungle to examine the riverbank. Draagan picked up a small stone and, while he still squatted, threw it across the river. It hit the mud near the croc harmlessly, so Draagan called across the water, "Has your big brother really returned?"

The croc didn't move; it didn't even open its eyes. In the end Draagan stood and stretched, looking around him for any sign of one of the others who had come looking for tracks with him. They kept pretty close whenever they left the stronghold, even though their weekly trip upriver to look for signs of the *salandra* had become somewhat routine. It felt a little strange to look around and see none of the others nearby.

He considered calling for them, and glanced at the original fragment he wore on his right forearm. When he did, a glimmer of movement between his feet drew his full and undivided attention. A moment later his knife flew down, and the slender black snake slithering toward the river was pinned to the ground as the blade went through its head. The snake might look nondescript, but it was one of the most poisonous creatures in the jungle—and that was saying something, for there were many poisonous creatures in this jungle. The snake would probably have kept going between his legs, all the way down to the water, but a bite from that little fellow could be fatal.

His attention returned to the *salandra* track, even as he reached down, picked up the snake that lay dead in the middle of it, and cast it away. He sighed. He could not reach any other conclusion—the great croc would have to be turned back upriver, and he would have to help. The rainy season was around the corner, and when the river grew swollen, a roadway for the *salandra* to move village by village, all the way to the sea, would open right up. It didn't matter if he was in hiding; he had a responsibility to use the power entrusted to him.

Draagan caught a glimpse of golden hair coming toward him through the dense green of the jungle, and he turned to go. He would tell the others about what he had found, and they might want to come view the evidence for themselves. Either way, it would be a quiet and sober trip back to the stronghold. A great croc was back, and they could not ignore it.

36

The Great Croc

Draagan couldn't see the *salandra* up ahead yet, but the swath of destruction it left in its wake made following its trail easy. It was moving fast, crushing the underbrush and knocking over any trees in its path, snapping them as easily as Draagan could break twigs. It was still moving parallel to the river, and if Draagan and the others didn't catch and turn it into the water soon, it would be beyond the trap. Then they would be out of luck.

Draagan saw the low hanging vine at the last second, and it was still almost too late. He was just barely able to duck below it, both he and the torch he was carrying. The great croc was long and wide and as strong as could be, but it was also so low to the ground that it hadn't cleared out all the vines strung across Draagan's path as he ran on the Arua. He'd had a few near misses so far, but none yet as near as that.

They had been so close to getting the *salandra* into the river, but the tribesmen who had been helping to funnel it toward the water had gotten too excited, and their line got bunched up on the riverbank. At the last minute, the *salandra*—perhaps aware at some primal level that it was being herded and therefore not wanting to go where it was being driven—cut back hard away from the river. A couple of shocked tribesmen in the place where the line had thinned out raised their torches to ward it off, but they were trampled by the great croc as it broke through and ran for its life along this very path, downstream and parallel to the river.

Draagan had hoped something like this wouldn't happen, but turning a *salandra* and getting him to go where he wanted was tricky business. There were only two things that would help him. The first, and the main, thing was fire, so the first step of their plan had been to use a large army of men to drive the *salandra* toward the river with torches. These were mostly tribesmen, but there were several Amhuru with Draagan helping, too. Getting to the water was imperative. It took an enormous amount of time, energy, and manpower to find, corral, and direct a *salandra* on land, where it could turn in any direction at almost anytime. So, the only hope of success depended entirely on getting it into the water.

At the same time, even though he wanted the *salandra* in the river channel where it would be easier to contain, once it was in the water, several new problems would emerge. The great croc would be even faster and more formidable in water than on land, so if Draagan or another slipped on a muddy riverbank and went in with it, they'd probably never get out again. The fires they set or carried to drive and herd it could no longer help except to keep it in the water, and, of course, every river goes in two directions. Invariably, one of those directions was precisely the way Draagan did not want the *salandra* to go.

So, to succeed, he had to employee the other thing that could help turn a *salandra*. The great croc liked to be in the water, but it liked to be submerged in the water; it didn't like to let much more than its head and back be exposed as it swam. Accordingly, the key was to find a place in the river where rocks and other natural barriers already existed, creating some kind of natural rapids, and then to submerge more large stones and whatever else they could find there to build up the underwater barrier. That way, if the *salandra* chose to go the way they didn't want it to go, they could either force him with the obstruction to turn around and go the other way or force him to climb up out of the water on top of the trap.

If they succeeded in doing that, in driving it up out of the water, then they could employ fire again. If the obstruction was big enough and solid enough, posted men with torches could block the *salandra* on it, though if it wasn't very wide, that could be especially dangerous. Draagan and the Amhuru didn't feel they could do that at the spot where they had built their trap. It just wasn't large enough or wide enough, and the surface of the exposed rocks was quite wet and slippery.

Instead, they strung a long rope over the river, just above the trap, along with a second rope about five feet above that. Rope bridges were used in many capacities by the jungle tribes, and they were as adept at running along ropes while holding the one above as Draagan was at running on the Arua. So, with a small army of tribesmen with torches near the trap, the idea was that if the great croc turned downriver, it would find its way largely blocked underwater by stone, with a row of flame hovering above the water. This, Draagan and the others hoped, would convince it to turn and head back upriver.

Once they had it going the right way, it would only be a matter of having enough men keep pace on either side of the river so that it didn't try to get out. Jogging along a riverbank while holding a torch and keeping the *salandra* in the channel of the river was much easier work than getting the thing in the river in the first place. That's why it was especially bitter to Draagan that they had literally been just a few yards away from having the creature in the water when it had broken free.

Now the great croc was approaching on land the place where the trap had been built in the water, and if it somehow got into the water below the trap, then the barrier they had constructed to keep it from going downriver would do just the opposite and keep the *salandra* from coming back upriver. That was always the danger of building a trap like this. It could backfire, and if Draagan and the others didn't get the *salandra* in the river soon, it looked like it was going to do just that.

Once below the trap, they would have to change strategies and defend the river to keep the *salandra* out, while also finding a way to drive it back the way it had come. Then, if they could do that, they'd have to try again to get it into the water. And if they failed, if it got to the water below the trap, then this wouldn't be about corraling or turning anymore—it would be about killing, and unless they could get the *salandra* into a confined space on land, that was a much more difficult task.

A great crack echoed from up ahead—another tree being crushed beneath the rampaging *salandra*—and Draagan knew he was close. He veered a little outside of the swath the creature was cutting, wanting to approach it on its left, since the river was on their right. If the creature reacted to him and his torch, he wanted to be able to turn it toward the water. There was still a chance they could get it in the water before the trap. He just hoped that if he did, the tribesmen by the rope bridge were ready.

Up ahead he saw the tail of the great croc swinging, whipping a small cluster of bushes that had escaped its direct onslaught, ripping them out of the ground. He reached through the Arua and tried to wrap its invisible substance around the creature's legs to slow it down, but it was so strong that it forged through and forward, slowing down only barely as it ran on.

But that slight slowing gave Draagan the chance he had been hoping for, and he drew up alongside the churning forelegs and head of the great croc. He couldn't turn to look for his brothers who had been running just behind him and to his side. He didn't dare take his eyes off the *salandra;* he just had to trust that they were still there. It was time to make his move.

He turned and darted almost straight for the *salandra's* enormous head. He waved the torch in the direction of the *salandra's* eye, and the creature whipped his head away as it turned on an angle toward the river. Draagan kept pace, sprinting to stay by the *salandra's* head and bracing for the creature to try to do to him what it had done to the tribesmen back upstream. Draagan, though, was ready, and he would not be trampled.

The *salandra* crashed out of the trees onto the upper portions of the riverbank, and for just a moment, Draagan thought maybe it wasn't going to try to cut back—that maybe, just maybe, it would actually go down the bank and into the water. He had just enough time to glance downstream and see in the distance, maybe fifty or seventy-five yards down, a solid line of torches in the hands of the men standing on the rope bridge. He felt a brief swell of elation at the thought that the *salandra* would soon be in the water and that the trap was ready. And, just as he did, the head of the great croc whipped back toward him, the terrible jaws open and poised to take him in whole.

If Draagan hadn't been waiting and looking for this to happen, he might have been lost. But, as soon as he saw the mouth gape and swing toward him, he reached through the Arua again. This time, it was not to wrap the creature's legs; instead he seized the Arua and pushed up on the great croc's jaw so that its whole head rose up and up until the bottom of its mouth was even with, if not above, the top of the Arua field.

Then Draagan jumped off the Arua and into the great croc's mouth.

He cleared the long row of jagged teeth, felt his foot touch down inside the mouth, and adjusted his grip on the Arua to try to slow down the *salandra's* attempt to close its jaws. At the same time, he reached up with the torch, driving the flame into the soft palate of the *salandra's* mouth.

As soon as he felt the torch touch, he let go of it and leapt forward through the quickly closing gap between the upper and lower jaw.

He waited for the jagged teeth to rip his legs open, but he must have aimed just right, for he dove down and out of the mouth without being bitten, hitting the sloping, muddy bank and rolling down it toward the water. And then, just before he was about to tumble into the river, he pushed up off the bank with a mighty leap, landing back up on the Arua. He turned downstream, running once more parallel to the water.

He couldn't see the great croc, but he heard the snap of its jaws over and over, as though the creature was trying to stop the burning inside its mouth that way. He also heard a sound erupt behind him that sounded somewhere between a hiss and a growl. It sounded to Draagan like fury and pain mixed. He turned up the riverbank to get away from the water, hoping, trusting, that the others would be there to do what he could not, which was to keep the *salandra* from turning up after him.

They were, and they did. The great croc started to turn, no doubt eager to avenge itself on the man who had dropped fire into its mouth, but four more Amhuru with torches blocked its path and it thought better of it, eyeing the flames even more warily than it had before. It swung back down the riverbank and shot straight for the water this time. The sound of the splash it made might have been the loveliest sound that Draagan had ever heard.

Tribesmen were running in now from farther back in the trees to line the riverbank and make sure the great croc didn't come back out of the water, and soon the near bank was lined with men with torches. Draagan lifted his eyes to look across to the far side. If that wasn't also lined with torches, and soon, the *salandra* would be able to simply swim across and get out again, and that was almost too painful to think about.

Fortunately, the tribesmen and Amhuru on that side of the river came pouring out of the jungle just a few seconds later, and the *salandra* did not head to the far bank. Now they would see, though, which direction it would turn. Draagan took another look downstream as though to be sure that he had really seen what he thought he had seen before. Sure enough, above the trap extended an almost solid wall of flame.

Draagan didn't know if the *salandra* could also see what he did—a wall of flame waiting for it downriver—perhaps glowing on the surface of the water from the *salandra's* point of view down below. Either way, it did not turn that direction. Instead, it turned upriver, swimming against the current with power and purpose.

The wall of torches on either side of the river began to move parallel upstream, beside and a little behind the great croc, but Draagan did not. He fell to his knees in the mud of the riverbank, suddenly exhausted and trembling. His legs and arms were shaking, and he thought, just for a second, that he might be sick.

"Are you all right, Keeper?" asked a voice he did not recognize.

"I am," he said, his voice shaky.

"It worked," the voice said then, and Draagan heard the tribesman's excitement, and perhaps a little surprise.

"It did," Draagan said, his head nodding, although he did not look up. "Kalos be praised."

As the tribesman walked away, Draagan wondered how far word of this night would spread. Most likely his secret was still safe, but some peace and quiet would be most welcome until word came from Telsiin that he could go home.

Deslo rubbed his aching shoulders. The scar from his wound in Sar Komen wasn't the problem—that had healed just fine. He had been carrying Kita for the last few miles, and even though she wasn't that heavy, it was remarkable how someone so little could come to weigh so much if carried too long. So he had handed her back to Kaden, and Deslo would enjoy this reprieve until it was again his turn.

Deslo looked at his sister, whose arms were wrapped around Kaden's head so her little hands could clasp his forehead, and Deslo found himself again wishing Kaden had carried him like that when he was a boy. Her head was down, her cheek against her yadi's soft hair, so that all Deslo could see were her blonde curls. He didn't begrudge her what he hadn't had; he was glad for her. He just felt sad for himself sometimes, for his own childhood.

Kita walked fine these days, now more than a year and half old, but she couldn't sustain the pace they were keeping without growing tired. Talking, though, that was another matter. She didn't say much, only a few words here and there, like "Yadi" and "Noni" and "Delo"—she couldn't get Deslo's name quite right, consistently leaving the "s" out. Deslo wasn't sure what to think about her relative silence, but he could see that Nara was worried. She tried sometimes to prompt Kita to speak when she would nod or use some other nonverbal form of communication, but most of the time these prompts were ignored. By and large, Kita seemed content to watch the world with her big, intense eyes and say nothing.

"She'll probably start any day now and never look back," Kaden had said the only time Deslo asked him about it. "She'll become a chatterbox, and then we'll think wistfully about the days when she didn't talk."

He smiled when he said it, but it had sounded a little too quick, a little too much like it might be a well-rehearsed line that he used to reassure Nara. Deslo didn't press the matter, as he figured they'd all find out in time. Kita would either start talking more, or she wouldn't.

Deslo realized as they kept walking that it wasn't just his shoulders that ached. His legs ached, his feet ached, pretty much everything ached. A couple months onboard *The Sorry Rogue* had not been enough to get him out of shape, not after spending all that time on land in Sar Komen. That wasn't the problem; the issue was the pace they'd been maintaining for the last month since going ashore. He knew that getting Tchinchura and the Southland fragment to this Telsiin was important, but he wished they'd take a few more breaks along the way.

Today had been especially brutal as they'd been working up a steady incline pretty much all day. The grade was steep, and whenever Deslo looked back the way they had come, the open grassland seemed to stretch down and away for as far as the eye could see. They'd been in open grassland for the past few days after working through dense woods most of the month. All of the terrain they had passed through had been devoid of settlements and roads, making the journey much more challenging.

That had been the whole point of going this way, of course. Amintuu had acknowledged that the most direct path from the closest seaport to the place where they were meeting Telsiin was just a little more than two and a half weeks. But, for all the reasons they wanted to be seen when leaving Sar Komen, they did not want to be seen arriving anywhere else. So, Kanns and D'Sarza had dropped them a good distance away from the seaport so they could make their way across country, steering as far clear of human habitation as possible.

In the distance, though, a lone peak rose above the sloping plain, a rough mountain of rock and scraggly plants, and Deslo knew without needing to be told that this was their destination. Amintuu had described the place when they left the woods behind and started across the plain, and now that it loomed before them, it was unmistakable—and, even better, it seemed to a weary Deslo to be close at hand. They'd be there soon, maybe even tomorrow.

By the time Amintuu called a halt to their march for the day, there was no doubt that tomorrow would be the day. Accordingly, the camp was more jubilant, as even the Amhuru were eager to be finished with the trek. The talk was louder, there was more laughter, and some of the Amhuru even dared to sing after dinner.

There were only eighteen Northland Amhuru still with them, as one of the squads of six that had rendezvoused with Amintuu in Sar Komen had been sent to bring Telsiin to the meeting place some time ago. They had gone with the third ship, and by Amintuu's reckoning they would have arrived at the meeting place perhaps a week ago. Deslo thought maybe he should be nervous about tomorrow; after all, he knew that Amintuu's decision that Tchinchura could be trusted and should be allowed to keep the fragment he bore wasn't final. But he just couldn't feel worried tonight. He was too happy to not be walking.

Still, as he sat by the fire after dinner looking up at the Northland stars, he felt a layer of melancholy beneath the jubilation.

Across the camp, sitting side by side and gazing at the same stars, were Olli and Maarta. He knew they weren't trying to exclude him. In fact he felt pretty sure they would have welcomed him if he walked over to join them. Nevertheless, he did not feel welcome and kept his distance.

At first, after leaving Sar Komen, things had been just like they'd been before on *The Sorry Rogue.* That is, Olli and Deslo spent most of their time together. Maarta, who traveled with them in place of Tchinchura on *The Lion's Mane,* would often talk with the Southland Amhuru and their apprentices, or the Kalosenes, or even the other exiles from Barra-Dohn. As time went on, though, he spent more and more time with Olli and Deslo.

Olli said this was because they were closer to Maarta's age, which was true, as he was just twenty-one. Still, Deslo was pretty sure that wasn't the only reason he sought them out to spend time together. Deslo didn't say anything to Olli, though, since he thought she already knew it wasn't the only reason.

And that was how it started. First Maarta was a guest in their fellowship, a definite third, an extra added to a strong, established friendship, but before long Deslo started to feel like the third. That feeling of being on the outside looking in had been clearest to him on Deslo's fifteenth birthday. His parents had been the only ones to remember it, at least until supper when they told everyone else and everyone onboard the ship congratulated him and wished him well. That the others forgot was no big deal—he didn't expect them to remember with everything else going on—but that Olli didn't remember had been disappointing. She had been an integral part of the happiness on his fourteenth birthday.

That had been a good day, Deslo thought. He could still see the happy images etched in his memory. He could see his yadi, up and about, largely recovered from the Madri crossing, joking with him about how far they'd come since Brexton and their scare with the gutsnakes. Kita had been gurgling and smiling as they passed her around, and Olli had joined them like just another member of the family. That might have been the day Deslo acknowledged to himself that he'd been wrong about her being a condescending nuisance—and it might also have been the day he realized that his feelings for Shaline now had competition.

After her relative inattention on his fifteenth birthday, though, he started looking for things to keep himself busy so he didn't have to hang around with Olli and Maarta, and most of those things turned out to be the same thing in the end—spending time with Kita. For their part, Olli and Maarta went out of their way initially to invite Deslo to join them in whatever they were doing, but after a while, they let it be. By the time they disembarked *The Sorry Rogue* to head across country, it was fairly natural for Deslo to travel with his parents so he could help with Kita, often lagging near the back, while Maarta and Olli generally moved with the main body of Amhuru, often near the front.

Deslo had made his peace with this, or so he had thought, but tonight's minor jubilee reminded him, in a way, of their first night in Azandalir. Thinking of Azandalir made him think not only of the place where his friendship with Olli had been forged, but of Trabor and Shaline. Thinking of Shaline, like always, brought mixed emotions.

Leaving her had been hard, one of the toughest things he had done since leaving Barra-Dohn—harder, in its own way, than fighting the grass gliders or the gorgaal. Even after waking in the Northlands, he'd missed her very much, but over time the heart-ache had faded. The closer he drew to Olli, the less he had missed Shaline. For a while he had simply told himself that Olli was "too old" for him, and that if Shaline were with them, she would be the only object of his attention, but he had begun to wonder about that. Looking at Olli and Maarta, though, made him realize that it didn't much matter what he thought. In the end Olli's heart was elsewhere.

So, thoughts of Shaline did not comfort him. He only felt guilty about his uncertainty and a little nostalgic. He hoped Shaline was all right, and Trabor, and Azandalir itself, for that matter. He also hoped that once they found Telsiin, things could get figured out and the Jin Dara be stopped so he could go back. He felt a rare but powerful urge, a feeling that resided deep, deep inside him, a feeling he could only understand and describe as the part of him that wanted nothing in this world so much as to go home.

He just didn't know where home was now, or how he could get there.

It was time for Kita to go to bed, so Deslo seized his opportunity to slip away from the celebration and took her. He lay down beside her, his head propped up on one hand, and he asked her the usual question. Kita nodded her head—yes, she did want a story. So, Deslo started working through the index of past favorites, some from their travels after leaving Barra-Dohn, some from the time when he lived in the city that Kita had never seen but that Deslo always insisted was her home, even if it was lost to them both forever.

Kita shook her head for all of these, though, and Deslo could see there would be no avoiding it—she wanted her favorite story, the story of how Deslo had woken up after crossing the Madri to find that he had a new, cute, adorable baby sister, the day he always told her was the best day of his life. Deslo didn't mind telling this story, but he always tried to sell her a different story first, as he had told it many, many times. But tonight it looked like he would need to tell it again.

He was about to suggest it, when Kita suddenly and without warning shouted, "Kiki!"

Deslo looked at her, stunned at the rare, verbal outburst, and a bit confused. "Kiki?"

"Kiki!"

"What does 'Kiki' mean?" Deslo asked, his confusion mingling with amusement. Kita's wide eyes looked at him with an excited intensity.

"Kiki! Kiki!" Then Kita pointed at herself, and Deslo understood.

"You want me to tell your story? How I first met you after I woke up?"

Kita pumped her head vigorously up and down in approval. "Kiki!"

"All right," Deslo said with a smile. "I'll tell your story, Kiki."

"Kiki!"

So he did. And when he was finished, he lay there while she settled and fell asleep, and then he rose to go tell his noni and yadi about Kita's new, self-appointed nickname.

Deslo had a feeling "Kiki" was going to stick. It somehow seemed right for her. He couldn't have said why, exactly, but as a name for this little bundle beside him, it worked.

He'd lost Shaline, and he was losing Olli, but not all was bleak. He had his Kiki, and Kiki had her Delo.

37

The Way of All Things

Up ahead, Zangira could see the mounds. There were twenty-eight of them in four rows of seven. He knew them all, of course, but when he visited, he always went right to the fifth mound in the second row. Today was no different. Today was, most likely, the last day he would ever come.

He squatted by the mound. The fire that had burned the length and breadth of Azandalir almost two years ago when the Jin Dara had paid his fateful visit had not only consumed every blade of grass and charred every tree from the slender olive trees in the vineyard to the great talathorne trees around the lagoon, but it had changed the nature of the soil. In some places the ground was slick and shiny and hard, like dark glass. These were the places where the fire had burned the hottest.

It wouldn't last, the infertility of the ground. It was the way of all things. People died and decayed, or burned and left their ashes behind, and this also returned to the earth and replenished what had been lost. One day Azandalir might be just as green and lush as it once had been, or so they said. Zangira wouldn't be here to see it, though. Nor would they.

The Amhuru were leaving.

"The last of us have come, my love," Zangira said to the mound. "We leave today."

He reached up and brushed away a tear. He had been here many times, and he never cried. He didn't even cry the first time, when they had buried their dead after the Jin Dara left and the survivors escaped from the caves which they had hoped would be their salvation but had become instead, for too many, their tomb.

Thinking of that made him shiver, even in the bright afternoon sunlight. The caves had become so terrifying when the rock grew hot, so hot they couldn't touch the walls without being burned, so hot that steam rose from the floor and their feet were burned no matter what they wore on them or how many blankets they stood upon to mitigate the effect. And then the caves started to collapse in places, crushing some outright and cutting all of them off from the outside world.

It became unbearable as the air grew so warm that it felt like it was burning your lungs to inhale, and then, after it cooled again, it became so stale that it felt like breathing death. His children had told him they had found themselves wishing for death, but neither they nor he had been the one to die. Zangira sometimes wished he had been, as the Azandalir he had emerged to find was not the one he had known.

All that had made it beautiful had been burned away.

He was weary. Weary of this world, weary of the conflict with the Jin Dara, weary of saying goodbye to his beloved.

"I know it's foolish," he said, "thinking I need to come here to say goodbye, even thinking that leaving is goodbye at all. I know you aren't here, anymore than the bones in this mound are really you. I know Kalos keeps you in the palm of His hand, and I know you wait for me there.

"We're going after him," Zangira continued. "We're all going—every last Amhuru of the Southlands. We're crossing the

Madri, all of us. It's bold, but it is the right thing to do. Our scouts are convinced he has crossed already, perhaps some time ago, so none of the Southland fragments are in the Southlands anymore.

"There's no reason for us to stay. What we were entrusted to protect has all gone north, and so must we. We will either find and kill him and reclaim what he has taken, or he will wipe us out. If he does, our failure will be final."

"You did your best, Father."

Zangira turned from his broken reverie to look at Trabor, standing silently on the Arua a few yards behind him, looking solemn.

"My best wasn't good enough."

"Perhaps not, but it was all anyone could have done," Trabor said, simply and with compassion. "We will make this right."

"Were you sent for me?" Zangira asked, noting the cold resolve in his son's voice.

"Yes," Trabor said. "It is time."

Zangira rose, stepping up onto the Arua to stand beside his son. He rested his hand on Trabor's shoulder. "Do you want to say anything before we go?"

"I have spoken my piece," Trabor said simply, and they turned to go.

Running one last time across the island toward the lagoon filled Zangira with a different kind of sadness then visiting the mounds. Since the fire, the island had been uninhabitable, so they had used it only as a place to meet and council with each other, usually staying no longer than a fortnight. Still, before today, he had always left it knowing that once they had achieved the goal of the scouting mission they were on, they would return to consult with the others. But not today. They were leaving with no definite plan to return.

And why should they return? The Temple had collapsed and lay in ruins, ironically just like the original it had been built to resemble. The Seat of Judgement was gone, as the fire that had raged across the island had burned so hot there that the entire side of the rocky ridge that surrounded Azandalir had turned into that dark shiny glass, and the mural of the six brothers had been burned right off the wall. The Springs had collapsed almost entirely, and their collapse had spelled doom for many of the Amhuru in the caves located in large measure right beneath them.

So Zangira ran with Trabor through the burned-out memory of their lost home, thinking that almost certainly it was the last time he would ever be here. They might succeed in finding and killing the Jin Dara, though that was itself very much in doubt, but even success didn't mean they'd be back. There wasn't anything but memories and graves to come back to.

As they ran through the midst of what had once been the talathorne wood that surrounded the lagoon, Zangira was impressed one last time by the still smoking trunks of the great trees. Many, indeed most, had fallen in the two years since Azandalir had burned, but a few of them still stood—great, black, charred poles rising into the stark sky. The ones that did stand still had wisps of smoke rising from them. He marveled at these trees, so big, so remarkable, that after all this time they could still stand, still burn.

Moored in the lagoon were five ships. What remained of the Southland Amhuru were all gathered here, and they could fit on five ships. Together they would sail for the Madri and cross it. Then, whatever happened would happen.

Zangira and Trabor ran up the gangway onto their ship, and not surprisingly, Shaline was waiting for them at the top. Her eyes were full of tears, and he wrapped his strong arms around her, pulling her tight. "We shall see her again," he said, "for Kalos holds her in the palm of His hand."

"I know," Shaline said, and she gave her father a hug. "I just wanted to say goodbye."

Zangira bent down and kissed her head in reply.

"It is time to go," he said quietly, and he turned to cross the deck.

Shaline watched her father cross the deck of the ship. His limp seemed more pronounced than usual. Perhaps it was psychological, as it was here on Azandalir that his foot had been crushed in the first place when the cave-in that killed her mother had almost crushed her father too.

As the ships headed out to sea, Shaline felt butterflies in her stomach. It wasn't just the unknown of the Madri and the crossing; it was the palpable sense of something waiting beyond. Destiny called, and she and her people were trying to answer it, but she knew there were no guarantees that they were sufficient for the task. To embark on a cause that you knew to be good and right did not mean you were equal to it. That much about life and the world, she knew.

Still, there was comfort in knowing the path ahead, if not the outcome. And there was also comfort in knowing they were not the first to go this way. Others had gone before. She found herself often, of late, thinking of them, of Tchinchura and the others—Nara and Kaden, Olli and Deslo. She wondered where they were and how it had gone for them, wondered if they were all right. She wondered if they would meet again, and if they did, what that would be like. Had Deslo changed? Would he still care for her, or was she forgotten by now?

The answers to all her questions lay ahead, and as Azandalir disappeared behind them, they sailed toward those answers. Shaline took comfort, amid all the uncertainty, in the knowledge that Kalos watched over her, for the Amhuru believed it was not just the dead that He held in the palm of His hand, but all things.

The climb to the top of the mountain—even if it wasn't a very tall mountain—was every bit as challenging as it had appeared from down below, and Kaden wasn't sure if he could have made it without Deslo to help with Kiki. The path they took up the side was only wide enough for them to move in single file, and still it was steep and full of switchbacks, so that Kaden and Deslo fell farther and farther behind the others, taking turns carrying their little blonde bundle.

For her part, Kiki seemed to be a bit afraid of the difficult terrain. It was probably the steep drop on the side, but she clung tighter and tighter the farther up they climbed, only reluctantly allowing herself to be passed between them, as though the insecurity of the handoff was too much to cope with up here.

Reaching the top, then, and its relative flatness, had eased Kiki's anxiety and provided relief to Kaden. He'd set her down and let her run ahead to Nara, who took her by the hand and smiled as Kaden doubled over to get a breather before coming to join the rest of them in front of the gates of the fortress that stood there well back from the edge.

The gates were open, and already the Amhuru who guarded them were mingling with Amintuu and the others who had escorted the Southlanders here. Telsiin had been sent for, but he had not yet come. He did so shortly after Kaden reached the main group, and introductions were made all around.

Perhaps because he had spent time at Azandalir and met Almaren, Kaden had expected Telsiin to appear more fragile. But if the chief elder of the Northland Amhuru was as ancient as his Southland counterpart, he did not show the mark of time as clearly. He was wiry and spry, and Kaden could see right away a look of hard determination that was quite different than the quiet gentleness that Almaren had exuded right up until the most difficult moments of the last meeting of the Azandalir elders before they left. Kaden had assumed it a foregone conclusion that Telsiin would concur with Amintuu's judgement about Tchinchura and what they had done, but watching the introductions take place, he was not now so sure.

But whatever misgivings Kaden had at first dissipated somewhat as the evening wore on. Telsiin was hard and determined, for hard times had befallen him and his people, but he was also an amiable host. He showed them around the fortress, which inside consisted of a large open area filled with several small buildings, little bigger than huts, ringed by a thick stone wall. The ground was dirt and rock without so much as a scraggly bush, and the huts were made of wood that must have been hauled up that same difficult path many years before, for they looked weathered and old, but how old Kaden could not have said.

They ate together with their hosts as the sun was going down, and the tone was very different than it had been the night before when laughter and singing had accompanied it. Kaden thought maybe it was weariness, or uncertainty, but whatever it was, all were subdued. After dinner, the few of the band who were not Amhuru retired to their huts so that Telsiin might preside over the formal discussion about what to do with Tchinchura, and beyond that, what to do in general.

The first order of business was to hear Tchinchura's story, and once again, Tchinchura told it in full. Telsiin did not interrupt to ask questions as Amintuu had; he only sat and listened. Not a word was spoken by anyone throughout, and when at last Tchinchura finished, the silence of the night wrapped around them all, and the crackling of the fire and the nighttime singing from the plain below of the insects the Northlanders called crickets were the only sounds that Kaden could hear.

"Your story has explained not one but two mysteries," Telsiin said, at long last breaking the silence, and when he continued, Kaden felt a chill inside. "For just over a year ago, on the same day, the two replicas of the other Southland fragments grew inert and fell to the ground. Now I know why all three fragments weren't brought across at the same time, as well as the story behind both crossings, for should I not assume that this Jin Dara has come pursuing you?"

"I would say, rather," Tchinchura said, "that he has come for me and for you. For I believe he desires the three Northland fragments as much as he desires the last of the Southland fragments."

"You think he would have crossed the Madri anyway, even if you had not come?"

"I do."

"Alas," Telsiin said, "we will never know, for you did come, and you have given him cause to come, too."

Telsiin stared hard at Tchinchura, but Tchinchura did not back down from that stare. He met the chief elder's eyes and held them, matching him stare for stare.

"I came at great risk, as did all who sailed with me, both to save the last Southland fragment of the Golden Cord, and to warn the Northlands of the danger the Jin Dara posed. I do not apologize for coming, for I believed—as did the Southland elders who sent me—that it was the right thing to do. Kalos will judge me when I cross over if it wasn't."

"And yet," Telsiin said, "it is I who must judge you now, and what you have done."

"Chief Elder—" Amintuu started, but Telsiin held up his hand, and Amintuu stopped himself short.

"There is a part of me that thinks this was a Southland problem that the Southland Amhuru should have dealt with. There are many places where one might secondguess the decisions that you and they have made."

Telsiin stopped there, and the silence deepened. Kaden felt it deepen, but he also felt anger rising inside him. Who was this man, who now had the benefit of hindsight at his disposal, to secondguess the decisions the Southland Amhuru had made? He glanced at Tchinchura, thinking that if he himself was angry, then surely Tchinchura must be, for he had been the one sent to look for the fragment Eirmon had stolen right from the beginning. Finding and recovering that fragment had been his consuming goal for many years before Kaden had even met him.

"And yet," Telsiin said when he started again, this time in a completely different tone as he gazed into the dancing flames of the fire, "that is ungenerous, and I know it. We, too, have had to recover fragments for one reason or another over the years, and I cannot say what I would have done had two been taken during my time as chief elder. Nor can I say what I would have done had two come into the hands of such a ruthless man. To cross the Madri and seek the help of my Southland brothers, no matter what the cost to myself, might well have been my choice."

He looked up from the fire and back at Tchinchura, now with sympathy and pity in his eyes. "I do not know if your decision to come has brought him or not, but I do know that you were right to come. We had to be warned, the last Southland fragment had to be protected, and we will speak no more about it."

"Thank you, Chief Elder," Tchinchura said, and Kaden thought perhaps he could hear in Tchinchura's voice the relief that he felt.

"It is well," Telsiin said. "We must leave the past behind and move on to more pressing matters—namely, what to do about this Jin Dara now that he has come?"

"Do the Keepers know that a second crossing was made?" Amintuu asked. "For I did not know until tonight."

"They should know by now," Telsiin said. "The first crossing set in motion several different things, from dispatching the kill squads to find whoever had crossed, to directing the Keepers to their current locations. We weren't prepared for a second, separate crossing. It took time to decide what message, exactly, should be sent to them and if the plan we had first conceived should still be followed."

"But you say they should know by now," Amintuu said, pressing the point.

"They should, but the Keepers, as you know, are each in remote strongholds, and the messengers have not had time to travel there and back, if they even return at all. I would not be surprised if they don't all stay to reinforce the guard where they have gone."

"They will need to be warned," another Northland Amhuru said. "They should know what kind of man has come, who it is that seeks them—and that he has two fragments."

"We should not send more messengers until we figure out what we want to do," Amintuu said. "We should rethink if hiding in separate strongholds is still the best plan."

"Yes, we should," Telsiin said, nodding. "Tell me, Tchinchura, for you know this man and his work better than any of us—what is your counsel?"

"There are many choices," Tchinchura said. "But in the end there are only two roads. All counsel must, after all is said, come back to these two basic choices—whether to hide or to fight."

"Do not even those two become one, in the end?" Amintuu said. "I have heard nothing that suggests that by hiding we will convince this man to stop looking, so is not hiding but a delay before the fighting begins?"

"I fear that it is so," Tchinchura said.

The silence that had held throughout this exchange did not hold now, as whispers and murmurs rose around the fire. Telsiin looked once more at Tchinchura, and he, too, nodded in agreement.

"I think the other Keepers must be recalled, for none of them alone is strong enough to resist the Jin Dara if he comes—or when he comes, for he will come. We will have to stand together, or I fear we will not be able to stand at all."

"Chief Elder, there is another choice before us," Amintuu said then, and there was a tone in his voice that brought the quiet back to the assembled Amhuru. Kaden found himself leaning in as though he was in danger of missing what was said.

"And what is that, Amintuu?" Telsiin asked.

"Whether we, too, will combine fragments."

Kaden's was not the only gasp that broke out around the fire.

"Hear me, I beg!" Amintuu added, as the rising swell of voices threatened to drown his voice.

"We will hear," Telsiin said, and again Kaden heard the hardness in Telsiin's voice that had been there before. "If you are sure of that which you would speak."

"I am sure of nothing, Chief Elder," Amintuu said, "except that this man and his soldiers destroyed with something approaching ease a force of Southland Amhuru almost as large as the one I led here. Did he not, Tchinchura?"

"His victory was decisive."

"So," Amintuu said, "if we gather the four remaining fragments into one place, but do not use their combined power to fight him, will we do anything more than make his ultimate victory easier? Should we not at least consider training with multiple fragments as he and his men have done?"

"But Kalos has forbidden us to combine the fragments!" one of the Northland Amhuru shouted across the assembly.

"We would be no better than the Jin Dara!" another said.

"We would be much better," Amintuu said in disgust, "for we would do this to defend the Cord, not to steal it. And besides, Tchinchura has already done what is forbidden by coming here. Can we not see that if we don't do this we will fail?"

Excited shouting and arguing broke out, and the exchange grew more and more tense, with a few supporting Amintuu and the rest trying to shout them down. It seemed to Kaden that Telsiin and Tchinchura alone kept aloof from the argument, but when it subsided enough for him to be heard, Tchinchura rose to his feet, and the assembly grew quiet.

"I am a guest to your council, my brothers," Tchinchura said. "And I do not take lightly the opportunity to be here. What I will say now, I will only say once, for the decision that lies before you is yours to make. Will you hear me?"

"We will," several of them said. "Speak."

"The great fear of the Southland elders, and my great fear as well," Tchinchura said, "was that by crossing the Madri, by disregarding the law that our ancestors made, we would open the door to disregard laws that they did not make, laws that came from Kalos Himself. I think, my brothers, that no matter how great the need that drives us, we must never do what Kalos has forbidden. If we cannot stop the Jin Dara and honor the law of Kalos at the same time, then we must not stop the Jin Dara. Whatever happens, we must be faithful, for that is the first and last commandment of Kalos for all men, but especially for the Amhuru."

Kaden watched as the assembly reacted, most nodded in approval, but those who had sided with Amintuu held back. He thought that Amintuu would argue with Tchinchura, and that the whole dispute would boil over again, but it was Telsiin and not Amintuu who spoke next.

"I am of a mind to agree with Tchinchura," he said, "but I do not think this decision has to be made tonight. We are agreed that the Keepers must be sent for. We will have time before they can come to decide what should be done once they arrive."

There was quick agreement on this point, and then the chief elder continued. "This is what I propose. Amintuu and his squad will stay here to help us protect Tchinchura and the fragment of the Golden Cord that he bears. The other squads will go to summon and escort the three Keepers here from their hiding places. While they are on their way, the elders will consider and decide this matter."

Telsiin's proposal was accepted without reservation, and the council was adjourned. Kaden made his way in silence with Deslo through the dark to the small hut they were to share with Nara and Kiki. As they walked, an unshakeable foreboding seemed to hang between them, an uncertainty that neither one could either voice or deny.

Finally, Deslo said without looking over, "What do you think, Yadi? Is Tchinchura right?"

"He has always guided us well," Kaden said, knowing this was not a complete answer, for in truth, he did not know what to say.

38

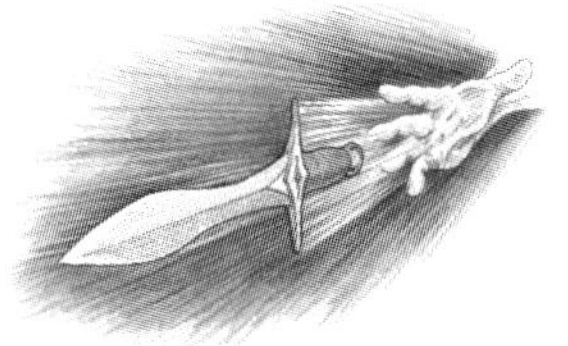

Casmir

The sky was overcast as a light rain fell. The Jin Dara looked up at the thick grey clouds above as tiny raindrops hit his face. The water felt real, and he could feel it run across the curve of his cheek. He was pretty sure he was awake.

Pretty sure seemed like the best he could do these days, ever since waking from those interminable dreams. The dreams had started awful and grown worse, each one darker and more terrifying than the one before it. He did not frighten easily, nor was he easily shaken, but the mere thought of the time he had spent trapped in that unreality almost made him tremble.

Several of his Najin had not survived the crossing. Oh, they had lived, but they had been broken men when they awoke—silent, staring, able to eat and walk and follow simple commands, but good for little else. Devaar had kept the dozen or so who had emerged from their slumber in this pathetic state under guard while he waited for the Jin Dara to awake, and once the Jin Dara had been strong enough to move about on the ship without help, he had gone to visit them.

The men were all below decks, sitting in almost absolute dark, staring at nothing in particular. He had walked among them, the light from his lamp illuminating their gaunt faces and casting their shadows against the hull of the ship. Below the empty, hollow stare, he saw in every man's eyes the fear. He saw the fear and knew it as fear, because he had felt and lived the fear. He looked and he shuddered, and he knew what he must do.

With Devaar's help, and the help of the crew and some of the other Najin, he herded these men up on deck. He stripped each of them of the Zerura that they wore, though this was more difficult than he had expected. They didn't fight it exactly, but each one of them pulled back when it was his turn, not in a way that suggested any of them were aware of what was happening, for they each stared forward with no expression. Instead, it was like an instinctive reflex was governing their actions with regard to the Zerura.

And then, once he had reclaimed the replicas they had worn across the Madri, he led them to the place where the rail could open for the gangway when in port, and one by one, he pushed each one of them off the ship, into the sea.

Their bodies hitting the water made splashes that were laughably small in the face of the large, rolling waves, and for a few moments, he could see them bobbing in the water beside and behind the ship. After a while, though, they disappeared from view. Their purpose had been served, and there was no point in drawing out their fate.

That had been months and months ago, and still the uncertainty about what was real and what wasn't lingered. Sometimes he wondered if he would ever truly wake, or if some part of himself had been left behind. That thought, when it came, made him secondguess what he had come to do. Most of the time, though, he understood that if he could succeed at the task that had driven him across the Madri, it wouldn't matter what price he had paid to get here.

So, he tried to focus on the task at hand, and for the most part, he was successful. The recruits he had added before sailing for Azandalir did not compensate for the losses he endured with the crossing. And as the ones who had been broken by the Madri in many cases were those who had worn the Zerura the longest, they were among his most adept. Now, with no idea how many Northland Amhuru he would have to face, he knew he would need more Najin. His first order of business, then, was to start replacing the men he had lost.

To train the new recruits, though, required that they go ashore. But where? That was the critical question. It would take time to turn these men into Najin, but he did not want this to be wasted time. He wasn't in a hurry, necessarily, but he liked to be efficient. So, after scouting several ports and talking to many ship captains, he decided that the port of Casmir would be ideal for his scheme.

Casmir wasn't a city that happened to have a port; it was a port that had become something of a city. It's location was such that it functioned as much like a crossroads for the sea as a port could, and most sea captains agreed that as a hub for ships in the area, it was as likely a place as any for the Jin Dara to find an Amhuru passing through—not that the Jin Dara had told anyone he spoke with that this was what he was seeking.

At the same time, there was a lot of open land inland from Casmir, and the Jin Dara found without difficulty an ideal spot for the training of the new Najin to take place. Meanwhile, he rented a house in town to house Devaar and the Najin he intended to keep with him there. At first he thought about simply taking the house, especially since the landlord annoyed him, but the death of the man, as enjoyable as it would have been, would also have attracted attention. Instead, he arranged to have a few wealthy merchants disappear—after they had left the port, of course—and the goods he recovered from them were sufficient to fund his stay in the town indefinitely.

Despite their best attempts to keep their presence in the town a secret, his men's physical features made this impossible. So their strategy was a simple one—patrol the quay and docks, being sure to keep a close eye on all newly arrived ships. If an Amhuru appeared, they would move against him immediately, and with any luck, he would be in their hands before he could even get into the town and hear that they were there.

And so today the Jin Dara strolled along the quay of Casmir, as he did every day, and he gazed up into the rain and let it fall on his face in the hope that it would prove that he was awake.

As he did, he closed his eyes and reached out to locate the Najin. He could sense every one of them, and knowing the quay and the docks intimately by now, he knew exactly where all ten of the Najin patrolling with him were. Not only that, but now he could reach farther out, having practiced this for so long, and he could sense the five he had left in town. Two he had left to guard their belongings at the house, and the other three patrolled the town on the off chance an Amhuru might somehow show up there without coming directly from a ship.

And, even beyond Casmir, if he really strained, he could sense the camp where the others trained the new recruits. It was almost an hour away by foot, and his feel for it and those who trained there was faint, but it was there, at the edge of his awareness. All of those who bore replicas of both fragments of the Golden Cord he wore were connected to him, no matter where they went, and he now believed that with time and practice, there would be no distance too great for his awareness to transcend.

He opened his eyes. Opening them did not affect his ability to sense the others, and a handful of them had started moving his way. He looked down the quay toward the end of the dock they were moving along, and sure enough, he saw the three who had been patrolling that dock jogging toward the quay. A new ship had arrived earlier that morning and was moored on that dock, but as of yet no one had disembarked. He wondered what had excited them, and he moved down the quay to meet them and see. He didn't have to wait long.

"They're here," one of the Najin said. "More than one."

"On the new ship?" the Jin Dara asked, looking down the dock. The new ship was way out there, but his eyesight had grown very keen.

"Yes."

"How many did you see?"

"Three, for sure," the Najin said, "but there could be more."

"Has anyone left the ship yet? Gone into town?"

"No."

"And other than the port official, has anyone gone onboard?"

"No."

The Jin Dara nodded. The port officials were all in his pay, and while it wasn't impossible that they might betray him, he doubted that any of them would. It seemed likely, then, that the Amhuru onboard that ship didn't know he was here. That there was more than one was a surprise, and it suggested to him that they might be expecting trouble. Why else would they travel in a group?

Then he realized that he didn't really know if this was unusual behavior for Northland Amhuru. He was assuming it was since Amhuru in the Southlands didn't normally do that, but how did he know what Northland Amhuru normally did or didn't do? This raised other questions, but all of them eventually led back to this—should he gather the Najin who were here and board the ship immediately? Or should he send for the others in town to come and join them?

No sooner had the question formed in his mind than he knew the answer to it. Including himself, there were eleven of them here. If they couldn't storm this ship and capture one or more of the Amhuru on it, then his mission here in the Northlands would probably fail anyway. He didn't care if the ship was teeming with Amhuru—he had the element of surprise on his side, as well as ten Najin. And, while being on the ship and not on land would affect his ability to manipulate the Arua, that was a knife with a double-edged blade, and it cut both ways.

"Get the others," he said, and he stood at the intersection of the dock with the quay. The three Najin who had brought him word of the Amhuru's presence scattered around the harbor, summoning the others who were there, and before long, all of them had come.

The Jin Dara started down the dock, his hood up to cover his golden hair and eyes. The others were likewise shrouded in the shadows of their hoods. What they looked like to the sailors and crewmen on the ships they passed, he did not care. Just so long as they were able to board the ship in question and take what they had come for, that was all that mattered.

As they approached the ship, the Jin Dara saw a head appear near the side, and he knew it immediately to be an Amhuru. The man looked down at the cluster of men, cloaked and hooded, walking briskly up the dock, and for a second a look something like puzzlement appeared on his face. And then—the Jin Dara could almost feel the moment of transformation—the puzzlement became alarm, and the man ran.

The Jin Dara knew what he was running for, and he ran too. He started up the gangway, and still about a third of the way up threw one of his knives and took the Amhuru in the arm—the arm that was trying to disengage the gangway. He then reached through the Arua, though it was harder to take hold of here—almost slippery above the water—and threw the wounded man back, away from the place where they would board.

There were shouts and the sound of movement on the deck, and the Jin Dara hung back now, motioning the other Najin to go up before him. He came up after, and what he saw was fighting that was both intense and short-lived. There were Amhuru and crewman fighting his Najin, and while he saw one of his men go down, the Amhuru were overmatched. Soon the fighting began to diminish, and as it did, the remaining crewmen surrendered.

He and the other Najin walked among the sailors, killing those that had surrendered, disregarding their screams and protests. As the last of them fell to the deck lying in his own blood, the Jin Dara saw movement out of the corner of his eye and heard a splash.

He whirled, noting as he did that he wasn't the only one who had heard it. Two of his Najin had turned toward the sound too. He ran to the rail and looked down into the dark, murky water. The rain made ripples on the surface, but he thought he could see a larger series of circles rippling out from a spot between this ship and the one next to it. A man had jumped overboard, he was sure of it, but had it been a sailor or an Amhuru?

"Go," he said, motioning to the two who had followed him to the rail, "find the man who jumped. If it's a sailor, kill him, and if it is an Amhuru—"

He turned and looked at the two wounded Amhuru they had captured during the fighting who were being bound by the other Najin even as he spoke. Around them a few more lay dead.

"Well, sailor or Amhuru, just find him and kill him."

They ran down the gangway, and he proceeded, with the help of the other Najin, to search the cabins and the rest of the ship. They found no more Amhuru onboard, and nothing of interest among their possessions. When he returned to the deck, he gave his attention to the two Amhuru lying there bound and gagged, under guard. He stooped beside them, pulled back his hood, and made sure they were both looking at him.

He smiled.

"I see by the look in your eyes that you know who I am," he said. "Oh, you may not know my name, but you know who I am. You know what I have. You know that I have dared to cross the Madri with them. You know."

His smile grew wider.

"And I know that you know many things that I want to know. Let me assure you that even though you will resist, sooner or later—probably sooner—there's nothing you know that you won't tell me."

He stood and turned away from them. As he did, he motioned for the Najin to pick them up and bring them along. Pausing at the top of the gangway, he looked back and said, "Leave the rest. Burn the ship."

Draagan sat in the open courtyard of the jungle stronghold. Around him on three sides rose the tall, strong, exterior walls, made primarily from the giant logs harvested from the dense jungle upriver and floated downstream to be used here. On the outside the walls had also been coated with a mixture the jungle tribesmen made primarily from river mud to seal the cracks in their own wooden houses, but this mixture grew very hard when dry and added an extra degree of strength to the dense wood.

Directly ahead of Draagan was the large gate, also wood, but not as heavy or thick as it would have been immovable by any ordinary human strength. Behind Draagan was the main building in the stronghold, a great hall with high wooden rafters and a ceiling unusually far off the ground. It had been built to feel a bit like the ceiling was a canopy of leaves, thereby replicating the feel of walking through the jungle when you walked through the hall, and the wooden rafters spoked out from the tall wooden pillars like branches from a tree.

The kitchen, training areas, and sleeping quarters for Draagan and the other Amhuru were all below the great hall. The stronghold wasn't terribly far from the river, but whoever had first constructed it had either been extremely careful to make sure they dug far enough away that water didn't get into the underground portions, or they had somehow reinforced the walls of those areas to keep the water out.

Draagan didn't know much about engineering or construction, so he didn't really understand how it worked. All he knew was that the halls and rooms down there were dark and narrow, and he greatly preferred being in the open courtyard where the sun sometimes, like today, could still shine on his face. This was the only place he could come for that, since he hadn't been outside the stronghold in more than two months, not since Breeson had come with the message that the other two Southland fragments had crossed the Madri, too.

That news had been a blow from which Draagan had not entirely recovered. The news that one had come, well, Draagan hadn't laughed that off, exactly, but it hadn't worried him too much. True, it had never happened before, but the whole "alarm" system his forefathers had established had been put into place precisely because it was possible. It was possible someone might take a fragment, maybe even a wayward Amhuru, and it was possible he might cross the Madri, perhaps in search of more.

And yet there were many Northland Amhuru, and they were forewarned and better acquainted with the Northlands—its climes, creatures, and hideaways. He just hadn't been terribly afraid. This turn of events, though, this second crossing, had really given him pause, and he couldn't stop trying to figure out the story that explained the facts. He knew there were many possible scenarios, but in the end he believed strongly that two of them made more sense than all the rest—either someone had stolen a fragment and fled across the Madri, and then some of the Southland Amhuru had come across in pursuit of that someone, or two of the fragments had been stolen by a single individual, and the Keeper of the third had fled from the one that bore them, crossing the Madri in search of help and, perhaps, safety.

He certainly hoped it was the former, but he feared it was the latter. If someone had stolen a fragment and fled across the Madri, he thought the Southland Amhuru would not have come after him. They would know that the Northland Amhuru would be alerted, and Draagan felt they would have left the situation to sort itself out—or at least left the Northland Amhuru to sort it out. He thought they would have focused on protecting the two originals they still possessed. At least, that was what Draagan would have done.

No, he didn't think he would take what he bore south across the Madri unless he thought that was an action of last resort. And he didn't think he would feel like he had no other option unless both the other two Northland fragments had been taken and he was the only Keeper who still had one. That would be unsettling, and he could imagine considering a crossing if it was the case.

But, if what he feared was true, then this second crossing would mean that someone other than an Amhuru already had two original fragments of the Golden Cord. It would also mean, most likely, that this someone wanted them all. That was why Draagan had not left the stronghold in over two months. He had been, some of the elders might say, cavalier with what he bore after the first messenger brought news of the first crossing and he had retreated here, but he could be cavalier no longer—even if that meant this courtyard was the only patch of ground where he could sit and enjoy a little sunlight for the rest of his life.

Draagan rose, stretched, and headed inside. He tried to push thoughts of what might be going on elsewhere in the Northlands out of his head, but he had little to distract himself with these days. The rainy season had passed, and with it the fear of flooding was gone, and in almost three months, there had been no sign of the great croc. He was glad, because if it came back, he would not be able to help this time. He could not now justify endangering the fragment he wore, even if the *salandra* returned and left a path of destruction all the way to the coast.

As he walked through the great hall to head downstairs, he saw Breeson, who approached and said, "Draagan, do you have time now to show me what you have been doing at the forge?"

"Ah," Draagan said with a smile at the irony—he had more time these days than he knew what to do with. "I do."

Breeson, who had decided to stay and lend his aid to Draagan's guard instead of return to Telsiin, at least for the time being, followed Draagan down into the network of halls and rooms below the great hall. When they reached his room, Draagan took up the pitcher of the pungent oil used for lamps here in the jungle.

He was well-acquainted with this jungle—one reason why he had come here to hide—but he had never quite gotten used to the smell of the stuff. The tribesmen harvested it and took it downriver to the cities on the coast, making it central to their economy and livelihood, but he often wished the lights here ran on corness like many of the meridium technologies in the middle latitudes of the north. They didn't, though, and since he wasn't prepared to live in darkness down here, he had to endure the smell.

Once the lamp was glowing brightly, he crossed to the small dresser on the far side of the room and lifted the box off the top. He carried it to his desk and set it down, then opened the carved lid, motioning for Breeson to come over. He reached in and pulled out a long, slender knife and handed it to Breeson, who took it from him and turned it over and over in his hands.

Draagan smiled as Breeson stared at the odd grey color, and opened his hand to let the blade lie there, moving it up and down as through trying to gauge the blade's real heft. He had felt much the same way as he examined the knives himself once they had cooled, for they looked and felt quite different then the meridium blades he had used and carried since childhood.

"What is it?" Breeson asked, turning to look at Draagan. "I mean, I know it is a knife, but what metal is this?"

"It is called steel," Draagan said.

"Steel? What is that?"

"Mostly iron," Draagan said, "but there are other things in the alloy that you would not have heard of."

"And Zerura?"

"There is no Zerura in this blade."

"I've never heard of steel," Breeson said, looking back down at the knife in his hand.

"It is still used here and there, I believe mostly by sailors and others who are on the water a lot and need meridium less," Draagan said. "According to some historians, steel was the most common metal used for weapons before meridium was discovered."

"I see," Breeson said, but Draagan could tell that he did not.

"Go ahead," Draagan said, encouraging the younger Amhuru to proceed. "Say what is on your mind."

"I am sorry, Keeper," Breeson said, seeming embarrassed to have to point out what seemed so obvious to him. "But if this steel doesn't have any meridium in it—and if you have not put any Zerura in it—how does it react to the Arua, and how can you control it with your Zerura? What use is it?"

"Ah, now you have come to it," Draagan said. He smiled at Breeson. "It does not react to the Arua, and I cannot control it—if by control it, you mean move it while in flight or recall it after I have thrown it. But, of course, while it is in my hand, it is mine to use as I will."

Breeson still looked perplexed, so Draagan added, "And if I can't move or sway it, no one else wearing Zerura can either."

There was a pause, and in the silence Breeson nodded, and Draagan knew that he saw, at last, the purpose of this blade. Indeed, the purpose of all the blades he had forged and placed in this box.

"Wouldn't regular meridium blades without Zerura work as well?" Breeson asked.

"Can you not control ordinary meridium blades a little when you seize control of the Arua field?"

"I can."

"As can I," Draagan said. He looked at Breeson hard to make sure he was listening. "Sometimes, when you have an advantage, you become so used to it that you do not see how depending upon it makes you predictable. And that, Breeson, can make your advantage a weakness."

He took the steel knife from Breeson's hand and threw it across the room. The strong, sharp blade embedded itself in the hard, wooden wall with a dull *thunk*. Breeson nodded in appreciation, and Draagan walked over to pry the knife out of the wall. When he had removed it, he turned to Breeson, grinning as he held the steel knife up for the other to see again.

"The kitchen knife is king, until it meets a sharper blade."

39 

Come

Kaden sat cross-legged on the ground, watching Kiki make shapes with the shadows her hands cast on the ground. He had shown her how to make a bird appear to fly, flapping its wings, and she had been delighted to learn how to do it. He had then shown her a few more, and now she seemed endlessly fascinated by her ability to make the shadows. He felt like he understood, since watching her delight was endlessly fascinating for him too.

The large white clouds drifted across the bright blue sky, and Kaden thought that it was afternoons like this that could make you forget that, just possibly, the world was hanging in the balance. Then shouts from the guards at the gate shattered the calm, and several Amhuru nearby ran to them. Kaden lifted Kiki and carried her to Nara, who was sitting not far away mending some of their more threadbare garments. He set Kiki down beside her, and without a word, jogged toward the gate. Deslo caught up to him from wherever he had been, and they both ran, axe in hand.

The first sign that there was no immediate danger was the fact that the gate was opening when they reached it, and the second was the solitary, exhausted Amhuru who stumbled through it. Two of the Amhuru guards ran out to have a quick look at the steep path that led up from the plain below, but they returned shortly after to confirm the man was alone. They closed the gate.

Kaden realized as the Amhuru fell to his hands and knees, so fatigued that he could no longer stand, that he knew this man or at least recognized him. He was a member of one of the squads that had come to Sar Komen to get them, one of the squads that had then been dispatched to the three Northland Keepers with the news that the first crossing of the Madri had been made by a friend, but that the second had been made by the Jin Dara, a man already in possession of two fragments of the Golden Cord and intent on getting more.

That had only been four months ago, and from what Kaden had gathered, that was not enough time for the squad to have gotten to their destination and back—not if they were going to travel in secret and avoid detection. The time frame just didn't work, and that fact, along with the man's ragged appearance and the fact he had arrived alone without any of the rest of his squad, did not bode well.

Telsiin, Amintuu, and Tchinchura were among the Amhuru who had by now crowded around the man, and Telsiin stooped beside him to offer water, which the man drank eagerly. When he had caught his breath, he spoke at last, looking at Telsiin, but speaking loud enough for them all to hear.

"We were ambushed . . . in Casmir," he said, still breathing hard. "It was him . . . the Jin Dara. I'm sure of it."

"The others?" Telsiin asked.

"Dead or captured."

"How did you escape?" Amintuu asked.

"We were docked, still onboard the ship," he said, and then proceeded to tell his tale in fits and starts. "I jumped overboard. I found my way under the ship, to a place beneath the dock, while they searched for me. When it was dark, I swam parallel to the shore, all night, only coming ashore at dawn. A fisherman, he took me to another island. I boarded a ship, began my way back."

There was silence as the assembly digested the news. When it was broken, it was Telsiin who spoke, still stooping beside the man. "You did well. Eat, and sleep if you can. We leave as soon as we figure out where we're going."

This last Telsiin said as he rose and started away, back toward the center of the compound. All around him Amhuru began to move, quickly and with purpose. Kaden supposed they had some kind of evacuation procedure they were following, but he and Deslo stuck with Tchinchura, who followed Telsiin, Amintuu, and a few of the others.

"Elder," one of the Amhuru began, "if one or more were captured—"

"Then we have to assume he knows where we are," Telsiin said, finishing the sentence. "Or soon will."

"And all the Keepers," Amintuu added, and that grim thought sunk in.

"He said Casmir, right?" Telsiin asked. "Do you remember which Keeper his squad was heading for?"

"Draagan would be the closest to Casmir," Amintuu said.

"Then we must assume Draagan is in the most danger," Telsiin replied. "So we need to figure out where we are going and who will warn the Keepers. Whoever is sent to Draagan must understand the urgent need for both speed and caution."

"Elder," Amintuu said, "should we not also consider whether or not—"

"No," Telsiin said, stopping in his tracks and turning toward Amintuu. "That was settled. I will not condone combining the fragments."

"But, Elder, things have changed—"

"Nothing has changed," Telsiin said, and he slowly turned to resume walking. "Nothing which would justify that. We must focus on the matter at hand. What is our course? Where do we go?"

"Our goal was to assemble all the Keepers," Tchinchura spoke up. "They were to gather here, were they not?"

"They were."

"Then we should now make our way to one of them," Tchinchura said. "Not this Draagan, perhaps, as we might be too late to help him."

"But all the Keepers then may be compromised," another Northland Amhuru said.

"We don't have to stay when we get there," Amintuu said. "But at least we will have brought two Keepers together. Then we can head somewhere else."

"Don't we need to figure out where that somewhere is? So we can tell the messengers we send to the other Keepers where to send them?"

"No," Telsiin said, stopping again, and turning slowly to look at them all. "We cannot, or we will have learned nothing from this. We will go to a Keeper, we will find a secret place, and we will keep it secret."

"Then how do we unite all the Keepers?"

"Maybe we don't," Tchinchura said soberly, nodding in aggreement as he looked at Telsiin. "Perhaps it was mistake to even try."

"We will pick two men to send to Draagan, and two to send to whichever Keeper we choose not to go to ourselves," Telsiin said. "Those four will decide amongst themselves before leaving where to take the Keepers should their missions prove successful. We will not know, and must not. Nor will they know where we are going after we find the Keeper we choose. That way, no one of us will be able to betray all the rest."

The group was silent for a moment, as the reality of what was happening settled upon them. It was Kaden who asked the final question.

"So which will we choose?"

"Maccado is probably the closest, so we could get to him

quicker," Amintuu said. "But Asantii might be the safer choice, since he is farther away from Draagan's location."

"Asantii . . ." Telsiin said. "Yes, it must be Asantii. If our messengers get through to Maccado and Draagan, it will be easier to bring them together."

"We are decided then?" Tchinchura said.

"Yes, we are decided," Telsiin agreed. "Now we must hope and pray that wherever the Jin Dara is headed, whether to Draagan or another, that he will fail. If he takes a third fragment, then I fear we are doomed."

The procession of small boats making its way slowly upriver, carrying both himself and his Najin, was a strange sight, of that, the Jin Dara was sure. He leaned over to say something to Devaar about it, but Devaar had fallen asleep beside him, his head drooping awkwardly as he slept where he sat.

He looked down on Devaar, and he wondered about the man. The Madri had changed them all, but perhaps none more than Devaar. He had even given up wearing Zerura, which the Jin Dara had reluctantly allowed since Devaar had been with him so long. Perhaps with time, he would get over the crossing and take it up again.

The Jin Dara's attention returned to the river and the boats. Down closer to the coast, there were roads through the jungle where faster modes of transport could be used, but this far inland, where the jungle was dense and forbidding, the river was the only road. Still, using the river to go upriver was slow business, no matter how you did it, and the people who lived in these parts did it in curious fashion.

A track just wide enough for a team of oxen to walk—oxen being the preferred beasts of burden in this corner of the world—ran beside the river. For each small boat in the procession, a long tether connected the craft to a pair of oxen. A driver walked behind each team, providing incentive in the form of a cracking whip for the oxen to keep pulling, and so the small vessels, laden with men, slowly crept upriver.

The Jin Dara was not a patient man, and this method of transportation might have driven him crazy—especially since he felt he was close, oh so close to finding a third fragment—had the jungle itself not been such a fascinating place. When he reached out through the Arua to get a sense of the creatures living nearby, to perhaps summon some to him, he was overwhelmed by the diversity. The jungle and the river both teemed with life, and he had spent the two weeks they'd been on this river so far examining that diversity, wondering if any of it might be put to good use, as he had used the hookworms and rhino-scorpions against Barra-Dohn, as well as the windrays against their ships in the bay.

There were any number of possibilities—from the small spiders and insects that were everywhere, to the many species of snake that were in the water and in the trees and everywhere in between, to the larger creatures, like the monkeys, the large cats, and the crocodiles that sometimes swam along beside the procession of boats when the Jin Dara bid them come. Yes, and he could imagine possible uses for them all, but what precisely he did not know and might not until he came to this jungle stronghold the captured Amhuru had babbled about once the Jin Dara broke him.

He swatted a mosquito away from his face—thinking, and not for the first time, that he should reach through the Arua field and obliterate every mosquito he could reach—and then he closed his eyes. Ignoring not just the mosquito but all the other creatures nearby, he tried as he had, every other day, to reach out upriver to see what he could feel up ahead. He stretched his mind, stretched his control, felt the Arua that radiated out of the ground sustaining and connecting and controlling the entire ecology of this jungle, and indeed the entire world, in ways the Jin Dara still did not fully understand, despite how far he had come in his use and mastery of it.

He reached out, farther, up and up the river, in and in toward the deepest center of the jungle, and suddenly he discovered something . . . enormous. Something . . . astounding. His eyes popped open, and he stared past all the boats, past all the oxen toiling beside the river. He stared, even though he knew that what he had felt, what he had touched, was so far beyond the portion of the jungle that he could see it was futile to even look.

"What are you?" the Jin Dara said softly but out loud. Devaar beside him did not stir, his head bobbing still against his chest.

The Jin Dara closed his eyes again and concentrated. He reached out, half expecting to find that he had imagined it—but he hadn't. It was still there, still lurking, sleeping, perhaps, dormant, near the very heart of this vast jungle world. It was so far away, he could get no sense of its size or shape in any concrete sense, but he knew that it was vast.

More than that, he knew that he wanted it.

Come, he called wordlessly across the distance between them, taking the faintest of holds upon the creature through the Arua, taking hold and tugging. *Come down the river. Come to your master.*

At first there was no response, and then the creature actually moved away. The Jin Dara almost let go of his hold in surprise. How long since a mere animal had resisted his will? What was this thing that even from this distance could resist his call? He tugged, harder, as hard as he could from so far away.

And then it happened. The creature stopped resisting. It stopped resisting, and it started moving down the river, obeying his summons.

Rika didn't fully understand just how *The Lion's Mane* and *The Sorry Rogue* came to be anchored offshore when they reached the edge of the wood, but then again she didn't care much for the trivial details of the Amhuru's business. All that interested her was information that might be of use to him, and she thought she was very close to having that. Very close indeed.

She imagined that when they'd left the ships in the first place, all those months ago, that Amintuu and Tchinchura had made some plan with D'Sarza and the other captain to keep the ships nearby if they were needed, and that someone had been dispatched to summon them. She didn't care how they got here, but she did care where they were going.

But about that, the Amhuru were being pretty tight-lipped. There was a distinct, deliberate, increased sense of secrecy among them, and she knew it wasn't anything personal against her. It was a reaction to the return of that messenger, and an understandable one at that. Some of their own, with knowledge of the whereabouts of all the fragments of the Golden Cord, had fallen into the Jin Dara's hands.

That could be disastrous, not just for them but for Rika as well. If he discovered where all the fragments were, and if he systematically took them, then she would have had nothing to offer him. But, if this mission to move Tchinchura somewhere safe was successful, then at least she would know where that was—once they got there. And that might turn out to be valuable information.

And yet she suspected that the situation might prove even better for her than that. She had caught the drift of a few conversations, and she gathered that the new strategy for the Northland Amhuru seemed to involve separating the four remaining fragments into two separate hiding spots, rather than gathering them all to one place as they had been trying to do.

If that was true, then it made sense that at some point they would rendezvous with one of these Keepers the Northlanders talked about. If that was indeed the plan, then she would potentially be able to lead the Jin Dara to not one but two original fragments. Surely that would be bait worth dangling.

But would the Jin Dara take it?

She couldn't afford to wait to find out.

40

Just a Chance

The Jin Dara walked cautiously along the line where the dense jungle gave way to the top of the riverbank. There was no track here for oxen to pull small boats upriver. That had run out well before the Amhuru stronghold, and the Jin Dara was a good ten days or more by foot farther inland than that.

When the boats had no longer served the Jin Dara and his Najin, they had disembarked, setting the oxen free to roam back downstream . . . and killing the hired drivers to leave no witnesses. They then made their way through the jungle on the side of the river that was opposite the Amhuru stronghold, staying as far back from the river as they could and still be within view.

Two days into their journey through the jungle, they had come upon the outskirts of a village of tribesmen, and they had paused there long enough to kill every man, woman, and child that they found in it. Four days later, after coming upon another, they had been forced to do it again, for the Jin Dara could not believe that the nearby villages hadn't promised to alert the stronghold should they detect an approaching force, and if he could keep word from reaching the stronghold before he did, he would.

Of course, he probably couldn't. He had no guarantee he'd fully exterminated either village, had no idea how much interaction these villages had with others he had not seen along the way, or how long the mass death he had left behind could remain a secret. Sooner or later a tribesman would head to the stronghold with word of what he had done, and the Amhuru would be on their guard. There was a chance he would get there first, but he figured the odds were against that, especially since he had taken this detour upriver.

Once they had found the stronghold, he had positioned the Najin around it, to keep an eye on it and to watch for any who might try to enter, but mainly to make sure that no one left. He had continued on upriver alone, for the massive creature from the heart of the jungle was still making its way slowly, relunctantly downstream, and he wanted to go and see it for himself. That, and he believed that he could overcome the last, stubborn portion of the thing's resistance and gain full control, both to bring it downstream faster and also to make sure he could direct it against the stronghold when the time came.

So, the Jin Dara crept along the edge of the jungle, along the top of the riverbank, knowing that around the next bend the object of his curiosity lay. His heart was beating fast, not because he was afraid but because he was overwhelmed with the joy of discovery. He hadn't come up this river and into this jungle to find this creature, but finding it gave him almost as much delight as finding and taking a third fragment would. Almost.

He started around the sharp curve of the riverbend, and his heart thumped louder and his eyes grew wide. A crocodile of unearthly proportions lay half in the water and half on the riverbank. It was a dark green, but there were brown-grey patches where the peculiar mud of this river had dried on its exposed hide in large clumps.

As he drew nearer, the crocodile opened its great mouth as though to yawn, but the Jin Dara did not believe it was a yawn at all. It was the final act of resistance and defiance from this creature, as though it believed that by showing him the mouth and the rows of teeth that could tear him and ten other men at the same time to shreds, that it would convince him to turn around, go back, and leave it alone.

Quite the contrary—that head and that mouth were perfect.

"You will do nicely, very nicely indeed," the Jin Dara said when the crocodile had closed his mouth and he could approach even closer.

He stood now, just ten or fifteen feet away. He had been holding the creature through the Arua field as he approached it, and now he held it completely. He could feel the crocodile submitting its mind and will to his control, and the Jin Dara knew that it would follow him back and do as he commanded.

"Come. You will be my battering ram."

Draagan walked across the courtyard to the Amhuru manning the stronghold gate. The tension among the others was high. The men who had been surrounding the stronghold for the last few weeks and keeping their distance had moved closer. It looked like the attack was finally coming, as they could all sense the manipulation of the Arua field that had been moving steadily closer from, of all things, upstream.

Breeson came up beside him. "Having second thoughts?"

"No," Draagan said, and he meant it.

"Really?" Breeson asked, sounding as though he didn't quite believe him.

"Maybe I could have slipped past them and gotten away," Draagan said. "But that would only delay the inevitable. A moment like this must come."

Breeson looked at him and frowned. "But isn't your chief duty to keep the Golden Cord safe?"

"It is," Draagan said.

"And wouldn't you be safer somewhere else?"

"I might be," Draagan said. "But we'll all be safer when the one who leads this rabble is dead."

"The plan is bold, Draagan, and clever," Breeson said, "I'll give you that. But there are more of them than us. There are no guarantees it will work."

"Of course there aren't," Draagan said. "And I'm not asking for one. I don't want a guarantee, just a chance."

"That, you will get," Breeson said drily, "and soon, I think."

"Yes, I think I will," Draagan agreed, and he grinned at Breeson, who then moved along. They all knew the plan, and they each had a station. Breeson headed to his.

The plan was a good one, but the problem with plans, even the best of them, was that something always happened that you hadn't planned for. Draagan felt the Arua being manipulated and wondered what surprise was coming. Still, they had surprises of their own for whoever had come for him, and theirs was not the only plan that could be derailed by the unexpected.

He climbed up the scaffold behind the wall to peer through the slits near the top at the jungle outside, but as he leaned against the wooden wall, he thought he felt it shake.

And yet what could shake the stronghold itself? It wasn't the men who encircled them, for they had been creeping around as quietly and unobtrusively as they could. Draagan peered up the river, in the direction of the source of the Arua manipulation, and what he saw coming around the far bend made his heart skip a beat.

The *salandra*.

They had found and brought the great croc. The fight hadn't even begun yet, and already there was a wrinkle—a rather large and deadly wrinkle—that their plan had not been designed to account for. He looked at the *salandra,* and he could see that apparently it had grown even larger since they had driven it back inland. What's more, it was so big now that, with the low water levels, it couldn't fully submerge in the river. So it came, half walking, half sliding downstream, and with each step its great legs took on the near riverbank, the stronghold shook.

Draagan dropped from the scaffolding, thinking both as quickly and as carefully as he could about what this would change and what it wouldn't. Strangely, the more he considered it, the more he thought the great croc—though very, very unwelcome here—might actually help with a few things. Specifically, he had been worried that the retreat from the gate and courtyard back into the great hall and the network of halls and rooms and chambers below wouldn't be convincing, that the invaders would sense the trap. But the *salandra* might ensure that it looked quite believable.

As for the *salandra* itself, it would be a pain to kill, but half the battle—or more—was getting the thing into an enclosed space. This one might come into the great hall quite willingly, especially if it was being driven by the will of someone outside who wanted to use it as a first line of attack, and the great hall was an ideal place to trap and kill it. The spears lining the wall of the great hall would come in quite handy for that.

Things could get tricky if they had to deal with the *salandra* and men bearing Zerura at the same time, but the close quarters in there might discourage them from coming in behind the great croc right away. At any rate Draagan and the others all knew to wait as long as possible to spring the real trap—ideally until they knew the one who had the original, or originals, was inside as well.

This particular strategy would probably only work once, and Draagan would only draw and use his steel blades under two conditions: if it had to be done to avoid capture and escape the stronghold, or if the one who bore a fragment or two of the Golden Cord was within reach and he had a chance to get it or them back.

It bothered Draagan that he didn't know if whoever was out there had one or two fragments of the Cord, even though he didn't know what difference his knowing would make. If he had two, and if the men with him were equipped with replicas of both, and if they combined their power, then all this might be for nothing, as Draagan couldn't even imagine how multiplying replicas from two fragments might multiply their abilities. Possibly, he thought, that might make them even bolder, even more susceptible to his strategy, but the boldness might be warranted if they had sufficient power to back it up.

The rumbling of the ground from the great croc's approach had been growing steadily louder, and from the movement by the gate, Draagan knew the time for planning and strategizing was about to end. A great cracking sound echoed through the morning, and shards of the gate broke off and flew across the courtyard. The Amhuru in and around the gate moved back, knowing it probably wouldn't survive a second blow.

Yes, Draagan thought, the time for planning had past. The time for fighting had come.

Olli sat quietly, enjoying the still, cold morning. Sometimes the others grumbled about having to spend so many nights out in the open air, especially in this brisk weather, but she still reveled in the freedom to be outside both day and night. Now that she had this freedom, she couldn't imagine going back to life in the caves. It was as though her early life had been a dream, and now, at long last, she was awake.

She looked across the camp at a small cluster of Amhuru, at Maarta who stood among them. He was clever and strong, but he was kind and gentle too. She had gravitated toward him right from the start, and she could tell he cared for her, too. She didn't want to presume on the future too much, not with so many uncertainties, but she wondered now, even if they could defeat the Jin Dara and take back what he had stolen, if she would ever go back across the Madri to the Southlands.

Maarta looked over in her direction and smiled. Olli smiled back. It occurred to her that home was a fluid concept, that it could be a person as much as a place. Had Nara and Kaden not found a home in each other since the destruction of Barra-Dohn, the great city that the Jin Dara had conqured? It was not so very strange, then, to think that she had traded the island in not for a better place but for a better life, even a nomadic one like this.

"I'm sorry, Jann," she said to herself. "I'm sorry you didn't survive to see the wider world with me."

Thinking of Jann still made her sad, but she no longer felt guilty for what had happened. He had come with her willingly, aware of the risk, even as she now traveled with the Amhuru aware of the risk. If the Jin Dara came, and if she was killed because she stood with them, so be it. She would not want any of them to feel guilty. What she did here she did of her own free will.

She rose, stretched, and walked toward Maarta. No doubt there was another long march ahead of them, but first she would enjoy some of this quiet morning with him.

Kaden stretched and yawned. The morning was very cold, and his back hurt after spending the night on a patch of ground decidedly less comfortable than it had looked. He understood why they were avoiding towns, but the knowledge that they were just a few miles away from the last real town they would pass before reaching the Keeper Asantii made him wish he'd been able to spend the night in a real bed and have a real meal. He closed his eyes and pictured a table in a nice, clean inn, laden with bread and butter, fruit, hot stew, and perhaps even a cup of that marvelous jonda that the Northlanders liked so much.

He sighed as he opened his eyes and returned to reality. There would be no jonda this morning, only dried meat and edible plants they had been gathering the last few nights to supplement their dwindling stores. The only good news was that they were perhaps only a month away from Asantii's hideout, a place called Berran's Point.

Of course, after their last council a few nights ago, in which they had finally decided where they were going to go after they reached Asantii and told him that the Jin Dara most likely knew of his whereabouts, it had become clear that they would not stay long and would soon be out on the road again. And though the Northland Amhuru assured him that the new destination was "not far," he had no idea what that meant. The place Telsiin and the others had decided on was just a name to Kaden.

The routine of breaking down the camp and preparing to set out after a quick breakfast passed uneventfully, and they were preparing to move out when Nara came to him, leading Kiki by the hand, with a look of some concern. "Have you seen Rika?"

"No, why?"

"I haven't seen her all morning," Nara said.

"I'll talk to Tchinchura."

"Kaden," Nara said, whispering urgently and leaning in as though to hide her words from Kiki, who wasn't really even paying attention. "She was sleeping kind of near the edge of camp. What if some wild thing came into camp and dragged her away?"

"It wouldn't have taken her stuff," Kaden said. "Let me talk to Tchinchura, see what he thinks."

Tchinchura didn't know what to think anymore than Kaden did, and most of the party spent the better part of the next half hour searching for Rika or evidence of her in every direction. In the end they did not find any, and when Tchinchura, Telsiin, and Amintuu conferred with Kaden after this search, it was with much consternation that they discussed their situation.

"No one found tracks of any kind, of an animal approaching the camp or her leaving it," Telsiin said.

"If she used her meridium-soled shoes when she left, there would be none," Tchinchura said.

"But why would she go in the night, without warning, without a word?" Amintuu asked, not trying to hide the frustration in his voice.

"Would she betray us?" Telsiin asked. "She spends a lot of time alone and, if I may say so, has always seemed to me to be not quite a part of your group."

Telsiin looked from Tchinchura to Kaden as he spoke, trying to read their reactions, but it was Amintuu who spoke. "It is true she was a loner, but she stood between my kill squad and the boy, alone. She saved their lives at the risk of her own. That hardly seems the act of a traitor."

"I agree with Amintuu," Kaden said. "She has been with us for five years, since the fall of Barra-Dohn, and while she hasn't always been pleasant company, I don't have any reason to accuse her of treachery."

"Though," Tchinchura said, "I don't know that Rika has ever been someone in whom any of us had a great deal of trust. She was caught in the act of betraying your father, remember."

"I know, Tchinchura," Kaden said. "But you knew Eirmon, even if only briefly. I would say that she was trying to use him even as he was using her. I don't know how much I blame her for that."

"But if it wasn't treachery, why would she go?" Telsiin asked.

"I beg your pardon, Elder."

They turned to look at Olli, who had approached while they were speaking.

"I may have the answer." Olli reached out her hand to Telsiin. In it was a small, folded piece of paper. The elder took it, read it, and then handed it to Tchinchura, who also read it, and he gave it to Kaden. Kaden quickly scanned the brief message.

> *Olli,*
>
> *I'm not really one for goodbyes. Please tell the others when you find this that I've gone and not to worry. I've been thinking about going for some time, but I didn't want to let everyone down. I do want the man who destroyed Barra-Dohn to be stopped, but I am a scientist and not a soldier. I miss feeling useful, so I've decided to go. I wish you and the rest the best of luck, as I know all too well what is at stake.*
>
> *Rika*

There was silence as the note was passed around, and then Telsiin said, "Where did you get this?"

Olli looked a little sheepish. "She slipped it into my coat pocket while I slept, probably thinking I'd find it as soon as we prepared to go. I am sorry I didn't find it sooner."

"It is well," Telsiin said. "At least you did find it before we spent much longer looking or deliberating. The real question is what do we do now? She is a member of your group, so I would know your thoughts, Tchinchura."

"We keep going," Tchinchura said without hesitation. "She was with us of her own free will, and she could leave of her own free will."

"Maybe Deslo and I should head toward the town we just passed," Kaden said. "See if we can catch up to her?"

"For what purpose?"

"Just to make sure this is really what she wants, maybe? She's a long way from the part of the world she knows, and she's alone."

"Which she knew when she left," Tchinchura said. "Whatever else we might say about Rika, she wasn't one to act hastily and without thinking things through. If she's been having second thoughts about committing the rest of her life to our cause, she has probably been having them for a while."

"Nara won't be happy if we just leave her," Kaden said.

"I am sorry, Kaden," Telsiin said. "But I agree with Tchinchura. We need to keep going. I'm sure Rika knew this, which is why she left the note."

Kaden returned to Nara, and as he expected, she didn't like it. She did acknowledge, though, and perhaps more quickly than he would have thought she would, that they had little choice but to go. Their mission was too important to delay, and if Rika had chosen another path, chosen to leave without a farewell, that was her choice to make.

The group took up their packs and headed out, but Kaden paused with one last look over his shoulder at the expanse behind him. He thought with an odd sense of humility that yet one more thread which had tied him to Barra-Dohn and his past was now cut, like so many others before. He whispered a prayer to Kalos for Rika's safety, realizing with gratitude as he did so that this no longer felt quite as strange as it once had.

Then he lifted Kiki onto his shoulders and set out on the day's march.

The great croc smashed through the doors leading into the great hall with even more ease than he smashed through the front gate. What's more, he took a large chunk of the front wall out too, as he didn't exactly fit through the doors despite the fact they were wide enough for ten men to walk in side by side when both were open. The Amhuru who were there to bait him dropped back ahead of his snapping jaws so that he pushed all the way into the great hall, just barely fitting between the two rows of columns that rose to the rafters above.

Once they had lured the *salandra* all the way in, the Amhuru who had hidden in the wings, waiting for this moment, moved in at once. They used the spears that lined the walls of the great hall to attack the *salandra's* feet and tail, trying to pin them down—the feet to limit his ability to back up, the tail because, aside from the creature's jaws, it was the most dangerous part of the great croc. In fact, in here, the tail might well have been the most dangerous part given the damage it could do to the great hall itself and its pillars.

The *salandra* roared with pain as spears stabbed down and through all four of its feet at the same time and as multiple spears pierced its tail. Still, the tail was not pinned down, and Draagan saw it swing to the side with ferocious power as it struck an Amhuru moving in to drive another spear through it. The man flew through the air and smashed into the wall on the side of the great hall, some twenty feet away, where he crumpled to the floor in a broken heap.

Draagan moved to the closest column, and, using the spikes placed strategically upon it as hand and foot holds, he climbed up into the rafters high above. Once there he knelt on a rafter and whistled to the Amhuru below. One came quickly to the floor below him and tossed up a spear, which he caught with his outstretched hand. He rose and ran forward through the great hall, jumping from rafter to rafter as necessary, until he stood in the air, far above the head of the *salandra*.

He heard shouts behind him, and he again knelt on the rafter as he looked back through the great hall toward the gaping opening in the front of the building. Some of the men in gold who had been outside the stronghold, surrounding it, had come at last. Now the real fight would begin, and he had to finish the *salandra* quickly so he and the other Amhuru could focus on springing their trap.

He looked back down. The *salandra* was turning its head to snap at an Amhuru that was baiting it. They knew their job was to keep its attention forward, so a handful of Amhuru were playing a deadly game of moving back and forth in front of the *salandra's* large and powerful jaws. It was dangerous but necessary, as the great croc, like his smaller cousins, could roll with little warning and much power, and if it tried that, it might well take down a row of columns and the great hall with it. Draagan watched and waited for his chance.

The mouth of the great croc closed, and its head swung the other way. At that moment, Draagan reached out through the Arua, knowing the *salandra* was being controlled by another hand. He didn't try to wrench control away, but he did try to tug against that other hand, in the hope that his interference would momentarily arrest the *salandra's* motion. And indeed, the large head stopped where it was, its two bulbous eyes seeming to gaze straight ahead. Draagan saw the eyes set well back from the jaw, saw the slight rise in its head between and just behind those eyes, gauged the distance and angle, and dropped from the rafter.

As he fell through the air, he raised the solid spear that he held tightly in both hands. As his feet struck the great croc's head, he plunged the spear down with all his strength. The sharp point pierced the thick hide of the *salandra,* met tougher resistance for a second, then pushed through into the softer material beyond, and the spear kept going until he had buried it several feet inside the great croc's skull.

The effect of this blow was instantaneous, for the spear had penetrated and pierced the great croc's brain. The *salandra's* head dropped downward with a thud onto the floor, throwing Draagan forward and off as he hit the ground and rolled.

The creature's body shuddered and lay still.

Draagan, though, had no time to survey or admire his handiwork. He motioned to the other Amhuru near the front of the great croc to follow him as he disappeared into the dark stairwell heading down in the halls below.

The *salandra* was dead, but a more dangerous confrontation was still coming.

The blow that killed the *salandra* reverberated through the Arua and struck the Jin Dara, almost like a slap in the face. He stood outside the stronghold, on the riverbank, and wondered how such a magnificent beast, which he had worked so hard to get down here to this place, could have been killed mere minutes after smashing through those massive gates like they were a thin and fragile glass.

The Jin Dara had felt the interference right before the end, felt someone momentarily wrestle with his control of the beast. It hadn't felt like a serious challenge to his strength or mastery over it, but whatever the goal of the maneuver had been, it had immediately preceded the death and resultant shockwave that came from it.

He found himself thinking back to the day he avenged his family's ancient grievance against Zeru-Shalim, when he stood in the desert controlling great whirlwinds of sand and directing hookworms and rhino-scorpions against the armies that thought they could stop him. He thought about how an unseen hand had interfered and taken control away from him that day, and he knew without knowing how that once more, after all this time, he had finally encountered another original fragment of the Golden Cord.

But this time the tables were turned. He had two fragments, and the one who opposed him had only one.

He walked up to the stronghold and stood in the gateway, which seemed to him to be much like an open and gaping wound through which the lifeblood of the Amhuru would pour when he and his Najin were finished with them. Even so, he hesitated. In just the few minutes since the death of the monstrous crocodile, he could sense that most of the Najin he had sent in had gone down below the ground. This didn't surprise him necessarily, as the stronghold wasn't terribly large, and the idea that there were subterranean levels made sense. That would, however, negate some of their advantage, as moving below ground would affect their ability to control the Arua, though not as much as being on water did.

He wondered momentarily if this might be deliberate, but he couldn't see a real adavantage for the Amhuru in it, as they would also be affected by being below ground. No, he thought; most likely the Amhuru had simply given way at the onslaught of the creature and his men, and they were fleeing to whatever dark and dismal corner of this place they could find in the hope of evading their doom.

They would not evade it, however, and the Jin Dara would leave none of them alive.

He walked in through the gate and toward the open hole in the building straight ahead. A third fragment was inside that building, and he would personally take it off the dead body of the Amhuru who wore it.

41

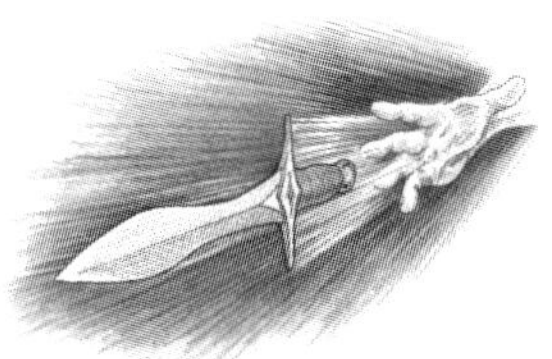

The Sharper Blade

There were two floors below the great hall, the main floor right below with the kitchen, dining room, sleeping quarters, and other various storage chambers, and the training area down below that. The training area had the forge, and in general it was open and full of various weapons and targets, designed by the people who had built the stronghold; they certainly hadn't been Amhuru, for they would not train so far below ground.

Draagan knew that the network of halls and stairs and rooms on both levels would be dark and full of danger, so he had been trying to move more or less in a circle and stay near the stairs that led up to the great hall itself. When the one he was waiting for came down, he would try to lure him back upstairs. Since he felt his adversary would feel most confident above ground, he wanted to face him there so he could best take advantage.

There was someone up ahead, he thought, so he ducked quietly into the dark storage room on his right, stepping over the body clothed in gold that lay slumped in the doorway. Though he preferred the light of a good, bright lamp when he was down here, of course, his eyes saw fairly well in the dark, just as his brothers' did, and, he imagined, just as their enemies' did. The Zerura they all wore had given that benefit to each alike, but while all could see with some success down here, he and his brothers knew this place so well they almost didn't need to be able to see. They had a definite advantage when it came to knowing how to get about and which doors led to dead ends and which did not.

He moved away from the doorway but pulled himself up as flat against it as he could, and readied his knife. The quiet footsteps were almost inaudible, though not quite. He readied for the blow, and waited. Time seemed to crawl, but eventually he heard someone right outside the door. The person stooped, and a hand reached out to roll the figure on the floor, perhaps to check the face. No Amhuru would care which particular man in gold the body was, so Draagan whirled away from the wall and struck.

His knife hit home, and the man, staggered by the blow, fell down upon his dead comrade. Draagan quickly finished him, and leaving the two bodies where before there had been just one, ducked back out into the hall, working his way back toward the rooms nearest the stairs to the great hall. The men in gold all had the look of soldiers; he was waiting for the man who would look, or at least behave, like a general.

He heard footsteps on those stairs, coming down, and he ducked again into a side room, a room used to store food supplies for easy access to the kitchen across the way. He crossed to the far side of the room and squatted down behind a table piled high with plates and serving dishes. He peered at the doorway from below the table, hoping for a glimpse as the man approached. He felt the figure on the other side reach out for and seize the Arua, and his excitement grew.

In the time since the battle moved down here, both the men in gold and the Amhuru had become reluctant to seize the Arua unless there seemed no other choice, as it was an effective way of alerting others lurking in the dark to your presence. He figured this man either hadn't thought about that, or he didn't care, perhaps because he felt he had no reason to be afraid.

The man glanced in the room, cautiously, and Draagan saw that his tunic was a similar color to the others, but there was insignia over his heart that he hadn't seen any of the others wearing. The eyes were gold and penetrating, and for a moment Draagan thought perhaps he had been seen, but then the man quickly darted past the open door and continued down the hall.

Sa, it was time to go. This was him. The trap was set, and he was the bait.

Draagan darted out of the room, glanced right at the man moving down the hall, then made sure that he was both heard and seen, running full speed back the other way as he bounded up the steps that led to the great hall. He emerged, saw no one waiting there, and darted forward alongside the now still body of the *salandra*.

He felt the man come up behind him, felt him reach through the Arua to try to take hold of him, and resisted his attempt while spinning to face him. The man did not have a weapon out, and Draagan knew that his assumptions about this man had been correct—knew that if he played this right, he would get his chance.

"You are the one," the man said. "I can feel it."

Draagan didn't say anything. He simply held his ground, staring at his opponent. He could feel the man probing him through the Arua, and he resisted enough to keep up appearances.

"You have something I want," the man said as he took a step toward Draagan.

"You should not have come here," Draagan called out as he stepped back, trying to make the step look difficult and forced to suggest he was unsure and uncertain, cornered and afraid. He lifted his meridium blade and held it aloft. "I am warning you. Go now, before the vengeance of Kalos falls upon you."

"The vengeance of Kalos?" the man scoffed. "I hate to tell you my friend, there is no Kalos, and I fear no vengeance."

He stepped forward again. “Oh, I almost believed it myself, once. When I put on the second fragment, I waited to fall dead. Or to have the ground open up and swallow me whole, or something. But nothing happened. That is, nothing except a remarkable increase in power. No, I don’t think I’m worried very much about the vengeance of Kalos.”

Draagan thought it was about time for his first move, and he stepped suddenly forward, throwing his bloody knife straight for the man’s head. The man waved his hand, almost casually, and the knife flew to the side as though it had been slapped out of midair by an invisible hand. It hit the thick hide of the great croc and fell with a clang to the ground.

The man laughed. “I don’t mind playing games, don’t get me wrong. Most days I quite like them. But let’s not play that game, you and I. Not today. I think you know there isn’t much point to it.”

For just a second, Draagan had to fight a smile. He tried to make it look like a grimace and fumbled for another meridium blade as he did so. He ran it along his fragment of the Golden Cord on his forearm and lifted it, holding the knife threateningly.

“Not willing to concede?” the man said, smirking. “I guess not. I wouldn’t give up what you have willingly either, even if I knew I was beaten.”

“Bearing a fragment of the Golden Cord is not a game,” Draagan said, stepping back this time before the man could take a step forward. He wanted to convey a measure of panic as well as fear.

“No, that’s true,” the man said. “It certainly isn’t. But the thought that with your one fragment you can withstand me with my two . . . well, that’s a game, isn’t it? A game you can’t win, I’m afraid.”

Draagan stepped forward again and hurled the knife, and this time, instead of simply swatting the knife aside, the man held up his hand, and the blade stopped. Then, suddenly, it was flying back at Draagan, who hadn’t been expecting that. Still, he had time and presence of mind enough to duck as the knife sailed high.

"I warned you about playing games with me," the man said, and some of the humor had gone from his voice.

Draagan knew it was almost time. He put his hand on the handle of one of his steel blades. "And if you had this," he said, indicating the band around his right forearm, "what would you do with it? Why do you want three pieces of the Cord?"

"I don't want three pieces of the Cord," the man said. "I want them all."

As he said that, the man took his biggest step forward yet. Draagan pulled the steel blade.

"You cannot have what I bear," he said, making a show of running it along the Zerura around his right forearm. Then he threw it.

The man raised his hand again, as though to deflect or redirect it once more. Draagan could feel him reach for it, could see the moment when his smirk turned to surprise as the steel blade flew on, impervious to his attempt at control.

The blade struck the man right in his chest, just below his collarbone. He staggered back, his eyes wide with terror and surprise and fear. Draagan watched all this as he moved, drawing another steel knife and running toward the wounded man. He intended to finish this now, once and for all.

The man tried to strike through the Arua at him, and indeed, he succeeded in slowing Draagan's approach, even as his hand clutched at the blade buried in his chest. Draagan would not be stopped, though, and soon he had reached the man. His first blow struck him in the stomach, and he drove the blade home as deep as he could.

The man fell to his knees, looking up at him with wonder as much as fear. Draagan thought the look said it all. Even as he pulled out the knife for another blow, the man still couldn't understand how this had happened. He had believed himself invincible, and now he was about to find out just how wrong he had been.

"The kitchen knife is king," Draagan said as he leaned over the man, "until it meets a sharper blade."

He swung down to plunge the knife into the man's throat and end this so he could take back what this man had stolen, take them and then go back and help his brothers, but the man lurched back in a final, desperate attempt to evade his fate, and swinging his arm wildly, he managed to deflect the blade enough that it missed his throat and cut a long and nasty wound up across the man's face.

The man fell back, and Draagan was about to pounce when a flood of men in gold emerged out of the stair. Some of them were wounded, some were not, but all were fleeing, pressed from behind by the Amhuru who were driving them up into the great hall.

The first of these saw him standing over their leader and let out a scream that drew all attention to him, and the next thing Draagan knew, he was running for his life. He scrambled up over the dead *salandra* and, reaching a column on the other side, climbed up into the rafters. Knives whistled by him, and multiple men behind him tried to seize hold of him through the Arua field.

Fortunately the emergence of more Amhuru and the call from some of the men in gold to help get their leader out of the great hall caused chaos all around. Some of Draagan's enemies seemed intent on merely taking the fallen man out, while others seemed intent on avenging him, but soon these latter seemed to accept that they had to unite against the Amhuru that remained and get out while they still could, for they had no defense against the steel knives now being wielded against them.

The men in gold gathered together around the body, and one of them heaved it up over his shoulder and fell behind the others, who made a living shield to protect their leader should he even still be alive to protect. There was a final act of violent struggle as both groups sought through the Arua to slow down if not stop and control the other, but the men in gold showed their superior strength in that struggle, and they threw back the Amhuru who strove against them. They backed systematically through the great hall and out through the hole that the *salandra* had created, until they disappeared from view.

Draagan dropped from the rafters, only then noticing the cut across his left arm that was bleeding pretty steadily. He guessed one of the knives thrown at him as he was fleeing his fallen foe had hit him after all. He would bind the wound, and it would heal just fine.

If he had done his work well enough, though, the wounds of the man who had led the men in gold here would not heal. But even if he died, would this end? Would another rise to take his place? The Amhuru needed those missing fragments back, but were they strong enough to do this, to defeat their enemies equipped with two fragments each and trained in their use? Even with the advantage of the steel blades, Draagan just didn't know.

He turned to Breeson and another Amhuru who were nearby. "Be careful. Don't let them know you are following, but follow."

"Yes, Draagan."

"I may have killed the man who bears the fragments," Draagan said. "Hopefully I have, I don't know. But either way, they still have them . . . which means our fight is not yet over."

Epilogue

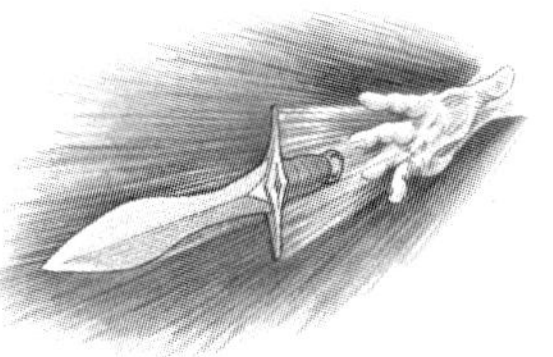

Beneath the Colder Moon

The camp was quiet as Telsiin and Tchinchura walked together away through aromatic pine trees, the snow crunching underfoot. They emerged from the trees and climbed to the top of a ridge, and from there they could see the sea down below, with the moonlight reflecting on the water. They had reached the coast at last, and tomorrow they would start moving north, parallel to it.

"We are close?" Tchinchura asked. As they looked down at the sea, his gaze strayed north.

"We are close," Telsiin said. "I think perhaps four or five days."

"From how you spoke of the desolate lands near Berran's Point, the . . . what did you call them?"

"Graymere," Telsiin said. "They're called the Graymere."

"Yes, the Graymere," Tchinchura said. "I guess I didn't expect the land here to be so beautiful."

"The land between here and Berran's Point is beautiful," Telsiin agreed. "Beyond it, though, the change comes. You'll see what I mean. For now, though, enjoy the beauty while you can."

"Sa, fair enough," Tchinchura said. "It is like a good rule for life—always enjoy beauty while you can."

The echo of thunder came rolling across the water, as though from somewhere distant, perhaps far out at sea. There were no clouds in the sky, at least none that they could see, and yet to Tchinchura the weather felt like it was changing. A storm could well be coming, and he thought it very likely that more snow would reach them before morning. It would be a long, cold night.

He looked up at the moon, noticing not for the first time, an odd halo of grey mist that seemed to surround it, so that it looked like a great white stone set in a grey metal ring. The sky was completely clear, so he had no idea what the misty grey ring was, or why it only wrapped around the moon but didn't cover any of it.

Tchinchura turned to Telsiin and pointed out the moon's strange appearance, and the elder looked up and nodded. "We call that a cold moon in the Northlands. I suppose because it happens most often in winter."

"A cold moon," Tchinchura said as he looked from the elder back to the moon. "Sa, it fits."

"Once, when I was boy, my grandfather told me about a prophecy that he had heard when he was a boy that was in fact already ancient by then." Telsiin paused, as though lost for a moment in his memories of his boyhood and his grandfather, but then he continued. "He said that one day the sun would rise beneath the colder moon, and that when it did, our doom would come."

As Telsiin spoke, a chill ran down Tchinchura's spine, and he felt goosebumps in his flesh. "Beneath the colder moon? Are you sure that was the phrase?"

"Yes, I'm sure," Telsiin said, turning from contemplating the sky to examining his companion. "Why, what is it, Tchinchura?"

"The Devoted," Tchinchura said, "with whom we travel . . . Marlo? I told you how I believed that he had been set apart to be a Guardian of Truth?"

"You did."

“He had a vision some time ago, before we crossed the Madri,” Tchinchura said. “In that vision, he heard a voice prophesying . . .”

“And that phrase was in the prophecy?”

“That phrase was in the prophecy.”

“Tell me,” Telsiin said. “Unless you have been bound by an oath of secrecy.”

“I have not,” Tchinchura said, so he told Telsiin about Marlo’s vision and the images in it, and then he finished with the words of the prophecy that both he and Marlo and Owenn had committed to memory. When he was finished, both he and Telsiin stood on the ridge, gazing at the sea in silence.

“I think,” Telsiin said at last, “that perhaps the fulfillment of both prophecies is near at hand.”

“Sa, I as well,” Tchinchura said. “Though I fear what that will bring.”

“As do I,” Telsiin said, turning away from the ridge to head back toward the camp. “But tomorrow, as all days, lies in the hand of Kalos.”

THE END

Glossary for *The Lesser Sun*

Alayna – Wife of Zangira

Almaren (ALL-mair-ren) – The oldest elder of the Southland Amhuru; resides in Azandalir

Amintuu (UH-MIN-too) – A Northland Amhuru

Asa – The Runners D'Sarza hires, they run Dengai

Azandalir (Uh-ZAN-duh-LEER) – Secret 'home' to the Amhuru who live in the southlands

Balaada Tree – Large tree in proverb spoken by Prince Hadaaya

Barra-Dohn (BEAR-uh-DOAN) – Once the center of power in Aralyn and home to Kaden and the Omiir family, the city has now been razed by the Jin Dara and lies abandoned; where meridium was discovered and where the Golden Cord was housed before Kalos separated it into the six fragments following the betrayal of Kartain

Ben-Salaar – the capital city of Prince Hadaaya's realm

Breeson (BREE-sin) – A Northland Amhuru

Brexton – Rough port in the Maril Islands; a place where our heroes get info about a the remote island in the Maril Islands where Jin Dara came from

Calamin – Southland Amhuru who accompanies Zangira in the mission to find the Jin Dara

Can'na – Slang for 'cannot'

Captain Elil D'Sarza (uh-LEEL duh-SAR-za) – Merchant and captain of *The Sorry Rogue*

Casmir (CAZ-meer) – Northland port city

Chokra – Fish the 'island of dreadful daylight' was once known for

Corness – Liquid made from corn that runs many meridium devices in the Northlands

"Cross over" – An idiom for death

Daala (DOLL-uh) – Fisherman who goes from Santago to the island

Dengai – Port operated by Asa Runners that Captain D'Sarza uses

Deras – The Kalosene killed by Eirmon & formerly the "Guardian of Truth" for the Kalosene community that Marlo & Owenn come from

Devaar (Duh-VAR) – the Jin Dara's second in command

Devoted – the – a term for Kalosenes

Draagan (Drah-GAN) – Northland Amhuru who has an original fragment of the Golden Cord, and for whom the Jin Dara comes . . .

Dreesen – Northland port

Ellenara Omiir (EL-len-NAR-uh O-MEER) – Known more commonly as Nara, the wife of Kaden

Garjan – Sailor & Maril Islander who points the Amhuru in the direction of the island of dreadful daylight . . .

Geffen (GEF-en) – D'Sarza's first mate on *The Sorry Rogue*

Golden Cord, the – a piece of Zerura given in ancient times to the king of Barra-Dohn; later separated into six pieces to prevent men from ever seeking to wield its united power again

Gorgaal, the (GORE-GAL) – albino gargoyle creatures that terrorize the island of dreadful daylight

Goya Fruit – a tropical fruit with dark juice

Guardian of Truth – Leaders of Kalosene communities (Devoted), they often have prophetic gifts; as Marlo receives in *The Lesser Sun*

Gutsnakes – small, slender brown snakes with silver markings on their heads. The snakes bite you and push eggs through the puncture wound into your bloodstream; the eggs find their way to your stomach where they grow until they hatch and the host vomits the new snakes out, a process which kills the host.

Hadaaya (Huh-DAH-YAH) – the prince of Ben-Salaar, old friend of Zangira

Honored One – An honorific among islanders/some sailors for Amhuru

"In the palm of His hand" – An Amhuru or a Kalosene idiom for what happens when the faithful die. They are in the palm of Kalos' hand.

"It is well" – A stock idiom among Northland Amhuru

Jin Dara, the (JIN DARR-uh) – Literally means "dark things." After razing Barra-Dohn, he executed Eirmon and stole his fragment of the Golden Cord; he now bears two fragments

Jonda – Warm beverage, a Northland favorite

Kaden Omiir (KAY-den O-MEER) – Son of Eirmon Omiir, king of Barra-Dohn; having renounced his father's throne in the fall of Barra-Dohn, he is now an apprentice to the Amhuru Tchinchura

Kalosenes – the religious sect dedicated to following and upholding the laws and decrees of Kalos, of which Marlo and Owenn are a part

Kanns – Merchant captain of *The Lion's Mane*

Keeper – the Northland Amhuru's term for those who bear original fragments of the Golden Cord; laymen use it for all who bear Zerura, regardless of whether it is an original or replica

Lion's Mane, the – a trading vessel that bears Amintuu and his kill squad to Sar Komen

Maarta – A Northland Amhuru

Maccado and Asantii – Northland Keepers

Madri, the (MOD-DREE) – an invisible barrier created by the Amhuru to keep the northern and southern fragments separate from each other; crossing the Madri causes those who bear Zerura to endure unknown but perhaps deadly effects

Maril Islands – Large constellation of islands, the island of dreadful daylight a remote part of the Maril Islands

Marlo – one of the Devoted that travels in exile with Kaden

Mirimae – Birds on Azandalir; sing in the morning

Na – No

Najin (NAH-jin) – the Jin Dara's specialized army

Noni – Another name for "mother"

Northlands, the – the name for all the continents and lands north of the Madri

Olli – Seventeen-year-old inhabitant of the island of dreadful daylight

Omojen – Prince Hadaaya's beasts of war; they are enormous, rusty red colored elephants, only much, much bigger than the 'ordinary greys.' Their tusks are massive

Owenn – the other Devoted that travels with the band of *The Sorry Rogue*; he is of large size and few words

Prince Hadaaya – Commander of the army helping Zangira as he hunts the Jin Dara

"Sa" – Yes (or, 'Sa, Sa' for 'Yes, Yes')

Saba – A word like 'sir' for many islanders/some sailors

Salandra – a great crocodile, large enough that a man can be trampled under one of his feet or be swallowed whole

Sar Komen – Large Northland city

Shaline (SHUH-leen) – daughter of Zangira & Alayna

Sorry Rogue, the – the trading vessel captained by D'Sarza on which Kaden and the other exiles sail to discover the origins of the Jin Dara

Southlands, the – the name for all the continents and lands south of the Madri

Talathorne Trees – Great trees in Azandalir; as old as Azandalir itself

Tchinchura (Chin-CHER-uh) – One of the two Amhuru who traveled to Barra-Dohn, he now leads the crew of *The Sorry Rogue* in their quest for information on the Jin Dara and to keep the third Southland fragment out of his reach; Kaden is his apprentice

Telsiin (TEL-sin) – Northland Amhuru elder, something of a counterpart for Almaren in the south

Trabor (TRAY-ber) – son of Zangira & Alayna

Trajax (TRAY-jax) – Southland Amhuru who accompanies Zangira

"What in the name of the six brothers?" – An Amhuru exclamation; as close to an oath as they get

"Winters" – A way for measuring age in the Northlands; how many winters a man/woman has seen. (Use "summers" in the Southlands)

Yadi – Father

Zangira (Zan-GEAR-uh) – The other Amhuru who traveled with Tchinchura to Barra-Dohn, he now leads a company of Amhuru on a quest to find the Jin Dara